Stealing Sunshine

A CHERRY PEAK NOVEL

HANNAH COWAN

First Edition

ISBN: 978-1-990804-50-2

Cover designed by: Andra Murarasu @andra.mdesigns

Edited and proofed by: Sandra @oneloveediting

Character Chapter Illustrations by: Jordan Burns @joburns.reads

Chapter Break Interior Illustration by: Madalyn McDermot @mads_forbooks

Also By

Swift Hat Trick trilogy

Lucky Hit

Between Periods

Blissful Hook

Overtime

Vital Blindside

Greatest Love series

Her Greatest Mistake

Her Greatest Adventure

His Greatest Muse

His Greatest Treasure

Their Greatest Strength

Cherry Peak series

Strung Along

Catching Sparks

Chasing Home

Stealing Sunshine

Amateurs In Love duet

Craving The Player

Taming The Player

PSYCHO - Hardy	3:19
Kiss Kiss - Madeline Merlo	3:12
Mess It Up - Gracie Abrams	2:51
She's So Mean - Matchbox Twenty	3:52
Intoxicated - Warren Zeiders	3:40
Femininomenon - Chappel Roan	3:29
Born This Way - Lady Gaga	4:20
I Hate Love Songs - Kelsea Ballerini	3:11
never til now - Ashley Cooke, Brett Young	2:54
BANKS - Jordan Davis, NEEDTOBREATHE	3:42
The Only Exception - Paramore	4:28
Better Than Words - One Direction	3:29
Cool Girl - Tove Lo	3:19
Sin So Sweet - Warren Zeigers	3:21
Somebody - Dagny	3:14

STEELE RANCH
STEELE RANCH
WELCOME TO CHERRY PEAK CANADA
TOWN HALL
FIRE STATION
BEAUTIFULLY BOLD
THISTLE & THORN
SCHOOL
ANNA'S HOUSE
POPPY'S HOUSE
COFFEE SHOP
FARMER'S MARKET
PEAKSIDE
BRYCE'S HOUSE
RUSTIC RIDGE
MADE BY @JOBURNS.DESIGNS

For those of us whose fires blaze behind thick walls of ice.

1

Bryce

"Ow! Shit. Fuck. Can't you be any gentler?"

I consider pressing the tip of the tattoo gun harder into the underside of my best friend's ass cheek before turning the idea away.

"You're the one who decided to get a tattoo here," I mutter.

"I didn't know it would hurt this bad!"

"It's two letters and a period. Suck it up."

Anna, another important member of our friend group, leans closer to both me and Poppy with blatant interest. She's got virgin skin, totally uninked, and while I'm itching to change that for her, I'm also not interested in pushing.

"Is it really that painful, or are you being a bit sensitive?" Anna asks her.

Turning her head to the side, Poppy glares at our friend. "How about you get a tattoo on your ass, Annalise?"

She's stretched out on the leather table without a shred of insecurity, a move completely in character for her. The hem of her sundress is flipped right up over her entire ass, a hot pink thong bright beneath the shitty lights in my basement.

Anna smiles, shaking her head while leaning back on the

storage bin she's sitting on. "Brody would like his initials there a bit too much, I think."

"It isn't too late for me to change the tattoo, Poppy," I remind her, half hoping she will.

"Cut it out, Ice. I'm not changing it."

"You can't honestly tell me he deserves his initials on your ass."

"Technically, they're not his initials," she rebuts.

I huff. "Might as well be."

S.D. are the letters she asked me to ink into her skin. A permanent mark that corresponds to the nickname she gave her boyfriend when they first met, Sir Douchelot.

"I think it's romantic," Anna says.

I wipe the *S* with a paper towel to clean the ink. "I don't see Garrison in here getting Poppy's initials on *his* ass."

"Would you like me to text him and ask him to come? We both know he'd be here in five seconds. He's probably waiting for me outside already," Poppy says.

Readjusting my position on my stool, I stretch my fingers out before gripping the gun again and bringing the needle back to her skin. The period is quick to ink, and then I'm wiping the skin again.

"All I'm saying is that he better appreciate this. It's going to hurt to sit and use a pole for a few days. You'll stretch this area constantly."

"Maybe just avoid going to the studio during that time, Pops," Anna encourages.

Poppy ignores our warnings. "No pain, no gain, guys."

Beautifully Bold, her pole studio, is her entire life. She's on a pole more than she is her feet at this point. Nothing and no one is capable of keeping her off it.

"Suit yourself," I grunt.

"So . . ." Poppy starts, wiggling slightly when the gun's needle passes over a sensitive spot. "When are you getting out of this basement and into a studio of your own?"

"I'm happy here."

"Here? You're happy doing tattoos for free in a dungeon?" she asks, calling me out.

"It isn't a dungeon."

"It is a dungeon, Bryce. And you should be charging people for your work. You're incredible," Anna says, watching me with that soft look of hers.

My skin tightens with discomfort as I continue to keep my late-night tattoo work to myself. They wouldn't judge me for tattooing those desperate enough to get one in the middle of the night, but I'm not ready to tell them about it yet. I haven't been ready for the last year.

"I'm tattooing two letters into Poppy's ass."

"So? Is that supposed to prove something?" Poppy asks.

"I tattoo to take the edge off. It's not a stable job idea in Cherry Peak."

"Neither was my hair salon," Anna says.

Poppy makes a noise in her throat. "Or my pole studio."

They're fair statements. Doesn't mean I want to take them into consideration right now. The thought of opening a tattoo shop gives me anxiety. In a town as small as Cherry Peak, the judgment is always there regardless of what you do or say. It's gotten better over the years, but with the number of wrinkled assholes packed into the streets on the daily, it's hard to believe it'll ever fully change.

I've watched Poppy be treated like a filthy freak for opening a pole studio and have received more than enough dirty looks for the ink on my skin. Their opinions don't matter to me, but they would have to if I were to open a real business here.

Not to mention, I have a terrible inability to keep my mouth shut when someone pisses me off. I've made my fair share of enemies in this town with my sharp retorts and middle fingers. A potential shop wouldn't last a week with how quickly I'd get myself in hot water. At least those who seek me out now know exactly who I am and love my work enough not to complain. A brick through my window sounds like a pain.

With a final glide of the needle, I finish the *D* and wipe it and the rest of the tattoo clean before turning the gun off. The cursive writing is clean and precise. Fucking pretty, even. I push away from the table and reach for my favourite ointment before slathering it over the raised skin.

"Do you want me to cover this? Or are you going to peel off whatever I put on the moment you get home?" I ask.

Poppy stretches her arms out in front of her and groans. "Since you're so worried about me, put the damn cover on, and I promise to leave it for a couple of days."

"So generous." I cover her tattoo with a sticky film and pinch the inside of her thigh. "You're done. And like I said before, it'll hurt to sit for a few days, so take it easy."

Anna giggles. "That seems more like a warning you should be giving Garrison."

I crinkle my nose in disgust. "Pass."

Poppy slides off the table and smooths down her dress before moving to the standing mirror I have propped up against a softened wooden beam.

Fine. Maybe dungeon isn't that far off after all.

With a tight grip on her dress, Poppy twists and lifts it to expose her ass again. Her eyes latch onto the initials that appear in the mirror when she bends slightly. I watch her face for a reaction, some small part of me always hungry for praise when it comes to my tattooing work.

"Yup. He's going to shit a brick when he sees this," she says, swaying her ass in the mirror. "It's perfect."

I take the compliment and leave her to continue checking herself out. Busying myself with cleaning up, I tune in to the music playing from my speaker on the small workbench left here by the previous tenant and fight a wince.

The country music is low and slow, the lyrics drawled in the way I can't stand. It's almost like nails on a chalkboard, but I've kept that to myself my entire life. Especially now that Anna's decided to marry a goddamn country superstar this upcoming summer.

"Are you sure we can't convince you to get something, Anna?" Poppy asks her, coming to my side, dress swishing at her thighs again.

"Someday, maybe," Anna answers.

Poppy yawns. "Boring."

"If I buy you a drink, can we forget about the whole tattoo Anna thing?"

"Depends on what type of drink."

"Whatever your heart desires, baby cakes."

Anna moves to my other side and gathers the ointment and stack of wraps from the table before putting them back where I grabbed them from.

After disinfecting the table, I take my makeshift station down quickly. The two women linger while I work, talking about their plans for tonight at Peakside, the only bar in town. Every Saturday, a giant group of us steals a table and stays until closing.

Over the past couple of years, less and less of us have stayed that long, though. Anna and Brody are getting married and have better things to do than hang around at a bar until the morning, and Poppy and Garrison can't make it more than a few hours without fucking, so they're out early.

Even Johnny, the town's sunshine cowboy with a mouth that rarely stops moving, isn't interested in staying late anymore. Not since he found Aurora and convinced her to give him a shot. He's had her on lock ever since.

It's been a long year of watching overly touchy and at times obnoxiously happy couples twist up our friend group. We're a far cry from what we used to be, and as one of the last single people around, it's becoming tiresome to go out with them every weekend.

I'm happy for them. Really. It just makes my lack of a dating life a bit more noticeable.

"Who's driving tonight?" Poppy asks once we've headed upstairs.

The stairs are old and creaky, the kind you find in a horror film with a blonde screeching while running from a possessed nun. I leave the basement light on at all times. Fuck my power bill. As someone who believes in all things paranormal, I'm too big of a wimp to ever turn the light off. Especially not while going up these creepy-ass stairs.

"Anna," I say.

She stops at the top of the stairs and glances at me. "Why is it always me?"

"Because we have to get our use of you in the summer, considering you're the world's worst winter driver," I state.

After bumping the door shut with my hip, I lead the way into my tiny bathroom to grab a couple of pain pills for Poppy.

"For your ass. We'll be sitting tonight, and the skin will still be pretty raw," I say before extending them to her with a flat palm.

"Thanks, Ice." She takes them from me eagerly before we step into the kitchen.

My fridge is as full as it ever is—and by that, I mean empty as fuck—when she grabs one of the half-drunk Fanta bottles from inside to help her swallow the pills.

"So, I don't think either of us are going to be driving tonight. You were right, Poppy. Garrison's leaning against Brody's truck with a scowl," Anna calls from the living room.

Spinning, I find her staring out my front window, which has been illuminated by the shine of headlights flashing down the street. I roll my eyes at the two men.

You'd think neither of them has ever had to leave Poppy or Anna before. How clingy can you get?

"Sorry, Bryce. Believe it or not, I did tell him to just meet us there," Poppy says, even though there's no disguising how happy she is to see him.

"Doesn't matter as long as there's room for me in that godawful fucking truck."

Anna gasps, her head whipping back, eyes wide. "Don't let Brody hear you say that. He thinks of that truck as a child."

"Congratulations. It has your eyes," I mutter before finding a pair of black boots and shoving my feet into them.

The other two finally peel themselves from the window and follow suit, and five minutes later, we're all stuffed inside the truck.

I tune out the sound of Garrison's dirty whispers from the opposite seat in the back as he squeezes Poppy's knee and twist to stare out the window.

Soon enough, I'll be able to sneak off to drink my cocktail alone and, for a few blessed minutes, not be constantly reminded that I'm destined for a life of singleness.

2

Daisy

I'VE NEVER BEEN MORE GROSSED OUT BY MY BROTHER THAN I HAVE this weekend.

I don't know why I thought staying with him and his girl-friend would work. Not with how every encounter I've ever had with them this past year has just been me third wheeling and listening to their sloppy kissing noises.

Johnny is my twin and, in turn, my best friend. But he's still gross as hell. Only now, it isn't because of the lack of showering or burping loudly in silence but because he's a stage five stalker obsessed with his girlfriend to the point of near insanity.

Still, Aurora is a good match for him.

They might be complete opposites, but she keeps him grounded and makes him happier than I've ever seen him. So, when she agreed with his offer to have me stay with them for the last couple of weeks and foreseeable future until I can find a place of my own, I accepted, not wanting to turn down their generosity.

That was my first mistake.

I should have said *no, thank you* and hurried up in my search for somewhere all to myself because now . . .

Another groan sounds from the room directly behind my

bed, and I squeeze the edges of the pillow harder against my ears. My breath is hot against my face as I consider suffocating myself before I have to hear my brother make another one of those noises.

"Are the walls made out of paper?" I whisper to myself.

It wouldn't surprise me if they were. This cabin is old as balls. Johnny's renovated almost all of it, moving room to room to make it feel more like a home instead of a creepy shack in the woods.

The guest room that I'm staying in is bright in the daylight, painted in soft greens and beige, with a shuttered window and sheer curtains. My bed is soft and cushioned, with a thick comforter that makes the bite of the relentless air conditioning not as noticeable. I always run cold, and even with this blanket, I've doubled up with socks to keep from freezing.

Moonlight streaks into the room through the curtains, keeping it from growing as dark as I'd like, so I add that to the tally of why it's past two in the morning and I'm still awake.

I should be grateful that I wasn't left with no option but to move back into my moms' house until I'm sorted in Cherry Peak, but as of this moment, I'm feeling grumpy. Sleep deprivation, stress, and cringe have turned my usual sunshine mood into a stormy one.

With a sigh, I grab my phone from the side table and wince at the brightness when I click it on. After lowering it until I don't have to shield my eyes, I'm opening the conversation I had two hours ago with my other best friend. The non-twin one.

Kiki: Sleep tight, babe. Imagine you're alone on a boat or something

Me: Oh perfect. Because we both know how much I love being on the water, right?

It's the opposite.

I'm terrified of bodies of water. Doesn't matter if it's a lake or the ocean, I get full-body shakes. It took me until I was five to stop screaming every time my moms put me in the bath. I'll admit that the ocean scares me more than a lake does, which makes complete and total sense. We're not meant to be in the ocean, *period*.

Kiki: Smart ass.

Me: Being alone on a boat scares me more than hearing my brother having sex with his girlfriend.

Kiki: Well that backfired then. Oops.

Me: Now I feel sick all over again.

Kiki: Night night, Didi *kiss emoji*

There's a slam against the wall, and I shoot up in bed, huffing my breaths. I whip my pillow across the room and hightail it into the hallway. If I didn't like Aurora as much as I do, I'd be slamming my fist against the door and telling them to keep it down, but I don't want to embarrass her.

The two of them were out at Peakside tonight and didn't get home until late, both sounding like giggling drunks. I should have known this was where their night was going and left earlier.

Not bothering with shoes, I unlock the front door and step outside. The porch is sanded to perfection, so I walk to the rocking chair in the corner without a worry of anything cutting into my feet through my socks.

With a long exhale, I sit and close my eyes, letting myself rock in silence for a few minutes. The house was built on Steele Ranch land but is far enough away from the ranch itself for any of the noise there to carry over. It also doesn't smell like cattle.

I've never liked the ranch much. Or animals, for that matter. My brother loves them and the ranch enough for the both of us. The only time I go there at all is to see him, considering he's been working there since he was a teenager.

It's been months since I've been back over that way. After graduating from the University of Calgary with my teaching degree this summer, I came back home with a new focus and drive. It was different passing the town sign this time around, knowing I'm here to stay.

I didn't rush to spend as much time as possible with my family out of fear of not seeing them enough before heading back to Calgary. Everything has been a bit calmer, and I feel steadier. Well, despite my nervousness about starting my new job in two weeks.

I went to the K-12 Cherry Peak Public School, and now I'm here to teach second grade.

The creaking of the porch door swinging open has me cracking one eye open. My brother offers me a soft smile and comes to lean against the railing. His hair is a mess, and he's wearing a pair of flannel pants and fuzzy slippers that I'm pretty sure belong to Aurora.

"Why aren't you asleep?" I ask softly, closing my eye again.

"Why aren't you?"

"Touché."

"You were stomping pretty loud when you passed our room," he says, and I pick up on the smallest hint of a slur in his words.

"Sorry. I didn't notice I was doing that."

"Nah, I'm sorry for not . . . uh . . ."

"Not remembering you aren't living alone right now?" I finish for him.

"Yeah. That."

"It's okay. It's your house. I'm just tired."

"'Cause of me. I'm sorry, Daisy. So is Rory."

"It's fine, really. I've cooled down since coming out here. But I think I'm going to find somewhere else to stay. Hopefully, I'll have better luck with my search soon."

The porch creaks under his weight, and I assume he's shifting around. "You're not being forced out because of my inability to be considerate for the little while that you're here. I'll keep myself in check. I want you here, Daisy. Missed you a whole lot."

"I missed you too. But I don't want to feel like a pest. And I'm not saying you've been making me feel that way. It's just the way I feel, all on my own. You and Rory deserve space for yourselves. I don't want to cut into that. And I have been," I say.

They may have been together for a year already, but somehow, they're still in their honeymoon phase.

Opening my eyes, I take in his frown and smile at him reassuringly. The crickets chirp in the fields around the cabin, and suddenly, I'm already missing the peace that comes with this place after only a month here. Despite the events of tonight, I really do like this plot of land my brother's got.

I stayed here a few times before Johnny met Rory and even a couple nights after that, but living here . . . that's completely different from a random sleepover.

"I don't want you to stay somewhere else," Johnny admits, almost pouting in his attempt to convince me to stay.

"I have to find somewhere else first. And it's impossible to find a place to live in this town."

He gnaws on his lip before sighing and saying, "What about Rory's old place?"

"The haunted one?"

"It's not haunted," Rory says, stepping onto the porch dressed in silk shorts and a massive sweatshirt. She crosses her arms and looks at me shyly. "If you want to stay there, I can talk to the owner. It's fixed up and liveable now."

"Thanks to me," Johnny boasts, chest puffing up as he sets an arm on her shoulders and pulls her into him.

I quirk a brow. "Are you aware that your favourite topic is yourself?"

"Not true. My favourite topic is Rory," he coos, planting a kiss to her cheek as it flames red.

There's a sharp sensation in my gut as I watch the look they share before dropping my eyes to my knees. It's envy brought on by the love and bond they share. I've never experienced one that strong before. Only dreamed of it. Wished that every relationship I entered into would be my final one, only to be heartbroken when each one ended.

"I appreciate the offer, Rory, but I'm terrified of ghosts. And that house gives me goosebumps. The bad kind."

"Despite what Bryce believes, it's not haunted," Johnny says.

Right. Bryce, the woman who's dressed up as a Ghostbuster every Halloween besides last. One of my brother and Aurora's friends, Bryce is always around. And despite my being Johnny's twin sister, she can't stand me.

I've spent too many nights keeping myself up over what I possibly did or said to offend her but have never come up with anything. From what I've put together, she just simply doesn't like me.

"Bryce would summon a demon to snatch my soul in my sleep," I say, pushing to my feet. It's getting chillier at night now that we're getting closer to September, and I'm underdressed in my nightgown.

"She wouldn't dare. I'd trade hers for yours," Johnny declares before curling an arm around me so he's sandwiched between Rory and me. "If you're serious about wanting to stay somewhere else, I'll ask around, 'kay? We'll figure it out."

I nod and pat his stomach. "Thank you."

"I'm sorry if I've made you uncomfortable, Daisy," Aurora apologizes, her voice revealing her embarrassment.

I shake my head and reach for her hand, giving it a gentle squeeze. "Don't apologize. Comes with the territory of living with a happy couple."

She appears reluctant to agree but doesn't push it any further. Rory is a closed-off person, but she feels just as deeply as the rest of us do. I wear my emotions on my sleeve the way my brother does.

"We'll do better," she declares.

"Thank you. I'm going to grab a glass of water and head back to bed."

My brother keeps me in his sights as I stand and reach for the porch door. He has a tendency to worry about me and our two older sisters a bit too much. It comes with the territory of being the only man in a family of five women, so I don't bug him about it too often.

Only when he steers toward unbearably protective.

"Night, guys," I say before stepping inside.

The porch door swings shut as they wish me good night. I wander into the kitchen and fill a glass up with tap water twice and then get back to bed.

Once I'm tucked in, I lie beneath the comforter and stare out the window, wishing that I'd chosen to sleep beneath the stars instead.

3

Bryce

I ITCH THE BLANK SKIN AROUND THE NEW PATCH OF INK ON THE back of my hand and strain my eyes to keep them from rolling at my mom's words.

She's dressed to the nines like usual in a knee-length, powder-pink, A-line dress and matching pumps. Her platinum-blonde bob is swept out of her face with diamond-encrusted butterfly clips ordered in the same pink as her outfit. One step into the town office and I could smell the old money wafting from her.

It's easy to recognize the scent when I've spent years scrubbing it off and extracting it from my blood with every prick of a tattoo gun.

My father is the mayor of Cherry Peak, but that isn't why they stink the way they do. This isn't a town where you'll find fame, riches, or glamour from that title.

Their old money comes from generations back when my great-great-great-probably even greater-grandparents bought up half of Montreal, specifically Westmount, where my mom grew up, when it cost two cents for a loaf of bread and ten dollars for a Summitt view.

Dad was born into his own family fortune here in Alberta,

but Mom's makes his look like pennies in comparison. When they married, they became moguls without having to lift a finger.

I've never gone into the financial details with my parents, but I know enough to realize my family name won't run out of funds for decades upon decades to come.

Big fucking whoop.

"He said you were quite rude, Bryce," Mom says, continuing to go on and on about the guy she forced me on a date with last week.

Her French accent should be watered down after two decades in Alberta and less than a few months spent back home in Quebec, but it's still loud and proud. Thicker in moments like this when her emotions get the better of her.

Much to my parents' disapproval, I don't have an accent at all. Worked hard to ensure that. If I hadn't been forced to take private French lessons growing up, I wouldn't have bothered learning the language either.

I slouch back in my office chair. "He also said he wanted me to date him *and* his brother and give them a family of eight starting immediately."

"Oh . . . and you didn't think the brother was an acceptable option? Did you ask to see a photo?" she asks, jumping right over the problem.

"No. I didn't ask for a photo of his brother. Do I really look like the right person to marry two men? And to birth not one but five kids? That's not ever fucking happening."

She tightens her stare, and I prepare for her scolding. "You really shouldn't be so picky, Bryce. You're not going to be in your twenties for much longer. Do you know how much harder it gets to find a man when you hit that number?"

"I only recently turned twenty-eight."

"So you think it will only take you two more years? I'm trying to help, darling. I simply don't want you to be lonely forever," she soothes, the Botox in her cheeks keeping her smile from spreading the way it did when I was a child. "You were already born by the time I was twenty-eight."

"Alright. Well, I'll be fine."

She turns her nose up with a scoff. "Of course you will be. You're a Lemieux."

"So, you understand that I don't need my mother setting me up on dates, then."

"No. No, that I do not understand. I am trying to help you, *ma belle.*"

"*J'veux pas ton aide.*"

She shakes her head, hair swishing. "Nonsense. I will tell Jean that you will meet him at the house for pastries on Wednesday afternoon. I'll have the cook prepare a spread for you."

It's only Friday, but Wednesday is still too soon. My skin crawls at the thought of not only entertaining another blind date but having it at my parents' house.

"Mom—"

"*Non.* You will not argue with me further on this," she snaps, accent growing thick enough to stick some of her words together.

I clench my hands beneath the office desk and swallow my anger. "Fine."

She grins, veneers blinding. A single clap of her hands, and she bends over the desk to kiss me on both of my cheeks.

"That's my girl. So thoughtful, hmm?"

I spread my lips in a saccharine smile. "I always am, Mom."

With a pat to my shoulder, she hums happily. Her expensive perfume slams into me, and I have to clear my throat to keep from coughing.

"Is that all you came here for?" I ask, pulling back and away from her.

"As if I would come here for anything else. Your dad is the only one of us who likes this place." Her nose crinkles, top lip lifting. "You do look mature in those clothes."

"If by mature, you mean sixty-five," I deadpan.

At the reminder of the clothes, I tug at the neck of my high-collar blouse where it cuts into my throat. The sleeves cinch in at the wrists the same way the collar does, hiding every inch of my skin from my hands up to my chin. My tattoos are left to suffocate beneath the scratchy material. They're "too inappropriate for the workplace," according to my parents. I cross my ankles, hating the way the loose skirt I'm forced to wear nearly drags along the floor.

My mom takes a long look at me from the other side of the desk and nods in approval. "You look professional. Much better than those tiny skirts and shirts you wear, hmm?"

"Hmm," I echo.

If she knew I had my black boots on beneath this desk, she'd lose a veneer.

"Maybe you will start dressing like this outside of work. I would love that. It would make such a beautiful impression on Jean to see you in such conservative, respectful clothes."

"You're feeling very assuming today, Mom."

"Assuming? *Non, ma belle.* Hopeful."

"Right. Well, I have to finish up here, so . . ." I wave toward the exit.

She tightens her grip on the strap of her purse. "Of course. Finish here and call me so we can speak details about Wednesday."

"Yeah."

"I'll see you, darling. Love you."

"Love you too, Mom."

She clicks her nails on the desk before flashing a final smile and stepping outside, leaving the office in blissful silence once again.

I let out a full breath for the first time since she arrived and hang my head back. Her intentions have never been cruel. They're just . . . short-sighted. My bisexuality isn't a secret to anyone, let alone my parents, but the constant shovelling of men down my throat has been something I've been dealing with for the last several months.

My dating a man is something that my parents understand. It's a comfortable situation for them. Me with a woman is harder to wrap their heads around.

Every time Mom sets me up on one of these fucking dates with another man she knows through her network and family ties, I humour her. It'll never be more than that. I know my mind well, and I know what I want in a relationship.

That'll never be a man.

I look forward when my phone buzzes on the desk.

Pops: Did you get the emergency text?

Poppy's text is confusing at first glance, but once I notice the dozens of others on my screen, I open them, expecting some shit to have gone down.

The group chat is flooded with messages all sent over the past few minutes. I silenced it the other night when they wouldn't shut up, so it makes sense I didn't hear anything while Mom was here.

Johnny: Emergency meeting at Peakside tonight at 6. @everyone

Garrison: I'm still in Toronto.

Anna: B + I will be there!

Poppy: I'll leave the house now. Miss u baby

Johnny: WBU Brycie?

Johnny: Bryce? Sorry, got rid of the i

Johnny: Miss you too Pops

Poppy: That was for Garrison, Johnny. I saw you last weekend

Johnny: And?

Garrison: Shut up, Johnny.

Garrison: Miss you more, honey.

Johnny: You tell me to shut up but call me honey? Mixed signals here people.

Anna: Will you tell us what this is about before we get there, Johnny?

Poppy: Where the f is Ice? As if the office is busy. Leaving now. TTYL xx

I roll my eyes at her last message. It's never busy here. I spend most of the day playing Solitaire on the computer.

Me: I'll be there. Need a drink or 10.

Johnny: KAY!

Anna: See you soon, Ice 🖤

Once the message comes in, I lock my phone and shove it in my bag before heading home.

Two and a half hours later, I'm a block away from Peakside when the sky opens up and starts raining on me. Thunder rumbles loudly as I curse and hurry my strides.

It would have been so much fucking easier to just drive, but knowing I'm planning on drinking my body weight in vodka, I didn't want to have to worry about my car afterward. Now, I'm wishing I'd used my head when I smelled rain the moment I left home.

By the time I reach the bar, I'm soaked. My denim skirt is chafing against my thighs, and my shirt is suctioned to my chest. There's water in my boots, and I'm positive my makeup is smudged.

"Fucking perfect," I mutter before pulling open the heavy wooden door.

My least favourite genre of music is playing, the country twang I hear on the daily whenever Brody speaks drifting from the speakers. It's empty besides the table of my friends past the double-sided bar.

I get a glare from the bartender, a.k.a. the mother of my ex-girlfriend, as I pass, my boots squeaking on the floor. I'd feel guilty for the mess I'm leaving if she and her daughter weren't on my shit list.

The bathroom sign is right ahead of me now. A beat later, I duck inside the ladies' room before anyone notices me and grimace at my appearance in the mirror.

I move quickly, wringing my hair out in the sink and dabbing paper towels beneath my eyes to clear away the smudged mascara. With my fingers, I comb through my wet hair and huff when it starts to frizz immediately after beginning to dry. Leaning over the counter, I rub my thumb on my temple where a streak of eyeliner has appeared before staring at my chest, grateful I wore a black shirt instead of white.

There's a flush, and then one of the stall doors rattles before opening. A small gasp has me looking behind me in the mirror.

"Bryce?"

My throat clogs at the voice before tightening to the point of pain when I meet Daisy Mitchell's eyes in our reflections. Static fills my ears as I narrow my stare.

Her hair is a deep, glossy red colour, and her piercing blue eyes are so intense they could shift planets with a single stare. Tall and slim, with a narrow, sharp jaw and a set of plump lips that I've seen blow bubbles in gum a hundred times, she's drop-dead gorgeous.

Her legs are miles fucking long and exposed in a pair of white cutoff shorts that I know must expose the underside of her ass cheeks with every step she takes. I tongue my cheek when I read the saying on the front of her waist-gripping shirt. *Too good for you.*

I almost laugh.

"Are you okay?" she asks, her voice sugar sweet and pure.

I swallow, glaring at the sink but watching her in my peripheral. "Fine. Just leaving."

She walks to the second sink beside me and turns on the tap. The way she shifts is awkward, janky. I made her feel that way.

"Were you caught in the rain?"

"Yep."

"Did my brother ask you to come tonight too?"

"Obviously."

She squirts soap into her palms and starts to lather it. The tap continues to run, and I snap a hand out to shut it off on habit. Silence hangs between us before she speaks again.

"I have a feeling that I know what this meeting is about—"

"I'm done in here," I rasp, snapping my eyes upward to look at her in the mirror one last time.

"Oh. Okay." Her expression closes down as she digs her teeth into her lip.

I keep my jaw shut to avoid saying something stupid and leave before I rip it open and speak anyway.

Daisy Mitchell has that effect on me. From the moment we met, I've had an annoying fucking impulse to blabber about anything and everything without a single reason as to why.

It doesn't matter.

I'm not in the mood to dig into that right now. She's right, anyway.

Too fucking good for me.

4

Daisy

People around town call Bryce the ice queen. Even her best friends have given her Ice as a pet name. They're not far off.

Her scowl is sharp enough to cut, and her words are cold, well-aimed bullets that never miss their target. Yet, I don't seem to care much about either of those things.

They don't intimidate me. *She* doesn't intimidate me.

Balling up the paper towel I used to dry my hands, I drop it into the garbage before following her out of the bathroom.

Johnny invited all of his friends to Peakside tonight because of me, even if he won't admit that yet. After our talk last week on the porch, he's been burning holes into the living room carpet with his feet while pacing and listing off every possible person I could stay with instead. It's a sweet gesture, but not needed.

I'm capable of finding somewhere on my own. It just might take me a bit longer.

Peakside is still as empty as when I arrived a half hour ago, but this time when I pass the double-sided bar, I stop and order a beer. I'm a bit frazzled after my run-in with Bryce, and a drink will hopefully help me shake it off.

The black-haired woman with eyes the same shade as glacial water and skin a shade paler than mine has never failed to snag my attention. She's gorgeous in that *look but do not touch* kind of way. There are icicles imbedded beneath her skin, just waiting to poke through and impale you, but the danger of that is almost exciting.

I've never been an adrenaline junkie, but when I'm intrigued by something—or someone—I can't help but want to test just how far I can push before the consequences appear. It's a personality trait I share with my twin.

After paying for the long neck, I make my way over to the table. It's packed full, both bench seats housing three bodies and a set of two chairs pulled from other tables to rest at the edge of it. There's one extra chair, and I would have laughed at the fact it's beside the one Bryce is sitting in if she wasn't already glaring at Poppy's brother, Darren.

He's sitting on the outside of the bench seat beside my brother and Aurora and is grinning smugly at her, almost as if he stole the spot on purpose.

"Enjoy getting a numb ass, Bryce," he says, the dig bright in his tone.

She licks her lips in a slow, vicious movement before baring her teeth. "Enjoy having a micro, Darren."

"Nah, I've got a—"

"Don't finish that sentence!" Poppy shrieks, hands over her ears. "Nobody wants to hear about your dick size, Darren."

I pull the empty chair further away from Bryce and set my beer on the table before sitting. She doesn't react, so I let it all go, focusing on everyone else now.

"Daisy!" Johnny exclaims, slapping a hand down on the table. "The guest of honour."

"I'm the what now?"

Rory smiles sympathetically at me. "I tried talking some sense into him, Daisy, but you know your brother."

"That I do," I agree.

Johnny addresses the entire table next. "As you all know, my twin is back in town to stay, and, well, she wants to move out."

"Move out of your place?" Brody asks.

The country music star leans back on the bench, his arm in its permanent place over his fiancée's shoulders. Anna leans into his body, her eyes bouncing around the table as we wait for Johnny to continue. The couple is a love story that will be told for a long while in Cherry Peak. A broody cowboy and the new girl in town running from a past with a man who didn't deserve her.

"Yep," Johnny answers.

"Have you thought about Rory's old rental?" Anna asks me.

I shake my head and cross my legs. "I'm not stepping foot in that horror story home."

"I don't blame you. I swear to God, I saw a woman in the upstairs window once," Poppy says with a shudder.

Rory snorts. "No, you didn't."

"I still don't know how you lived there for so long," Anna says before pointing at Johnny. "And I don't know how you let her."

My brother throws his hands up. "Hey, don't take shots at me. I tried to get her out of there, but you know how my woman is."

"And how is that?" Rory asks him, an eyebrow cocked.

He smirks before leaning to whisper into her ear, and a beat later, Rory's cheeks flame a bright red. I smile softly at the way their eyes meet, and despite the no doubt dirty words he's just spoken to her, I can't help but feel really, really happy for them.

"You're going to talk like that right beside me? Really?" Darren cries, twisting his face in disgust.

Bryce stares at him and bluntly says, "Shouldn't have stolen my seat."

"Shouldn't have stolen my seat," he echoes in a high-pitched voice.

"Mature."

Darren flips her off and takes a long drink from his glass. Their dynamic is interesting. I've noticed it a few times in the past, but mostly in passing. Getting a chance to watch it up close makes it easier to see that they share a similar brother-sister relationship to the one he has with Poppy and I have with Johnny.

"Anyway, back to why I called you here," Johnny says, guiding everyone back. "Anyone have an open room for Daisy?"

My stomach swirls with nerves and a bit of embarrassment when he drops the question. Everyone besides Bryce turns to look at me, and I keep a brave face despite feeling like a child who needs to be taken care of.

"I'm capable of finding my own place. I don't want anyone to feel forced into housing me," I add, tucking a piece of hair behind my ear.

"Nonsense!" Johnny declares.

I meet his eyes and subtly shake my head. "Johnny."

He looks a bit scolded when he nods. "If anyone would be *open* to letting my sister stay with you for a few weeks, we'd both appreciate it."

"Did you kick her out?" Darren asks him.

"No. But she hasn't . . . been sleeping well at our place."

Poppy tries to hide her laugh but fails when it escapes her sealed lips in a cough-like sound. "So, you two have been keeping her up all night with your fucking."

"Don't laugh, Poppy," Aurora mutters, cheeks still that deep red hue.

Poppy pulls her hair behind her shoulders and leans forward over the table. "Oh, I'm going to laugh. For all the shit y'all give me and Garrison, this is just too good."

"It's a blessing he isn't here to hear this," Brody notes.

Johnny huffs. "I'm sure Poppy will give him the rundown the minute she gets home."

"Of course I will."

They continue to pick on my brother for the next few minutes, and I let them, sitting back in silence. They're all really nice people. The best Alberta has to offer. But they're not really *my* people. Not the way they are my brother's.

Darting my eyes from the table, they land on the crossed, bare legs of the woman beside me. She bounces the one she has beneath the other, and I focus on the black cowboy boots that cup her from foot to calf. A dark denim skirt has risen to midway up her thigh, and even with her sitting position, her black band tee is cropped short enough to expose an inch of her toned stomach.

Her attractiveness is obvious, but as I lift my eyes higher and higher, so is the way she's looking at me right now, all cool irritation and a sharp bite of curiosity.

An apology gets stuck in my throat when she tenses and looks away. I release a long, quiet exhale and glance back at the table.

"I'd love to help you, Daisy, but unless you're willing to commute from Calgary again, me and Garrison are out," Poppy says.

Darren speaks next. "I've got a pull-out couch in my office, but it's pretty shit."

"We have two extra rooms," Anna pipes in.

Hope swells in my chest. "Really?"

Brody finishes his beer and reaches for the tray of nachos on the table. "We're up through the ranch. Past the main and guest houses. Down from the shop."

Living on Steele Ranch . . . My hope deflates.

"I appreciate the offer, but living on the ranch isn't really *me*," I say, shoving the guilt away that follows my statement.

Brody shrugs me off, unbothered. "It's not for everyone."

"What about you, Ice?" Poppy asks.

I stare at her, trying to analyze the barely there twitch of her lips. Bryce adjusts her posture beside me, her leg no longer bouncing.

"What about me?"

"You have an extra room, don't you?"

Anna gasps before glancing between Poppy and Bryce. "Yes!

That's right. You said you were using it for what again? Your clothes?"

I don't dare steal another look at Bryce. Not even when she shifts again, this time planting both feet on the floor.

"Would you do me this favour, Bryce? Please?" Johnny asks, excitement ramping with every word.

When I feel the weight of her eyes on my face, I look over. The vividness of the blue is startling this close up and without the dull, yellow lights of the bathroom to drown them out.

"It would only be for a couple of weeks," I say softly.

Her tongue presses against the inside of her cheek. Everyone's watching us, not a single word spoken. It's eerie, and I itch at my forearm when my nerves become relentless. Something about this woman shocks my system. Makes me shy, almost.

Maybe I should just take Brody and Anna up on their offer.

"Oh, for fuck's sake. Just say yes, Bryce," Poppy mutters, the first to break the silence.

Bryce's nostrils flare with her short sniff. "Fine."

With a quirk of my lips, I offer her a thankful smile. She doesn't return it before darting her eyes away and toward the bar. Then, she's up and away from everyone.

Discomfort nips at me, but I ignore it. Bryce can hate me all she wants as long as I can sleep in peace. Besides, it will only be for a max of two weeks. Not a day more than that. We can deal until then.

"Sorry, Daisy. She takes her personal space seriously," Poppy divulges.

"It's okay. I get that."

"I'll talk to her. Straighten her out," Johnny says.

Poppy twirls the tiny straw in her red drink. "No, I'll do it. She's just not the most welcoming to people she doesn't know well."

It's a lie. I've heard the opposite from my brother and his girlfriend. If that were the case, Bryce wouldn't have taken in both Aurora and Anna as easily as she did when they moved into town. Yeah, she's guarded and brutally blunt. That's obvious. But rude? Down to her very core? That's still to be decided.

It seems that I'm an exception to her usual behaviour, and I'm curious enough to want to know why. She can be warm to those she cares about as I've seen a handful of times, and I want to know why I've been written off as someone who can't be tucked into that category the way my brother and everyone else has.

"Thank you, everyone. I appreciate you helping me out. And for offering me a place, Brody and Anna."

"Anytime. We've got a soft spot for the Mitchells," Anna says with a wink.

"If I didn't mind the smell of cattle or being woken before sunrise, I'd have moved in without a second thought."

"I'm with you, Daisy. When we stay in the guest house on the weekends, I've started wearing earplugs," Poppy says.

Brody laughs. "You get used to it after a while."

"Only if you want to." Poppy finishes her drink and pats Anna's shoulder. "I'm going to check on Bryce."

"Want me to come?" Anna asks.

"No. I've got it. Just let me out."

Brody and Anna exit the booth long enough to let Poppy out before sliding back in. I watch Poppy head right for the side of the bar not visible to us at the table and then drop my gaze.

I feel bad that this has upset Bryce so much, but she could have turned my brother down. Something tells me that Bryce isn't one to fall under the trap of peer pressure.

So why didn't she just say no?

5

Bryce

I'M THREE VODKA SHOTS DEEP BY THE TIME I FEEL POPPY SLIDE ONTO the stool beside me at the bar. I wave at the bartender who took over for Vic's mom for the night for a fourth before facing my best friend.

She's watching with a soft, concern-lined expression, and I huff at her. "Whatever you're planning on saying, don't."

"I wasn't going to say a word," she lies.

"And I wasn't about to have another shot."

The bartender slides another glass across the counter, and I take it, shooting it back without a flinch. It burns like a mother-fucker, but that's the best part. He chuckles at my eagerness, and I glare at him.

"Can I get a water, please?" Poppy asks before he disappears.

"'Course."

I tap my black-painted nails on the bar, leaning my body weight against it. "Water?"

"For you, asshole."

"I don't want water."

"And I don't want you to wake up tomorrow with a hang-over from hell, but here we are."

"I'll keep my complaining to myself."

She sighs, placing a hand on my shoulder to spin me around, bringing us face to face. "I'm sorry I offered your room. Is that why you're like this right now?"

"She could have stayed in the guest house. You're hardly there."

It's the place she and Garrison stay at when they're in town on the weekends. But recently, they haven't been staying on the ranch long enough to use it. Not with Mr. Fancy Pants CEO whisking her all over the world on these endless fucking trips of theirs.

She scrunches her brows, frowning. "Are you mad at me?"

I spot the brown hair of the bartender and shout, "Can I have a bottle?"

"Of water!" Poppy adds.

Pinning her beneath a harsh glare, I try to shake her hand off my shoulder. "Don't mother me right now. I can handle my liquor."

"I know that. I've been drinking with you since we were fourteen, sneaking pink Sour Puss into my parents' garage. This isn't about that."

The mention of the watermelon-flavoured poison rolls my stomach. Bartender #2 hands her a glass of water, and she pushes it directly in front of me before I can tell him to dump it somewhere.

Eyes zoned into me and the glass of water I haven't moved to grab yet, she doesn't look away until I've lifted it to my mouth and drank it. It's not the taste I'm searching for, and before she can mother me again, I order another shot.

"You want to talk about this, Poppy? You can wait. I'm not interested right now."

"What exactly do you think I'm wanting to talk about, though? Your feelings about me not using the guest house enough or the fact I didn't suggest it to Daisy? Because if it's option number one, then you're right about not getting into it here and now. But option two? That's something I'm curious enough about now to dig into. You heard her just as well as I did. She isn't interested in staying on Steele Ranch, and last time I checked, the guest house was smack dab in the middle of it."

"It's nicer than my place," I mutter, ignoring everything else she's said.

I reach for my last shot of the night and tip it back.

"I don't think she'll care about that."

I grunt in response, the effects of the vodka starting to make the world a bit smoother. Or softer? Rougher? Fuck knows.

"Okay."

"Is there a reason why you don't want her to stay with you, besides the fact I was the one who suggested it?"

"Don't give a shit that you suggested it, Pops."

She leans against me when I face forward, her cheek on my shoulder. "So what, then? Worried she'll add a couple too many throw pillows to the couch? Or that she'll host wild parties while you're gone and offer free tats to randoms? Come on, Ice. She's Johnny's twin and one of the sweetest people I've ever met. I don't think you'll have to worry about much."

"Don't know what you want me to say. It's already done. She's staying whether I want her to or not," I say, my voice sounding a bit garbled.

"You don't want her to, then?"

"Stop analyzing me," I snap, stumbling off the stool to stand. "It's done. Over with."

She reaches out to steady me. I slap her hand away and step back.

"Just let me breathe," I plead.

Her confusion is obvious. I'm confused too. I just don't want to talk about this. Not with her, not with anyone. My problems with Daisy Mitchell are mine alone. I'll deal with them sooner or later.

"Alright, Ice. Can I at least get you a ride home?"

"No. I'm good on my own." It's probably still pissing rain outside, but fuck it. "Text you when I get home."

"If you're sure . . ." She trails off, glancing behind her at the sliver of the table we can see.

I leave her there while she's not paying attention. Slipping outside is easy. I'm not drunk enough to be tripping over myself yet, but I brace myself on the railing as I move down the steps.

"Bryce! Wait up for a second!"

My mouth grows dry. I freeze on the sidewalk, rain pelting my hair and face, soaking my clothes. The street is empty, quiet, and wet with rain puddles.

"Oh crap. Do you have an umbrella? Are you walking home?"

Daisy's a rambler. I've picked that up over the past three, almost four years. Doesn't seem to matter who she's speaking to, if she wants to talk a mile a minute, she will.

"Let me drive you home."

"No, thanks" are my first words to her.

"At least take my jacket. It's in my car."

"Why did you come out here?"

I recognize the sound of her yellow high-top Converse clapping against the wooden stairs. The ones with the daisies painted on them in white and stars in black.

"I realized that I don't have your number. Or know where the house is. I don't need to see it before I move in, but I do need to know when I can actually do that."

Goosebumps cover my bare arms as cool rain freezes my cheeks. I shiver. "Poppy can give you my number. And move in whenever you want."

"Maybe we could meet up for breakfast and talk details another day?"

It's a really fucking sincere offer. I'd have to be a heartless bitch to turn it down.

"I don't eat breakfast."

What?

"Oh."

"I mean, I don't like breakfast. Obviously, I eat breakfast."

"Well, I actually like cooking breakfast. It's the easiest meal to cook. It's hard to go wrong with pancakes or toast or eggs. Maybe a smoothie too, depending on how you're feeling. Just dump a bag of frozen fruit into the blender with some milk and you're set."

I twist, looking back toward the building. Suddenly, the liquor sets fire to my blood, and I'm burning deep in my chest.

She's stepped out from beneath the awning of the bar and lingers on the bottom step in the rain. Her hair is drenched, draping over her shoulders as the thick strands drip red-tinted water onto her shirt, staining it. I've always known she isn't a redhead. The black roots that appear in between dyes tell on her.

The pink at the tip of her tiny nose is concerning. She could get sick standing out here talking to me. Johnny wouldn't let me live that one down.

"You're getting wet," I blurt out.

Her round cheeks pinch when she smiles at me, a small laugh escaping. "That's okay. I don't mind."

"Go inside. I'll text you tomorrow. No breakfast, but I'll tell you when to move in."

"Okay. That works."

"Great."

I turn around and start down the sidewalk. I'll be too drunk to get home on my own if I don't leave now.

"Bryce!" she shouts, and I stop automatically, waiting. "Get home safe."

Thump.

With a weak wave, I leave. The movement in my stomach has to be from the booze. Not her.

THE RAIN STOPPED ten minutes ago.

My lips are probably blue, but I don't get up. The curb is

hard against my ass, and the inside of my boots are full of water. I have a chill despite how hot I feel beneath my skin.

Victoria's old house is behind me, the fence Poppy, Anna, and I painted pink out of spite a couple of years back brown again. The lawn is overgrown, weeds sticking up through the longest pieces. I fucking hate this house almost as much as the woman who doesn't even live inside of it anymore.

She's been gone for a while now. Off somewhere with the man she chose over me. I don't love her anymore, but the wound she left is still there, just scarred over.

My first and only long-term relationship with a woman was torn out by the roots by a man. It wasn't the start of my annoyance with all things men, but it did spark a deep-seated hatred. The good for fucking nothing, shit for brains, goddamn assholes have brought me nothing but headaches since I was a teenager.

In a perfect world, they'd disappear from the Earth with a snap of my fingers. But the world is far from perfect, and now, all of my friends have found themselves ones to make me suffer with forever. Anna first, then Poppy. Aurora moved here and fell prey to Johnny within a few weeks. And now, it's just me.

Well, me and one of the only men I can stand who's currently driving down the road to pick me up.

Darren Huntsly is a good guy. I've known it since Poppy and I were kids and he'd punch any classmates who tried to come near us on the playground. I've grown to accept him as both a brother and a best friend, despite every rule I've ever made for myself telling me I'm a fool for it.

When Victoria cheated and tried her best at convincing me that we couldn't be happy together without a man in our relationship, Darren was the first one I called from the police station after I . . . made a mess of things.

He was on the phone with the officer who took me from the scene of my crime within seconds of us hanging up, trying to get me released without having spent even an hour in a cell. Of course, Poppy doesn't know that detail. As far as she's concerned, she was my first call from the station.

It was instinct to call him when I found myself parked on this curb, too drunk to risk walking home on my own.

He's got a sleek black car that costs . . . a lot. If it isn't raining, I force him to let me put the roof down so I can feel the wind on my skin. Even the seats are expensive, a deep brown leather with cooling and heating and massagers for long drives.

I'd marry this car. Yeah, I would.

The headlights are tinted blue when they fan over me and then illuminate the street. I wait for him to put the car in park before trying to stand.

A car door slams. "Christ, Bryce. You're going to get sick."

"Yeah, Dad. I am."

He holds me up with an arm around my middle before we're moving. I lean against him and keep my protests hidden when he lifts me off my feet and carries me to the passenger door.

"I was going to follow you, but Poppy told me to leave you be. Clearly, I should have listened to her," he says.

I roll my eyes and tuck myself into the seat once the door is open. He reaches in to help with the seat belt, but I push his hand away.

"She was right. I called you, didn't I?"

He sighs, backing up. "Yeah, you did."

The door shuts, and I close my eyes, leaning my head back. It smells faintly like the cologne he always wears, but it doesn't irritate me. Probably because I bought it for him.

I keep my eyes shut as he slides in beside me and clicks in his seat belt. The radio goes so quiet I can barely hear the song playing before he asks, "What's up with you?"

"Not you too, D. Not right now."

"You called me to pick you up in the middle of the night, drunk off goddamn vodka when you know it has this effect on your body, and you don't want me to ask what's wrong?"

I swipe a hand down my face and look at him. He's waiting

for me to speak, two eyebrows lifted expectantly and lips slightly parted as if he's got a rebuttal at the ready.

"I don't want to share my place with someone I hardly know."

The words feel sticky coming up, and they sound the same. I'm a pathetic liar on a regular day, but under the influence, I'm just plain ridiculous.

"You sure it has nothing to do with who you'll be sharing a place with? Daisy is—"

"Yeah, I know what Daisy is, Darren," I hiss before he can finish. "Just take me home, please."

"It might help to say it out loud, Ry. It's only a matter of time before everyone else pieces it together. My sister already has an idea."

I tense, whipping my head to scowl at him. "Don't tell anyone if you want to live."

"Not planning on it. I'm just saying, maybe you wouldn't get into these moods if you weren't—"

I stick my hand out and tug at his beard hair. When he curses and shoves me off, I smirk, crossing my arms.

"Take me home, D."

He does, and in a town the size of Cherry Peak, I'm being tucked into bed in ten minutes flat. With a kiss to my forehead that I wipe off immediately, he leaves, locking up as he goes.

The last thing I think about before I crash is *fuck vodka.*

6

Daisy

"So . . . you would really rather stay with Bryce Lemieux than me? I'm trying not to be offended here, but damn."

Kristen—Kiki to me—kicks her legs out in front of her and sighs. She's lying beside me on the football field, both of us staring up at the clouds in the sky. The grass is thick beneath our backs, groomed to perfection by the old man who runs the rec centre in town. Cherry Peak might be small by design, but it doesn't lack the necessities.

There's a fire station, town hall, small RCMP office, and locally owned supermarket to start. Add in the coffee shop, diner, bar, Poppy's pole studio, and Anna's salon, and I've never felt like I didn't have what I needed here.

Well, other than a university or a single decent rental.

The football field is empty today, but it won't stay that way much longer. Once school starts next week, everything is going to get a bit crazier. My life especially.

"You know I'd rather live with you. But while I mean this with all the love in the world, your place is . . . a little . . . rough around the edges," I say carefully.

She whips her head to the side so fast one of her blonde curls slaps me across the face. Her glare is weak, more for show than anything else.

"That's rude."

"I said I meant it with love. It's better than the haunted house, at least."

"That's literally the whole reasoning behind saying 'no offense' before dropping a serious insult."

I laugh. "Yeah, you're right. I'm sorry, but even you can admit your place needs some love."

Love and a bulldozer.

The one and only apartment building in town is two stories tall with eight one-bedroom rentals inside. It hasn't been updated since it was built forever ago and is cheap for a reason. But in Cherry Peak, you can't be picky about your housing unless you plan to buy instead of rent. Most of the people who live here have been residents for generations and were either handed down property or have the funds to build something new.

"It's just classic, Didi. You know, *original*."

"Originally a dump."

"Daisy!" she scolds, giving my arm a shove. "At least I have a place."

"Can't argue with you there."

"So, Bryce?"

I wince as memories of the last time I spoke to Bryce come spiralling back. I'm beyond nervous to stay with her, but that doesn't mean I'm not going to do my best to make it work. My only other choice is to move back in with my moms.

"Yep," I say.

"And? When are you moving in?"

Kristen keeps her eyes on me, her interest in this situation obvious. I don't blame her for it either. It'll be an interesting next few weeks.

"She said she'd text me with information."

"Alright. Well, it's not like you have a lot of stuff to bring. All of your furniture from Calgary was included in your rental, right?"

I nod. "All I'll take are my clothes, shoes, and toiletries. Things like that."

"Obviously, I'll be helping you."

My lips curve into a grin. "Obviously."

"I'll feel out the big bad ice queen while I'm there. Make sure she isn't going to turn you into an ice sculpture in your sleep."

"I think she'd most likely freeze and shatter me before bothering to sculpt me."

She snorts a laugh and looks up at the sky again, her hands folded over her stomach. "Just make sure you don't stay there if you're going to be unhappy. I'll buy you some heavy-duty earplugs for your brother's house before watching you suffer somewhere."

"Thanks, Kiki. But I don't think it'll be quite that bad. We'll both be working during the day, and I'm not looking for another best friend or anything. It'll be fine."

"What does she even do for work? Do you know?"

"I think she works at the town office. Her dad's the mayor."

A pause. "I'm sorry for her loss, then. That man leaves a lot to be desired."

"Really? I've never met him."

"I've only met him once, but he didn't exactly leave the best impression."

I huff, my nerves growing. "Great."

"But it's not like you'll ever have to see her parents. Not unless you're planning on being more than roommates," she teases, looking toward me with a devilish grin.

"Don't start with the matchmaking. You were just talking about her carving me up into an ice sculpture."

"I was just joking about that."

Pushing up on my hands, I glance ahead of us at the goalposts before meeting her green-eyed stare. "I'm not looking for anything more than roommates."

"Boo. You never are."

"You're supposed to be grateful for that. It means you don't have to share me with anyone."

"Seeing you in love wouldn't be too bad of a trade-off," she says.

"I'm content being single."

"For now," she sings, sitting and pulling her legs into her body. "Don't you ever feel lonely not having somebody?"

I soften my expression at the emotion in her voice. "Do you?"

"Honestly, yeah. It's not just having a boyfriend that I want but the love, I guess. The emotional connection to someone. Does that make sense?"

"Of course it does. I think we all want that."

"Even you?"

Exhaling, I lean forward and rip a handful of grass out of the ground. "Even me. I just don't want to prioritize finding that right now. Not with everything else going on. I'm too busy trying to get ready for my new job and this whole roommate situation to handle much else, let alone another entire person."

"I get it, Didi."

She leans against me as I say, "Thank you for caring."

"Shut up. I'll always care about you. Even when you leave me behind and move away to Calgary for four years."

"You'll never fully forgive me for that, will you?"

"Nope," she answers, popping the *p*.

"I'm here now."

"For good."

"For good," I promise.

TWO DAYS LATER, I'm spending my Monday morning at my moms' house, grabbing the rest of my things before heading to Bryce's place. Her text came only yesterday, and while it left a lot to the imagination, I decided not to waste any time before moving in.

Bryce: Hi. This is Bryce. Monday is fine. Lock code is 1031. I left your bedroom door open. Mine is shut. I work til 4:30.

The address to her place was attached in a separate message, and I thanked her immediately before jumping into packing. The two suitcases in my parents' living room, in addition to the one from Johnny's, are all I've decided to bring, other than my laptop and all the paperwork and lesson plans I have for school.

Johnny's off moping somewhere, more upset that I'm moving out of his place than I am. It wasn't like I planned on staying there for very long, anyway, but I do wish I could have stayed a smidge longer. There's no one that gets me the way my twin does.

"This is the last time I'll ask, but are you sure you don't want to just stay here, Daisy?" Mom frowns at me from her spot on the couch. "Is there a reason you aren't?"

My mom and mama have both been bombarding me with these questions the past couple of days, but where one lacks subtlety, the other does not.

"If there was a reason, I'm sure she'd have told us. Right, baby?" Mom asks, her lifelong experience as a youth therapist paying off in the way she words her questions.

I can tell it frustrates Mama sometimes to see her wife understand us in a way that she doesn't always, but she never makes a big deal out of it. And I try my best not to make her feel like she's doing anything wrong simply because she doesn't know the exact right way to handle certain situations.

I tighten my hair tie and then slip my shoes on. "I'm just ready for something else. I'm home now, and I don't want to have to move backward from where I was in Calgary."

"You wouldn't be. It's perfectly healthy for adults to move back into their parents' house at any time if they need to," Mom argues.

"Jen," Mama says on a long outward breath. Focusing on me

now, she steps around my suitcase. "We support your decision, Daisy."

Mom gets off the couch and rushes toward me. Once I'm in her arms, she kisses my head a half dozen times. "Of course we support you. Doesn't mean I love the idea."

"I'm not a kid anymore. None of us are," I whisper.

Her arms grow tighter around me. "I know. I've already said goodbye to you a million times and just hoped it would be a little longer before I had to again."

I let all my arguments die.

It doesn't matter that I've been moved out for years or that I've been staying with Johnny and not them since I got back. The few minutes it'll take to drive from Bryce's house to this one is a pointless fact.

My moms have been without kids in their house for a while now, and I think they just miss us. We're a big, close family, and now, the house is empty and quiet.

"We'll cook your favourite meal this week. How about that? You can tell us all about your new classroom and how you're feeling before the first day of school," Mama suggests.

Mom pulls back but doesn't release me fully, keeping her hands on my arms. "That wasn't really a question, by the way. It's a summons."

"Good thing I was going to say yes, then," I tease.

"Let our baby go so she can get out of here. You can't keep her stuck to your side by grasping onto her like that," Mama says.

She closes a palm over Mom's hand and gently pulls it from my arm. The wedding ring on her finger makes my chest swell with emotion, a fierce sense of happiness filling me. They've been married for what feels like ever, and I swear they look more in love every passing day.

"Thanks, Mama. I'll be back soon. I promise."

Mom looks around the room, brows furrowed. "We'll help take your suitcases out to the truck. Where's your brother?"

"Johnny! Come here, turd face!" I shout.

"C'mon, I could have done that," Mama mutters.

With a shrug, I walk around them to lift the handle of my first suitcase. "He's hiding somewhere pouting."

"Probably in the backyard," Mom huffs before disappearing in search of him.

Once she's gone, Mama comes closer, pulling me into her arms with tight squeezes. I release the handle of my suitcase and breathe in her perfume, shutting my eyes.

The bond I share with Mama is something I would go to the ends of the Earth to protect. Mom is an incredible mother, but Mama has always got me in a way that I feel deep in my soul. Maybe it's all of her counselling experience or something bigger than that; I'll never know.

I've been lucky enough to be raised by two amazing women who I've grown to idolize. But it was Mama who I sat down with first on my sixteenth birthday and came out to as a lesbian. I don't have an explanation as to why I didn't go to them both together other than I felt like Mama would understand me the best. She reacted the way I expected her to and hugged me so tight I thought my bones would pop out of their sockets. Five minutes later, Mom was joining us, and they were telling me how happy they were that I felt comfortable enough with them to share that part of myself. I don't think I've ever told them just how much I appreciate their support.

"Daisy, please tell Mom to stop bringing up why you're moving out of my place!" Johnny yells, his footsteps heavy on the floor as he heads our way. "She's embarrassing me!"

Mama laughs into her hand as I roll my eyes and drag my luggage with me to the front door. Johnny appears with a huff and takes a long look at my suitcase.

"Don't huff at me," I say. "And you don't get embarrassed by anything."

"I'll huff if I want to. Now, come on, I need to have time to give Ice my big brother speech before you kick me out."

"Your big brother speech? Why does she need that?" Mom asks, eyes narrowing. "Isn't she one of your friends?"

Johnny waves a hand through the air. "She is, but that doesn't mean she doesn't still get a good ol'-fashioned talkin'-to."

"Oh, please. Don't start," I warn.

He grabs the second suitcase and rolls it toward where I stand in front of the door. "Start what?"

"Don't give her the talk, Johnny. I'm serious."

"What talk?" Mom steps closer to open the door for us. Mama smiles coyly at her. "Don't look at me like that, Rachel. What talk is going on about?"

"*The* talk, Jen," Mama says.

"Oh." Mom blinks a few times. "*Oh*."

"You'll keep your mouth shut, Johnny. I'm serious," I threaten.

He shrugs me off and shoves open the porch door before yanking the suitcase down the stairs. I wince as the wheels clang on the cement, but when he starts to whistle, I'm chasing after him, doing the exact same thing to the suitcase I'm hauling with me.

"Don't act all innocent, Jonathan. You will *not* make this awkward for me. Got it?"

Unlocking the truck, he lowers the tailgate and starts tossing the first suitcase into the bed. "How would I make it awkward?"

I set my hands on my hips and try to look as intimidating as I can. Compared to my twin, that's hardly ever possible. He's a mammoth, with the stubbornness of the mules on Steele Ranch. Shifting his body toward me, he leans his hip on the edge of the tailgate and cocks his head.

"If you bare your teeth a little and work on your death stare *a lot*, you might have a shot at giving your new roomie a run for her money," he says, poking fun at me for the millionth time in our lives.

"You're so annoying. Just keep your bro speeches to yourself, please. At least until I can make her like me a bit. If you go in there now spouting your mouth off already, she's just going to hate me even more than she does."

The humour in his eyes fades. "She doesn't hate you, D."

I make a disbelieving noise in my throat. "Maybe *hate* is a strong word. But she strongly dislikes me. And that's fine, but just please don't make it any worse."

"Maybe it's another speech I need to be giving her altogether," he mutters.

"You're not giving a single one. I'm serious. I can handle myself."

"I know you can." He takes the suitcase from me and puts it in the bed before slamming the tailgate shut. "But you'll let me know if you need anything, right?"

"Of course."

Nodding, he reaches for me and pulls me in for a hug. "She's good people, D. Rough around the edges but real good to those she cares about. You'll be fine."

"It's not my first time with a roommate, J. It'll be good. And short-lived, hopefully."

I squeeze him once before turning to face our moms. They're standing together on the sidewalk, hands linked with gentle expressions on their faces. Mom adjusts her glasses up her nose before speaking.

"Call us when you're settled."

"Or just come back over," Mama suggests casually.

I smile, heading to my car. "I'll call."

"Loosen the reins a bit, you helicopter moms," Johnny calls.

Mama doesn't hesitate to flip him the bird, making him burst out in loud, booming laughter before I'm hopping into my car and waiting to follow Johnny to Bryce's place. A beat later, we're gone.

7

Bryce

My parents hate my car. They'd prefer I drive a gas-guzzling SUV with bulletproof windows and tires meant to handle rough-as-fuck terrain than a small electric one. Being protective and judgmental are their love languages. I pieced that together when I was just a kid and have been rebelling since. Purchasing a small black car that would most likely crunch like a hard tortilla shell in a collision drove them mad, and I like watching them sweat a bit. I'm pretty sure *that* is my love language.

When I pull up along the curb outside my house, I linger longer than necessary just to avoid joining the people I know are already inside. The old truck in front of my car is Johnny's, and the dainty blue one across the street I recognize instantly as Daisy's, but I don't know the vehicle in front of it. Or understand how someone could be blind enough to park in front of a bright red fire hydrant. It'll get towed if an RC sees it, but it's not my business.

It's unsettling having so many people at my place while I'm not there, but I can either get used to it now or let it eat me up inside.

Fuck it.

I get out of the car and lock it twice before slugging my way up the sidewalk. The front door is unlocked when I turn the handle and push my way in.

"Maybe you could ask her to give me a free tattoo. She gave Poppy one, but when I asked, she told me to stop talking," Johnny shouts, his voice slightly muted, as if he's in one of the rooms down the hall.

I don't see anyone as I shut the door and kick off my boots, so my muscles loosen slightly. There aren't a bunch of boxes all over, and from what I can tell, all of my things are still in their rightful place. My black couch doesn't have any colourful throw pillows on it, and the skull-shaped candle I impulse ordered online the other night is still on the fireplace mantel.

Wandering into the kitchen, I search the counters for anything new, but they're bare of anything besides a fruit bowl with a single banana inside. Curiosity fills me as I leave the kitchen and start down the hall toward the mix of voices.

"You're not unpacking my clothes, Johnny."

"Why? I'm just trying to help."

"Go put my tampons beneath the sink, then."

A heavy sigh. "Fine."

I wait in the hallway, a few feet from the open bedroom door. There's a slam of a cabinet, and then a voice that doesn't belong to either Daisy or her brother appears.

"Am I allowed to help with your clothes, or am I on tampon duty too?"

Kristen Newberry, Daisy's best friend, isn't someone I'm very knowledgeable of, but I still recognize her voice. I've heard it around the diner and at Johnny's family barbeques that I'm always brought to.

She's a stranger in my home, but then again, isn't Daisy one as well?

With a stretch of my neck, I walk into the spare room and get my first look at the people there. Kristen's the first I see. She's stretched out on the bed, wrinkling the comforter I washed last night. Two suitcases are beside her, but only one is open, exposing the clothes inside.

It's damn near impossible to keep my eyes from snapping to the pile of hot pink panties and nude bras inside the left of the suitcase. They're just there. Obvious and free for everyone to see.

I clear my throat and look at Daisy when she swings around from her place in front of the dresser. Her smile is wide and genuine, and I swallow twice.

"Hi, Bryce!"

I swallow again. "Is the room fine?"

"It's great. I wasn't expecting it to be so spacious," she says.

"Yeah. The place is pretty big."

"Jeez, Brycie. Why are you still wearin' that? You're scaring me," Johnny states, exiting the ensuite bathroom.

Daisy looks at him with narrowed eyes. "Johnny! That's so rude."

"It's true," I mutter.

The high-collared button-down blouse and pencil skirt that falls to my ankles feel like a prison jumpsuit more than a work uniform. Every day, it seems to grow harder and harder not to rip them off and burn them in a field.

"The clothes look uncomfortable." Daisy slides the dresser drawer shut and moves closer.

Kristen stares at me, a subtle, calculating gleam in her eyes. It's not enough to annoy me, so I let it be. If she's anything like me, she's trying to send a warning in regards to her best friend.

I've done far worse to make others treat my friends with respect than simply stare at them. I can appreciate her effort. As weak as it may be.

Daisy stops beside the bed and lays a hand on the mattress. Five sparkling, yellow nails gleam beneath the ceiling light. Her twin follows behind her but doesn't stop at the bed. He comes right up to me and flattens his massive hand on the top of my head before moving it around.

I pinch the underside of his arm, and he squeals like a pig

before yanking his hand back. "Don't do that again, or I'll shave your hair off in your sleep."

"Aurora wouldn't speak to you again if you did that," he tosses back with an arrogant lift of his voice. "She loves my hair."

"She would get over it."

"You don't have the face for a bald head," Kristen tells him.

Daisy fails to hide her amusement. "She's not wrong. Don't risk it."

"You know what? I'm leavin'. First, I'm on tampon duty, and then this? I need to go home to my woman," he says.

Smile drooping, Daisy asks, "You'll come by soon?"

"'Course, D. Whenever you want." He side-eyes a look at me. "Bryce won't have a problem with my surprise visits, right?"

My brow twitches. "Even if I said yes, it wouldn't matter."

"Great. I'll take that as approval. Walk me out?" he asks.

Once again, he isn't really asking me, so I just nod and lead him out of the room. We don't make it three steps before Daisy's stopping us.

"I'll come too!"

I glance over my shoulder and see Johnny shake his head at her and lightly push her backward into the bedroom.

"Nah, you unpack with Kiki. Call me tomorrow. Love you."

He kisses her head and then nudges me forward. I tilt my head and watch the two of them, intrigued with what this is about.

"Johnny," Daisy says, his name spoken with obvious warning.

"Are these all thongs, Didi?" Kristen asks loudly. "Ooh, a strapless bra. And a—"

Daisy loosens a sigh and then leaves. "Yeah, I get it. Stop going through my intimates."

"Intimates? How very modest of you."

Johnny settles at my side as we continue down the hallway.

The longer he waits to speak, the more intense my curiosity grows.

"Did you get piss on my toilet seat or something? What's up with you?" I ask once we've made it to the entryway.

"I'm not a dog, Bryce."

"Depends on the circumstances."

His laugh is more snort than anything else. "Alright. You know I like you, Bryce. Wouldn't have let Poppy suggest Daisy stay here otherwise."

Leaning back against the wall, I cross my arms and nod. "Alright."

"Be nice to her while she's here. Drop the ice queen act a bit."

"Ice queen?"

"Yeah, ice queen. I know better than to tell a woman she should smile more, but just . . . warm up a bit around her. Try to have a conversation every once in a while. Get to know her."

"She'll be fine here, Johnny. You've got my word."

The corner of his mouth tips up. "Thank you."

"You're welcome. Now, I really want to change."

"Yeah, I don't blame you. It's hard to have a serious conversation with you when you look like that."

My lips flatten in a scowl. "Like what?"

"Your shirt is buttoned up so high I'm surprised it hasn't choked you out. How much longer do you have to wear this shit?"

"I don't know. I thought I'd be used to it by now, but I think it grows itchier every day."

Sliding a nail beneath the tight cuff around my wrist, I scrape at my skin. The tattoo on the back of my hand has healed a bit and is less itchy than the rest of my body.

"Can't you just not wear it? What are your parents going to do? Fire you?"

"I'm picking my battles."

And right now, I need to focus on getting my mom off my back with this blind date nonsense.

"Well, glad to see you've kept the boots, at least. Maybe you can get Daisy into a pair. I've been trying for a long fuckin' time with no luck," he says before offering me another grin and slipping past me to the door.

His boots aren't inside, and while I didn't look for them outside, I'd bet they're on the other side of the door. He was raised proper despite his sometimes annoying demeanour. Dirty cowboy boots on my floor would have made me have a stroke.

"Your sister wears hand-painted Converse. I doubt she'll ever slip on a pair of boots," I state.

"Worth a shot. Thanks again, Bryce. Means a lot to me that you took her in. I know you like your space."

"Stop thanking me."

He chuckles and grips the door handle. "You got it. I'll see you soon, I'm sure."

"Bye, Johnny."

"Bye, Brycie."

Once he's gone, I pop open the top two buttons of my blouse and head for the kitchen. My collection of Fanta cans in the fridge is a welcome sight, and I snag one before cracking it open.

Skull aching from having my hair up all day, I tug the elastic from it and moan at the instant relief.

"Am I interrupting?"

I tighten my hold on the cold can in my hand and meet Daisy's stare. With one leg in the kitchen and the other still in the hall, she visibly hesitates to join me. Even her expression is nervous, all rolled lips and hopeful eyes.

"You can come in," I say.

She accepts the invitation she didn't need and eyes the drink in my hand. The corner of my mouth twitches slightly as I twist and pull her a can from the fridge. Face carefully blank, I offer it to her.

"Thank you. I love Fanta."

It sounds like a lie, but I can't quite tell.

"I thought you'd be a Crush kind of girl."

"Orange or cream soda?"

I cross my ankles and tap a nail against my can. "Cream soda."

"Care to elaborate on that?"

"No."

She slides a sparkly nail beneath the tab on her can and cracks it open with a soft smile. "Do you want to know what kind of pop I thought you'd like?"

"Something fucking boring like Pepsi?"

Her nose wrinkles. "No. More like sour apple. A flavour only available in one of those fancy glass bottles."

I blink at her, tonguing my cheek. "Should I be offended?"

"You tell me," she teases before taking a sip of her drink.

"I don't get offended by much."

"What's your secret?"

I pause. I've always known it would be easy to talk to Daisy, and I'm being proven right with each passing minute we stand here. My edges soften in her proximity, and fuck, that's dangerous. That's why I sharpen them again before she has a chance to do any damage with her toothache-inducing sweetness.

"It's not giving a shit, Daisy. You should try it sometime."

She doesn't so much as flinch at my harsh tone. "Isn't that boring? Maybe it's easier not to be bothered by things, but I like caring."

"Your loss, then." I finish my drink and drop the can in the blue bin beside the fridge. "I don't have many rules, but I like to keep to myself. Sometimes I have friends over, and they can be loud, as I'm sure you know. There's only one bathroom, so keep showers quick in the morning. I work weekdays from eight 'til four thirty and am off weekends. There aren't a lot of groceries in the fridge—"

"I can buy my own groceries. And just give me a list with my share of the rent and utilities and when you want them paid by. I'm not a freeloader, Bryce. Cleaning up after myself and being respectful of others is something that comes naturally to me," she says, clutching her can to her chest.

"Alright. Then, we're good."

"We're good," she agrees.

Swiping my tongue over my lips, I nod, glancing around the room. "The code will get you into the house whenever you want, but if you want a key, I can get one cut. Poppy and Anna are the only two other people with keys."

"Your parents don't have one?"

I laugh. "No. And that's a good thing."

Her lips part twice, as if she's trying to think of what to say before finally asking, "Are you okay with my moms coming over? They're a bit . . . They just like to see me often. I can always just go over to their place if you're not okay with that."

"They're welcome here. All the Mitchells are."

"Thank you." Her smile warms the room and knocks at my chest. "I'll let you go get out of your work clothes. I've got some unpacking to do."

"Kristen didn't want to stay and help you?" I ask before I can leave her there without another word.

Fuck. This is exactly what I was talking about.

"I wanted a bit of time alone to speak with you first."

"Are you always so straightforward when someone asks you something? We hardly know each other."

She laughs softly, moving toward me at a casual pace. The first touch of her hand to my arm makes my throat sticky. It's hot and gentle. Calm and searing.

"I don't think that's true. But even so, I'm excited to change that."

With a stiff arm and the lingering heat of her touch burned into my skin, she leaves me standing in the kitchen. This time when I reach into the fridge, it's a beer I'm gripping.

8

Bryce

THE ONLY THING MORE RIDICULOUS THAN BEING SET UP ON A DATE with a man your mother picked for you is to have him pick you up and drive you to your family home for it.

Not only do I not like random people knowing where I live, but I really, really fucking hate it when I don't want this man to be anywhere near me to begin with.

My family home is about fifteen minutes north of town in a small community of exorbitantly built designer homes. It faces the golf course that loops through the entire community and a man-made swamp that I bet Darren to swim in years ago. The HOA fees are disgusting, and the rules that go along them with are just as bad, but my parents love living there.

I've always thought it was ironic that the mayor of Cherry Peak doesn't even live in the town, but fuck if anyone else cares about that.

The inside of the sports car is stuffy and uncomfortable, but once Jean steps out, I take a full breath and shake some of the tension from my shoulders. He's heading for my side, so I pop open the door before he has a chance to do it for me.

The man my mother set me up with today is tall and lanky

with classically handsome features, boring brown eyes, and a clean-shaven jaw. The lines of his white dress shirt and matching linen pants are crisp and perfectly ironed.

There are brown loafers on his feet.

Loafers.

I'm more concerned about how my mother thought for even one half of a second that I would like this guy than I am about how I'm going to ditch him in a few minutes.

Jean grips the side of the door and pulls it as far open as it'll go before I step out. My boots scuff the driveway as I sidestep the hand he offers to me and tug my denim skirt further down my thighs.

"May I at least open the front door of the house for you?" he asks, half teasing, half begging.

I linger, waiting while he shuts my car door and uses an app on his phone to lock both of them. "I like to open my own doors."

"We're on a date. I will open the door for you always."

His French accent is so thick all it does is remind me of my mother.

"No, thanks," I say before beginning the walk to the house.

The stench of flowers from the bushes lining the edges of the curved driveway has always been overwhelming. I've never seen my mother watering them once in my life, and I doubt I ever will.

Jean catches up to me quickly, and I shove my hands in my pockets before he grabs one of them the way he tried to on the drive here.

"Your mother told me you do not like kind gestures. I thought she was lying," he reveals.

"My mother lies about a lot of things, Jean, but that wasn't one of them."

"It's rude to deny genuine gestures."

"I never said I wasn't rude."

He clucks his tongue to the roof of his mouth. "It would be a lie."

I stop moving, coming to a stop before the cement stairs leading to the massive double doors leading inside the house. The tall columns on either side of the stairs are thick and round, supporting the balcony that faces this side of the property and connects to my parents' room. If I thought for a moment that my mom was up there, I wouldn't bother with my next words, but I'd bet she's on the other side of the front door, waiting and watching for us to come in.

Turning to face the bureaucrat wannabe, I set my hands on my hips and keep my expression stiff.

"Listen, Jean. The only reason I'm here is to get my mother off my back for a little while. I don't know what you did to deserve being forced to take me out on a date, but whatever it was, I'm sure it wasn't terrible enough for you to stick this out. You're more than welcome to leave if you're going to sit and complain about my rudeness for the next hour. Whether we finish this date or not, I came, and she'll take that as a win."

He stares at me for a few moments, surprise and almost a bit of humour appearing in his eyes before he clears his throat.

"I am not leaving."

I shrug a shoulder. "Your funeral."

The front door opens, and a beat later, my mother's face appears. Her makeup thick and flawless, she beams at Jean and gestures for us to come in with a hand heavy with diamond rings.

With her hair curled tightly and pinned at the base of her skull in an intricate bun and makeup giving her the appearance of a younger version of herself, I wonder how long she spent getting ready this morning.

"Jean! It's such a treat to see you again," she welcomes, voice high and bubbly.

Jean takes my hand and tightens his grip when I try to tug it free, smiling sweetly at her. "Thank you, Mrs. Lemieux. Your home is *magnifique*."

My mother looks at him with a sense of pride I've never witnessed in the same way. I've grown tired of being jealous of such stupid things. It's easy to brush off.

She pins me with a stern look, one that says *Look! Someone with manners.* "Oh, you're a delight, Jean. Come in, come in. There's tea and biscuits on the back patio."

"I hate tea," I say.

"Coffee, then," she pushes through flat lips.

Jean stares down at me. "Shall we?"

I carefully pat my pocket, checking for my phone without drawing attention, and then hum in agreement. "I have to use the bathroom first."

"I'll lead Jean to the backyard. You remember the way there, Bryce?" Mom asks.

I fight off an eye roll. "Yeah, I remember."

Without needing further confirmation, Mom takes Jean's other hand and starts guiding him through the door and into the house. He's forced to release me, and I stretch out my fingers before turning down the first hall.

I'm not fifteen steps from the entry when I pull my phone free and send a text.

Me: SOS. You know what to do.

I duck into the bathroom and lock the door behind me. The typing bubbles appear on the screen before a reply pops up.

Darren: Again?

Huffing, I lift the toilet lid with the tip of my toe and let it bang closed. I wouldn't put it past my mother to have followed me.

Me: He's wearing loafers.

Darren: Yikes. Alright. Ten minutes?

Me: I'll make it work. Thank you

Pocketing my phone, I take a breath before flushing the toilet and washing my hands. There's no one on the other side of the door when I leave, and my relief is instant.

There's no sound in the house besides the clack of my boots on the floor. Probably should have taken them off at the door, but the prospect of getting mud on my mom's shining floors fills me with too much excitement.

"Bryce?"

I stop at the sound of my father's voice and inhale a long breath. "I didn't know you were home."

"I'm happy I was."

He comes around to face me and inspects me with deep blue eyes before pulling me in for a hug. It's mostly comfortable. I even return the gesture.

"Not that I'm not pleased to see you here, but why are you home? I didn't know you were going to be here," he says.

"Mom didn't tell you?"

"Tell me what?"

I leave his arms and arch a brow. "I'm on a date."

His expression levels out. I take that as a good sign. Maybe he'll tell Mom to stop it with all of these terrible potential matches.

"I see."

"You see?"

"Your mother just wants you to have someone," he explains.

I lick my lips before letting my words out. "Tell her to expand her criteria, then. No more finance bros. I'd appreciate if she included a few pageant queens as well."

"Are they not just opposite sides of the same coin?"

"Maybe. But at least she wouldn't be blatantly making a show of which gender she'd prefer I wind up with," I mutter.

Dad reaches out and drags his thumb over the edges of my forehead. He's always been the more affectionate one, but that isn't saying much. Mom hasn't hugged me since I was a little girl. I doubt she even remembers how. Dad being a hugger doesn't mean he enjoys my company all that much, so really, I could do without the empty affection.

"You know how she is, Bryce," he says, stepping back.

I realize I've been dismissed and grit my teeth, passing him on my way to the backyard. The lack of family photos on the white walls and shelves should make me sad, but it just . . . doesn't anymore. I don't have any photos of them in my house, so why should they have to have any in theirs?

I'm incredibly aware of the weight of Dad's stare on my back until I turn and it's gone. He doesn't follow after me. He never has. Mom can be cruel to both of us, but for some reason, I'm the only one who won't stand there and let it happen. It's always been this way. I resent my dad for it sometimes.

From my side of the patio doors, I can see Jean and Mom sitting at the patio table, a kettle and tower of fancy fucking pastries resting between them. The teacup in front of Jean is more than likely topped to the rim with tea and honey. Probably cream too. I crinkle my nose and join them.

"Your mother was telling me about your passion for stocks? Is that true?" Mom asks, her cup poised at her mouth.

"Ah, yes. It's a newer hobby for me. Something to kill the time."

I hover by the doors, not letting them know I've stepped out yet. This conversation is exactly the one I thought they'd be having.

"I suspect you don't have a lot of that with your career, right?"

Jean smiles bashfully at her. "Oh, I make the time for my favourite things."

Her cheeks tint with a soft pink that makes me move toward them, done watching. The last thing I want is to see them continuing to . . . flirt?

Fuck's sake.

"You started without me," I state bluntly.

They both turn to face me, and Mom gets up instantly, taking her cup with her. Jean jumps up and pulls the chair closest to him out from the table.

"Just waiting for you," he says.

I reluctantly take the seat and push it in before he can. "What were you talking about?"

"Jean was telling me about his interest in the stock market. Have you ever thought about investing, Bryce?" Mom asks pointedly.

I meet Jean's waiting stare. "No. I've always hated numbers."

"Oh. Well, that's alright. They aren't for everyone," he says a bit too quickly, face growing a bit weary.

"My only hobby is tattooing. Do you have any ink?"

He blanches. "No. I don't, actually."

"What a shame."

The air grows awkward as neither of us speaks, and I think I enjoy the silence more than I did the conversation. Mom fiddles with her teacup, a nail tapping along the edge. Her stare is hot and angry on my face, but I ignore it.

"Bryce has an interest in art," she puts in, trying to spin my love of tattoos into something more proper. "Do you have that in common?"

Jean's eyes light up, colouring coming back to his cheeks. "Yes, I think we might. What type of—"

Having left my ringer on after leaving the bathroom, it begins to go off, cutting him short. I pretend to look apologetic as I pull it free of my pocket and answer it.

"Hello?"

"Is it going that badly? You can still say this is just a scam caller," Darren says, his voice a familiar comfort in my ear.

"Oh shit. Really? Is she okay?" I ask.

Jean keeps his stare on me as I speak, his curiosity sharp. Mom doesn't buy it. I'd be concerned if she did, considering I've done this to the past three guys she's set me up with. But she won't say anything about it in front of Jean.

"You owe me a day of free babysitting, Rye," Darren says.

"Yes, I do need a ride. I'm at my parents' house. See you soon." Hanging up, I meet Jean's waiting stare. "Something's come up. I have to go."

"Let me wait outside with you," he offers, already standing.

"That's okay. I don't need company."

"He'll wait outside with you, Bryce," Mom tells me.

Gritting my teeth, I nod once. "Fine."

I move quickly, wanting to get away from her as soon as possible. Jean follows at my heels, not giving me an inch of space. It'll take Darren fifteen minutes to get here, and that's fourteen too many.

"If you don't mind me asking, what's happened?" he asks.

"Something involving my best friend's daughter," I lie, stepping through the patio door. He tugs it from my hand and holds it for me.

"Is she alright?"

"Yes."

"Am I really that bad?"

The question stuns me enough that I turn my head to look at him. Guilt twitches in my gut.

"It's not you."

"No?"

"Honestly? I'm bi, Jean. And I swore off dating men a long fucking time ago. You and me? We wouldn't work. I'm sure you've pieced that together by now too."

He doesn't answer for a minute. Still, he opens the front door for me and waits until I've stepped out to follow. His manners are immaculate, but unfortunately, that isn't enough.

"Does your mother know about what you've told me?" he asks gently.

"Do you think it would matter either way?"

Another pause. "I'm sorry. I didn't know."

"How were you supposed to?"

"Still, I am sorry for putting you in an uncomfortable spot. It wasn't my intention."

I peer up at him, taking in his sincere expression. "Thank you."

"Can I wait for your ride with you now? Maybe we can speak about your hobbies while we do?"

"You want to know about my hobbies?"

He nods. "Yes."

I give in. And for the next thirteen minutes, I divulge more about myself to a stranger than I think I ever have.

9

Daisy

I'm not a snoopy person.

Well, actually, that's a lie. I totally am. But in my defense, I'd love to meet one person who wouldn't take the first opportunity to do some snooping around the home of someone as elusive as Bryce. It's like dangling a deep-fried pickle in front of my face and expecting me not to snap my teeth at it like a rabid animal.

I've held myself back for the past two days, but after watching Bryce slide into the passenger side of a sports car that I'm sure costs more than this house, I sat in the living room for two hours until finally, I gave in and sprinted to her closed bedroom door.

The door handle is cool in my palm, and as I turn it just slightly, I don't feel a lock engage. It's surprising, considering how adamant she was about keeping her space from me. I tongue my cheek and stay still, waiting for my conscience to catch up with me.

It doesn't, and I take that as a great sign before I'm pushing into Bryce's room.

The past two days I've been staying here have been awkward. After our single conversation in the kitchen the first night, we haven't spoken much at all. Bryce comes home from work and goes straight to her room. I've even started leaving my bedroom door wide open every night in hopes that she'll pop in and say so much as a hi.

I knew it would be a bit weird living here, but I'm more desperate for person-to-person communication than I've been in a long time. When I was in Calgary, there were always people to see and speak with, places to go and hang out after class or on the weekends. I know I have my family here in Cherry Peak, but I don't want my only friends to be my moms.

Maybe taking a look into Bryce's room will give me an idea of what to talk to her about. A hobby I could try and offer to join her for or a favourite show we could watch together. I'm not picky. Rather, I'm damn desperate.

How am I supposed to show her how thankful I am for her letting me stay here if I can't even speak to her?

With a puffed exhale, I slip into her room and blink at the darkness. Blackout curtains drawn over the windows, there's not even a sliver of sunlight slipping through. I slap a hand to the wall and flick on the light.

"Wow. Okay."

It's . . . very Bryce.

A massive bed is set in the centre of the room with a black felt headboard and matching bedding. The dressers are, surprise, *black*, along with the nightstands and the thin table against the wall and beneath the hung flat-screen. Two thick, deep purple rugs cover the cool wood floors on either side of her bed, matching the lampshades on the nightstands.

I make note of the pops of purple and step further inside. The floors creak beneath my feet, and I make note of that too. Just in case . . .

The accordion closet doors are shut, and I keep them that way. I'm a snoop but not a creep.

Swallowing, I slide my palm across the top of her dresser and notice the lack of dust. Even the black-limbed, spider-looking light fixture above her bed seems clean, like she dusts every inch of her room on the daily. I can't relate, but I won't lie and say that I'm not impressed.

The laundry basket beside the closet doors is full of folded clothes, so at least we have one thing in common. I'll have three baskets of clean, folded laundry before even thinking about putting it all away.

A half dozen pictures hang on the walls, each one focused on a body part decorated with black ink. The two thighs above her bed are hers. I'd recognize the tattoos anywhere, even after only seeing them in person once. Twin snakes curling around flesh, teeth sharp and buried in the flesh of two dripping peaches. The juice pooling around their mouths is almost indecent, and I think that was the point.

I flick my eyes between the different portraits, trying to shove each one into my memory, categorizing them. Black letters in the webbing of each of her fingers, an ankle piece with a date and time, a . . . set of boobs? Blinking hard, I take a step toward the photo and let my lips part in surprise.

It's the ink wrapped around them that draws my focus and keeps it there until I'm unable to look away.

A full chest piece covers the swells of each breast, with a bull skull centred between them. Grass and tall flowers with small petals wrap around the horns and trail down and around her boobs. The word *home* has been spread throughout the design, almost as if it's meant to be hidden. I gulp to dry my suddenly overly wet mouth and bite down on my lip.

The dual hoops through each nipple complete the image somehow. A part of me expected to find ink on the breasts themselves, but they're bare.

Bare and perky with blush-pink nipples decorated in black jewelry that I've never thought to find attractive before. Until now.

Maybe I shouldn't be surprised to find such open and proud art in Bryce's room. She doesn't seem like the type of person to share these parts of herself with just anyone, and now I'm hit with a wave of sharp guilt. There's a reason the door was closed, and I've just peered into more of her soul than I was intending to.

I back out of the room before I'm aware that I'm moving. With a wince, I pull the door shut behind me with more force than necessary and run my hands over my hair and face, every inch of me hot with shame.

Tucking tail, I make a beeline for my room. Kristen would shit her pants if she saw me running out of Bryce's room like a naughty child, but I can't help it. It's that or—

A door closing outside makes me freeze. The rich notes of Bryce's voice follow after, and I stop breathing, my muscles locked up tight.

"You can come in if you want, D," she offers.

"Thanks, but I've got to meet with Sasha, and you need a moment to yourself."

It's easy to recognize Darren's voice despite not knowing him that well. He's got one of those deep and dark timbres that I'd bet turns straight women feral.

Bryce replies, sounding angry now. "Want me to come? She'll piss off quick after seeing me."

"Yeah, with my daughter in tow."

"Not if Abbie has a say. She loves me."

"She could, if you'd let her."

A scoff. "It's a kid thing, Darren. I'll be her favourite aunt once she's a bit older and doesn't smell like sparkles and cheap lip gloss."

I barely manage to hide my laugh.

"Alright, Rye. But don't get butthurt when she chooses Poppy over you. She loves her cheap lip gloss scent."

"I love Abbie. Don't be an asshole. I'm just . . . not the best with kids. Leave me alone about it."

There's a moment where I can't hear either of them, and I manage to take two steps toward my room. I'm almost there when the front door opens, and Bryce calls out.

"Text me later."

"Yes, ma'am."

I squeak and reach for my door seconds before the air shifts. It grows cooler, sharper. Pulling myself together, I smile and turn my head to look at Bryce.

"Hi."

She stands at the end of the hall and watches me. Silent but with eyes that speak for her, she inspects me, brows low.

"Hi."

"How was your day?"

Her mouth twists at the question, unease heavy in her eyes. For a moment, I wonder if she's about to tell me something real and unrehearsed, but disappointment hits a beat later.

"Fucking fantastic."

She goes to walk past me, but before she can, I reach out. My fingers glide across hers before I grasp onto them, risking having them bitten clean off. Her head snaps in my direction, mouth parted in surprise despite the tight coiling of her shoulders. For a long few seconds, neither one of us speaks. The warm fingers in mine are small and strong, flexing and growing damp.

"You look pissed off, Bryce," I say softly, cautiously. "Not fantastic."

She tugs her hand free of mine, leaving me clutching the empty space left behind. "Do you want to have a heart-to-heart or something?"

I recover by leaning my shoulder against the wall and tipping my chin. "I'm up for it."

"I don't know you."

"You could."

She glances up at the ceiling before dropping her ice-blue eyes back to stare at me. They've dulled slightly, no longer sharp enough to cut, just scrape if necessary.

"I need a drink first."

Spinning on her heels, she leaves me in the hallway. I follow quickly, not about to miss my chance to dig into her head.

There's a clang in the kitchen when she grabs two beers from the fridge and opens them, offering me one without so much as a glance in my direction.

"Thank you," I say, accepting the bottle.

"Have you ever been on a blind date?"

The blurted question takes me by surprise, but I hide it with an open expression. "No."

"Lucky you."

"Is that where you were? On a blind date?"

She takes a long pull of her beer before making a low humming noise in her throat. "One of many. My mother has a passion for them, apparently."

"I take it that this one was bad?"

A tiny flicker of humour travels through her expression as she sets her bottle on the countertop and then grips it on either side of her body. The movement forces her tight black denim skirt to stretch as she spreads her legs. Her cropped shirt is tight over her chest, and I focus on not looking for a hint of the piercings from the photo in her bedroom.

"My mom hopes that if she shoves enough posh, finance-loving boys under my nose, I'll have an epiphany and suddenly want to date one," she explains.

"She's wrong?"

"Yeah. You could say that."

I swallow my nerves and take a drink from my bottle before placing it on the kitchen table. It's warm in here, and I'm suddenly wishing I could crack open a window. Too bad the only one in here is right behind her.

"Have you spoken to her about it? Told her to knock it off?"

What a stupid question.

Bryce wets her lips and drums her fingers along the edge of the counter. "Listening to me and my feelings isn't my mother's specialty. As far as she's concerned, my infatuation with women will pass. Once I'm done with my . . . *phase*, I'll be ready for one of the men she's tossed at me."

"Shit. I'm sorry."

I can't imagine my moms feeling that way about my life and plans. My siblings and I got lucky with them. We've never had anything short of full support when it comes to every aspect of our lives. Sometimes it's hard to remember not everyone grew up the same way.

"Can I do anything to help?" I offer before she's had a chance to reply to my apology.

She pushes away from the counter and tugs at the hem of her cropped shirt. The band on the front of it isn't one I recognize. I'm not a risk taker when it comes to music.

"There's nothing anyone can do. I'll keep putting up with it until she gives up."

"That's not fair to you."

With one brow climbing her forehead, she says, "Don't tell me you believe life is fair, Daisy."

"No, I don't. But that doesn't mean we have to lie down and accept all of the shitty things that come our way," I argue, lurching forward on my toes. "Especially when it comes to family."

"I'm sorry to break it to you, sunshine, but there isn't a damn thing you or me can do to make my mother let this go."

Maybe in a few hours, I'll regret not taking her words to heart and leaving it be. We'll go back to not speaking to one another and co-living in awkward silence. But for now, I can't seem to help myself. That's my only explanation for what happens next.

I snatch my beer from the table and take two gulps of it before cringing at the foamy taste and blurting out, "What if you weren't single anymore? Would she stop then?"

10

Bryce

I STARE AT DAISY FOR TOO LONG WITHOUT SPEAKING. MY BRAIN churns and churns through several replies, but they're all muddled with too much confusion to make sense of.

It's an out-of-pocket suggestion, considering my lack of love life. I'd be offended if it were anyone but her asking. The woman wouldn't know what it means to purposely offend someone if it bit her in the ass.

"Maybe," I manage to say once I've cleared my throat.

"Are you up for trying?"

"Where do you suggest I find a girlfriend? The supermarket?" I ask stiffly.

She worries her lip, eyes darting around the kitchen before landing back on me. The gleam in them has me standing straighter, a tight feeling growing in my chest.

"What about me? Would I do?"

I choke on air. Spit, maybe.

She opens her mouth, but I spin away from her before she has a chance to speak her next sentence. I beat my palm to my chest in hopes of soothing my coughing, but it only makes it worse.

"Drink this," she orders before my beer is shoved in my face.

I take it and drink, focusing on swallowing instead of spraying it out all over the kitchen counter. My hand is sweaty around the glass as I clue in to how close she is to me.

Fruity perfume swirls in the air around me, and I breathe it in despite myself. She's warm, the heat from her body trying to tug me into an embrace that feels as appealing as it always does. As *she* always does.

The thought has me shoving away from her. With space between us, I suck in long, non-Daisy-soaked breaths, no longer coughing. She doesn't try to come closer, and I avoid looking at her to confirm whether I've hurt her feelings or not.

"You don't want to date me," I tell her bluntly, staring at the wall across the room instead of at her.

"Why not?"

She's so inquisitive. It's a piece of her personality that I noticed the first time we met.

"Why would you?"

"Touché." Her laugh is soft, nervous. "I was thinking more in the fake sense."

That has me snapping my head to the side. She doesn't balk at my confusion and jostles a shoulder instead. Appearing nonchalant, she holds my stare and tugs her mouth up at the corners.

"I've been thinking of a way that I could pay you back for letting me stay here besides the bare minimum things, and, well, you need help with your parents. It's a win-win. You let me stay here, and I'll pay you rent, of course, but I'll also help with this. It's the only way I'll feel like I haven't taken advantage of you," she adds.

A win-win.

"You're fucking crazy, Daisy."

It's the wrong thing to say. So wrong on too many levels to count. But I'm unable to say anything else. If she knew what I thought about her, she'd rescind the offer and leave, never looking back.

The hurt that flickers across her pretty features makes my jaw tense, teeth grinding. I hate that look on her. Lips no longer upturned but tugged down and curled the wrong way. Her blue eyes a shade darker than usual, more ocean at night and less clear summer sky. I struggle with the weight of the knowledge that I've tarnished the bright aura she always has pulsing off her.

"Why is it crazy? Because you don't think it would work or that you'd be fake dating me?" she asks, straightening her posture just enough for me to notice. Like she's preparing for a fight and doesn't plan on losing.

I like the sight of her backbone. Always knew it was there, but having it in play with me brings something hot and heavy to my gut.

With a firm grip on the counter, I hop up and sit on the edge of it. She watches me move, lips twitching. I pat the space beside me, and she doesn't hesitate to join, her legs swinging in the tiny shorts she always wears around the house once she's comfortable.

"It's crazy because nobody would believe it just suddenly happened. Let alone my parents," I tell her, clarifying.

"I think we could do it. You've dated women, right?"

I chuckle. "Yeah, Sunshine. I've dated my fair share of women."

With a glance over, I catch the slight flush of her cheeks before she dips her head and lets her hair hide them from me. The deep red waves are thick and shiny, healthy in the way they bounce even with the slightest movement of her head. I'd bet it feels just as smooth between my fingers as it looks.

I curl my hand into a fist and shove it beneath my thigh.

"Well, then I think we could pull it off," she states.

"You don't need to pay me back for staying here. It's not some huge burden, and you're not getting a room for free."

"Maybe not, but I feel like I do. And this is the perfect way to do it."

"No," I say, deciding for the both of us.

She scoffs in her throat. "Yes. Unless you have some serious reason as to why you can't, then we're going to be fake lovers."

"You're pushy."

"Thank you."

My laugh is genuine but short. "It wasn't a compliment."

"I'm not pushy. I'm just sure of myself and what I'm offering. It will work, I'll make sure of it. And once your mom grows to realize that you're not interested in any of these men she keeps feeding you, we'll call it off and go back to whatever we are now."

"Feeding me?" I ask, stuck on that one part of her statement. "I'm not a succubus."

"No? Could have fooled me."

"Now I'm the one getting offended."

She hits my arm with hers and laughs louder. Fuck, she has a pretty laugh. Like a wind chime blowing through a quiet, dull night.

"Don't be offended. Look at you, Bryce. You could eat men for breakfast, lunch, and dinner. Late-night snack too," she teases.

"I prefer fruit to vegetables."

"Oh yeah? Do you have a favourite fruit?" she asks. If I didn't know better, I'd say she's baiting me.

"Peaches."

Her throat bobs, eyes darting to my thighs. I follow her stare and realize how high my skirt has ridden up. The denim is tight, but I like it that way. And right now, it's high enough that both of my thigh pieces are fully on display. Peaches, juice, and fangs.

My body is covered in sexual innuendos. From my first piece, I knew I wanted every bit of ink to mean something. And once I got started, I couldn't stop. An addict in every definition of the term. The rush I feel with the press of a needle to my arm is the closest thing to an orgasm that's available without fingers in my pussy.

I'm proud of every design on my skin and always make sure

all of my favourites are placed somewhere I'll be able to see them at any given time. My twin cobras are no exception.

"Did they hurt?" she asks, voice airy.

I twist the thigh closest to her, showing the inner parts of the design with a risk of flashing my panties. She doesn't tell me to stop, so I don't.

"Like a bitch. Especially right here." I trace the underside of the peach where it curves high up my inner thigh, exactly four inches below my bikini line. "The nerves here are incredibly sensitive."

"I bet."

She's leaned in to see, and I don't move in fear of scaring her. With her eyes so focused on the area between my legs, I fear they'll start to shake. When I can't help but clench between them, I decide we're done and slam them shut.

"Anyway. We'd have to convince everyone. Your brother included," I say, changing the subject.

Daisy sits back, nodding almost to herself before pushing her hair behind her neck. She smiles at me, shifting on the counter.

"We could tell him the truth."

I shake my head. "He'd tell Rory, and she'd tell the rest of the girls. From there, everyone would know."

"I could swear him to twin secrecy," she suggests, too damn hopeful.

"If we do this, nobody knows the truth. Not your siblings and not my best friends. It has to be real to everyone. The moment someone learns the truth, the plan is ruined. If my mom figures out that I turned to fake dating to get out of these dates . . . I'd rather suffer through a million more of them than suffer that embarrassment."

She chews on that for a moment. "Alright. Okay, nobody will know. But that means our story has to be perfect. No holes, and we have to be ready to explain it a thousand times without getting our facts mixed up."

"Easy enough."

"What is our story, then?"

"You don't have anything to suggest? This was your idea."

Daisy exhales, jerking her chin in agreement. "That's true. Well, we're already living together, so we could say that it just happened naturally?"

"What happened naturally? You took one look at my empty fridge and decided you wanted to be the one to fill it?" I ask sarcastically.

She hits my arm again, and I think I like when she does that. "Not exactly. How about you just let me come up with something in the moment. It will feel more genuine that way. We don't bring it up to anyone alone before then, and we'll just make note of the story we tell the first time so neither one of us forgets."

"Will that work?"

"I'm a pretty good actress."

"I hope so." I hold her stare with one that I hope she can understand the seriousness behind. "How long will we date for?"

"As long as it takes. I don't have anything else to do besides work. School starts Monday."

"Okay."

She does a double take. "Okay?"

"Okay, we'll do this. Fucking fake date."

It sounds ridiculous, yet my heart is thrashing at the agreement. The crush I've had on Daisy Mitchell for the past three years should have made me turn this idea down and build a permanent wall between us. Instead, it's encouraging me to go along with this.

It's going to get messy. I'm going to torture myself by picking at an unhealed wound over and over again. I've thought about Daisy in the exact way I'm going to be "pretending" to over the next who fucking knows how long. If she ever found out that I agreed to this, knowing that I want her for real, she might never trust me again.

It feels dirty and sneaky. But I'm not doing this just for my own selfish reasons. It's more than that. The idea of telling my mom that I'm no longer able to entertain these blind dates feels like a well-deserved fuck off. Having my fake girlfriend be Daisy is just a bonus. Even if I know that by the end of this agreement, I'll be left worse off than how I entered it.

For three years, I've successfully hidden my affection for the sunshine girl beside me. Every blunt, cold reply and blank expression were my only ways of keeping my cards hidden. I've never reacted to someone the way I do her, as if she'd somehow already burrowed herself into my life without my knowledge by our first meeting.

Nobody knows how I truly feel. Not Anna or Poppy and Darren, despite their suspicions that I may be playing a little too hard against Johnny's twin. I wasn't planning on confirming those feelings, and now, it seems I have no choice.

They'll believe me when I say that they were right. This plan could actually work, but I fear it will break me in the process.

Too bad I've never feared a little pain.

11

Daisy

I'M UP EARLY THE NEXT MORNING. AT THE FIRST CREAK OF THE floor in the hall outside my room, I sit up in bed and attempt to push my bed-head flat.

Yesterday, I woke up single, and today, I have a girlfriend. A fake one, to be specific, which I guess I need to be when we're not in private.

Blowing out a breath, I cringe at my morning breath and slip out of bed. Toes curling into the plush carpet with every step to my dresser, I yank clothes out and get dressed. The bathroom is across the hall, and I don't think I'm quite ready to be wandering Bryce's halls in only my panties just yet.

I tuck the strings of my sweatpants into the waistband and open my door slowly. It's silent, so I slip into the hallway, eyes set on the bathroom—

"Good morning."

I jump and spin, my hand slapping at the wall to stabilize myself. Bryce watches me with a straight face, a coffee mug in her hands. Her outfit is the same one she's worn every day since I've been here, but I swear it keeps getting worse. I know that shirt has to be itchy.

"Morning!" I cheer, cupping my throat where I can feel my pulse hammering away.

"Was I loud?"

"What?"

She shifts, putting her weight on one foot. "Was I loud enough to wake you up?"

"Oh. No, you weren't."

Nodding, she looks past me at the empty hall, fingers tapping her mug. My lips twitch at her shifty behaviour.

"Did I wake *you*?" I ask.

She blinks, looking at me again. "What? No. I work at eight."

I don't bother telling her that I already know that. I've heard her leave the house at seven forty-five every single day. She's nothing if not punctual.

"Do you walk or drive to work?"

"Walk."

"Fancy some company this morning?"

Her eyes widen slightly, but she recovers quickly, clearing her throat. "Nobody will be up and watching this early."

"Are we not allowed to get to know each other while we're doing this? If I don't know anything about you, I won't be able to make the relationship look genuine. My brother will know something's off right away."

She scrolls her eyes down my body, and suddenly, I feel like a complete slob. The baggy shirt and sweatpants I pulled on are nothing compared to her proper clothes, even if they are completely wrong for her.

The jean skirt from yesterday is long gone, replaced with a long, loose one that's only an inch from dragging on the floor. Her blouse is ridiculous and hides all of the artwork that I now know lies beneath. It feels like a crime to hide such beautiful designs with something my great-grandmother would probably turn her nose up at.

"Why do you agree to wear that?" I blurt out. With a wince, I add, "I mean, it's just not *you*. Not at all."

She slides a finger into the collar of her shirt and pulls at it as if that's the only way she can breathe properly. "I pick my battles."

It's a rehearsed line that I'd bet she's spoken a million times. When I don't look convinced, she grips the fabric of her skirt and lifts it to expose her from the knee down. The black cowboy boots on her feet have me giggling.

"I rebel in my own way, Sunshine," she states.

I stare at her boots, lips spread into a smile. "I see that."

She appears more relaxed now, just a fraction of her icy exterior warming. "If you're walking with me, we leave in five. The first thing you need to know about me is that I don't like to be late to anything."

"Got it. I'll put something else on and meet you by the door."

I'm already halfway to my room when she says, "Don't change. You look fine the way you are."

I lift a brow and glance at her over my shoulder. "Like I've just rolled out of bed?"

"Like you don't feel the need to dress to impress anyone. Let alone on a walk to the town office at 8:00 a.m." She puts her weight on her other foot. "It's nice."

I can't help the way my chest warms at her words. A subtle compliment from Bryce? Yeah, I think I'll survive the next few weeks. It feels good to hear that from her.

"Alright, you win. But I need to sort my hair, at least. I'll be quick."

She doesn't smile, but I don't expect her to. "Three minutes."

I salute her and disappear into the bathroom instead of my bedroom. The floor doesn't creak for a few moments after I've closed the door, but when it does, I swear I hear her muttering to herself.

If only I could hear the words.

"Do you have a favourite colour?" I ask five minutes later.

With fall rolling in, the leaves are orange and crunch beneath my Converse, where they've fallen on the sidewalk. I pinch my cardigan together at my chest to fight the chill and wait for Bryce to speak for the first time since we left the house.

She didn't put a sweater or coat on before we left, and it doesn't look like the cool morning affects her. Maybe she has goosebumps beneath the sleeves of her blouse or on her tattooed thighs. Or maybe she truly is the ice queen and doesn't feel the shift in temperature.

"Yellow," she answers.

"Really?"

"Black would be too obvious."

I twist my lips to hide a smile. "I'll admit that I thought it would be black."

"It's been yellow for a while now."

"I'll make a note of that. Can I ask another question?"

She stares ahead at the row of shops on our right. The Beautifully Bold swinging sign is behind the Thistle and Thorn one, two thriving businesses run by two badass women whom I've come to know. I get hit with a blast of pride when we pass both shops, and Bryce straightens, as if feeling the same thing.

"You don't have to ask whether you can ask questions. Just do it," she mutters.

"I don't want to be rude."

"You're not," she states simply.

"Good to know." I walk around a missing chunk of concrete on the sidewalk and fall back to her side, making sure to keep some space between us. She watches me, eyes heavy and focused on my movements. "When did you get your first tattoo?"

"My fifteenth birthday."

My lips part in surprise. "Fifteen? How did you get away with that?"

"Wade Steele forges a great signature."

There's no stopping my laugh. It punches out of my lungs, leaving me breathless. Wade Steele, the owner of Steele Ranch, is the world's biggest hard-ass, but somehow, his kindness knows no bounds.

His wife, Eliza, wouldn't have put up with him for the duration of their marriage if he wasn't soft and squishy beneath his hard shell.

"Where is the tattoo?" I ask, the words airy as I catch my breath.

She licks her lower lip, tugging at her shirt collar again. "Nowhere I can show you in public."

My cheeks start to burn at her bluntness, but I blame it on the chilled breeze that's begun to pick up. "Can you at least tell me what it is?"

"A middle finger shaded in pink, purple, and blue."

The bisexual flag colours. "You knew when you were fifteen that you were bisexual?"

"Fourteen, actually, but nobody would tattoo me then. I found a spot in Calgary that would ink me at fifteen, but it was a grungy fucking shop with a creep of an owner who just wanted to get his hands on a teenager. It's a miracle I didn't get an infection afterward," she says with a huff.

I shiver at the thought of an infected tattoo and what sort of man she's talking about. "I think I knew at fourteen that I was a lesbian, but I wasn't ready to announce it until I was sixteen."

"I get it."

"My moms weren't surprised when I came out, so I don't think I was all that subtle about it before then either. But they didn't force me to move faster than I wanted to. How did your parents take it?"

From the corner of my eye, I see the way she visibly locks up at the question. I want to curse myself out for overstepping, but it's too late to take the question back.

"We're almost at the office. I told you nobody would be out at this time to see us."

I turn and flash her a gentle smile. She's got a couple of inches on me height-wise, but it's not enough to have me looking up at her. Even if her gaze is intimidating enough on its own, making my confidence waver beneath it. I don't let it crumble, though. That's not me.

"Just because no one saw us doesn't mean it was for nothing. I learned some things about you, so I'll take that as a win," I declare.

We stop in front of the small office building, and while it feels a bit awkward between us still, I don't let that deter me. Especially not when I see someone walking out of the coffee shop down the road and toward us.

It's go time.

"Don't look, but there's someone coming," I whisper, keeping my eyes on Bryce's.

Her jaw ticks. "Who?"

"I'm not sure. Nobody I know, at least. But we should still do something, right?"

"Do something? Like what?"

Her nose twists when she sniffs, and it's adorable. We're close enough that I can see every mark on her face and wrinkle in her lips. I've never seen skin so clear yet textured in a way that proves she's a real person and not the robot she sometimes pretends to be.

Brows thick and manicured, they sit confidently above her kohl-lined blue eyes and draw together slightly the longer I stare. I dig my teeth into my lip just once before blinking and diverting my gaze.

The scuffing of shoes on the sidewalk has me acting before I can think twice about it. If it's not me that makes the first move, something tells me that it won't be Bryce.

Swaying onto the balls of my feet, I lean close and press my pursed lips to her cheek. Warm and smooth beneath my mouth, her skin heats as I'm pulling back. Her simple, spiced berry perfume sticks to my throat, and I risk a final sniff before giving her space.

She's frozen in place when I meet her eyes and say, "Have a great day, Frosty. See you at home later."

"Frosty?" she croaks.

I wink, my smile sly. "Sunshine?"

"What a fucking pair," she says absently.

Wiggling my fingers in a wave, I start moving backward, a pep in my step that electrifies me. The newfound energy in my bones has me pressing my fingers to my lips and blowing her a kiss before spinning and leaving her there before I can see her reaction.

I don't question the way I'm feeling.

Not once.

12

Bryce

I FUCKING HATE SOCIAL MEDIA.

That sentence is as much of an "I'm not like the other girls" one that I could say, but I'm only being honest. Once I get started with scrolling, I get lost stalking every single person I've ever known in my life who's upset me in one way or another.

I analyze their posts from the moment we grew apart to now. Are they happy? If so, how? Why do they deserve good things when they've hurt me?

There's one profile I stray to more than the others. Victoria Clarkson is my archnemesis. With her tight black curls and sleek jaw and cheekbones, one look at her is usually enough to spoil my day.

Exes aren't supposed to make you happy, *obviously*. But are they supposed to make you so lightning mad years after a breakup? No, they're not.

Yet, I can't stop my teeth from grinding as I swipe past the latest photo update of her and the man whose cock probably still has the shape of my foot imbedded in the shaft.

I might appear like I find it easy to hate people, but that's not the case. In order to hate someone, you have to care about them in some way, shape, or form. Past or present. Usually, I can't be bothered. But with Vic, I've long since accepted that I truly do hate her. If that makes me a bad person, then so fucking be it.

She's to blame for the pain I experienced for months after learning she'd taken my refusal to start a three-way relationship as a reason to cheat. Only she didn't believe it was cheating. Not when she'd been *honest* about wanting more than just me.

Could have broken up with me first before jumping into bed with her now fiancé, but what the hell do I know.

I squeeze my phone tight enough I'm surprised it doesn't shatter in my hand and toss it across the desk.

"If I pick up your phone and I see a picture of Vic, I'm going to take it away from you for the next two weeks," Poppy warns, appearing in front of the office door.

I scowl, leaning back in my chair. "What are you doing here?"

"That's a terrible way to greet your best friend," she says with a dramatic pout.

I eye her outfit, making a conclusion as to why she's here just by the tight spandex shorts and cropped tank top. Her hair is in a tight, slicked-back ponytail, and her cheeks are still pale instead of flushed, so I must have been her first stop.

"It's not Saturday. Don't blame me for not expecting you."

"You're in a cranky mood today."

I inhale, my eyes shutting as I reel myself back in. "Sorry."

"You're forgiven. Wanna talk about it?"

She rounds the desk and props herself against it, legs crossed at the ankles and expression open as she stares down at me. I lean forward and prop my chin in my palm.

This should be when I tell her that I have a "girlfriend." It's as good a time as any, but the longer it takes me to speak, the harder it is to tell the lie to her.

"You can tell me anything, Ice. You know that. Even if you think I'll bug you about it, I promise to wait until you're feeling better," she adds teasingly.

I tilt my head and meet her eyes. A stab of guilt deep in my chest has me deciding to hold off on telling her about Daisy.

"I haven't been sleeping well. And every time I go on social media, I see Vic and realize that I should just be the bigger person and block her," I say.

"But if you block her, you won't be able to see what she's doing. I get it. We're too snoopy for that."

I nod. "If she posted something about me, how would I know if she's blocked?"

"That's valid. I'm all for keeping things the way they are as long as the real reason you haven't blocked her is because you're still into her. If there are feelings there—"

"I'd rather pull each one of my nails off than have feelings for her again. That's not it," I declare.

And it's the truth. I don't want anything to do with that she-devil anymore. From the moment I caught her cheating and wound up spending a night in jail for breaking her now fiancé's dick, I've written her off. The time apart has only furthered the chasm between us, and I'd rather slip inside of it and fall to my death than ever go back to the person I was with her.

But that doesn't mean I don't get random bursts of curiosity that lead me to her social media profiles.

Poppy laughs loudly, her face lighting up with humour. "Fair enough. Why aren't you sleeping well? Your new roommate keeping you up?"

It takes more effort than it should to keep my breathing steady at the question when my heart jolts. I flatten my lips, contemplating what to say. How can I tell her that, yeah, it is because of my new roommate that I haven't gotten more than a handful of hours of sleep at night?

Knowing Daisy is sleeping in the room beside mine is a temptation that I didn't need. It's a pain in my fucking ass and one that I know isn't going away anytime soon.

Wetting my dry lips, I rip the Band-Aid off and get this over with. "She's not only my roommate."

Poppy waves me off. "Yeah, yeah. She's also Johnny's twin and our friend. I get it. But that doesn't answer my question."

"She's my girlfriend."

Out of every reaction Poppy could have had, I wasn't expecting the belly-deep laughter that explodes out of her. She curls over and wraps her hands around her stomach, as if her laughter is so strong it's started hurting.

"Fuck off, Poppy," I huff, using my foot to push away from her and the desk.

Her eyes widen as she watches me roll away, laughter slowly dying. "Cut the shit, Bryce."

"You're not supposed to know yet."

"Stop lying to me."

I itch the back of my hand. "I'm not."

When she reaches for both of my hands and uses her hold to roll me toward her, I know I'm fucked. She narrows her eyes and thins her mouth.

"The truth. Now."

"You sound like a parent."

"I'll punish you like one, too, if you don't explain yourself. And I'll add that I've known you way too damn long not to be able to smell a lie a mile away. And right now, you reek," she scolds.

"You're such a pain in my ass."

She ignores me. "Explain, Ice."

I pull my hands free of her tight grip and run them down my thighs. My clothes are too restrictive for me to relax, and I've never hated them more than right now.

"She is my girlfriend. But it's not that simple," I begin, replicating her glare with one of my own. "You're not supposed to know anything more than that, Poppy. And I swear to God, I will lose my shit if you share this with anyone. Even Garrison."

She worries her lip. "What about Anna?"

"No. No one else can know. I mean it. Even just you knowing makes this all the more complicated."

"Maybe you shouldn't tell me anything else. I don't know if I can lie to everyone," she says in a rush, standing tall before starting to pace the office.

"That would be easier."

She shakes her head furiously, the slick ponytail whipping through the air. "No, now I have to know. I won't be able to let this go. But goddammit, Bryce! What is this? Some task from the FBI?"

"Not quite."

With a long exhale, she comes back to my side of the desk and props herself against the edge. Her eyes are so focused they make me queasy.

"Tell me everything," she demands, and I don't make her ask again.

With a look around the office to make sure I haven't missed anyone else entering, I say, "Daisy is my fake girlfriend. She's going to help get my parents off my back with all of the blind dates by showing them that I'm content with a woman. Once they realize I'm not looking for anything they've been offering, we'll fake a breakup and go our separate ways," I explain, hating how devious it all sounds.

There's so much that can go wrong here, and with my family involved, I'll never live any of this down if the truth gets out. I'll be a complete laughingstock to them and everyone in town, and the last thing I want is to drag Daisy down with me.

Poppy doesn't say anything for a long moment. Her lashes flutter as she blinks furiously. I bury my head in my hands and groan.

"She offered. I should have turned her down," I speak into my palms.

There's sudden warmth on my back as Poppy starts rubbing my spine. "Maybe it isn't such a bad thing."

I whip my head to the side, staring up at her in disbelief. "Be serious."

"I am. I was shocked at first, but I know you, and you've liked her for a while, right?"

I put my face back in my hands in hopes she'll drop this. "You're wrong."

"No, I'm not. Whether you admit it to me or not, I'm not blind like everyone else is. You're into Daisy Mitchell, and that's *okay*. You know that, don't you?"

"Stop it, Poppy."

She doesn't know the whole story, and I don't plan on explaining it to her anytime soon.

"Why? Because you'll have to finally admit it if I push you far enough?" she asks, voice lifting in volume.

I spin to face her, forcing her hand to fall from my back. My skin flushes with an angry heat as I swallow my frustration. "She's my fake girlfriend. That's it."

"Fine." She raises her hands and shakes her head, brows high. "Daisy is your fake girlfriend. Now what? We just lie to everyone now? For how long?"

"You don't have to lie. Just don't say anything. Pretend you don't know the truth and behave like everyone else. As far as how long this will take, that's up to my mother." And Daisy.

The moment she decides we're done, we're done. I'll respect her wishes without hesitation. This is for me more than it is for her. Fuck, I've already told her she doesn't owe me anything for letting her stay at my place.

Poppy rubs at her temples. "This is a terrible idea."

"I know."

"So call it off!"

The words are sticky in my throat. "I can't."

I don't want to.

Her eyes dig deep into mine, searching for everything I'm refusing to say. But I hide my secrets so well even she can't find them.

With a heavy sigh, she palms her hip and drops her stare. "I love you, Ice. Even when you do stupid shit."

"I know."

"The least you can do is say it back."

I roll my eyes. "I love you, you needy bitch."

"That's better." She flashes me a smile and pets my head. "But really, I hope you know what you're doing here. This isn't just some random girl. She's Johnny's twin and a member of our little family."

"You don't have to remind me of that."

"Yes, I do."

"It'll be fine. I've got it handled."

Her expression tells me she doesn't believe me for shit, and in all honesty, I don't believe myself either. I feel completely out of control already, and we haven't even really started.

"I'm here for you always. Don't forget that," she says.

"I won't," I swear. "Now, tell me what you're doing here during the week. BB okay?"

She shrugs. "BB is great. I just missed teaching class here. Calgary is so busy that I feel like I don't have as much one-on-one time like I used to in Cherry Peak."

"Can you shrink the class sizes in Calgary?"

"Not until this one finishes. I will be for the next few. But until then, here I am. Are you busy, or can you join?"

"Right now?"

She looks around the empty room as if to show me how unbusy I am. "Yes, right now. There's a class at one, and I thought you might join me."

Fuck it. "Fine. But I'm throwing you under the bus if I get in trouble for leaving early."

"Bring it on. I've never been scared of your mom."

"What's that like?"

Her laugh is soft. "For what it's worth, I hope this plan of yours works. Your mom is unbearable."

I stand and reach for my phone, the app still open from earlier. Surprise ripples through me when it isn't a picture of Vic on the screen but one of Daisy. It's a close-up selfie from . . . my couch? My breath is caught in my throat as I stare at her flawless skin and bright eyes. Her smile is wide and honest, and the dimple in her right cheek threatens to make me weak in the knees.

I've never been into dimples until Daisy.

Poppy's laugh startles me, drawing my attention from the picture.

"Fake," she says, rolling the word around on her tongue like it's something foreign. "Right."

13

Daisy

I'M APPLYING THE FINAL LAYER OF YELLOW POLISH TO MY TOENAILS when Bryce gets home. My older sister, Giana, is rambling about one of the players on the Vancouver Warriors hockey team who won't stop ruffling her hair every time she asks for him to pose for a photo, but I've given up listening. She loves men, but they're also one of the only topics she'll call me just to complain about.

I screw the top of the nail polish bottle tight and set it on my nightstand before leaning forward to try and sneak a look at Bryce walking down the hall. The longer I wait for her to pass the door, my back hunched over and toes spread to avoid messing up the polish, the louder my sister gets until I can't ignore her any longer.

"Hello? Sorry I'm so boring. You could have just hung up instead of ignoring me."

"What?"

I lean back and bring my eyes back to the screen, giving up on seeing Bryce. Giana's scowling at me, her dark brows scrunched together and green eyes sharp behind her long lashes.

"I wasn't ignoring you, Gi."

She scoffs loudly. "Yes, you were."

"Okay, I was a little bit."

"First, Johnny doesn't pick up the phone, and now, you don't even pay attention to me when I'm ranting about a total bugger of a goalie."

"This is what you get for moving away," I poke.

She jams a finger into the screen and hisses, "Don't start with me, Daisy. You know how I feel about Cherry Peak."

"Small town with small dreams, Gi. Yes, I know."

It's the reason she left the moment she graduated high school. We all saw it coming, but it still sucked. Giana has always had big plans for her life, and while some people get lucky finding success in Cherry Peak, she didn't want to risk it. Vancouver was somewhere she always wanted to go despite the skyrocketing housing and gas prices.

She attended university there and worked incredibly hard to nail a job as the social media coordinator for the Vancouver Warriors NHL team.

We're proud of her, but the distance sucks. Our family is very close, and not having her nearby weighs on all of us. Especially our moms.

"Don't say it like that," Giana pleads, eyes softening.

"I didn't say it like anything. You're happy, and that makes me happy."

I flash her a supportive smile and relax into the pillows at my back. They're pretty flat and uncomfortable, but on my list of things to purchase, pillows aren't anywhere close to the top. Until I start working again, I'm going to have to be pretty frugal. Just like when I was in university, I'm ready to live off ramen and no-name cereal.

"Are you going to tell me why you were so distracted just now, or do I have to dig?" Gi asks.

I'm not ashamed of the way I'm keeping an ear out for Bryce. She still hasn't walked by, and I'm a few minutes away from going to see why.

"I just thought I heard my roommate get home."

"Right. Bryce?" She waits for me to nod before continuing. "How is that going? I don't blame you for not wanting to stay with Johnny and Aurora. It was bad enough having to when I was down for Christmas."

"Yes, Bryce. And they're in love, Gi. I'll suffer if it means Johnny's happy."

She rolls her eyes at me. "You're too nice. He's your twin, but it's okay for you to still get annoyed with him when he's being inconsiderate."

"He hasn't been inconsiderate."

"Keeping everyone up at night with his sex noises *is* inconsiderate."

I reach down to touch my toenails. Once I've concluded that they're dry enough, I tuck my chilled feet below my blanket.

"You sound jaded. When's the last time you dated?"

"We're not getting into my dating life right now."

I lift a brow. "Oh, we're not? Why?"

"Back to Bryce. You didn't answer my question. How is that going?" she asks, putting the pressure on me instead of her.

I let it go. "It's been good."

"Good?"

"Good," I reply coyly.

She leans close to the camera, trying to stare into my soul. "Nuh-uh. Tell me everything."

I don't have a chance. As if summoned by Giana's demand, Bryce finally walks down the hallway. I lurch forward on the bed when she goes to pass my door without stopping, searching for a glance of her ugly work attire.

"Bryce?" I call.

She stops instantly and then takes one step backward, looking into my room. It's her house, but she inspects the space like she's never seen it before. I haven't done much to it besides add my thin, cheap pillows, bedding, and thick blackout curtains. The desk was already here when I moved in, but I guess maybe it does look different with my school calendar spread over it and my cup of pens and markers in the corner.

The two tubs of school supplies I've yet to bring to my classroom are shoved into the corner of the room, but she doesn't pay that mess much mind.

"Hey," she says once she's finished looking around.

"How was work?"

Once I ask the question, I realize she's not in the same clothes she was this morning. I'm instantly alert as I stare—or more like gawk—at her new outfit. I've never seen her in anything like this before. Short jean skirts, yes. But not tight spandex shorts that ride high on her thighs, exposing the exact curve of the peach tattoos she told me hurt to have inked, and a tank top that's been chopped right under the bust.

My pulse quickens, and I snap my eyes upward, finding crystal-blue ones waiting. At first, I think she's annoyed with me for staring at her, but when she slips inside my room, hovering at the door, I start to doubt that.

"Poppy dragged me to pole," she says, explaining her outfit with a wave of her hand down her body.

"Ignore me one more time, Daisy, and I'm going to block your number," Giana threatens.

I wince, remembering she's still on FaceTime. Bryce cocks her head at the other voice in the room with us but doesn't say anything.

'Sorry, Gi. Do you want to say hi to Bryce?"

"I mean, it would be nice, yeah" is her answer.

Before I turn the phone, I focus on Bryce, waiting for her to shake her head or tell me outright she doesn't want to speak with my sister. We're supposed to be making it known that we're together, but if she isn't ready, I won't push.

I'm still working on getting over the guilt that comes with the whole lying to my family thing, but I know they'd understand if they ever did find out the truth. Until then, they're not going to know that we're not really dating. It won't last forever, and once we've "broken up," everyone will forget about it.

Bryce holds my stare and nods. It's hardly more than a sharp jerk of her chin, but I have a feeling I won't get more than that right now.

She crosses the room and hovers at the edge of the bed. For someone who was just working out, she smells really good. Like her usual spiced berry perfume, but with something almost a bit sweet thrown in.

Definitely *not* paying too much attention to the inches she keeps between her arm and my bent knee, I bring the phone between us so we're both visible and grin at my sister.

"Say hi, Giana," I muse.

My sister huffs a laugh. "Hi, Bryce."

"Hey," Bryce says.

"Daisy was just telling me all about you."

"I was not!" I argue, my neck warming. Swinging my head, I stare up at Bryce. "I definitely was not."

My new roommate and fake girlfriend watches me for all of three seconds before asking my sister, "What did she tell you?"

"Just that you keep a jar of old fingernail clippings on your bedside table."

The corner of Bryce's mouth twitches, and I itch to reach up and lift it higher, curious as to what a real, happy smile looks like on her.

"I hope you don't mind that I only told her that once she admitted how you keep a tooth from each of your exes in a sock under your pillow," Bryce replies, completely straight-faced.

Giana covers her mouth, gasping loudly. "Daisy! That's a secret!"

"Oops."

"It seems that my girlfriend has loose lips," Bryce states.

I press my lips together to hide my sharp inhale when she just flat out drops that bomb like it's such an easy, casual thing to say. I'm grateful that she was the one to bring it up, but damn. I wasn't expecting it.

"I'm sorry, what?" Giana asks, all signs of her humour gone.

I smile too big, hoping it will help her relax. "Surprise!"

Giana clears her throat, eyes blinking furiously. Bryce doesn't waver beneath my sister's heavy gaze, but that doesn't surprise me. She's got a backbone that I would kill to borrow for a day or two.

"Is this a prank?" Giana accuses.

I fidget on the mattress and reach for a pillow, tugging at the edge of its cover. "No, Gi."

She focuses harder on us, nose crinkling slightly. "Then why are you standing so far apart? Do you not like to touch one another? Because touch is an important part of a relationship. Momma taught us that."

The question startles me. It's a valid one, but not one I'm sure how to answer. Thankfully, I'm pretty quick with thinking on my feet.

While Bryce stands frozen in place, her tongue jabbing into her cheek, I slide to the edge of the bed and grab her hand. She jolts at the contact but hides it with a twist of her body, posture loosening muscle by muscle. I thread our fingers together and rest them gently in my lap.

Her breaths are audible, heavy, and I'd bet mine sound the same. I'm content with the small contact, and when Giana leans back from the camera, it seems so is she.

"New relationship jitters? Been there," she says.

I blow out a relieved breath. "Yeah, we're still a bit awkward."

"How did it happen? And why wasn't I called immediately after?"

This is what I was waiting for and thought about all morning. Every word falls off my tongue like a well-rehearsed script.

"It only happened a few days ago, Gi. Once I moved in and we got to spending time together, it was obvious that Bryce was someone that I wanted to get to know even better. And the connection was just . . . instant. I've been away for so long, and I decided I didn't want to waste any time beating around the bush."

"And that was that? You both felt the same way?" She's speaking to Bryce now.

"I've felt that way for a while now. I was waiting for Daisy to catch up."

Bryce's statement sounds incredibly honest. So much so that my cheeks heat despite the lie I know is hidden within it. Maybe I didn't have to worry about us being able to pull this off after all.

Gazing up at her, I let loose a lazy smile and hope it helps convince my sister that we're not lying out of our asses right now.

Bryce might very well be the selling point here because the way she stares at me, a foreign spark in those guarded eyes of hers that drags a soft touch along my rib cage, has me wondering if I'm going to survive the next few weeks or find myself chewed up and spit out.

Is it bad to consider if that would even be a bad outcome? Call me a glutton for punishment, but I could think of worse ways to go.

I try not to focus on the soft, strong hand in mine and turn back to my sister. She may as well be audibly swooning as she stares back and forth between us. It's a win as obvious as any.

One down . . . only a dozen more to go.

14

Bryce

Daisy hangs up with her sister and slowly sets the phone on the bed between her bent knees. She hasn't released my hand yet, and I tell myself that I'll pull it free in a minute.

One minute turns into two, and two must turn into three by the time she clears her throat and slips her fingers free of the hold. A flash of heat rolls down my body as I put some extra space between us and decide to leave.

"Do you think the story I made up is easy enough to remember?" she asks abruptly. "I tried to keep it easy and not give too many details."

"Yeah. Instant connection. Easy enough to sell."

"Okay, great! That's what I thought too," she says, smiling softly.

"I think I'm going to . . ." I jab my thumb toward the door, suddenly awkward as fuck. "Gotta shower."

Her eyes widen in realization. "Right. You were at pole, I take it?"

"Yeah. Poppy's here early. I couldn't pass up spending the afternoon with her."

"That's sweet of you. I've never been to her studio before."

Is she saying that because she wants to go? Does she need an invitation? Am I the one who should be doing the inviting? For fuck's sake, why are my hands always so goddamn sweaty?

"It's a nice place. Very pink," I blurt out.

Holy fuck, Bryce.

Clapping my hands together, I swing my body around and walk right out of Daisy's room, not another word coming out of my mouth.

I don't stop walking until I reach my room and shut the door with my back. As I linger there with my eyes shut and cheeks pulsing, embarrassment makes a mess of my insides. Never have I dealt with such a terrible case of word vomit and anxiety in someone's presence. Daisy is the exact personality that should make it easy to be myself. Yet, that's not at all my reality.

I'm a tongue-twisted teenager around her, and I'm supposed to be able to pull off a fake dating ruse? At the rate I'm self-destructing, it's going to be an absolute disaster.

There's a knock on the door against my back, followed by a soft "Bryce?"

My mouth is scarily dry. "Yeah?"

"I'm sorry I didn't ask if it was okay to hold your hand like that."

"It's fine."

"No, it's not. We haven't discussed boundaries, and we should have. I'd like to do that now, if that's okay with you."

I glare at the black-and-white photo of my tits on the wall in front of me and inwardly curse my lack of shame. The moment I open my door, Daisy's going to get an eyeful of my body whether she wants to or not. Talk about overstepping boundaries.

"We can talk in the living room," I suggest.

"I don't mind talking in your room. Unless that's a boundary?"

I roll my lips together. "No. It's not a boundary."

Cracking the door open a few inches, I'm greeted with a soft-featured Daisy. She's still in her sweat shorts and baggy shirt, but the way they hang off her is nice, easy. I'm used to seeing blue eyes reflected in mirrors and windows, but there's something about hers that are intriguing. Bright without being blinding and soft without losing all their edge.

"Actually, do you want to go out? Get out of here for a little while?" she asks, a nervous flutter in the words.

"To do what?"

"I've got to bring my supplies over to the school and start getting my room set up. It's a bit last-minute, but I've been kind of . . . procrastinating it. New job nerves and all that. I could use the support, if you were up for a bit of a field trip?"

If it means we can get out of this room before she can get a good look inside, then yes. "I need to shower first."

"Totally fine! I'll get everything together and wait," she rushes out, her soft smile growing into one that makes me glad I didn't turn her down.

My stomach feels tight when she grips the doorframe and her sunbeams threaten to spill into my room.

"See you soon!" she squeaks.

I watch her leave and, a beat later, listen as her bedroom door clicks shut. It takes me a minute to gather myself enough to shower and get dressed, but once I'm finished, I put my hair up and slip on my boots.

Time to myself has dulled my nerves, leaving me cool and collected once again. Back to the person I've always been.

Wiggling the silver belt buckle at the front of my straight-cut jeans, I let out a slow, controlled breath at the familiarity of my outfit. The bleached black Linkin Park band tee is comfortable and couldn't be further from the frilly, white blouse I'm forced to wear during the week.

Daisy's already waiting in the living room when I get there. The two blue tubs that were in the corner of her bedroom are by the door, overflowing with school supplies and thick paper shapes that I assume are supposed to get hung on the classroom walls.

"Ready?" I ask, snatching my keys and wallet from the coffee table.

She jumps to her feet and reaches for the first tub before lifting it into her arms and starting toward the door. "Ready."

I move past her and hold it open for her to walk through before unlocking my car and grabbing the second tub. She's just set hers down on the street when I drop mine beside it, and then we shove them into the car.

Luckily, it's only a three-minute drive from my place to the school, and we're not suffocating in awkward for silence for too long.

"Before my interview, I hadn't been back here for years," she says once we've started our walk toward the front of the building.

"I've come with Darren a few times. For Abbie."

Her first Christmas recital was . . . surprisingly well put together. For a bunch of five-year-olds, they followed their choreography to a T and hardly missed a lyric of "Jingle Bells."

"That's right. She's going into first grade now, right?"

"Yeah."

"Maybe I'll get to teach her next year."

"You're planning on staying in Cherry Peak?" I ask before I can stop myself.

Daisy balances her tub on her knee in order to scan her pass to get into the school and pull open the door once it unlocks.

"I would like to. My family is here, and I won't tell Johnny this, but being away from him was the hardest out of everyone and everything. It's absolutely a twin thing, but he'll get arrogant about it."

The hem of her long cardigan brushes my thigh when I follow her inside and adjust the tub in my arms. Our fashion senses couldn't be more opposite. I've never worn a cardigan in my life, let alone a thick wool one that reaches my ankles or heeled booties with zipper charms. I've always preferred something made from jean material, T-shirts, and cowboy boots. Easy and simple.

Daisy isn't simple in the slightest, and easy? Not a fat fucking chance. It's not a bad thing. Just different.

"He missed you too. Couldn't stop telling us how proud he is of you," I tell her.

I don't have to be looking at her to know she's smiling. "He's a great brother."

"Seems like it."

"Alright . . . I think my classroom is just over here," she directs, turning left down a forked hallway.

I follow behind her, every inch of this school and its white-painted walls bringing back memories that I thought were long forgotten.

Sneaking into the bathroom to kiss my first girlfriend during free period, stealing the quarterback's stupid football he used to toss in class and throwing it at Poppy's face when I saw him chasing after me.

School was here and gone so quick that sometimes it feels like it never actually happened. I don't miss it, but sometimes I do regret not taking advantage of how easy life was back then.

"It's here!" Daisy squeals, using the toe of her boot to push open the door. "I'm excited but also nervous. There are so many things that I worry about, but—"

We step inside and freeze. Daisy's shoulders slump immediately, her excitement squashed with the disaster in front of us.

Like it was rented out to a group of asshole college kids over the summer, the classroom is almost unrecognizable as a place for second graders. Every desk has been turned upside down and looks like they've been drawn on with thick, permanent markers. Chunks of gum are so big they stick out like sore thumbs on the corners of them, and the chairs have been scattered all over the place.

A whiteboard is stained with old writing from neon-coloured pens. The biggest desk at the front of the classroom has a bent leg, making it lean at the corner with a collection of pens and papers scattered on the floor from where they must have slid off.

I place the tub of supplies on the floor by the door and move through the room, anger beating like a second pulse beneath my skin.

While the blinds appear to be down, I tug at them and realize that one of the windows is open, the screen missing.

"The window's open. My guess is a couple of kids broke in over the summer and no one noticed," I grit out.

"Oh." She hides the devastation I know I'll find when I turn around with fake nonchalance. "Well, it's a good thing I didn't wait any longer to come, then. Now, at least I'll have time to clean this up before Monday."

"You're not cleaning this up," I snap a bit too quickly. Turning to face her, I softly add, "The school should have been checking the rooms. This isn't your mess to fix."

"I don't want to make a bad first impression. I'll spend today cleaning and tomorrow unpacking and decorating. It's fine."

With a fake smile, she searches the room, throat straining. "I'm sorry you wasted your time coming to help me unpack. I'll get someone to pick me up later once I've finished up. You can go."

Yeah fucking right. The first thing I do is slam the window shut and make sure it's locked up tight before pulling the blinds up. The view outside is of the school's football field, but the lights are off during the summer, and unless they've added them over the past few years since I graduated, there are no cameras on this side of the building.

I feel Daisy's eyes on me while I grip the closest upturned desk and flip it onto its thin legs. Working my way down the line, I do the same to four others before she speaks.

"You really don't have to do this, Bryce. I wouldn't even expect this of a real girlfriend, let alone a fake one."

"Is that a joke?" I ask, not a lick of humour in my tone.

She keeps her lips flat and shakes her head.

"If my girlfriend didn't offer to help me when I needed it, I'd kick her ass to the curb. I'm interested to hear what you think is something a partner should do for you if this doesn't count," I say.

She swallows loudly. "I've always felt guilty asking others to help with things that I know I can do myself."

My eyelid twitches when the tip of my finger touches a gob of gum before I slap my hand down on my pants, rubbing the sensation away. "You'll need to cut that shit out."

"It's not that easy, Frosty."

Her laugh is a welcome sound. I relax slightly.

"We'll work on it."

Glancing across the room, I focus on the nervous twist of her mouth and looped fingers pressed to her stomach. She kicks the first tub of supplies against the wall and heaves a sigh.

"Should we get started, then?"

15

Daisy

I THINK I'M STARTING TO FIGURE BRYCE OUT.

I've heard the term Rottweiler boyfriend before, but in this case, it's Rottweiler *girlfriend*. While fierce enough to appear mean to those who don't know her, she's actually a giant squish ball that would roll over onto her back for some affection from those she trusts.

I'd enjoy being one of those few. Something tells me that I'd never have to handle a single battle alone ever again.

My classroom is coming along, but without proper cleaning supplies, we've only managed to get everything back in their proper locations. That hasn't stopped Bryce from becoming completely focused on fixing a mess that shouldn't be her concern.

I keep sneaking looks at her, my entire body flooded with warmth as she tears between the desks and arranges them in the way I told her I wanted them. Once they're organized in groups of four, she narrows her eyes on my desk and kicks its broken leg.

I stifle a laugh behind the back of my hand. If she had access to a jug of gasoline, I'm positive the desk would be up in flames by now.

"I'm sure we can find something to stick underneath it for now. Just to even it out," I suggest.

"Absolutely fucking not. Darren's coming with supplies to fix this mess."

"He is?"

She nods, keeping the desk pinned beneath her scowl. "He should be here soon."

There's that warmth again . . . "When did you ask him to come? I don't want to bother him. I know he must be busy with work."

"I texted him a few minutes ago. And don't flatter him. Darren works for a max of three hours a day unless he's in the middle of a project. If he wasn't coming here, he'd be going to fiddle around at the station."

"I've never actually known what his career is. Just that he volunteers at the fire station sometimes."

It's common knowledge that Bryce is close friends with him. They might bicker like an old married couple, but even I knew as someone from the outside looking in that there would never be anything more than that between them. And the more I think about the potential of that, the likelier a funeral seems because Bryce would rip that man to shreds and leave nothing behind for the birds to pick at.

I'm concerned that I'll have the same fate unless I keep my guard up. But at the same time, maybe I could use a bit of a challenge in my life.

"He works for an architecture company that runs out of Calgary," she says.

"Oh, wow. Good for him."

"He's good at what he does. Real fucking good. But don't tell him I said that, or he'll never let me live it down."

My lips part on a soft laugh as I pull the end of the string of multicoloured letters out of one of my tubs. "Want to help me hang these while we wait for him?"

"Did you bring tacks or something?"

"A giant container of them. They're in the tub," I confirm.

She abandons the broken desk and digs through the tub, gripping onto a clear container a beat later. When she takes the letters from me, I grab the other end and tug it free of all the other decorations. I choose the wall above the dirty whiteboard and drag a chair over before standing on it to reach where I want them to start.

"We should talk about boundaries now. Before Darren gets here," I say before dropping my palm for a tack. She sets one in my hand with careful fingers, keeping the sharp side up. "I don't want to overstep."

The tack takes a bit of a shove to go into the wall, but it gives eventually, keeping the Z hung in place. I step off the chair and push it to the other side of the whiteboard.

"My usual boundaries would have us looking like strangers," Bryce mutters.

"Well, what are they?"

She hovers close to my back when I step onto the chair again and take the opposite end of the string. The corner of the *A* bites into my fingers as I wait for her reply.

"I don't love physical contact with people outside of my closest friends. I'm not the touchy-feely type of person."

"That was obvious, Frosty."

She stares into the container of tacks in her hand, eyes cloudy. "I wasn't raised around a lot of physical affection. It doesn't come naturally to me."

"That's alright. You don't have to want to be that type of person. I'm certainly not going to force you to be. I just want you to be comfortable with me because, obviously, I *am* a touchy-feely person. It's second nature for me to reach for someone's hand or hug them whenever I get the urge to, and sometimes I don't always remember that not everyone is like that," I explain, the backs of my eyes burning with guilt.

It's a character flaw. I've tried to become more conscious of my actions, especially around those I don't know all that well, but with Bryce, I kind of just act off impulse. It's careless of me.

She moves then. I don't see her come closer, but I feel it. The container of golden tacks shakes, and then a warm, steady hand closes around the one I have hanging at my side. My breath stalls in my throat as I slowly look down at where she's standing, eyes no longer shadowed but clear.

"I don't think I have boundaries with you," she says, her voice the softest I've ever heard it. Almost like she's trying to soothe me.

Before I can think too much into that, someone clears their throat. I wait for Bryce to yank her hand away, but she rubs her thumb along the back of mine instead.

"I knew something was off about you being at the school, but I can't say that I expected to find this," Darren says.

I opt to give him a thankful smile instead of waving, deciding not to release Bryce's hand just yet. He needs to believe what he's about to learn.

"Did you bring everything?" Bryce asks.

"Yes, your majesty." He examines the room and the mess that was left for me and frowns. "Someone had a good time in here."

"I'm glad they enjoyed themselves, at least," I say, keeping my tone light despite my strong displeasure with the state of my first classroom.

Bryce scoffs. "I'm not. Whoever did this is a bunch of fucking assholes."

"They were probably just kids looking to have fun," I argue gently.

She snaps her eyes to me, clearly frustrated. "If they're old enough to break into a school and vandalize it, then they're old enough to know better."

"She's right. Even Abbie knows better than to do something like this," Darren says.

My exhale is far too heavy. They're valid points, but it feels wrong of me to be angry with a bunch of children for something

I'm capable of fixing. Maybe that makes me a pushover. I don't know.

I flex my fingers, and Bryce releases them before handing me a tack. Stabbing it through the *A* and into the wall above the whiteboard, I say, "Either way, it's done with. The only thing I want to do now is finish this classroom and start looking forward to Monday."

Darren sets his bag of tools on one of the clusters of desks. "Fair enough."

Bryce is more reluctant. She tongues her cheek the way I've noticed she does when she's thinking or struggling with something while shooting daggers at the crusted writing on the whiteboard.

I'm struck with another burst of realization as to the person Bryce is beneath the rough exterior that keeps most people at a distance. She's angry for me, appearing ready to march an army on my behalf, and we've only been roommates for a week. I haven't done anything to earn her protection, but she's given it to me anyway.

"It's okay, Frosty. Really," I urge, stepping off the chair.

She glances at me from the corner of her eye. "It's not. But I'll let it go."

Mouth tugging up, I brush my hands over my cardigan before palming my hips. Darren starts to pull everything out of the bag he brought, and I rush to grab the cleaning spray and a cloth, handing them to Bryce.

"For the whiteboard. Maybe once it's clean, you won't look like you want to rip it off the wall and break it in half?"

"No promises," she grumbles but takes the bottle and cloth from my hands.

"Thank you, Bryce."

I plant a kiss on her cheek before she gets too far away. Bryce doesn't freeze up this time. A squeak escapes me when she takes my hand and slants her lips over my knuckles, leaving them there for a breath.

I'm not imagining the smirk that appears just as she drops my hand and turns to the whiteboard, giving us her back.

Darren's chuckle is loud, but I continue to stare at the black shirt clinging to Bryce's back. It shakes slightly, and I swear I can hear the ghost of her laughter.

"So, when did that happen?" Darren asks.

At a snail's pace, I turn around and come face to face with his lazy grin. I shrug loosely and wink.

"Wouldn't you love to know?"

"Actually, yeah, I would."

"Say please, Darren," Bryce throws over her shoulder, scrubbing at some blue swirls with the cloth.

He rolls his eyes. "Please."

I take the paint scraper and rubber gloves from the pile of supplies and prepare to start scraping gum from underneath the desks while he heads toward my broken desk, a couple of types of tools in his hands.

Darren Huntsly is a handsome man. Tall with wide shoulders and a bulk to him that isn't the typical buff type, but the kind that tips the scale toward dad bod status. He shares some physical characteristics with Poppy, but not many. It's easy to tell they're siblings but also that they're still very much their own people.

When I look at Johnny and me, I feel the same way. He got his looks from Mom, and I just . . . didn't. Whoever it was that our moms used during their IVF journey, I imagine I look more like him.

"It happened recently. Still really new, D. Don't push," Bryce says, an obvious threat in her tone.

He jerks his chin at her, and something passes between them that I don't know the meaning behind.

"So, it's new and what? You're just going to try it out?"

His instant belief in what he's just learned isn't what I was expecting.

"I think so. We still have so much to learn about one another, but we have a connection that I didn't want to waste by beating around the bush," I answer.

Dropping to my haunches in front of the first of many desks, I snap the rubber gloves on before gripping the paint scraper. I hold my breath and run the blade beneath a gob of gum.

"Does anyone else know?" Darren asks.

Bryce moves down the whiteboard. "Only Poppy and Daisy's sister."

"Poppy knows and didn't tell me?" He gapes.

It's news to me too. I mean, I kind of assumed Bryce would tell Poppy, but she hasn't brought it up to me.

Bryce flashes me a quick, almost apologetic look before saying, "I told her not to."

"When are you guys telling everyone else? You won't be able to keep it a secret if that's what you're hoping to do."

"We haven't talked about that yet," Bryce mutters.

"I suggest you do it at Peakside. Hit everyone at once."

I pinch the gum that's fallen and set it on top of the desk. "That's a good idea. Saturday nights, right?"

"Always," he confirms.

The underside of the second desk is worse than the first, but I make quick work of scraping it clean. I watch Bryce's legs move, carrying her away from the whiteboard and toward the desk Darren's crouched in front of.

"We'll think about it," she says.

Darren clucks his tongue. "Fair enough."

Suddenly, a ball of nerves fills my stomach. It's not like we're in a real relationship, but nobody else will know that. Once we've told everyone about us, it'll be the real deal. Next will come her parents.

But I'm excited for that part of our agreement. It's about time they learn what it takes to support their daughter, and I'm more than up for the task of being the one to teach them.

16

Bryce

We didn't leave the school until long after the sun had set. Darren's babysitter needed to be relieved at dinnertime, so he left hours before we did. I wouldn't say it was awkward per se once he was gone, but there wasn't a lot of conversation happening.

We went home exhausted and disappeared into our rooms the moment we could. I woke up this morning before I heard Daisy so much as stir in her room and went to the only place I knew she wouldn't.

Steele Ranch. The guest house, specifically.

My furious knocking on the wide front door lasts for a while before finally, footsteps sound on the other side. The sight of a half-asleep Poppy wrapped in a puffy pink robe doesn't shock me.

I push past her inside the warm house. "Is Garrison here?"

"He's in bed. Like I wish I still was," she croaks.

Good enough for me.

The guest house is bigger than you expect when you first hear about it. It rivals the size of the main ranch house but lacks the same rustic charm. Updated with gleaming gray wood floors, white walls, and appliances that belong in industrial kitchens, it's the second-newest building on the ranch.

Brody and Anna's place makes this one look like a ramshackle cottage.

I turn into the living room and collapse on the massive sectional. My back sinks into the cushions as I slap my hands over my face and groan.

"What's wrong? Not that I don't love seeing your beautiful face, but I'd prefer not to do it so early in the morning."

"I shouldn't have agreed to this," I say, the words muffled in my palms.

"To what exactly? You're not prone to always making the best choices."

I want to glare at her, but that would mean uncovering my face. "I kissed her hand."

"You kissed her hand?"

"She kissed my cheek."

"Oh-kay . . ."

"Do you think we should go to Peakside tonight?"

"Who? You need to slow down and look at me." Suddenly, she's tugging my hands down my face and sitting beside me, expression open. "Explain what's going on."

"Your brother knows and suggested me and Daisy make our couple debut at Peakside."

"You told my brother?" she asks, nose scrunched.

"This isn't the time for you to be jealous. He doesn't know that it's fake."

Her entire face lights up. "Okay, he can know that slim bit of info, then."

"This is serious. Do we go to Peakside or not?"

"Why wouldn't you? There's no better place to do it."

I grip my knees and huff and huff like I'm trying to blow the goddamn house down. "My parents won't be there. This is supposed to be for them."

"They'll hear about it. I'd be surprised if they don't already by the time you get home afterward. Are you worried about them finding out, or is this all because you don't want to lie to everyone?"

I wish that was it. Lying to all of our friends should be what's making me doubt this plan, not that the longer we continue to act on it, the closer I'm moving into obsession territory.

Finding Daisy attractive was one thing. Watching her from afar and yearning for the right time, if *ever*, to make a move is another. But having her so close while knowing I'm supposed to make our fake relationship real enough that I can touch her body and kiss her skin . . . I'm completely and utterly fucked.

One taste and I'm contemplating putting a stop to this before I wind up lost and broken.

"You know the truth. The only people I feel guilty lying to are Anna and Darren," I mutter.

She leans against me, shoulder to shoulder. Her puffy robe is thick and warm, too bulky for my personal preference. It looks expensive, and I'd bet that's because it is. Garrison isn't frugal with his billions when it comes to her.

"They'll forgive you if they ever find out you lied. And I've got your back. I think my brother is right. Peakside is the smartest idea. Not to mention, it'll be loud and busy, so you can always sneak off if you need to," she says.

"Do you think I can pull it off?"

Her eyes lift to my face, but I don't turn my head. "Are you finally admitting what I've known for years now?"

"What's that?" I ask, needing her to be the one to say it.

"That you want Daisy Mitchell."

The statement is like a pipe straight through the chest. I struggle to breathe around the intrusion and instead sound pained when I finally find words.

"I want Daisy Mitchell."

Poppy's arm slides below my chest as she hugs me from the side and squeezes tight. "I'm proud of you."

"It's not that big of a deal."

"It is," she soothes, pressing her cheek to my arm. "Even if you think it isn't."

"After this is over, it won't matter whether or not I want her. It's fake in her eyes. Like we agreed it would be. And I feel fucking creepy now."

"You're not creepy, Ice."

I make a deep noise in the back of my throat. "I am. Agreeing to this while having pre-existing feelings for her is fucking creepy. I'm not only lying to everyone else but to her too."

Poppy twists, leaning over my lap with a hand on the armrest. Her frown is one I've seen a million times over the course of our friendship, but it feels different this time. Like she's disappointed in me or something.

"You're plenty of things, Bryce Lemieux. Blunt, stubborn, crass, a connoisseur of vibrators and horror documentaries, but you're absolutely not creepy. It pisses me off when you speak negatively about yourself."

"Connoisseur of vibrators?"

Her frown breaks, flipping up into a slight smile. "That is all you would pay attention to."

"Don't act innocent."

"I prefer dildos. Vibrators are plain."

"You have a living dildo in your bed right now," I point out.

Leaning back, she settles beside me once again and laughs. "The best one on the market too."

"Fuck off." I jostle her with my arm and tip my head back to stare at the ceiling, exhaling. "What do I do here, Poppy?"

"Stick to the plan while opening yourself up to her. Give her the chance to learn who you really are. Once she does, that's when you'll have a chance to convince her to be yours for real."

Goosebumps explode over my arms and legs, followed by a dull voice in my head that tells me to listen to her.

"You've gotten wise," I say.

"Love does that to you, I think. Makes you see the world a little brighter."

"Sounds . . ."

"Fun?"

"Terrifying," I correct her.

Her eyebrows jump up quickly. "You're not wrong. Relationships are terrifying. Especially after one like you went through. I don't blame you for being extra guarded when it comes to letting people in. You've always kept most things close to your chest, but it's been worse since you and Vic broke up."

"She's marrying that guy, you know?" I mutter.

"Good. I hope they have a terrible life together. They deserve each other."

"Yeah."

"Hey," she says, a bite in her tone. I meet her waiting stare, somewhat comforted by the fierceness of it. "Don't. She wasn't meant for you. It's time that you found out if you're close to finding the person who is."

It sounds easy enough. But if it was, I wouldn't be in the situation I am right now.

Daisy didn't need to be convinced to come with me to Peakside.

The moment I asked, she was agreeing and heading off to her room to get ready. I went to the basement, an itch beneath my skin that I knew I needed to ease before attempting to go out tonight.

When I turn my tattoo gun off and look at the clock, it's been over an hour since I've been down here. A buzzing sensation lingers in my bones as I set down the gun and pick up the paper towel to wipe my ankle free of ink.

My back aches, and there are pinpricks in my calf as I stretch it out and blink the daze from my eyes. The flower on my ankle is small, hidden beneath a veil of black vines. I didn't even realize I'd begun inking it until I got to the fifth petal. By then, it was too late to change course with the time I had. So, I hid it beneath the vines and hoped like hell nobody would get close enough to my feet to tell.

And Poppy said I wasn't creepy.

The floor creaks above me, and I start to clean up my mess. We need to leave in an hour to be on time, and I've just created an open wound on a part of my body that's going to be rubbing against a pair of cowboy boots all night. Even with the wrap I stick on, it's sensitive and will be that way for at least another day. Fucking incredible thinking that was.

An hour later, I'm as ready as I'll ever be. After showering with my foot held out of the tub, I've already had to replace the wrap around the new tattoo and clean up a giant puddle from the floor before I slipped on my ass.

It kept me busy. Helped keep my mind off tonight and what's going to happen the minute I step out of my room and head to Peakside with Daisy at my side.

The sock on my left foot is folded once at the top to keep from rubbing my tattoo, but the moment I slip my boot on, it'll be going up and over it. I'm not going to risk wearing anything else just in case someone notices the new design. Especially Daisy.

After shrugging my black leather jacket on, I untuck my hair from the collar and linger with my hand on the door handle. Fake or not, this is my first date in a long time. I'm not a nervous person by nature, but the last few days have proved that I'm not immune to that feeling. It's been one of the only things I've managed to feel at all.

With a shake of my head, I open the door and stride down the hall.

I don't make it far before Daisy's door opens. She sounds breathless when she says, "I'm ready! Are we leaving now?"

Any type of mental preparation I've done prior to this moment goes out the window the moment I turn around. Poppy's speech about my worthiness is shoved to the back of my mind, replaced with an incredibly striking sensation of incredible *un*worthiness. It has nothing to do with me and all to do with Daisy, though.

I doubt a single living person would ever be worthy of her right now.

She's pulled her deep auburn hair up into space buns, leaving loose curls draping both of her cheeks. Her skin glows, lips painted a bubble-gum pink that matches the flowy romper she's wearing. Bare legs that go on for miles despite her slightly shorter frame have my mouth filling with cotton. White tennis shoes are on her feet without a stain in sight.

I'm underdressed despite the simplicity of her outfit.

This is me. The black jeans and boots, cropped shirt that's a size too big, and tonight, a leather jacket instead of the jean one that was hung beside it because I knew Poppy would hate the jean on jean. I'm confident in my style, and I won't change it.

"Yeah," I say on a loose breath. My throat is clogged, something thick stuck inside of it. "We're leaving."

Her soft blue eyes roam over my body, and I stand frozen in place. The flush on her cheeks is from her makeup. I wish it was because of me.

"You look beautiful, Frosty," she says, a soft smile playing with her lips.

My heartbeat is in my ears. "You too."

"Thank you," she chimes. "Shall we go?"

Her hand hangs between us once she's extended it toward me. I take it, my middle tightening at the contact as I shove down a shiver.

"Do you want to bring a jacket?" I ask.

The house is silent, and every clap of her shoes on the floor echoes. Silence has never bothered me so much before. Usually, I like it. It means I'm not being forced to speak with someone I don't want to. Yet, with Daisy, I'd speak about anything if it meant it was her voice I was hearing.

"If I did, then you wouldn't get to offer yours to me when we leave Peakside tonight," she teases.

We move into the front room, and I bend to slip on my right boot. "So you want me to freeze instead?"

Her laugh is bright and clear, taking my question as the joke I intended it to be despite the poor execution. I swallow a whimper of pain when I roll my sock up over my tattoo and shove my foot into the other boot. The boots are well broken in, but I've never worn them with a fresh ankle tattoo before.

"It's not my fault your jacket looks so warm and inviting," she says, opening the front door for me to walk through first.

"I hardly ever wear it."

"Well, then it can be like a letterman jacket. I've always wanted to wear one of those."

I stand beside her on the porch and lock up before we start our walk. "They smell like sweat. You haven't missed much."

"Let me guess—you dated a jock in high school?"

My laugh comes out of my nose. "Fat fucking chance. I messed around with one, though. Wore the jacket once with nothing beneath it."

"So you went for jocks, and I went for their cheerleaders."

"I didn't think Cherry Peak even had cheerleaders," I say.

Daisy swings her arms at her sides, every bit of her appearing as joyful as usual. That sates me, somehow. Knowing that her time with me this past week hasn't caused her to act any differently.

"Has Johnny ever told you that I used to do track and field?"

I glance at her, surprised. "No."

"I did a lot of high jump and hurdles and went with the school team to regionals in twelfth grade. Calgary cares a bit more about sports than we do here, and that's where I met the cheerleaders," she explains, the humour in her voice also lining her lips with a devilish smile.

"You used the school trip to get laid, then."

A slight pain blooms in my side when she leans over and jabs me with her fingers. "Don't say it like that. It makes me sound dirty!"

"Who knew innocent Daisy Mitchell was such a perv." I cluck my tongue and watch as her neck pinkens. "We've got a real Cherry Peak scandal on our hands."

"I'm not *that* innocent, just for your information," she clarifies.

"Apparently not. Tell me something else to help your case."

"Help my case? Am I being graded on my perv level right now? Are you approving of my actions after all?"

"I never said that, Sunshine."

Daisy licks her lips, and I watch the entire motion of her tongue as it slips over every pink inch of them.

"But you're thinking it," she counters.

I lift a coy brow. "And if I am?"

"I'd say not to get your hopes up for more juicy details. The cheerleaders are my dirtiest secret."

She quickens her step, like she's trying to leave me behind, and I huff a silent laugh while matching her pace.

"I don't believe that."

The setting sun casts a glow over her face, reflecting the soft sense of longing in her eyes. "Johnny is the twin that got the risk-taker trait. I sat back and let him run loose most of the time. Majority of the stories from my teen years are the ones I told our moms to cover for him when he got home late or not at all."

"You don't have to do those things for him anymore. There's time for you to make some stories of your own," I state.

Daisy's steps falter, the curled pieces of hair framing her face whipping when a gust of wind drags over us. "Why does that matter?"

I stall. The idea that slammed into my subconscious just seconds ago refuses to flutter away. We're close to the bar, and any minute now, we won't be alone. Someone will pop up, and we'll have to drop this conversation. I'll be let off the hook.

I speak anyway. "Is there anything that you've always wanted to do but never did?"

"Of course. Most of them are small and kind of stupid, though."

Doubtful. "Like what?"

She tucks the loose hairs behind her ears. "I've never gotten the chance to hike up the side of a mountain and dip my toe in a glacial runoff."

"That's not stupid."

"Have you forgotten where we live? There are mountains everywhere."

To emphasize her point, she reaches out and points at the peaks towering over the edge of town. They're snow-capped right now, but in a couple of months, they'll be painted white from the narrow tops to the thickly treed bottoms.

"I'll hike with you," I offer, launching the words off my tongue. "I told you that you didn't owe me anything more than rent money for letting you stay with me. So, if you insist on helping me with my parents, then I'm going to help you with this to make us even."

"What?"

"Just say yes so we can go inside."

She stares at me, looking from one eye to the next, as if she's searching for the hidden meaning behind my impulse offer. Frustration lines her face when she doesn't find it. I like the sight of her pouting.

"You'll really go hiking with me?" she asks softly.

"I will."

"Then you have yourself a deal, Frosty."

17

Bryce

It's like something out of my worst nightmare, the way everyone turns to look at us when we walk in. The gawking eyes feel like sandpaper rubbing up and down my skin, but I keep myself in check instead of telling them all to fuck off the way I want to.

I touch Daisy's lower back with a firm hand and guide her through the bar. It's not the first time I've witnessed people staring at her, but it's for an entirely different reason this time. While I'm used to them pausing to take a look at her breathtaking beauty whenever she steps into a room, this time, they're pausing to wonder why she's here with me.

Smug isn't an emotion I'm familiar with, but maybe I'll have to get used to it. I think I might like it after all.

Daisy scoffs under her breath and rolls her eyes at a couple I recognize from the town office as they observe us from their booth without a care. The woman tugs her phone from her purse before we've even made it past them, and my gut tells me that it isn't the babysitter she's texting.

"I'll never get used to how nosey everyone is here," Daisy says beneath her breath, words just for me. "In Calgary, you could walk into any busy spot, and nobody would know who you were or care why you were there."

"You forgot how small a small town really is, Sunshine. It's spending a night out drinking and constantly reminding yourself not to get crazy out of fear of waking up the next morning to every single person in town knowing and judging you."

"You're right. It was easier to forget about the pains of this place the longer I was away. But I still missed it."

"I wouldn't miss the town. Just the people," I say, letting her see something deeper inside of me.

The bartender glares at me the way she always does, but once she notices Daisy beside me and the hand I have on her back, she strays from the usual. With a sharp laugh, Victoria's mother, Pamila, makes a scene, shouting to the second bartender words that she hungers for me to hear.

"Look at this! Another victim for the infamous cold-hearted bitch to sink her teeth into. Is she the first Mitchell daughter you'll be testing out, or have you already sampled the others?"

My throat constricts with a mixture of anger and embarrassment, the former being my focus. Daisy is stiff as a board beside me, but I don't spend time contemplating the reason behind it before dropping my hand and storming over to the bar.

My skin beats with a pissed-off flush. Pamila is more immature than her daughter. I should have expected something to have been coming all this time. She's been too quiet about my relationship with her daughter for too long not to have been itching to cause a scene. Seeing me with Daisy—the first woman since Victoria—has struck a chord.

Pamila doesn't know the truth of what happened between me and her daughter, and I haven't given enough of a shit to tell her differently. Victoria is a coward when it comes to her mother, and for a while after our breakup, I hated the part of myself that didn't want to ruin their relationship the way I knew would happen if the truth came out. It shouldn't have mattered what damage I left behind after she broke my heart, but for some fucking reason, it did.

I'm paying for that now.

"Wait!" Daisy calls before her fingers curl around my bicep. My attention snaps to her touch, my anger gone for the briefest of moments. "We're not here to deal with that woman. She's not worth it."

"It is worth it. I've waited a long time to put her in her place."

"Not tonight, Bryce. Please. This isn't how it's supposed to go," she pleads, face scrunching painfully.

It's that expression that has me turning my back on Pamila. I suck in a long breath and try to ignore the eyes I can feel sinking into me from every direction as I focus on Daisy's.

"She has it coming. I'm not someone to hold my tongue, Daisy. I'd rather chomp it off than do that. Especially when people I care about are brought up to piss me off," I snap, hoping that she doesn't remove her hand as a result of my anger. "I've walked on eggshells in this place for years despite that. Just trying not to start shit with people who more than deserve it."

Her fingers loosen before drifting up along my sleeve and settling on my shoulder. My chest grows tight, too tight to get a full breath in, but I keep completely still.

"Just one more night. There's something more important about tonight than a cruel person who clearly thrives on attention. You want to make a point to parents? Let it go one last time, and tomorrow, you can make her life hell and teach her not to mess with you."

"I want a drink," I mutter.

She laughs, and it pushes back the black clouds in my mind. "Poppy's already got it handled."

With her hand on my shoulder, Daisy urges me to look back at the bar. The sight of my best friend leaned over the bar with a finger jabbing into Pamila's chest is more than enough for me right now, but her words soothe the sharp edges inside of me that hadn't quite dulled from Daisy's.

"Keep your poison tongue inside your mouth, Pamila, or I'll encourage that 'cold-hearted bitch' to cut it off and shove it up your ass."

There's a hush around us, but Poppy doesn't care. She grabs two beers from behind the bar and takes them with a toothy grin.

"Consider this the start of an apology," she drawls before turning to wink right at me and Daisy and gesturing around the bar toward where I know our group of friends are waiting.

Daisy strokes a hand up my spine and dips her chin at my best friend. Poppy leaves us then, her hips swaying confidently.

Pissed off doesn't begin to describe my feelings, but fuck if I'm going to let it ruin my night. I'd rather be pissed than know I've hurt or disappointed Daisy by not being the bigger person here.

"Are you ready?" she asks.

"I'm sorry she brought you up like that. I've never thought about any of your sisters in that—"

Daisy cuts me off with a finger to my mouth.

In the middle of Peakside, she touches my lips with the pad of her finger and steps close, closer than she has before.

A boulder smashes into my chest, stealing my breath. Something warm and charged fills the space between us and brushes my body with electric fingers. She's not much shorter than me and probably weighs as much as one of the bar stools nearby, but she watches me with the determination and focus of someone ten times her height and size.

My mouth is dry, lips aching for me to reach out with my tongue and wet them. I'd taste her then. Probably wind up sucking the tip of her small finger into my mouth and moaning at the new connection.

Fuck, my entire pussy clenches at the idea. Would she like if I bit down on the soft pad of it? Just gently . . . enough to have those pretty blues widening and pupils expanding with a dangerous mix of shock and lust.

"Don't apologize for the actions of others, Bryce. We're not responsible for anyone besides ourselves. Everyone has their own mind and their own conscience, even if they choose to ignore it," she murmurs, eyes flitting between mine before drifting down to where we're connected.

Her cheeks turn pink as she applies pressure with her finger, forcing my lips to part enough for it to press against the bottom more than the top. I exhale over the dainty fingertip, and her breath hitches, gaze bouncing back up to snag on mine.

I've dreamed of being this close to her. Of what the heat from her body beating into mine with wild fists and attention fixated on me and only me would feel like. What I was wishing for was nothing compared to the real thing.

"You're blushing, Sunshine," I breathe out.

The pink deepens and spreads to her ears. "You don't blush."

"I don't?"

She touches my cheek with her other hand, using the backs of her fingers to stroke the length of it. I shiver from head to toe, unable to hide such a visceral reaction this time.

"Maybe you do," she whispers, stroking my skin again where I know it flames as brightly as hers. "Pink looks good on you."

My laugh is rough, but as she stares at my mouth with a startling sense of awe, I don't think she cares how it sounds.

"Your smile looks better, though," she muses, one of her own appearing.

"I've smiled around you before."

"Hardly. Not like that."

Cool air attacks my hot skin when she removes her hand and uses the other to trace the shape of my bottom lip and pull up the corner of my mouth.

"I'm more of a scowler," I say bluntly. Aiming for it to sound like a joke, I hope it doesn't sound as self-deprecating as it feels.

"I like your scowls too."

If we stand here like this any longer, I'm going to start thinking too far into these comments and find meanings behind them that don't exist.

We're in public.

This is all for show.

An act for or Pamila and the couple that I'd bet have already told my mother everything we intended her to learn.

I'm not interested in hurting myself.

Daisy's forced to stop touching me, our connection breaking when I take a step back. My neck is hot, and I feel how damp it is with sweat as I pull my hair into my hands and drape it over my shoulder.

"If we don't go now, someone will have drunk our beers," I mutter.

She blinks a few times, her face unreadable for the first time since I've met her. "You're right."

I hesitate to touch her now.

In front of Darren, we were able to keep our distance in the classroom. But we aren't in a classroom this time, and we're about to do this in front of everyone important in my life. Her twin brother included.

"What do you need me to do?" Daisy asks, reading my mind. She looks like herself again.

"Do we hold hands?"

"We do whatever feels natural."

But what if everything feels natural with her? I'd hold her hand every day if I could, even if my palms grow sweaty in seconds.

"Start with this," she adds, threading our fingers.

I focus on every point of contact we have, from our hands to our arms that are pressed together, and take a deep breath.

We head straight for the table around the bar, and every step settles me somehow. Despite what we're doing here tonight, the people waiting for us are my family. They bring me a peace that isn't possible to replace.

"Daisy, you've officially made the most punctual person I know late for somethin'," Johnny says, the first one to notice us approaching the table.

Brody barks a laugh. "Fuck, you're blind as hell."

"What?" Johnny appears dumbfounded by the comment.

Garrison's pressed to the wall beside Poppy on the other side of the table, but that doesn't stop him from reaching across it to snap his fingers in front of Johnny. Daisy's twin brother frowns at his friend.

Aurora, like everyone else at the table besides Johnny, is ping-ponging her eyes between Daisy and me and the hands we have interlocked. She smooths a hand down his arm.

"Hands, Johnny. Look at their hands."

He whips his head in our direction and sucks in a breath at the sight pointed out to him. I avoid his attention and glance around for two available chairs to haul to the table.

"What the fuck, Bryce?"

Having only found one chair not already taken around us, I release Daisy's hand and pull it from a nearby table before meeting Johnny's stare.

"Surprise."

"Surprise?" he echoes, voice climbing an octave. "This isn't a surprise! This is a blindside!"

"Calm down, Johnny," Daisy tells him.

I place the empty chair at the edge of the table and gesture for her to sit. She furrows her brows and shakes her head, waving me off.

Leaning toward her, I lower my voice. "Sit down."

She cocks her head at me before spreading her lips in a smirk. "Fine."

"Thank you."

"After you," she adds coyly.

My breathing shallows momentarily once I piece together what she means. There's no time to deny her suggestion with everyone staring at us with blunt curiosity. Panic flushes through me as I sit on the chair and wait for her next move.

I exhale tightly when she plants her ass on my lap and beams at everyone. Head swinging, I look to Poppy for help, but she's too busy giggling into her hand to be of use.

Johnny shakes his head frantically. "I'm gonna ask again. What the fuck is happening?"

He's pale, shell-shocked as he stares at us like he's seen a fucking ghost. Dramatic as hell, that guy.

"I thought it was pretty obvious. Bryce and Daisy are together," Anna says with outward approval.

The guilt I was dreading hits at her words and the tone with which she says them, but I keep my face blank.

"When did this happen?" Brody asks.

"You've only been staying there for what? Two weeks? I want to know how this happened and why I wasn't told way sooner!" Johnny adds.

Garrison clears his throat. "One week."

Johnny points across the table at him, the sharp lines of his jaw loose. "One!"

"Not helpful," Poppy scolds her boyfriend. "Not everyone acts like a total ass when they meet someone they're interested in like you did. I'd bet it's a lot easier to fall for someone when there isn't so much tension."

"You weren't complaining about the tension when I was hate fucking—"

Poppy shoves her hand to his mouth and flashes an apologetic smile at Daisy before Johnny steps back into the conversation.

"So, you moved in and immediately decided you wanted to date one of my closest friends?" he asks his twin.

I swallow past the tightness in my throat and cut in, continuing to keep my expression carefully closed off. "Does it matter? You can either approve or not. I don't really care either way."

Johnny gasps again, this time with a hand slapping his chest.

"You know, I'm the closest thing to a dad that Daisy has. Is this how you'd speak with her father?"

"Yes."

Daisy's body shakes with a gentle ring of laughter as she leans against me, back to my chest. The ease of her movements strikes something inside of me. A click of a lock moments before it swings open. On a wild fucking whim, I release the tight grip I have on my control and give in to my impulses.

Winding an arm around her middle, I rest my chin on her shoulder and inhale the sweet scent of her perfume. One by one, I meet the surprised and elated stares of everyone at the table, letting them see some of the truth that lies behind the mask I've slipped on.

"Well, I don't plan on being the one to argue with Bryce on this," Brody says, a beer pressed to his mouth. "Congrats."

Poppy holds my gaze, pride and peace amongst the emotions in her eyes. "I don't think anyone should feel the need to argue."

"You're really dating the one person I can't intimidate?" Johnny asks Daisy, slouching back in the booth.

Daisy turns her head, and I look away from Poppy to stare at her instead. She looks honest, and I wish she weren't such a natural at this.

It looks too real.

For them and for me.

18

"I'VE GOT TO HEAD BACK TO TORONTO NEXT MONTH," GARRISON says after finishing the last few drops of amber liquid that were in his glass.

We've been at Peakside for a while now, and thankfully, everyone has moved on to topics that don't involve me or Bryce. It was quite entertaining to watch Johnny think that for even a second, he'd be able to intimidate her, though. He deserved a chance to flex his brother status.

I already knew everyone here was welcoming and kind, but they've proved once again that that quality about them isn't ever going to change. Similar to the last time I was here before the fake dating agreement, I've been included in conversations and given the opportunity to add my two cents to every topic.

It's nice to feel accepted. Especially by these people.

Poppy rubs her cheek against Garrison's bicep. She's been dozing on and off for a few minutes, snuggling close to him while her eyes flutter shut.

Her words are slurred with sleep. "We'll be gone for a few weeks."

Bryce grows alert beneath me, like this is news to her. The

arm that hasn't moved from its original place around my middle stiffens, tightening slightly.

"Why?" she asks cooly.

Poppy blinks open her eyes and frowns. "Swift Edge needs him there in person for a few things."

"Okay. Like what? Why do you have to go with him?"

"Because I'm clingy as fuck, Ice. That's not news."

Garrison, seeming to feel the same sharp tension growing between them that I do, adjusts his position in his seat and interrupts their discussion.

"I asked her to come with me. I don't like to be separated from Poppy longer than absolutely necessary. If I didn't have to leave, I wouldn't. The reasons behind my requested presence are not negotiable."

Bryce laughs deeply. It's a cold, empty noise. "Don't use your CEO tone with me."

Unease swishes through me. Her tone is too devoid of emotion, even for her. Something's wrong, and from the complete silence around the table, everyone else has realized that too. Including Poppy.

No longer dozing, she sits forward, forearms digging into the edge of the table and brows crinkled. "What's going on, Bryce?"

I wince. Bryce's arm turns into a vise around me, but it's not a painful hold. My wince stems from the question being asked in such an open environment.

Maybe I'm overthinking it. I don't know Bryce even a quarter of the way Poppy does, but it doesn't seem like a question Bryce would ever answer in front of everyone. If anything, I would think being asked this way would make her more upset.

"Dance with me."

Nobody responds to the demand spoken from behind me.

"Please," Bryce adds, her voice dipping into a soft, desperate murmur that slips over the back of my neck like warm wax.

It takes me a moment to realize she's speaking to me.

I turn my head and focus on her, tuning out the rest of the

table as my gut cramps with uncertainty. The walls behind her eyes have lifted as they dig into mine, exposing a small flicker of . . . pain?

I'm more alert now than I've been in a long time. There's not an ounce of hesitation inside of me as I hop off her lap and give the table my back. The moment I extend my hand for her to take, she smiles at me in thanks, and my pulse stutters.

It's nothing more than a subtle tug of the corner of her mouth. A blink-and-you'll-miss-it reaction from someone who makes a habit of keeping their emotions well restricted. But despite that, I think it might be the most honest smile I've ever witnessed.

"You'll have to lead. I've got two left feet," I confess, almost shyly.

Bryce clasps my fingers and stands, her gaze piercing. It's almost relieving to see the intensity returning to her eyes, even if I'm the one trapped beneath it like a spider in a glass with no way out.

"I enjoy leading."

It sounds like more than a simple statement. Like a declaration or even . . . a promise.

She steers us away from the table without a word to anyone else. I offer her friends a very fake, apologetic smile before looking forward to where we're going.

We don't go undetected by the tables overflowing with busybodies and drunks. Most give us quick once-overs as we pass by, and I keep waiting for someone to make a no-good comment, but either they just don't care enough to, or Bryce's curled lip has struck fear in them, keeping their mouths sealed shut.

I giggle to myself at the death glares she's shooting in every direction but mine. It's nice being around someone who isn't afraid to stand up for not only themselves but you too. It could be presumptuous of me, but I feel very confident in thinking that for as long as I'm filling the role of Bryce's girlfriend, she'll keep me safe from as much as she can.

A Rottweiler girlfriend for sure.

The square dance floor is crowded when we slip between stomping bodies and find a space to stand. A line dance comes to an end as "Cadillac Ranch" by Nitty Gritty Dirt Band rolls into a slower love song. A few people take a break from dancing and head back to their tables for a drink, creating more room for us to stand.

A place like Peakside doesn't stray from country music, mixing the old kind with the newer pop style. Bryce's expression slips when the current song hits the chorus, revealing an annoyance that intrigues me.

Still hand in hand, I give her a tug. She stumbles toward me, free hand coming down on my shoulder and boots scuffing the floor. I look down between us at our feet before letting loose a laugh.

"You wear cowboy boots every day, but you don't like country music?"

A muscle ticks above her brow. "How do you know I don't like country music?"

"Lucky guess."

We must look awkward, neither of us swaying to the music and instead standing in place. Bryce sucks her cheek and keeps her hold on my shoulder loose, unsure, before our eyes catch. In a blink, she's dipping her hand to the inside of my waist and palming me there, the heat from her skin a shock to my system. My inhale is sharp, and she focuses on my mouth with smothering blue eyes.

"I hate country music," she confirms in a low voice, using her chin to gesture to the hand I have lying limply at my side. "Hold my shoulder."

"Why do you get the waist and I get the shoulder?"

Her mouth tips in a tiny, crooked smirk. "I'm leading, Sunshine. If you want to give it a try, we can swap."

My face feels hot as she teases me. I don't want to think about how red it is. Hopefully, the dull lights help drown it out before she notices.

"Back to the country music thing. Why don't you like it?" I ask, shifting the spotlight to her.

She waits for me to hold her shoulder before guiding us into a gentle sway. One step to the side and then back together before doing it again and again.

Her body is fit and slim but still muscled. I noticed it before when she came home from pole in her workout clothes but also when I sat on her lap earlier tonight and felt the way her thighs contracted beneath my weight. And now, as my fingertips dig into her shoulder with an exploratory touch, her muscles bunch and strain with her movements.

It's wrong of me, considering our fake relationship status, but touching her this freely, the way I've been doing over the last few days, has made it hard to keep from wondering what she feels like elsewhere.

Above the cropped hem of her band tees and the edges of her tight jean skirts. Where her tattoos disappear, hidden from the public eye.

Obviously, Bryce is ridiculously gorgeous. I've known it from the moment Johnny introduced us three years ago.

Back then, she was more intimidating than anything else, with her startlingly blue eyes the colour of cracked ice deep below the surface of a glacier and full, peach-shaped lips that she kept stretched thin. One minute in her presence was all it took to feel the raw power that ran below the surface. How in control of herself she was and confident in both her appearance and attitude.

There's not a person alive, man or woman, who isn't secretly struck stupid at the sight of her. I'm no exception to that, and I wouldn't want to be.

Bryce is a woman that anyone would be lucky to have in their life. Stunning in the way that doesn't seem real or possible sometimes, protective to a fault, and passionate. Her art is masterful, and I'm itching to see more of it. Not only what's on her skin and hung on her walls, but the stuff in her mind and soul. The ideas she's waiting to put to skin and the ones that haven't been discovered yet.

"It feels surface level. I like deeper music. The kind that rips emotion out of you."

I blink the glaze away from my vision and smile timidly. "What?"

"You asked why I don't like country music."

The humour in her tone makes my stomach swoop.

"Right. It makes sense. I think there are country songs out there that portray emotion, though. You just have to find the ones that speak to you."

"Which speak to you, Daisy?"

"What if I write you a list?"

"Like a playlist?"

"Yeah. I can never think of my favourite songs off the top of my head, but if you think you'd actually listen to them, I can put together a playlist."

Her thumb sweeps along the curve of my waist. "Do you listen to rock at all?"

There's a hidden question in there that I don't miss. No, I reach for it with desperate hands instead.

"I'd love a playlist of all your favourites, Bryce."

"Alright," she replies, voice hushed but pleased.

"Have you always liked that genre of music?"

"Despite how badly my mom tried to brainwash me with classical jazz when I was an infant, yeah. I think so."

"Classical jazz?" I ask, baring my teeth in a winced smile.

Bryce huffs a laugh and turns us around the dance floor, guiding us in another direction. "It's fitting, considering how boring she is when she's not busy complaining about me."

"Did you ever used to get along?"

"When I was really young and didn't know myself or what I wanted yet. I wore the dress-up gowns and plastic heels with the pink puff balls on top. Asked Santa for tea sets and fairy-tale books and spent hours brushing my Barbie's hair."

"Everything a little girl is told she should want," I say with a weighted sigh.

Bryce rolls her lips and fixes her features, closing her emotions off. The sight of her hiding herself from me is a kick to the stomach, even though I know she doesn't owe me honesty in that way. It's intimate being familiar with someone's innermost thoughts and emotions, but that doesn't stop me from wanting to see them. If anything, every little look inside of her mind and heart has me craving more.

Just one more peek. Then another, until I'm as familiar with her as I'm willing to allow her to be with me.

"I grew into my own person early on and realized I didn't like the things she wanted me to. Instead of brushing the Barbie's hair, I chopped it off and coloured it with Sharpie. The teacups started to go missing, and I snapped the heels off my shoes. That's the end of all those memories," she mutters.

It's not, but I don't push. She's already opened up to me more than I was expecting her to, and that's good enough for right now.

"When do you want to break the news to your parents? Think they already know?" I ask, finding a groove with the easy swaying motion. Maybe I'll be able to step it up next weekend.

"If they don't already know, they will by the end of the night. But sooner is probably better than later. Otherwise, I'll get a text telling me the time and place for my next blind date."

"Is it bad that I'm kind of excited?"

"To stick it to my parents?"

I tip my chin.

"Fuck no. I've been waiting for a chance to tell them to shove it for years."

I feel the vibration from my laughter all the way down to my toes.

"There's no better time like the present, then."

She holds my excited stare and squeezes my fingers before releasing my waist and rolling me out along her arm. I squeak in surprise and nearly trip over my feet but steady myself at the last minute, choosing to trust that she knows what she's doing with this new move.

With our arms forming one long, straight line, I come to a stop and suck in deep breaths, my chest rising rapidly. Bryce keeps her sights on me and only me. Just like that, time stalls, as if it's as surprised by this moment as I am.

Lips parting before spreading into a tooth-flashing grin, Bryce laughs with the entire force of her being. I freeze at the happiness vibrating in the freeing sound and allow myself to be pulled back into her body.

Only this time, the strength of her tug brings me closer than I was moments prior until our breasts smoosh and mouths hover close enough for me to taste her next words.

"Yeah, I think the present is a pretty fucking good place to be right about now, Sunshine."

19

Daisy

I GET TO SCHOOL MONDAY MORNING EARLY ENOUGH THAT THE parking lot is completely empty and the prime spots are mine for the picking.

I'm not the worst driver per se, but it's definitely nice to have the time to get my car perfectly straight and in the centre of the yellow lines without anyone watching and judging how many attempts it takes.

My book bag is heavy as hell as I pick it up from the ground and drape it over my shoulder. A stack of Duo-Tangs, binders, and my planner fill my arms next before I head for the school doors.

A deep magenta and fiery, orange-coloured sunrise streaks across the crisp fall grass, and as the biting breeze nips at my cheeks, I'm grateful I tossed on a jacket before leaving the house.

Bryce's leather jacket that I never returned after stealing Saturday night.

The same night I felt a few of the bricks from Bryce's walls crumble to dust with our conversations. We've never spoken so much about ourselves before. It was like we were interested in digging deeper than what I had originally thought when we first agreed to this.

With a bit of struggle due to my full hands and aching shoulder, I make it inside the building and down the hall to my classroom without dropping anything. It's completely silent besides the squeak of my Converse on the freshly waxed floors, and I smile, taking a long breath, soaking in the first-day nerves.

My inhale rips right back out of me the moment I see my classroom.

Yes, I did put a bit more work into finishing it before we went to Peakside Saturday night so that I wouldn't be embarrassed to have students and parents come inside, but it wasn't perfect yet.

There certainly weren't new chalkboards hung for the kids to scribble on between lessons or multicoloured lounge chairs and a rainbow bookshelf in the corner of the room for reading and visiting. I know for a fact I hadn't purchased a yellow, flower-shaped rug for beneath my desk either.

Pinching the skin of my wrist doesn't change the view in front of me. It's not a dream, then. I clutch the binders and books into my chest and gawk at the classroom of my dreams.

"Oh, wow! You totally beat me in the classroom department. It's so cute."

I jump and spin around, the unfamiliar voice coming from behind me. The woman leaning in my doorway isn't one I remember ever meeting before, but she seems kind enough at first glance.

She has her bright blonde hair up in a braided ponytail and deep emerald-green eyes open and clear beneath lightly mascara-coated lashes. Cheeks pinkened with a natural blush and freckles splattered over her narrow nose and forehead, there's something incredibly dainty about her. Her height adds to that, and it's almost hard to believe that someone can be *that* much shorter than me.

Dressed in a loose-fitting, ankle-length skirt that matches the mossy colour of her eyes and a white blazer with a simple top beneath, I feel an instant comradery with her and her sense of style. My vintage, light-washed jean overalls with hand-painted daffodils are a bit more casual than her attire, but I have a feeling we'll match often in the future.

I keep my voice light as I skip toward her. "Hi! Thank you. I can't take full credit for it; I believe my girlfriend and her best friend had more to do with this than I did. I'm Daisy Mitchell. I'd shake your hand, but I've got my arms a little full."

"Here, let me help you." She reaches for my binders and takes two from my arms before striding past me and setting them on my desk. "I'm Delaney. It's nice to meet you. Any relation to Rachel Mitchell?"

I drop the rest of my things on the desk beside the binders and huff, leaning back against the side of it. "She's my mom, actually."

Light sparks in her eyes. Recognition, rather. "That's right! She mentioned her Daisy girl to me a few times in the past."

"How do you know my mom?"

It's not a surprise that Mama's been talking someone's ears off about her kids. She doesn't need much provoking to do it the majority of the time. But I am curious why she would tell this woman in particular about us.

Delaney's easy stare sweeps over the classroom as she takes her time answering. I don't push, but my curiosity does grow an inch at her silence.

"She was my therapist for a few years. When I moved back to town after graduating university."

Regret slashes through me like a knife. "I'm sorry. I didn't mean to push. We just met!"

Her laugh is delicate, like the ice on a lake after winter's first overnight freeze. "It's alright. I'm not ashamed of seeking therapy. Your mom helped me a lot back then."

"Still, I shouldn't have pushed. I'm glad to hear that, though. I'm sure she'd feel smug about knowing she left a lasting impression on you and your life."

Delaney smiles reassuringly. "Anyway, I'm teaching third

grade right next door. If you need anything, just wander on over. Is it your first school year teaching?"

"What gave me away?"

"Honestly, nothing. It's just a feeling I have."

"Do I look prepared enough? I feel like I've forgotten a million things," I admit, rubbing my hands together nervously.

"One of the things I've learned with teaching, especially when it comes to little kids, is that you're never properly prepared. Every group of students is different, and what works for one won't work for the next. The best thing to do is just feel it out as the days come. You'll adapt to their craziness."

"You know what? I think I like that perspective," I say, grinning in appreciation. "I sense a budding friendship here."

"Yeah, so do I, Daisy."

"Do you have a lot to do before class, or are you up to grabbing a coffee with me first? I thought I had more to do, but actually . . . I'm feeling pretty confident now."

I need to text Bryce. My gut is telling me that she was the one behind this classroom transformation, and if I'm right, she deserves the world's biggest thank you.

This wasn't part of our agreement. She didn't have to take time out of her weekend to fix my problems for me. But . . . she did, and my chest feels entirely too small to confine my swelling heart. Combined with the fluttering sensation in my belly, I fear I'm one second away from floating into open air like a balloon.

Her absence from the house on Sunday makes sense now. I hadn't wanted to ask where she was or what she was doing out of fear of looking like a real-life clingy girlfriend. Now, it's looking like I won't have to.

"I wouldn't mind a coffee," Delaney accepts my offer.

I beam at her while shrugging off my bag and letting it fall to the desk with a clunk. The only thing I grab from inside of it is my wallet before leaving the room with a new friend at my side.

"Walk or drive?" I ask.

"Drive. Always drive."

"Mind if we take your car, then? Trust me when I say that you don't want to have to watch me try to park again once it starts to get busy here."

"Only if you excuse the mess. I've got a big dog, and she's one hell of a shedder."

I keep my pace easy and languid despite my growing excitement. Without thinking twice about it, I decide she's going to be my friend and seal the deal with a nickname.

"Sounds good to me, Della."

"So, you mentioned a girlfriend?" Delaney asks. The mug in her hand is full to the brim with a steaming latte decorated with an elegant sketch of a leaf made from cream.

I went with a shot of espresso and a croissant to soak it up with after contemplating ordering a drink infused with more sugar than coffee. That's more my brother's preference. Our sisters are similar to me in their coffee tastes.

My teeth sink into the cushion of my lip. "Yeah, I guess I did. Her name is Bryce."

"Lemieux?"

I don't miss the tightness in her voice, unable to skip over it. She might as well have told me she doesn't like Bryce, which doesn't sit well with me. Straightening in my seat, I lean over the table and pin her in place with an expertly disguised smooth stare. I'm not angry, but I am on high alert.

My gentle, welcoming persona isn't to be mistaken for weakness or acceptance.

"Yes. Is that a problem?"

She toys with the end of her braid, expression flighty. "The friend that helped with the classroom . . . is Darren?"

"It is."

The colour leaches from her face, her natural flush disappearing in the blink of an eye. My oversensitive heart doesn't like knowing that I've upset her. It's a curse.

Delaney hasn't taken a single sip from her latte before she discards it on the table and checks her watch. Wetting her lips, she swallows hard and stands, hovering.

"I remembered that I have a few more things to do before class this morning. We should go now."

My stomach falls when suddenly, her flighty attitude makes a bit more sense. The emotion in her voice isn't kind. It's brutal.

Soul-crushing agony that has me flinching back in my seat.

Bryce has nothing to do with it. She can't. While Delaney was stiff about her, I hadn't sensed this . . . tortured brokenness scraping below the surface.

This is all because of Darren.

I immediately rise from my seat. "Do you want me to ask the barista to transfer your coffee into a takeaway cup?"

Delaney softens a smidge, a flicker of light appearing through the thickness in her eyes. "You wouldn't mind?"

"Not at all." I take the cup from the table and bring it to the front counter.

The barista gets to making the swap with a simple smile. Inching over to the waiting section of the counter, I pull my phone from the side pocket of my overalls and open my messages with Bryce. There's a new one waiting from her, and I smile like a fool as I read it.

Bryce: You didn't pack a lunch. What's the point of a lunch box if you forget it in the fridge and don't bring it with you to actually eat at lunch?

My reply comes easily.

Me: I was a little nervous this morning and must have forgotten about it. I'll find something for lunch. Have a good day at work!

"Your to-go cup, ma'am," the barista says, drawing my attention.

The "ma'am" makes my skin itch. I'm way too young to be

called that, but I take the cup from her with a thankful nod as my phone buzzes.

Bryce: See you later.

It sounds ominous. Or maybe that's just me hoping that it means something more than it does. There's nothing quite like pushing through a nerve-racking day and being comforted with a surprise visit from a friendly face.

Is Bryce that type of person, though?

Two weeks ago, from what I knew about her in passing, I'd have said it's unlikely. Now? My gut reaction is to expect the best from her. The caring actions that I've seen from her over the past few days have me wondering if everyone's too quick to judge her. Myself included, even if I'm not someone who naturally expects the worst of a person.

What a stressful life that would be.

Bryce might look and act tough, but I'm certain there's so much more hidden below the surface, and I wouldn't mind being the one to test that theory.

I think I've already decided that I will be.

"I said I needed oat milk. Not regular. Are you incompetent, or can you follow a simple instruction? Redo it."

The cruel tone is all wrong for a place like this, a soft, comforting coffee shop nestled into the only busy street in all of Cherry Peak. While I may only remember having heard this voice once before, there's no mistaking the owner of it.

Peakside Pamila scorns the sweet barista with a jabbing finger and square-shaped nail hovered above the counter. The barista looks mortified, her ears and nose tipped with red as she shakes like a leaf behind the cash register.

Not only is it too early for this type of behaviour from anyone —let alone a grown woman—but it's completely uncalled for. I kept my mouth shut at Peakside when she insulted not only Bryce but me as well. It wasn't my place to start an argument in such a public setting when I didn't even know half the story behind her disgusting comments, but that didn't mean I hadn't wanted to.

For the first time in my recent memory, I contemplated what it would feel like to slap a woman across the face. I've never turned to violence for anything. Not when I was an angry child and Johnny would pull my hair and pinch me when he didn't like something I'd done or later on when he'd use our sisters against me to get what he wanted. He was always the more impulsive twin. I enjoy thinking things through so I don't wind up in situations that I won't know how to maneuver my way out of.

But seeing Bryce upset because of someone else's ignorance and hatred? That pushed me further than I'd been pushed in a long, long time. I felt . . . *stabby*.

If I hadn't been shoving all my focus into keeping her from jumping over the bar and doing something that would have absolutely crushed our night, maybe I would have been the one to stand up to Pamila instead of Poppy.

Is it normal for me to have been jealous of Poppy in that moment? I don't even know anymore.

Not having been the one to stand up for Bryce has unsettled me a little. It feels like it should have been my job.

There's an odd burning sensation in my chest, and I linger behind Pamila, not going back to Delaney yet. My body is on a different wavelength than my brain. If it weren't, I'd be doing what I always do and leaving this to the people involved instead of butting in.

"I'm sorry. I'll make you a new one now," the barista rambles, her sneakers squeaking on the floor as she rushes off.

Pamila chuffs at her and waits at the counter with her nose in the air like she's the queen of goddamn coffee or something.

"You know, it costs nothing to treat people with kindness."

I know my eyes have blown wide at my outburst. It's so unlike me that I'm not prepared for her to whip around and glare at me.

"What did you say?"

My swallow is thick, but I attempt to play off my nerves with a shrug. "She didn't mean to mix up your order. I'm sure if you had noticed it wasn't right and asked her nicely, she would have still fixed it for you. Instead, you chose to belittle her."

"Mind your own business, Daisy Mitchell."

"You're a bartender. Do you appreciate it when customers speak to you like this when you make a mistake?"

"I don't make such stupid mistakes."

I fold my arms over my chest and keep my head high, not allowing her to make me feel weak. "Lucky you. Not everyone is as perfect."

She scoffs coldly and faces forward, opting to give me her back instead of responding. It's sad, really. How angry people can get at others over problems with such easy fixes. I feel bad for her. You have to be incredibly upset with your life to take your pain out on others this way.

Something angry and not yet sated pinches at me. An urge or pull that might as well be forcing my jaw open with eager fingers.

"Just a bit of advice, Pamila, but from now on, I suggest you keep your snide remarks inside when it comes to Bryce. She's not a person you want to be attacking like that."

Fascination lining the dark, ugly brown colour of her eyes, Pamila gawks at me over her shoulder. "I'm not afraid of her or her sidekick, Poppy."

"Good. Be afraid of me."

Holding her gaze, I do something I've never done in my entire life and bare my teeth at her.

In my head, I imagine that I look vicious. Like a savage beast standing over an unprotected cub ready to fight my way to the death.

In reality, I know I've got to be nowhere close. A yappy dog nipping at someone's heels, more like.

But still, Pamila's scowl wavers before she twists forward again, a silent way of telling me to screw off. This time, I let her.

I catch the barista's watery eyes behind Pamila and give her a thumbs-up. This is only a job for her, but she's still a person with real feelings, and I don't enjoy the thought of them hurt because of this woman.

She tugs her mouth up into a small smile before mouthing *thank you* to me and finishing up the new drink. That unsettled feeling from earlier smooths out slightly, enough for me to stop thinking about it.

Delaney is waiting for me by the door, appearing naive to what just happened. I think there's too much going on in her mind right now for her to have been paying attention to me.

Yanking open the door for her to exit, I keep my sights trained forward instead of back to gather one last glance at Pamila. It's not worth it, and as I follow behind Della onto the street, I make a silent promise to myself.

The next time someone attacks a person I care about, I'll be just as brave as I was just now for that stranger. Especially when it comes to a certain ice queen who really isn't all that frozen after all.

20

Bryce

I'm a godawful fucking cook.

I used to blame my inability to create anything even half-edible on my parents, my mom specifically. She didn't cook for shit. Still doesn't. Instead, she orders in from every place willing to deliver to their Cherry Peak–adjacent neighbourhood and dumps hefty tips to those who initially refuse. My dad is either purposefully naive to her antics or just doesn't care enough to question why the garbage is always taken out right before dinner is served and the same meals are on a constant rotation. As long as he's fed, anything is fair game.

Personally, I'd have preferred growing up eating peanut butter and jelly sandwiches or hot dogs instead of the dishes Mom ordered. I've never liked fish. Not salmon or cod or any other variation of it. But every second night, it appeared on a plate in front of me.

"Don't complain and just eat, Bryce," she'd say, her frown lines deepening as she shook her head at me.

So, I did, and the moment I left home, I wrote that shit off. I'll go as far as to do an entire lap around the supermarket just so I don't have to pass the fish department and get a whiff of its smell.

Amongst other things that I focused on once I escaped my childhood home, I made an effort to teach myself kitchen basics.

Eggs, boiled or scrambled. Grilled cheese, soup from a can, and a handful of different easy recipes that I found online or begged Darren and Poppy to teach me. It's pathetic, really, how little I've managed to teach myself and master, but it's something. A tiny, stupid fucking skill that I was never all that grateful for until today, when I saw the pale yellow lunch box on the counter while I was grabbing my to-go coffee cup for work.

It was empty inside. Not even a single non-refrigerated snack packed and ready to go.

Daisy was in a rush all of yesterday, holed up in her room finishing plans and colour coding her planner, so I shouldn't have been surprised to find that she'd forgotten a lunch. Regardless, it still frustrated me to think of her putting herself and her body's needs on the back burner.

That's when I texted her. It was an impulse decision driven by pure concern. I didn't need her to text me back before I decided that I would be the one to fix the problem for her.

Leaving work early was an instinctual reaction that snapped into fruition once my mother started to call and text, demanding a meeting.

What am I hearing about you and a woman?

Is this an attempt to scold me? A punishment?

Daisy Mitchell? That's who you were with last night?

Why have I heard this from anyone other than you? Tu m'as blessée.

Answer my calls. Come to the house right now.

I didn't.

Instead, I turned my notifications off for her number and ignored her completely.

Both my mother and the state of the kitchen are disasters that I've been conveniently blocking from my mind as I sit in my car in the school parking lot, hesitating to go inside. All of my prior confidence that led me here has scuttered away, turning me into a coward once again.

Two plastic containers filled with a couple of sandwiches and fruit salad sit on the seat beside me and in Daisy's yellow lunch box in the fridge back home, ready for tomorrow.

Home.

Mine, and hers for right now. For a while still. Longer if it were up to me. It's only been just under two weeks, but I've grown to like the sight of her in my place. Even with the mess of colours she's brought with her but has tried to hide.

Like the massive, fluffy starfish slippers I've found under the kitchen table or tucked beneath one of the couch cushions, as if she kicked one off and lost it while watching one of the musicals she seems to love.

I've noticed several new things about her since she moved in. Her habit of pretending not to be cold all the damn time and instead mentioning that she's freezing, wrapping herself up in one of her thousand heavy blankets for one.

She's been bundling up less since I started keeping the heat turned up a couple of degrees, but that doesn't mean the multi-coloured blankets have stopped appearing everywhere throughout the house. On the back of the kitchen chairs, flung over the couch, or even on the back porch, layered with frost.

Getting a basket to keep them all in one place is on my list of things to do.

The time on the dash is a reminder that I have to get my shit together and go inside. As if sitting outside of a school with my car idling isn't creepy as fuck on its own, being here without a kid of my own only serves to make it worse.

It takes me too long to gather everything from the passenger seat and head into the school, but once I'm there, I feel even less comfortable than I did outside.

A bell rings as voices shout and scream amongst booming laughs and giggles. Lockers slam shut, and kids run past without a care as to the way they knock into me and have me rocking back and forth on my feet to keep my balance.

Slowly, I slip through the small openings that appear between students and retrace my steps from yesterday. It was far quieter then. No kids sniffling their runny noses or shrieking when they realize they've forgotten something in another room or their locker. I prefer this place at night.

"Auntie Bryce!" I hear through the noise once I've turned down the hallway leading to Daisy's classroom.

Abbie is the only child I've spent more than a few minutes of time with in my life. My best friend's daughter is a smiley thing with bright emerald doe eyes and hair so curly and thick that it's broken too many elastics to keep track of.

A spitting fucking image of Darren, she stands beside an open classroom door and waves wildly at me. A stuffed skeleton is clutched in her hands, and my heart pangs in recognition. She's had that since she came home from the hospital. The only gift I've ever given her that she refuses to let go of, despite the rude comments I've heard Darren complaining about from the older kids at school.

"Hi, Skelly," I say, jumping back a step to avoid smacking into a child who rushes past us. "Are you going for recess?"

She juts her chin. "Yep! Daddy made me a sandwich with blackberry jam for lunch. Nana's jam! He cut it into a pumpkin."

"That's nice."

"Do you like blackberry jam?"

"Not really."

Her entire face scrunches. "Why?"

"It's too bitter."

"Mom says Dad's bitter. Is that the same?"

"Your dad isn't bitter, Abbie. Don't listen to your mother."

It's terrible advice to give a six-year-old. Incredibly terrible advice. Too bad her mom is a bitch who won't ever stop trying to ruin Darren's life.

The little girl pushes her finger into the top of the skeleton's eye socket and hums. "I still will."

My hands sweat around the containers in my hands, so I adjust my grip on them and look to Daisy's classroom just up ahead. The door is open, and as much as I care for Abbie, I don't want to lose my time with Daisy discussing Darren's ex-wife.

"You better go, Skelly. And make sure your dad knows how much you loved the sandwich he made you," I tell his daughter.

Her eyes brighten, a grin forming. "Okay! Bye, Auntie Bryce!"

I freeze for a beat when she plows into my legs and squeezes them tight. With a pat on her head, I send her on her way and slip into Daisy's classroom before another kid has the chance to get too close.

Abbie might be my exception when it comes to children, but I'm still not all that comfortable around them. If I hadn't been there from the day after she was born, I doubt I'd have gotten close enough to let her hug or tease me.

"Bryce?"

There's a clang, and then I'm coming face to face with my girlfriend for the first time in two days. My *fake* girlfriend.

It takes me a minute to blink, and by the time I do, my eyes are so dry they burn. Overalls have never done it for me before. Not even close. But with the way my nipples tighten beneath the work blouse I still haven't changed out of and I lose my breath in a sharp puff, it's safe to say she's altered my view of them.

She has no defined shape in them with how baggy the thighs and waist are, but somehow, she's never looked more beautiful. The messy, clipped-back hair and rosy cheeks add something to her appearance that makes it nearly impossible to breathe properly.

"Sunshine," I mutter, my voice sounding as strained as my chest feels.

There's a shine to her eyes today that makes the blue stand

out, almost like it's taken on a completely different shade. One more vibrant. Alive.

"What are you doing here?" she asks, standing from behind her desk.

"You said you were going to find something for lunch."

Her lips part before she tugs the bottom one into her mouth and then lets it go. "I was."

"Do you have food in your desk?"

"No. I was going to . . ." She trails off, focusing on the containers in my slick palms. "Is that food?"

I flush with heat. The kind that smothers. "It's just something small."

"That doesn't matter. Here, pull up a chair and eat with me. I have about fifteen minutes before the bell rings."

She wheels herself to the far end of her desk, leaving me a small space beside her. I avoid eye contact while I grab an extra chair from one of the sets of desks and pull it beside her.

I'm stiff as I drop into the chair and place the containers in front of us. Thankfully, Daisy doesn't hesitate to lean close and snap the lids off the containers, giving me a hit of her sweet, floral perfume. She stares at the food with a soothingly warm expression and takes a sandwich for herself.

I should look away when she raises it to her mouth and sinks her teeth into the white bread, but watching her eat food that I made for her is one of the sexiest situations I've ever found myself in.

Perfectly manicured nails dig into the bread, keeping it in place as a moan slips out of her, and I jerk in my chair, a pulse thumping between my legs. My gaze tightens, refusing to have it drift so much as a millimetre.

Her tongue slips out and drags across her lips when she pulls the bread away, and then her jaw is working. The strain of her throat as it pulls and releases with a swallow threatens to have me collapsing onto the floor at her feet.

Begging for a chance to taste and savour her the way she's doing to her food.

For just one fucking opportunity to learn if I was right all along in knowing that she'll taste like my biggest temptation and desire. My undoing or revival.

"Eat, Frosty. You've got to be hungry. Did you come straight from work?"

My throat hurts from how dry it is when I speak. "No. I went home first and made lunch."

"Oh. Right. That makes sense."

"But I am hungry," I add quickly.

My fingers tremble when I grab the second sandwich. Clenching them to hide it, I take a large bite of the sandwich and struggle to chew it with the lack of moisture inside my mouth.

"You know, I was hoping you'd come today," she reveals casually.

My first swallow is a struggle with the dry bread. "Why? Are you okay?"

"I am. It's just been a bit overwhelming. I didn't student teach with kids this young, even though I knew I wanted to teach them. It's kind of luck of the draw with placements, so coming here and being around so much energy and excitement was a lot to take in. It still is. But it's been a very good day so far. Despite forgetting my lunch, of course."

The giggle at the end of her sentence fills the classroom as fully as it does my mind, having become one of my favourite sounds in existence.

"Plus, it's nice to see you. Especially considering all you did for me to get this place finished for today."

I lift my eyes and find hers waiting. Like an expert in all things Bryce, the aspects of myself that I don't reveal to fucking anybody, she bypasses all of my safety protocols and makes a home for herself in the pits of my insecurities and worthlessness that I've tried to bury for over a decade. They don't feel so heavy once she's reached them, like she's transferred some of her colour into their black holes.

It should be enough to have me taking off. To give me the push I need to reinforce my security.

I bring my walls down a little lower instead.

"You deserved a finished classroom. It should have been like this from the very start," I declare.

"It should have. But it wasn't. And I have you to thank. So, thank you, Bryce."

Staring helplessly into the endless depths of her eyes, I can't be bothered to look away. Even when I discard my sandwich on the table and take her cheek in my hand.

It scorches against my palm, threatening to brand me with her initials. My heat sparks in answer as she leans into my touch instead of away, accepting it and nuzzling closer, eyelids drooping.

"This is just one of the many things I'd do for you, Daisy."

"Because it gives us something to use as proof?"

I stroke the corner of her mouth with my thumb, aching to tug it up just so I could see her smile again.

Poison slithers up my throat as my lie builds, leaving a sour taste behind.

"Yeah, Sunshine. Just proof."

21

Daisy

When I was a teenager, this would have been my idea of a regular workout. At one point, I was spending two hours a day running through the wooded areas outside of town, taking in the fresh air and burn in my calves and chest.

I never ventured up the mountains, though. My moms took to threatening me with Johnny's mandatory company on my runs if I even dared think about heading up one on my own. The threat worked because there was no way my twin brother—who might actually run slower than our ninety-year-old grandmother —was going to ruin my afternoon routine. Kiki loathed exercise and was out of the question, and Josette was my only sister still at home. She was too busy volunteering as the photographer for all the school sports teams to join me.

Then, by the time I headed off to university, I stopped running, and the prospect of hiking the beautiful mountains I grew up gawking at seemed completely impossible.

Until I blabbered to Bryce.

And now, I'm paying for my loose lips.

Folding my body over a massive rock, I heave breaths into

my tight, burning lungs and wipe the sweat from my forehead with the bottom of my shirt.

"Will you make it to the top?" Bryce asks with a tinge of humour.

I shoot her a weak, playful glare. "How are you so unbothered right now? Don't tell me you're secretly a pro hiker."

She props her foot onto the trunk of a tree and leans forward to grab the toe of her sneaker for a stretch. Like the first time I saw her in workout gear, it's a completely different experience than the typical jean skirt or work blouse.

Even with the fall chill in the air, she opted for a pair of tight, high-cut spandex shorts and a cropped shirt that's been torn at the arms in the same style my brother loves. It reveals the muscles in her biceps, the band of her black sports bra, and the detailed artwork all over her skin.

I settled for regular leggings and an old, baggy shirt that I'm pretty sure belongs to my brother. It wasn't until I was digging through my dresser drawers after work today that I realized I don't own any allocated gym wear, and that told me all I needed to know about how this hike was going to turn out.

"Poppy keeps me in shape. Pole is the hardest workout I've ever done."

"Really? I've never tried. But from the fact I could collapse here and not get up ever again, I don't think I'd do very well," I joke.

"She isn't at the Cherry Peak BB location much. If you want to attend one of her classes, you should head to Calgary."

"Is that where you go?"

She drops her leg and props the other, stretching it just as hard. "No. I haven't gone a lot since Poppy left. If I go, it's when she's in town and is leading a class."

"Do you not like the new instructor?"

"I like her fine. It's more so that I don't want to attend with anyone else." She stares straight ahead at the tree trunk, stuck in her thoughts for a moment. "It was our thing. I started out of support for her, and it's not the same now. Anna thinks it is, and she attends class here more than I do. It's just not as easy for me."

My smile is one of understanding. "I get it. It's sacred to you."

She sets her foot on the ground and reaches behind her head to tighten her ponytail. Her eyes flick between mine. "Yeah. Exactly."

"Well, I'd love to go up sometime and try one of her classes. Maybe we could go together? The next time you go up to Calgary?"

It's obvious that I'd like to be her friend. We may be pretending to be something more than that, but I enjoy Bryce's company outside of that agreement. She's surprising. A person that I didn't expect to be able to find such a calm and comfortable connection with but have. I've already begun holding that bond close to my heart.

Bryce holds my eyes for a few beats longer before nodding. "I'd like that."

She'd like that. Not just a simple yes.

Success.

I beam at her and plant my hands on my waist. Jerking my head at the sloped trail we've swerved off, I say, "I guess I should get in better shape first."

"I was terrible at it for a long time," she reveals, falling into step beside me as we start up the trail again.

Given that we chose to go after I finished work, there isn't much time left before the sun begins to set on us. I'm not familiar with this trail, but Bryce seems to be, and that's good enough for me. Getting stuck in the woods after dark isn't on my bucket list.

"Is pole where you got your abs from?" I ask, stepping over a thick tree root.

She curves a manicured brow and glances over at me. "Have you been checking me out?"

"As if you don't have people checking you out all the time.

You're gorgeous," I blurt out, waving a hand down her body to emphasize my point.

Bryce cuts me a surprised look, her cheeks taking on a deep red hue. My stomach pinches, happiness flowing freely through me.

"So are you," she murmurs, dropping her head, eyes on the dirt trail.

Mischief twirls through the happiness, creating a mess of bright and exciting feelings. "I didn't take you for the shy type."

"I'm not."

"You can be."

"Don't tell anyone. It'll ruin my reputation."

Despite her attempts to hide her face, I catch the twitch at the corner of her lips.

"Your secret is safe with me," I promise.

She points to the right at the fork in the trail, and we pause. "There's a mountain-fed river about a minute down that path."

"Let's go!"

I'm already headed down the path when she huffs a laugh and jogs to catch up. I take a deep inhale of the mountain air and make a promise to myself that I'll come out here more often. We live in one of the most beautiful places in the world, and I haven't been taking advantage of it.

"How many times have you hiked this trail to be able to remember where this river is?" I ask.

"Too many to keep track of. But I haven't come here in a couple of years. I've been too busy with work to find the time."

"Office work keeps you that occupied?"

She kicks a rock off the trail. "No. I do other work on the side. My job at the office isn't important. To the town or me. It's just something I agree to do in order to keep my parents off my back about the tattooing. There are other people who work for the town that do everything from home. I'm just a face for the front desk."

"Tattooing? You mean you tattoo for a living too?"

Why didn't I know that? It seems like something a girlfriend should be aware of.

"It's just a side gig. Something I do to keep myself busy and scratch an itch."

I know she's playing it off. If tattooing wasn't something she truly loved, she wouldn't be sacrificing her soul working at the town office just to keep your parents from giving her hell about it.

"If you love it the way it seems you do, then you should be tattooing full-time, Bryce. Your work is phenomenal. It's the best I've ever seen," I tell her, not a trace of a lie in my words.

"It's not possible in Cherry Peak. The town is too small."

"It could be. I mean, how many people do you have that are requesting house calls?"

A sound of rushing water becomes audible the further we get down the path, and I swing my head to the right just in time to spot a flash of turquoise blue amongst a forest of deep green.

I spin to face Bryce, excitement leaking from my every pore as I pick up my pace.

"Be careful, Sunshine. I can't fake date a dead woman," she warns.

"I'll be fine. Now, answer my question before I get too distracted by the pretty blue water and forget about it."

I watch her contemplate allowing me to do exactly that, but when I threaten her with a stiff pointed finger, she rolls her eyes and answers me.

"I have ten clients that are on a steady rotation. But even that isn't enough. Not when a steady rotation in the tattoo world is having an appointment every few weeks. It's not a cheap hobby."

"How many would you need? Eleven?" I ask, waggling my brows.

"You'd let me tattoo you?"

"Is that so surprising?"

Her throat works with a strained swallow. "You don't have any tattoos."

It's my turn to tease. Before we leave the cover of the trees and cross onto the rocky slope surrounding the river, I pause, tipping my lips in a smirk.

"Have *you* been checking *me* out, Frosty?"

"I already said you were gorgeous, didn't I?"

She passes me then, holding my gaze as our shoulders knock. I'm a breath away from reaching for her in an attempt to keep her close when she stares past me, wonder lighting her eyes.

I turn, too curious to learn the reason behind her reaction. My mouth falls open at the magnificent sight in front of us.

"Yeah," she whispers knowingly. "It makes the hike worth it."

It's jaw-dropping. From the crystal clear, bright blue water that nearly matches the exact shade of the sky to the small but fierce white rapids that crash amongst the tallest rocks and the floor of dainty pebbles beneath the surface, it's a spot that's impossible to forget.

A sanctuary guarded by lush greenery and endless patches of flowers. White, purple, yellow. They're everywhere, scattered along the riverbank and threaded through the forest that's home to the various chirping birds and wildlife that I'd bet are watching us right now.

"That's an understatement," I murmur in awe.

Not wasting any time, I toe off my sneaker and remove my sock before moving to the water's edge. The river is freezing when I dip my toe into the lapping current and grin.

"Mission accomplished," I announce.

Her next exhale is heavy, a weighted noise that draws my attention. She follows me and stares out at the river, lips parted and the cold nipping at the tip of her nose. I grow entranced at the sight of her fully relaxed, as if that exhale was her way of expelling every one of her troubling thoughts in the safety of this piece of paradise.

Folding my fingers in the hem of my shirt, I let myself lean closer to her, just enough for our arms to touch.

"Thank you for sharing your special place with me, Bryce."

She turns her head, eyes calm as they brush over my features, the storms from within them gone for this moment in time.

"It's not just my place," she argues half-heartedly.

My sigh is soft in the river-kissed air. It's not nearly as cold anymore with her by my side.

"It's somewhere special to you. That makes it somewhere worth sharing. Even if it is just with me," I declare.

"It's not just you, Daisy. It's *only* you. I've never brought anyone else here, and I don't want to. I like it like this. With only us."

I do too.

I CREEP out of my room and down the hall, careful not to make a sound once I realize Bryce's bedroom door is cracked open. It's late, but insomnia doesn't care much about the numbers on a clock. Apparently, the same can be said about Bryce since there's a soft light escaping the crack in her door.

With a flick of the lights in the kitchen, I roll some of the soreness out of my shoulders. It's not the part of my body I expected to be sore after a hike, but honestly, every inch of me is sore.

The hour-long bath I took shortly after we got home didn't do much for me other than tease sleep I knew wouldn't come.

My favourite brand of iced tea—the kind in juice boxes—is stocked in the fridge, and I grin at the twin rows of them on the top shelf beside Bryce's cans of Fanta. She must have picked them up earlier because I remember taking the last one with me to work this morning.

I steal a box and rip the straw off and out of the wrapper before plunging it deep. The cool, sugary liquid coats my throat as I gulp it down, and my eyes droop. Another tease. I'll be half-asleep out here before heading back to bed and spending the next three hours staring at the ceiling.

My inability to sleep is an on-and-off issue that I only started suffering from in my late teens. Like a timer finished ticking, it hit out of the blue, taking nights of peaceful sleep with it.

I finish my drink too quickly and pull open the fridge to grab another. Only this time, I hover my hand over a chilled orange can, contemplating bringing it to Bryce as another thank you for today. Even if I already know she'll tell me not to waste my time thanking her again.

It wouldn't be a waste, though. Not to me.

Decided, I turn off the light and retrace my steps. When I reach her door, I ignore the way my pulse speeds with nerves and knock twice, keeping it quiet in case she just fell asleep with the light on.

No answer comes, so I do it again. Another minute passes without a word, so I push open the door just an inch and peek inside.

I think my stomach tries to climb out of my throat.

Blood cranking to a boil beneath my skin, I try to turn and leave but find that I can't. My feet are glued to the floor while I focus on what's happening, unable to do anything else.

The buzz is nearly silent. So quiet I only pick it up when I strain to hear, my fingers wet with sweat as I grip the edge of the doorframe. Tension coils in my belly, my nipples tightening and scraping against the soft material of my nightshirt.

Bryce is turned away from me on the bed, one hand draped down between her legs while another grips onto the headboard so tight her knuckles and biceps strain. The slow, controlled rocking motion of her body makes it obvious what she's doing, even without the low buzz of the vibrator.

She's a straight line from the base of her spine up her neck, rigid in a way I've never seen her. But this isn't the same rigidity as when she's uncomfortable or frustrated.

This is from pleasure. A drive to find release.

I gulp down the moisture in my mouth and press a hand to my chest, the innocent touch feeling anything but. My teeth scrape my bottom lip as I slide my hand an inch to cup my breast, squeezing just once.

Bryce releases a heady, desperate moan and drops her head forward, her rocking growing in intensity. I wish I could see past the mountain of blankets at her feet just to catch a glimpse of what she's using between her legs. What's prying these sounds from her throat and transporting her somewhere far outside of this dark room.

A deep blue shirt hangs off her body, hitched at the hips and sagging off one shoulder. The top curve of her ass is exposed, bare for my prying eyes. While pale like the rest of her, it's completely uninked. My fingers twitch to whip off the blankets around her to see if the rest is as void of designs.

My head swims, emptying of warnings and demands for me to leave. It's an invasion of privacy to be standing here, but I'm not thinking logically. If I were, I wouldn't be slipping a hand between my legs to press a single finger against the slick material of my panties, feeling how it molds to my slit and makes my knees shake with the force of the sudden relief.

The headboard creaks, thumping against the wall once as she shakes and lurches forward. Muscles straining in her jaw, she lets her mouth fall completely open and whimpers, the entire length of her body trembling.

"Fuck." She bucks, abandoning the space between her legs and using both hands to gain balance against the headboard. Her head turns my way slightly, but full, dark lashes brush her cheeks, giving the appearance that her eyes are closed. "Fuck—*Daisy.*"

Panic restricts my airway as I duck out of the doorway and hightail it back to my room. I don't make a sound as I close the door behind me and sit on the edge of the bed. Pressing my thighs together, I try and ward off the incessant throb between them, but it doesn't work.

I'm flushed, so hot beneath my shirt that I rip it off and throw it across the room. My nipples are sore and as hard as the pebbles in the riverbed earlier.

Disbelief rattles my every thought. Fear follows when everything starts to sink in. She saw me. She had to have known I was there. My name was a warning because she was . . . orgasming, and it was too late to yell at me to leave. Right?

I press a hand to the mattress and shake my head.

No.

I'm going to forget this ever happened and hope that she does too. If not, I'm going to be packing my things up tomorrow and crashing back at my brother's house.

Bryce and I have made too much progress to revert back to how we used to be. I won't let it happen.

It's only one more thing I have to pretend, so why does it feel like the most challenging of all?

22

Daisy

A WEEK PASSES IN A BLUR. MY FIRST FIVE DAYS AS A REAL-DEAL teacher are over, and it took me all of my Saturday to recoup half of the energy I spent.

Bryce hasn't mentioned what happened the other night at all. Not the next morning or the following one. It was a relief not to have her sit me down and call me a creep before kicking me out, but then again, she'd have to be home sometime to speak with me. And I haven't seen her since the night of our hiking trip.

I've missed her company, and I can't seem to shake my disappointment at the realization she doesn't feel the same.

Every evening this week, she's been gone doing what I can only assume is her part-time tattooing gig. I've spent them all alone, only finally reaching out to Kiki yesterday for some company. We fell asleep mid-*Fifty Shades* marathon until we were woken by what I swear was Bryce's fist slamming into my closed bedroom door at midnight.

She hasn't said anything about the spying or the fist slamming thus far this morning, even with me staring at her across the kitchen table like a crazy person and slurping from my juice box. Sure, she's given me cool, distanced looks here and there, but in all honesty, I'm sensing a bit of an angry vibe brewing. I can only hope it isn't because of what I've done.

"What did you get up to last night?" I ask, done with the silence.

Even beneath her oversized tee, I can see the shifting of her shoulders as she adjusts her position on the dining chair. Lifting her eyes from her phone, she quirks a brow.

"I was working."

"Until midnight?"

"Why does it matter? Were you waiting for me to get home?"

I bite the straw in my mouth. "No. But your whereabouts are something a girlfriend should know."

"It's been a long time since I've had one. You'll have to tell me all of the rules you have for me to follow."

She's trying to annoy me. Testing her limits, maybe, to see how much I can take. Excitement sparks in my blood.

"If you want rules, we can make some. I just want to know if you're going to be home late every night in case I'm asked about something you've done and have to keep up appearances. I wasn't aware house calls took place until the early morning hours."

A muscle twitches in her cheek as she sets her phone down on the table, the weight of her full attention smacking me right in the face.

"What about you?"

"What about me?"

"Am I going to be asked about why you're spending your nights boarded up in your room with another woman while I'm gone?"

The question makes me pause. I knew there was something off about her this morning, but the whip-like tone of her voice is far worse than I'd have expected.

"Is that why you haven't spoken to me this morning?" I ask, fully aware of how carefully I should tread here.

"No."

"Then what is the reason?"

"It was Kristen, right?" she asks stiffly.

"Yes. She's my best friend."

Bryce hums, shifting her gaze away from me. I inch forward in my chair and lay my palms flat on the small table. She's not that far from me, but I can't reach for hands that aren't available for me, even if I want to take hers and squeeze until she opens up to me.

"Is it not okay if I invite people over? In that case, all you have to do is tell me that. I wouldn't want you to punch a hole through my door next time."

I'm already starting to smile when she looks at me again. The ice in her eyes is sharp, though not cutting, and I take that as a good sign.

She scratches her cheek and pulls her hair over her shoulder. It's loose this morning, even a bit messy as some thin strands stick up near her scalp. It's like she rolled out of bed and came right to the kitchen this morning, not expecting that I'd be awake as well.

"You can have people over. I just don't want to look like a fool if you have something going on with another woman," she says, the words brittle.

"Something going on with who? Kristen? You think me and Kristen are together?" I sputter.

Tension grows in her expression. "Should I think differently? I came home late at night and learned there was another woman in your room while the door was shut."

"I don't know whether to be offended that you think I'd offer to enter into a fake relationship with you while already being in a real one or curious as to why you didn't just barge into my room to see for yourself."

"I'm not the barging type."

"Just the banging type, then?"

The innocent question drops to the tabletop like a boulder. An awkward giggle bubbles from my lips, and Bryce's attention zeroes in on my mouth. It's impossible not to watch hers right back, mesmerized by the way they part around laboured breaths.

Now . . . despite my lack of love life as of recently, I haven't exactly forgotten what sexual tension feels like. It's one of those things that becomes ingrained into the core of your memory. A sensation that may feel distant and foreign at times but is quick to flip into recognition during moments like these, where you consider pouncing at someone like a wild beast.

At least, that's what I think.

I can only speak for myself with absolute certainty, but from the tightening of my lungs and the moisture soaking into my panties as I stare at Bryce's mouth, there's no doubt I'm feeling a startling attraction to her.

My fake girlfriend.

This isn't the first time either. Far from it after what I witnessed the other night and the way my body responded to it. I didn't sleep at all and went to work with heavy bags beneath my eyes and an irritability that I put all my focus into not showing in front of a classroom of children.

For some reason, I think this is the strongest wave of attraction I've fallen prey to. From the sheer effort it's taking to keep my breaths steady so my lungs don't shrivel up and the subtle press of my thighs together beneath the edge of the table, it's safe to say I'm in dangerous territory. It's worse than the other night, and I'm hopeless to thinking of why that is right now.

Bryce doesn't appear as affected as I am. If it weren't for the streaks of red climbing her neck and the strain of her jaw, I would have thought she was simply staring at me.

Her ability to keep a straight face doesn't seem to matter right now. It's silly, but I take that as a compliment. Like I'm an exception to her usual façade.

"I don't refuse anyone when they ask for a tattoo," she

reveals, slowly slipping her eyes up my face. "They ask, and I take my shit and go where they want me whenever they want me."

"Are they taking advantage of you, then?"

Her brows knit together. "No."

"So, you're okay with being out all night every night going house to house? You don't get tired of getting home late or missing conversations with those around you?" I ramble, my buried irritability seeping through.

"Are you upset with me because I'm gone late, Daisy?"

I avoid eye contact, suddenly feeling small beneath the fierceness of her stare. "No. I just need to know if I should stop leaving the lights on once I've gone to bed."

"You won't have to. I'll be home earlier from now on."

"Don't feel obligated. I'm a big girl."

"It's not obligation. I forgot what it was like to have someone at home waiting for me," she states, finally looking elsewhere.

Unsure what to say back to that that wouldn't be too heavy for this moment, I change gears a bit. "Just try to save a day for your newest client."

Her choppy chuckle is a welcome sound after the previous few minutes. "Any day is yours, Sunshine. Just tell me when and make sure you're absolutely sure first."

"You got it." Smiling softly, I pull my hands back toward me and fold them. "I thought that maybe you'd gone to your parents' house and spoke to them without me."

"I've been dodging my mother all week. I wanted to talk to you first before I dragged us into that fucking mess for real. Give you one last chance to back out."

The invisible arms that have been wrapped around my middle for the last few days loosen inch by inch. "I think it's too late for that. And I want to meet them."

"You *want* to meet my parents?" she asks, visibly taken aback.

"Well, not because I think they're nice people but because I want to make sure they know the way they've been treating you isn't right."

"My mother is a lot to take in. She'll curse you out in French simply because she knows you won't understand, and then she'll drive her point across in English. I can't promise that she won't try to hurt you as a way to get to me. I'm not planning on letting her do that—"

I interrupt her rambling with a shake of my head and soft words. "I can handle myself. I'm not someone who lets others walk all over me."

And after missing my chance to stand up for Bryce in Peakside, I made a promise to myself that I wouldn't miss another.

Bryce keeps narrowed, curious eyes on me for a few moments after I've spoken. I don't try to sneak out from beneath them and let her stare for as long as she needs to believe me.

Finally, once I've grown a bit fidgety, she leans back in her chair and blinks, shutting down the intense connection.

"What about tonight?"

My eyes bulge. "Tonight?"

"Unless you're not ready," she adds, giving me another chance to back out.

Her doubt jabs a sensitive spot inside me. I've never been someone with a hard shell, and because of that, yeah, I'm gentle natured. But I'm not afraid to use my voice when need be. I grew up with too many siblings who loved to hear themselves speak not to have grown a backbone over the years. It was that or grow comfortable in the shadows.

Yanking my spine into a straight line, I inject as much power and confidence as I can into my voice.

"I'm ready. I'm your girl, and I'll make sure they know that you won't be accepting another from anyone else. Let alone them."

Disbelief floods her eyes. It's there and gone so suddenly that I wonder if I made it up, even as I struggle not to chase after it.

I could have clarified that I'm not really her girl . . . but when it sounds so good the way I said it, it would be a waste to change it now.

I'M SUCH A HORNY FREAK.

My two-year sex detox has affected me way more than expected. That's the only excuse I have for why I'm walking half a second slower than Bryce, just so I can catch a glance at the bare curves of her inner thighs as they appear below her short jean skirt when she sways her hips.

My belly is on fire, something forbidden gaining in intensity the more she walks and the higher her skirt shifts and climbs up her butt. I'm being the opposite of respectful right now as I ignore the desire in my blood and look up at the sky, begging for it to swallow me.

Ever since I was smacked in the face by how truly attracted I was to Bryce, I've been obsessively aware of her beauty and all the little things about it that won't seem to let me get one moment of peace.

She's so pale that every scar and imperfection on her body stands out like it's been circled in red marker. The thick mass of black hair that she hardly ever puts up appears heavy, and while I've never been interested in wrapping anyone's hair around my knuckles and using it for leverage during sex, suddenly, the images are there in my mind. The outright craving to try it just once to see if I'll enjoy it after all.

There's so much endless ink on her body, from her ankles to her throat, and holy, I've never been so intrigued by art before. The memory of what I know hides beneath the shortly cropped band tee she's wearing lingers in my mind like a stubborn cold.

She's so damn confident in herself and her body that it's that much harder not to gawk at her and wonder what it would take to replicate the same feelings within yourself.

I consider asking her to strip me bare and teach me how to embrace those things, but if I did, I don't trust that it wouldn't lead to other things.

Not right now.

And that's absolutely not very fake, is it?

"This house is insane," I throw out in an attempt to cool myself down with a subject change.

"More like ridiculous."

"No wonder your parents don't live in town. There's nothing like this there."

Bryce jerks her chin and slows her steps, walking in pace with me. The change of speed helps me focus on what I should be paying attention to. *Not her ass.*

She calls the house ridiculous, but at least it's beautiful. A little too similar to a castle for my taste, with the rounded entrance and sharp roof peaks, but still breathtaking. It's grand and white and bright, appearing far more welcoming than it is. A smokescreen like the witch's house from *Hansel and Gretel*.

I can't imagine a woman like Bryce in this place. Not happily.

"It paints the perfect family picture my mother loves to project."

"That it does. I mean, there's a literal"—I squint past the giant stone with matte-black letters that spell out the Lemieux name—"gazebo over there."

Bryce releases a harsh breath. "Yeah."

She slows her steps the closer we get to the house. The driveway is round and dramatic, made of tiny little pebbles that have been squashed down to be completely flat, but the toe of her boot catches on one, sending her stumbling.

"Woah," I say, shooting my hand out to grab her elbow before she can fall forward.

Her skin is hot beneath my grip, even as the colour leaches from her already pale cheeks. Concern slashes through me, and I take her hand in mine, stroking the back of her knuckles until she meets my waiting gaze.

"It'll be fine, Frosty. I've got you," I promise.

Palm slick with her nerves, she swallows harshly and squeezes me back. "I trust you."

"Then, let's go meet with the Devil."

23

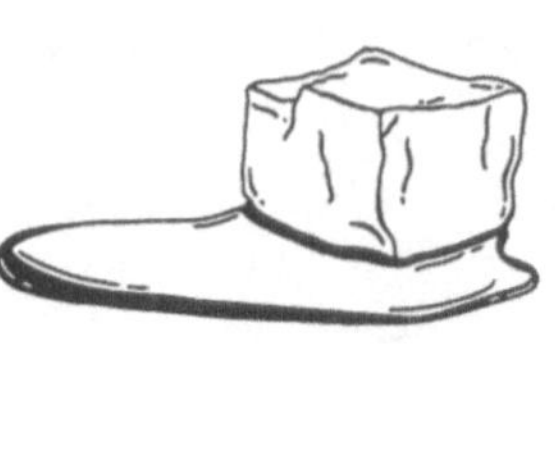

"*T'ES ENFIN ARRIVÉE.*"

"No pleasantries today, Mom?" I ask, ignoring her dig about our intentional tardiness.

I learned my punctuality from her, which is how I knew that showing up today fifteen minutes late would piss her off. My bad.

Dressed in a simple white sundress with her ears and neck weighed down with pearls, Claudine Lemieux welcomes us into my childhood home with a hidden grimace.

"Good afternoon, Mrs. Lemieux. You have a beautiful home," Daisy says brightly, not waiting for me to give a forced introduction before stepping in.

I walk into the house with stone legs, but she floats in, a soft, natural smile on her face as she stares at my mother. It's hard to tell if this is an act or if, like usual, this is just Daisy being herself.

"Daisy, I presume?" Mom asks absently.

"Yep. Daisy Mitchell. Again, I just want to say how nice it is to meet the woman who raised the one I've fallen head over heels in love with."

I don't breathe.

Can't.

The statement pounds in my mind, already on its own memory reel and tucked in an easy-to-reach shelf for later.

Warmth slips up my arm before a solid pressure envelops my entire side. Floral perfume soaks into my clothes and imbeds itself in my skin as Daisy leans into me and palms my opposite hip.

It's nearly impossible for my chest to expand on a breath, and when I finally figure it out, I'm gulping air.

"Love? This is the first I'm seeing of you," Mom guffaws, letting the door swing shut with a slam.

Leaving Daisy and me behind, she stalks through the entrance and disappears into the formal dining room. I wait for Daisy to release me, but she doesn't even spare me a glance before dragging us after my mother.

I'm dead weight, my feet moving of their own violation. My reaction to Daisy's easy, flowing words is alarming. I'm not a fool. I know she was lying. But that doesn't mean that they didn't still rip my chest open and leave me standing here with my heart on full display.

"Tell me something about her that I can use to start a conversation," she whispers.

"She has three siblings. All brothers."

"Really? You have three uncles?"

"Yes."

Her thumb drifts above my skirt, grazing my bare stomach and the goosebumps that cover it. "Alright. We have a big family in common. What about your dad?"

"He won't be here."

A low, deep rumble of a voice floats from the dining room, and I pause. Daisy laughs quietly.

"I saw a pair of men's shoes by the front door," she answers the question I haven't asked.

I clear my throat. My stomach churns in a weird way, a wave of nausea storming in that I force to the back of my mind.

"He's never home."

"I imagine being a mayor is a busy job."

"It's Cherry Peak, not Toronto," I mutter.

Her grin is big enough I can see it clearly from the corner of my vision. "Fair enough."

There are quiet words being spoken when we enter the dining room. They come to a stop immediately as two sets of eyes fall on us.

"Mr. Lemieux. I'm Daisy Mitchell."

She releases me to step forward and offer my father her hand. I'm struck by how large of a man he is when he accepts her hand and dwarfs her in size. Her hand disappears in his, and he stares at me above her head, curiosity blaringly apparent in his aged features. I roll my eyes.

Out of both my parents, my father has always been the one most accepting of me. I always told myself that he just didn't give a shit enough about me to care one way or another who I was attracted to. It was easier than believing he actually might have cared enough to think about my life and what I wanted.

It's a bit more settling to see him here with Mom. While she's never outwardly said anything to admit that she would prefer if I were straight, sometimes it doesn't take those exact words. Her obvious favouring of men and disinterest in my life where women are involved explains more than an outright admission would.

I've long since stopped caring what she thinks, but my father makes it harder to do the same. At least until he forgets how to stand up to her and instead lets her walk all over me without saying a fucking thing.

"Hello, Daisy," Dad says, releasing her hand a moment later.

She moves back to my side without hesitation, holding me the same way as earlier. As if it's easy to touch me like this.

As if she likes to.

"You have a beautiful home. I noticed a gazebo outside. Was that here when you bought the house?" she asks.

"No, actually, I put it in a few years later. Bryce was always playing guitar outside when she was young and kept burning her scalp in the sun because she refused to wear a hat. It was my attempt to keep her out of the sun while still letting her be outside."

Daisy twists to face me, eyes bright with newfound information. "You play guitar?"

"No. I gave it up when Mom told me it was a ridiculous hobby. And I don't remember the gazebo being for me and not just a decoration piece." My words bite as I flush hot, the back of my neck growing damp with sweat.

It's not an angry heat despite how fucking annoyed I am with my parents. There's something off about it. Same with the tightening of my stomach, my skin cooling despite my rising temperature.

Mom sucks in a loud breath. "Not in front of guests."

"Do you still remember how to play?" Daisy asks me, not sparing my mother a glance.

I curl my arm around her back and tug her the slightest bit closer, hoping she can't tell that I'm using her as comfort. There's something about touching her like this that warms the innermost parts of myself, as if her sunshine is able to slip through the cracks and blind the darkness.

I may be a hard, cruel person, but I still believe I have a fragile, battered soul. The kind that strikes first out of fear and doesn't allow for any prisoners. My defenses are high, but once you manage to slip past them, you're granted free rein.

Daisy's so far past my defenses that she's not even detectable anymore.

Eyes fixed on her, I lower my mouth to her temple and breathe in, hoping her smell will settle my stomach. "We'd have to sit down one night and see."

"I'd like that," she murmurs, the tops of her cheeks taking on a pink hue.

"Bryce is right. The gazebo has become more of a lawn decoration these past few years, I'm afraid."

Dad steals Daisy's attention, and I glare at him before I'm fully aware of what I'm doing. He's too tuned in to those around him to miss it. The curiosity I saw moments ago returns, now higher in intensity.

"Enough of the gazebo. I've arranged a light meal for us. Sit," Mom demands.

On the ridiculously long dining table, she's arranged four place settings, complete with fabric napkins and pale blue cushions on the chairs. My stomach rolls at the food already plated up, an invisible fist punching me deep in the gut.

I didn't pick up the scent of fish when we arrived, but now that I see it, it's everywhere. In my hair and on my clothes. Even on my lips, the remembrance of the taste seeping onto my tongue.

Pressing my lips together, I fight back a gag and divert my stare, focusing on the bottle of red wine already uncorked. It doesn't help. The thought of eating or drinking anything makes me sway on my feet.

Daisy steps into me and softly taps my cheek. "Are you okay?"

"Yep," I croak.

Mom hovers on the other side of the table, waiting for Dad to finish pulling her chair out. Smoothing down the puffy skirt of her dress, she sits and presses a kiss to his clean-shaven cheek.

"Sit down, Bryce. *Arrête avec ton attitude.*"

"What did you say? I'm sorry, I don't speak French," Daisy says.

"Oh, nothing. Now, don't be rude, Bryce."

"You look a little green," Dad points out, pretending to be worried.

Daisy presses the back of her hand to my scorching hot forehead and furrows her brows. "You feel really warm. Are you sure you're feeling okay?"

I roll my eyes up to stare at the ceiling and take a small inhale before nodding and looking back at the food on the table. My stomach thrashes so violently I have to press a hand to it as I take the chair opposite my mother.

Daisy follows close behind me, not allowing more than a couple of inches between us. Even as she sits on my right, she doesn't stop looking at me, not even bothering to pretend to believe what I'm trying to sell everyone.

Her hand clasps on my bare thigh below the hem of my skirt, and my stomach has a fit for a completely different reason.

The smell of fish is so much stronger at the table. My lips part as I'm forced to breathe through my mouth and swallow the burn of vomit creeping up my throat. It's almost worse this way.

Risking a look at my plate, I see the roasted asparagus tucked beneath the edge of a thick piece of salmon. The yellow sauce that's been drizzled over the top seems to make my nausea worse, and before I can stop it, I gag.

Loudly.

Daisy's head swings in my direction before she's leaning over and bringing her face close to mine, our noses almost touching. "Bryce?"

"I'm going to be sick," I whisper.

Scrambling back from the table, I get the fuck away from everyone and the food that's driven me to this point. Jogging out of the room, I slap a hand to my mouth and dive into the closest bathroom.

My knees slam against the floor so hard pain splinters up my legs as I flip the toilet lid and heave the contents of my stomach. It's one of my most embarrassing moments, and I couldn't even get up to shut the door if I tried.

Nose burning, I manage to drape my hair behind my shoulders. I'm going up in flames as I continue throwing up, my body hunched over the toilet.

"Oh, Frosty."

I squeeze my eyes shut and lean my forehead on my arm, hoping I've just made her up and that she isn't actually here to see this.

"Here," her gentle voice chimes.

Shivers zip up and down my body when my hair is pulled back with careful fingers and an elastic is wrapped around it.

"I knew you weren't okay, but I didn't know you were sick like this. We wouldn't have come here if I had, sweetheart."

A very real, very non-imaginable hand sweeps up and down my back, even as I hurl again, sweat clinging to my face and neck.

"My parents aren't here," I mumble.

"No, they're not."

So no nicknames, I almost say. Should plead. Especially not one like sweetheart.

"I didn't feel sick earlier."

She keeps stroking my back in slow, comforting circles. "Good. I wouldn't have wanted to make you feel worse just to come here of all places."

"It was the fish."

"Just the fish? You feel really warm, Bryce."

I hum, my throat raw and sore as I close my eyes. "I don't get sick."

"Nobody is exempt from getting sick. Not even stubborn women," she teases.

With weak arms, I push myself back enough to flush the toilet but don't look at her. I'm a fucking mess right now. And despite throwing up everything I've eaten in the last fucking week, I don't feel any better.

I'm sluggish and dizzy, like I've run a marathon on an empty stomach. My muscles feel like jelly, making it near impossible to keep myself upright as I collapse against the toilet, my ears ringing.

"Mr. Lemieux!"

I stop fighting the pull of sleep and close my eyes. Just for a second.

When I open them again, I'm not in the bathroom.

A searing pain lashes through my head, the focal point

behind my eyes telling me it's a migraine. My stomach is sensitive, clinching as I shift on a . . . bed? There's a pillow beneath my head that smells like the essential oils my mother drenches the house in.

With a cough to clear my throat, I attempt to open my eyes. It hurts like a bitch, and the throb behind them pushes harder, forcing me to squeeze them shut with a groan.

"Bryce? What's wrong?"

"You're still here?" I scrape the question up my throat, hating how weak I sound.

The bed shifts, and I flinch when a cool cloth is placed on my forehead. Warm breath puffs across my cheek.

"Of course I am. I'm not leaving you here alone, and there was no way I was risking waking you up to go home," she says sternly.

"What the fuck happened?"

And why do I feel like I've been hit by a truck?

She smooths my hair out of my face, a lone finger tracing the edge of my hairline. "I'm pretty sure you have the flu. Are you sure you were feeling okay when we left the house?"

"I was fine. I thought I felt sick when we got here, but I'm used to feeling some sort of discomfort whenever I'm here."

She sighs, scraping her nails against my scalp. I swallow a moan before it can slip out and squeeze my eyes shut tighter.

"Does your head hurt?" she murmurs.

"Like a bitch."

"How's your stomach?"

"Sore."

It feels like someone's used the inside of it for punching practice.

"I'm going to get some supplies, and then I'll be right back, okay? If you need me, please call. Scream if you need to. This place is a serious castle, and I might get lost."

"I want to go back home. Don't get shit from my parents."

Forcing my eyelids open, I wince at the pain the small stream of sunlight brings to my head and curse. My stomach folds in on itself as I lean forward and curl my fingers in the thick duvet thrown over me.

"Don't. We're not going anywhere until you're not one step from falling asleep on me again."

She leans over and pushes me back down with a hand on my shoulder. I know I won't be able to keep my eyes open for much longer, but I refuse to shut them again without looking at her.

Concern is etched on every inch of her face and lies heavy in her eyes, deepening the blue. The downturn of her lips is so subtle that I have to stare to realize she's actually frowning. Emotion clogs my throat, guilt slapping me across the face.

"I'm fine, Sunshine. A few painkillers and I'll be good to go."

It's such a fucking lie. My eyes slide shut, and I clench my teeth as much as I can, given how tired I am.

"No, you are not fine, Bryce. But I will find you some painkillers. I'll be right back."

Somehow, I'm able to lift my arm enough to reach for her before I fall asleep and she disappears. Her fingers are so cold when I cover them and bring them to my chest.

"Don't go yet."

"Let me help you," she whispers, the heat from her other hand so close to my cheek but not touching, just hovering.

"You're better than medicine."

"Sleep, Bryce. I'll be here."

Her cool fingers trace the corner of my mouth, and then— then I swear I feel her lips replace them. Just the ghost of a touch, but it's enough to make my cheeks burn as I grin in my sleep.

It's the best kiss I've ever had. Even if I am dreaming.

24

Daisy

Bryce's smile lingers after her breathing evens out in sleep. I'm held captive by the sight of it, unable to look away as I continue running my fingers through her damp hair, trying to untangle it without a brush.

Her smile is as rare as the peace in her expression and lack of thoughts that keep her brows in a perpetual state of tugged inward.

Being this close to her while she's in such a vulnerable state is something I doubt many can claim to have experienced. I feel an overwhelming sense of appreciation knowing that I'm now one of those few, even if the circumstances are less than ideal.

Her parents being on the other side of this room grinds my gears. I'm on high alert, my protective instincts blaring. It's upsetting that I feel the need to protect her from her parents in the first place, but after only spending a few minutes with them, I recognized that they aren't the right people to take care of her right now.

Her mom is too pompous and high on herself to realize that she's ruined her relationship with her daughter, and her father turns a blind eye to everything her mother says. He might very well have a good heart and genuinely care for Bryce, but he's doing a terrible job of showing it.

She deserves more from them. Love and understanding and support.

Everything that I've been lucky enough to receive from my moms. There hasn't been a single day in my life where I didn't feel like they were my biggest fans. Sometimes it's easy to take for granted the relationships we have, but after today, I'm realizing how blessed I am.

Our parents hold such an important position in our lives. They're supposed to love us unconditionally, nurture always, and teach us right from wrong. The world around us will always change, but family is supposed to be everlasting. So why does Bryce's appear as though it's one wrong comment away from crumbling?

Stroking her hairline, I let my gaze linger on the slow droop of her smile. The damp cloth on her forehead is warm now, so I peel it off and reluctantly get off the bed. She doesn't move a muscle as the mattress shifts with my weight.

There's no one in the hallway when I step out and shut the door behind me with a soft click. The Lemieux house is intimidating enough on the outside, but inside, it's somehow worse. When Bryce's father carried her into this room, I wasn't bothering to make note of which hallways we were heading down or how many doors we passed. Bryce was my focus.

Now, I realize it would have been easier if I had been more aware of my surroundings.

The hallway is long, with too many doors on either side and a bright light shining at the end where it curves. My socks hide my footsteps as I pad along the sleek floors.

A staircase is down the curved hall, and I make a beeline for it. White walls are everywhere with boring, minimalist artwork hung on them. The lack of family photos on this floor would be alarming if I were anywhere else. My childhood home, for example.

There were a few on the main level that I noticed when we arrived, but other than that . . . it's been quite sad.

Gripping onto the staircase railing, I take the stairs carefully, not wanting to make enough noise to draw attention to myself. I'm not doing anything wrong, but I'm a stranger to Bryce's parents and could do with avoiding any weird encounters right now.

I need to find medication, a bowl for Bryce in case she can't make it to the bathroom next time she has to throw up, and to cool this cloth back off. Then I can go back to her.

The main floor is as empty and quiet as the second. No chatter or television noise. I'd even settle for some soft music just to fill the void as I slip into what I hope is the kitchen and freeze.

Grabbing the doorframe, I keep still, as if that'll turn me invisible or something.

Bryce's mother must have some freaky motion-detecting superpower because the moment I take a silent step backward, she's whipping around and pinning me with sharp, distrusting eyes.

"What are you doing?" she snaps.

I wet my lips and release the doorframe. "Bryce needs medicine. And a bucket or a bowl."

She hums, patting the skirt of her dress. "We don't keep medication in the kitchen."

"What about a bowl?"

"We don't use bowls. There should be a bucket in the garage. I'll have my husband find and bring it to you."

Who doesn't have a family puke bowl? Geez, we are from completely different tax brackets.

"Thank you," I say and then turn, prepared to leave.

Something stops me. A tug deep inside myself.

Facing her again, I flex my fingers at my side and lift my chin. "Did you know that Bryce doesn't like fish?"

"She is too picky."

"Actually, she's not. But you took the one food she doesn't like and made sure it was here today. Why? Just to upset her?"

Claudine sets a hand on the kitchen island and leans against it, hip popped. It's a position that's so Bryce-like it's almost hard to believe. The tight pull of her features should have me abandoning this conversation before things get out hand, but again, something stops me.

"Who are you to judge me, Daisy Mitchell?" She sneers my name as if that'll intimidate me.

It doesn't. Not even close. "I'm your daughter's girlfriend. Someone important in her life that looks out for her. And right now, that's exactly what I'm doing. Don't push me, Mrs. Lemieux. Bryce is worth protecting."

"She doesn't need protection from me! I'm only looking out for her as a mother should."

"You're not looking out for her, though. You're hurting her."

The apples of her full cheeks glow with a flaming red. Knuckles white from her grip on the island, she knots her eyebrows.

"You know nothing. *Rien du tout.*"

"I know more than you think. And I can confidently say that you continuing to disregard her sexuality and preferences has broken her trust in you. There's strain on your relationship that's obvious to everyone. Even a stranger looking in. And it won't go away until you leave your ideologies at the door and embrace her for who she is and what she wants," I say, unashamed of how loud I've gotten.

She turns her nose up at me, completely disregarding everything I've said. I don't know why I was hoping she would take my advice into consideration when clearly, she's too stuck in her own ways and beliefs to care at all about Bryce's.

I swallow my frustration before adding, "You may think that by not telling her you wish she would just like men, that you're being supportive of her bisexuality, but in all honesty, Mrs. Lemieux, you're not. What she needs to hear from you is that she's accepted the way she is, regardless of who she wants to love. And if you can't do that, then you need to leave her be. Setting her up on blind dates with men when she's been vocal about not being interested in a straight relationship is not allyship, and it certainly isn't parental support."

My chest rises and falls quickly, every inhale shaky and exhale confident. It's a lot to drop on your fake girlfriend's mother upon first meeting, but I couldn't hold it back any longer. This is the reason I'm here right now, and while I'm playing the part of Bryce's girlfriend, not a word I just spoke wasn't true.

Regardless of what our relationship may be, Bryce is someone who's important to me. And I'll always take care of those who matter, even if they don't quite know that yet.

When Claudine turns away from me and a reply doesn't come, I leave the kitchen. She isn't my priority right now.

Her daughter is, and I refuse to be another person in her life who lets her down when she needs them.

AFTER WHAT FEELS LIKE AGES, I step back into Bryce's room with my arms full of items. Pill bottles, a new cool cloth, a bottle of water I stole from the mini fridge in the living room, and a bucket to rest beside the bed.

My hair is up messily on the top of my head to keep it out of my face, and I shrug out of my cardigan before draping it over the black velvet chair in the corner of the room.

It's obvious that this is Bryce's old room, even if her parents have scrubbed most of her out of it. Whether on purpose or purely just to turn the space into something impersonal for guests, they've stripped all of her personality from the décor.

After living with Bryce and snooping around in her room, I know what to expect from any space where she's spent long periods of time. Dark vibes with some hidden pops of muted colour. Graphic artwork, loud patterns, and sleek furniture. She's completely her own person with a unique style, and it feels like a loss to sit in here and see how bare it is.

Everything may reek like lavender, covering the spicy scent of Bryce's perfume, but my gut tells me that this used to be her space. Even stripped of personality, they've left nail holes in the wall and the black furniture. Even the bedding is still dark. Not black, but a deep purple. The small collection of guitar picks in a glass dish on the long dresser draws my attention.

In a beat, I'm in front of the dresser, staring down at the collection. I dig through the different shapes and styles before pinching the smallest of them all, a bright yellow one.

"I thought she gave up guitar," I whisper.

"I did."

With a gasp, I have the guitar pick smushed to my chest and am whirling around. Bryce watches me from the bed, eyes cracked open just enough for the blue to appear amongst a whole lot of red. Her lips are nearly as pale as her face, and I abandon the guitar pick where I found it.

"How are you feeling?"

Her tired gaze tracks me across the room as I go to her side and perch on the edge of the bed.

"Like shit."

"Here, sit up." I reach for the items I left on the floor and grab all the pills she needs before cracking open the bottle of water and bringing it to her lips. "Take these and drink some water."

"I don't need all this," she argues, brows furrowing even as she pushes up on the pillows as much as possible.

"You do. So shut up and take your medicine."

Her lips part, eyes blowing wide. "You just told me to shut up."

My lips twitch with the threat of a smile, but I keep firm. "I'll do it again unless you listen."

"I liked it."

"You like hearing me tell you to shut up?"

"I like your backbone, Daisy."

I flush beneath the intensity of her lingering stare and opt out of replying to that.

Tapping her bottom lip, I hold out the first pill and then push it inside her mouth. The water is next, and I don't let her stop drinking until she gently nudges the bottle away. By the time she's taken all the medication, she's collapsing back on the mattress with a groan.

"Get some more sleep, Bryce," I say softly, pushing her hair back, unable to help not touching it again.

She struggles to keep her eyes open, fighting sleep. "Don't go this time."

"I won't. I'll be right here."

"Lay down with me."

Before I can argue against that, she spits a curse and rolls over, panting at the effort it took. I let my laugh fill the quiet room and adjust the blankets that she's pulled beneath her body.

"I'll get sick lying on your pillow."

"If you do, I'll take care of you."

I pull my lip between my teeth and bite down on it. Bryce doesn't look away from me, even as she lifts a weak hand and pats the empty spot beside her.

"Please," she mumbles.

My resolve crumbles with that single word.

Knowing exactly well how bad of an idea this is, I climb in beside her and decide that I'll deal with the consequences of this once everything goes back to normal.

25

Bryce

SOMEONE FILLED MY EYES AND MOUTH WITH SAND.

Or buried me alive in it, more like.

I'm unsure how I wound up in the bathroom again or how I didn't notice myself puking all over my shirt. From the smell of myself, it's no wonder Daisy's asking if I want to have a bath.

"I'll shower," I manage to say, surprised I can get my crusted lips to form words.

"You can barely stay awake sitting on the floor. I won't stay in here if you don't want me to, but at least let me help you run a bath and actually sit in it."

Taking these clothes off is all I want. I smell putrid, and the longer she sees me like this, the easier it's going to be to scare her off. Somehow, I've managed not to do it already, and if this is what takes me down, I'll never recover from it.

"I'll be naked," I blurt out.

Humour lines her eyes as she reaches around me to flush the toilet and releases her hold on my hair. I want to ask her to wrap it in her hands again. Her touch soothes me. Doesn't matter where.

"I can cover my eyes," she offers.

Another wave of nausea hits, and I grip my stomach in an

attempt to fight it. There's nothing in my stomach but water, but even that hasn't been lasting long before it's flying back up.

Daisy brushes a hand over my shoulder, and then the tub behind me begins to fill. The sound of the water running makes my head pound, the migraine of all migraines lingering.

"You don't have to do this, Daisy."

"Do what?"

I choke on a laugh. "All of this. Take care of me like I'm a child."

She moves around the tub, the sound of a hand cutting into the steady stream of water coming from behind me.

"I wouldn't be here if I didn't want to be," she murmurs.

"That was out of obligation," I state, trying and failing to sound unbothered. "My parents wouldn't have cared if my girl-friend had left once dinner was ruined. It wouldn't have changed our plan."

A pause, and then she's crouching beside me and taking my hand from where I have it resting on my knee, pulling it into her lap.

I have to strain to see her properly, but she's so beautiful that it's worth it. Somehow, she doesn't look tired, just focused, worried. The healthy flush of colour in her cheeks and lips is a welcome sight.

"There's no obligation, Frosty. Just concern. Now, let me help you up so you can strip and get into the bath."

My chest tightens, and I speak without thinking about the consequences.

"I need your help."

She blows out a soft, panted breath. "With getting in?"

I dip my chin. "With everything."

Her eyes dart to the side, and I worry I've blown it before she worries her lip and slowly brings them back. My hand is so fucking sweaty, but I have the flu to blame it on.

She doesn't. And I'm not that out of it not to realize how slick her palm is against mine.

"Let's worry about getting you up first."

I grip the edge of the toilet and hoist myself up as she tugs on my hand. My balance gives, and my vision blackens with fuzz that takes a few seconds to clear. She's there to stabilize me before I tip over.

"Sorry," I grunt, sidestepping her to lean against the sink. The sight of myself in the mirror above it nearly has me crumpling to the ground. "Fuck."

I look like shit. Worse than shit. Like a corpse that's been dug out of the ground a few days after a burial.

My hair is a giant tangle, and the mess of puke on my shirt is enough to have me fighting a wretch. The blue bags beneath my eyes are deep and dark, bringing attention to the red tinge around my pupils. Daisy ignores both my apology and curse, seeming unbothered by my appearance.

That makes one of us.

She squats and starts digging through the cabinet beneath the sink before pulling out a new toothbrush and toothpaste.

"If you strip, I'll get this ready, and then you can brush your teeth before getting in the tub. I can even get it ready for you in the hallway," she offers, tone so soft it's almost a whisper.

"I'll brush them first."

Don't leave the room.

She's quick to open the packaging on the toothbrush and smothers it in minty paste. I take it from her and scrub my mouth until I'm sure my gums are bleeding, while she stops the tub from filling any higher.

"You're sure you don't want me to leave and come back when you're in the tub? I've put bubbles in," she says once the toothbrush has been placed on the edge of the sink and the scent of bubble bath fills the room.

Shaking my head once, I lower my hand to the hem of my shirt and inhale a long, steady breath. I curl my fingers in the fabric and start sliding it up my abdomen.

Daisy doesn't move, although her gasp is hardly loud

enough for me to catch it. I've never cared much about the opinions of others when it comes to my body. I've stripped for and flashed tit at more people in a tattoo studio than society would consider normal, but Daisy's different.

Her opinion of me is the only one that matters.

In all of the dreams I've had where she's played the leading role, my first time naked never occurred in a situation like this. One where sex and desire aren't at the forefront of our actions.

Goosebumps pop up on every inch of skin, covering me head to toe. I swallow and tug the shirt over my chest, more aware of my surroundings than I've ever been.

The spike in my temperature isn't from the flu. It comes from low in my belly and spreads like wildfire between my legs and up into my chest.

She doesn't back away. Doesn't move a muscle until I reach up to pull my shirt over my head and my muscles start to shake. As she reaches forward to help me, her forearm brushes the swells of my breasts, and I gulp down the scent of her, subconsciously arching my back to get closer.

My shirt goes over my head, and my hair rains down over my neck and chest, creating a barrier between Daisy's wandering eyes and my bare tits.

Her pupils expand, and my nipples tighten to the point of pain. The metal through each one is cold and heavy, weighing them down and intensifying the pulse in my pussy.

A swallow fills the space around us, and I'm not sure if it's mine or hers.

"Can you do your skirt?" she asks on a loose breath.

"No."

Her nod is absent. Small, thin fingers stroke the rough jean material, then pop the button and pull down the zipper.

I squeeze the sink so tight it could crumble and hold my breath, watching as she lowers herself to her haunches. Her pace is a punishment. But I take it.

"Are you sure you want me here doing this, Bryce?"

My hand drops to her head, and I smooth the top of her hair before cupping the back, my eyes blazing in a way I've never experienced before. I ache so deep, like I'll never be able to find relief.

Daisy leans further into my hold, and I moan without having a chance in hell of holding it in.

Her eyelids droop, and she dips her fingers beneath the waistband of my skirt before she slowly starts inching it down my hips. My panties linger behind, but before I can let my tongue run free and tell her to take them off as well, she rectifies her hold and grips them tight.

They come down with my skirt, and the air around us disappears. Every breath is a struggle. The burn is everlasting.

I keep her trapped beneath the weight of that burn, and she doesn't drift. My nausea lingers, buried beneath the desire and arousal that's taken over every inch of my system. For now, I'll do my fucking best to keep it at bay. Just for another few minutes.

It feels like hours, but finally, the skirt falls.

Daisy keeps her eyes on mine, not straying even as I stand naked in front of her. I don't risk looking down to see how wet I've left my panties, but I want her to. The longer we stand here, a barrier shattered between us, the harder it is not to tell her the truth about my feelings.

"Can you make it to the bathtub?" Her voice is so fucking breathy, the words almost whimpered.

"Yeah, Sunshine, I'm good," I rasp, giving confirmation for far more than just her question.

Blinking once, then twice, she releases my gaze and lets hers drip down my body. From my heaving breasts and the metal hoops in my nipples that are visible through the dirty strands of my hair, the straining muscles in my torso, to the smooth, wet area between my legs.

A voice in my head tries to scream at me that this isn't right and that things are going to be different in the coming days. I drown it out with the heavy sounds of her breathing.

I'm not prepared for her to cup my calf in a hot hand. I chomp down on my tongue and narrow my eyes, unsure if she's playing with me or just that interested in touching.

The ink on my body is a lot to take in, and usually, I like that.

Not now. It's stealing her attention and inviting her to dig into the reasons behind each design when that's the last thing I want us to focus on.

I angle my body toward the bath and release her head when my stomach lurches, a sore discomfort returning. If I don't pull myself together quickly, I'm going to risk ruining the moment with vomit.

Daisy watches me stumble to the tub and ungracefully stabilize myself on its edge, my ass perched in the air. It's one of the only areas on my body that's nothing but boring, pale skin.

"Let me help," she rushes out, snapping into action.

In a blink, she's crouching beneath my arm and holding me up. I lift a leg over the edge and step into the hot, bubbly water. It only reaches my knee, but I assume she doesn't want me to fall asleep and drown with it too high.

"Easy, easy. I don't want you to slip and hurt yourself."

I'd do it on purpose if it meant she'd heal me afterward. *Fuck, that sounds dark.* Maybe just a knock of my knee on the porcelain or something.

By the time I'm sinking completely into the water, I'm battling exhaustion again. All sexual thoughts have floated back to where they came from, too far to call upon them without risking passing out.

"Is the temperature okay?"

I make a noise of agreement in my throat and rest my head against the pillow slung over the back of the tub. The water slooshes up over my tits and against my collarbones, and I let my arms hang loose beneath it.

When I tilt my head to look at Daisy, I find her sitting on her knees beside the tub with her arm draped over it, fingers playing in the bubbles.

"My parents," I mutter.

She twists her mouth in distaste. "What about them?"

"How did you find all the shit you gave me?"

"I found it."

"You searched through the house on your own?"

"Would you have a problem if I had?"

I smirk sleepily. "No. Not at all."

"I found your mom in the kitchen. She told me where to find most of the supplies, and your father gave me the bucket," she reveals, almost cautiously, like she still doesn't believe that I don't give a shit what she did here.

She could have set the house on fire, and I'd have probably thanked her for taking away a place full of so many upsetting memories from me.

I bring my knee up and rest it against the wall of the tub she's perched over. "How was that?"

"As great as you'd expect. I kind of chastised her."

"Chastised how?"

She takes the fingers running through the clouds of bubbles and swirls them over my exposed knee, igniting another round of raised skin. "I did what we were here to do."

"Thank you."

"You're welcome. Anyway, she deserved a piece of my mind. Dinner was uncalled for."

"Don't remind me."

She giggles, propping her chin on the tub. "Sorry."

Looking up at the ceiling, I say, "I made you your playlist."

"You did?" The excitement in her voice speeds my pulse.

"Yeah. It's not just rock. I kept getting sidetracked."

"I can't wait to hear it. I've started yours, but I'm not quite done yet."

I jostle my shoulder. "No rush."

There's not a chance I'm telling her that I stayed up until 4:00 a.m. finishing it the same night she said she'd like one.

"Do you want to get your hair wet? I don't have shampoo, but we can at least scrub it a bit."

Of course, my mother has the bathroom stocked with bubble bath but not shampoo.

"I'll fall asleep."

"Let me worry about that," she argues lightly.

I give in embarrassingly easily and let her guide me in the water until my hair sinks below the surface. She dips her hands into it and starts scrubbing my scalp, drawing small moans and sighs from me that I'm too exhausted to be ashamed about.

Too soon, she helps me sit up and squeezes the excess water from my hair. I feel the change in the air the moment her eyes find my bare chest as it hovers over the water, bubbles almost completely gone.

My nipples are hard from both the sudden chill and her attention, and slowly, I bring my eyes to hers, not hiding from the attention.

Her pink tongue darts out and slides across her lips, nose burning red. "Do you love Cherry Peak that much?"

"What do you mean?"

"The tattoo. The bull skull and the word 'home.' Is Cherry Peak an important part of your life?"

She's asking about my tattoo when my tits are on display? For fuck's sake, this woman is going to drive me mad.

With a huffed laugh, I tip my head down and stare at the tattoo. I designed it myself, but an old friend put ink to skin.

"Cherry Peak is where all of the important people to me are. It's not so much about the place but those in it. The bull was the only physical thing that reminded me of here that I haven't already put on my body." I lift my arm and rest it beside hers on the edge of the tub. "My first idea was the cherry tree."

She thumbs the outline of the tree on my forearm and leans in close, breath warming my skin. "It's beautiful."

"It could use a touch-up or two."

"Either way, it's gorgeous. You're incredibly talented."

I hide my reaction to her compliment by closing my eyes. "It's a hobby."

"Just take the compliment, Frosty. I promise not to let anyone else know that you did," she teases.

"Thank you," I say, exaggerating the words.

Silence falls, and I keep my eyes shut, letting it settle over me. With the knowledge that Daisy's beside me and I'm taken care of, I let the promise of sleep sweep me away.

26

Daisy

I'VE LOST TRACK OF TIME. NIGHT FELL HOURS AGO, BUT I CONTINUE to fight my exhaustion, not wanting to miss Bryce needing me. She's hardly moved since she fell asleep again after getting out of the bath, but what if she did and I wasn't conscious?

The soft pink pajamas I found for her in the dresser are hideous, but thankfully, she was too tired to notice them before crawling into bed. They looked wrong on her, another variation of the uniform she's forced to wear at work. All frills and lace and scratchy material that cover too many of the tattoos I now know exist.

My hand began cramping a while ago, but I haven't been able to stop stroking her head and running my fingers through her hair. The largest part of myself, the one that's constantly needy for attention and physical affection, is thriving yet still craves more from both of us.

Wiggling my toes beneath the heavy blanket, I strain to make out the shape of Bryce in the dark room. I feel her more than I see her. Steady, hot exhales warm my thigh, and her hand grips my shin, fingers curled even in sleep.

She's had her head laid on my lap for a long time. A few minutes after falling asleep on the pillow that's lying cold and empty beside me. I didn't dare move her, not only because I didn't want to disturb her but because having her cheek on my thigh filled my chest with a dizzying warmth. Even in sleep, she reached for me. Trusted me.

So, I've been sitting up against the headboard, fully aware of the kink in my back and the cramp in my hand because I can't make myself move.

This isn't how either of us expected to spend our weekend. After a long, draining week, I was looking forward to rotting the weekend away on the couch. Instead, I'm here.

It would be normal to feel frustrated about that, right? But if so, why am I the opposite? I'm tired and sore, and even a bit uncomfortable being in this house with Bryce's parents.

It all pales in comparison to the peace I feel in this moment.

I wouldn't trade this weekend for anything. The thoughtful conversation, gentle touches, and the inside look at the version of Bryce not many get to see. We've bonded. Both emotionally and physically, if what happened in the bathroom wasn't just a figment of my imagination.

God, the bathroom. I can still feel the raised skin on her legs and waist beneath my fingertips. It wasn't my intention to touch her chest with my arm, but when she arched into it, I forgot how to breathe.

Tipping my head back to rest against the headboard, I press my tongue to the inside of my lip and gently curl my fingers in the thick mass of her black hair. Heat crawls up my chest and neck as arousal floods my stomach.

It's wrong, completely uncalled for in the situation I'm in.

Yet as the memory of taking her clothes off comes barrelling in, I struggle to think of anything but the most beautiful body I've ever seen. Have ever dreamed of or imagined.

Muscled stomach and shoulders, curvy hips and thighs, and breasts the size of generous handfuls. I'd have had a much better chance of shoving my interest out of my mind in the bathroom, crouched in front of her, had I not pulled down her skirt.

It was intimate in a way that should have been terrifying. Something that should have taken place between lovers and not two people still getting to know one another. The brief moment outside of her room last week doesn't come close to that.

And I wouldn't take it back.

Not the feel of her skirt in my grip or the familiar sensation of lace panties scraping my skin. She was so hot it burned as I brought them both further and further down, until she was bare before me, all smooth, puffy skin that glistened in a way that threatened to undo me completely.

For a moment, I considered staying there forever, doing nothing more than staring at her from my place on the floor, her hand steady on my head like a guiding force.

My attention snaps to my lap when Bryce grows restless. With a turn of her head, her face is pushed between my thighs instead of on them. I hold as still as possible, muscles quivering with the strain of keeping them tense.

She lets out a soft noise and then slides her hand up my leg, over my knee and to the squishy part of my thigh. It disappears beneath the hem of my skater skirt, which has already risen on its own. She lingers only a couple of inches from my damp panties, and my pussy sings at the closeness, a sharp prick of desire following.

I swallow thickly and attempt to lift my thigh in hopes of pushing her head upward. Instead, she tightens her grip on it and stretches her arm out, encouraging my leg outward to create a much larger gap between them that she groans into.

"Bryce," I squeak, all too aware of how bad it would be to allow her to do what I think she might be trying to do to me in her sleep.

In her sleep.

She probably thinks I'm someone else, and that's more than enough of a reason for me to tug her carefully by the hair and repeat her name, louder this time.

Bryce jolts up and off my lap, the skin of my leg where her

hand was growing ice-cold. "Jesus fucking Christ. What the fuck?"

My body shakes with silent laughter at her outburst, and even though I can't see her scowling at me, I know she is. Call it intuition.

"What's wrong?" she asks hoarsely.

"Has anyone ever told you that you get touchy when you're sleeping?"

Her hair whips around her face as she tries to stare at me in the dark. "What did I do?"

I scoot further down the bed now that she's not on my lap. The relief in my back from the new position is instant.

"So, is that a yes?"

"Tell me what I did. If it was something that freaked you out—"

"Are you hungry?"

She pauses, the confused scrunch of her features obvious, even with the lack of light. "No, I'm not hungry."

"Are you sure?"

"Daisy, stop fucking with me," she warns with a slight hiss.

I swallow a giggle. "I'm pretty sure you were five seconds away from trying to eat me for breakfast."

Silence.

More silence.

Then, the crinkle of sheets as Bryce reaches behind her for a pillow and shoves it into her face. Her groan is so loud it's hardly muffled.

I roll my lips together and reach for the blanket before tugging it up my body and nestling it beneath my chin.

My lashes flutter as I wait for her to finish freaking out, my patience everlasting when it comes to this woman.

Finally, she pulls the pillow from her face and rests it on her lap. Eyes trained forward, she says, "You could have punched me for that."

"Why would I do that?"

"Because I just tried to touch you without your consent."

The frustrated bewilderment in the words is reassuring in a way. It's a reminder that she isn't the type of person to take anything like this lightly or do something that I'm not okay with. I don't need the reminder, but knowing it's there is comforting.

"Well, you didn't. And you hadn't even actually touched me anywhere that I hadn't touched you earlier. You're a good person, Bryce. Even when you have dirty dreams."

"I wasn't having a dirty dream," she denies gruffly.

"No?"

"No."

"If you say so."

"Daisy," she scolds.

The deep, chastising sound of her voice does nothing but spark the desire that's been lying dormant since she got off my lap. If anyone should be scolding themselves for sexual behaviour, it should be me based solely off my dirty thoughts.

"You know, considering we're supposed to be in a relationship, it would be really bad if someone learned that we haven't even kissed before," I ramble, letting my tongue run free.

Excitement rams into me head-on.

God, I'm pushing my limits here. This is not what I should be encouraging. Especially after all that's happened since we got to Bryce's parents' house.

Bryce hesitates for a beat, but no immediate refusal comes. "How would they find that out?"

"It could come up in conversation and slip out."

"What do you suggest, then?"

She's looking down at me with those cool blue eyes that I wish I could see more clearly. At the same time, maybe the darkness is a blessing. It gives us the opportunity to hide some of ourselves. A reassurance that this isn't the time for us to expose our souls to one another or turn this into anything it doesn't need to be.

"Practice. If you're feeling up to it," I murmur.

"That's all it'll be?"

The lie feels as forced as it does wrong. "That's all."

I don't know if I believe what I'm saying. It doesn't matter, though. Not when I'm scorching hot and fidgeting with the need to maul her.

"I have to brush my teeth first."

Before I can offer to help her out of bed, she's up and swaying into the ensuite. I take it as a good sign that she's regained enough of her strength to walk on her own. Maybe we've been here longer than I thought.

I'm a mess of nerves and sore, sensitive nipples by the time she stumbles back to the bed and sits beside me. Replicating my position from when she slept on my lap, she keeps her back propped against the headboard and legs pressed together.

"Are you okay? Maybe you should sleep some more," I offer, pushing myself up and out from beneath the blanket, too hot for it now.

Bryce doesn't answer with words. She reaches out and palms my cheek, guiding me toward her. I move onto my knees and shuffle closer until I'm no more than a pinky's length away, and I can smell the mint toothpaste on her breath.

"Ready?" I ask.

My eyelids fall, hiding her expression as we hover, tasting each other's breath but not moving for anything more. I'm not touching her, and I want to be. The rules that are supposed to be keeping us in line are non-existent in this moment. They might as well have not existed in the first place.

I'd have broken them anyway.

"Not really."

Bryce strokes my cheekbone with her thumb, and then our lips are meeting. It's just a soft, curious press of mouths, but it unlocks something inside of me.

She pulls back after the smallest of moments, and I push forward on my knees, digging them into her thigh before kissing her again. It's less curious and more confident, starting gentle but growing firmer as I realize that the sensation I'm feeling is interest.

A genuine romantic interest in Bryce that spreads far beyond the physical desire that's grown hopeless to ignore. It was so obvious, yet I'd ignored it. Three weeks and I've already lost any hope of keeping my heart out of this.

The sudden, steady grip on my waist pulls me out of my thoughts. I bump my nose against hers when I lean further into the kiss and throw my leg over her lap, keeping myself up on my knees.

"Just more practice," I whisper.

She pulls at my waist, and I jerk forward before collapsing onto her strong thighs, my knees giving out.

"Practice." The agreement is nothing more than a rasp.

Finally, I find something to do with my hands and place one around her bicep while the other returns to her hair, my nails scraping against her scalp.

Lips part against mine, and Bryce huffs a breath into my mouth. Her fingers tense on my jaw, and then they're cautiously drifting. Down my neck, over my rapid pulse, and to the hollow of my throat, she touches me with pressure so gentle it's nothing more than a ghost of the one she's applying to my waist.

I tremble under her touch, every inch of my body burning hotter and hotter the longer we kiss and she keeps her hands on me. The constant pressure of my nipples against the pads of my bra is nothing compared to the one between my legs. It takes everything in me not to adjust my position and ride her thigh so I can feel some reprieve.

She appears more in control than I am. Every innocent brush of her fingers over my skin is a piece of kindling thrown onto the flaming need in my every molecule, and I don't think she has any clue the extent of my desire.

The feeling of her nail drawing a line up the back of my ear is enough to yank a whimper from me. My hips roll, and I drag my lips down her chin and duck my head, shaking like a leaf.

"We've practiced enough. They'll know we've done it before," she says so softly I almost don't hear her.

I squeeze my eyes shut and freeze, almost wishing that I hadn't heard at all.

A myriad of emotions hits me as I slowly push back to my knees and swing off her. It's stupid to feel rejected. I was the one who said this was all for practice. She's just following the rules when I'm incapable of doing so.

That doesn't stop me from aching in a completely different way than I was a moment ago as I sit on the opposite side of the bed, keeping a healthy bit of space between us.

"I'm going to get you some more meds. Do you need anything else?" I ask, putting on a brave face.

"I'm okay."

Well, that makes one of us.

I swallow any and every potential reply and leave the room. It's a while before I come back. Not until I'm sure that Bryce is nearly asleep again, too tired to bring up what just happened and to realize that I've curled up on the armchair instead of the bed.

Where I stay for the rest of the night.

I thought the dark would have been helpful, but we may as well have been directly beneath the sun.

27

Bryce

Anna and Rory hog the majority of my bed and giggle over whatever they're looking at on the phone held between them. From the Brody Steele tour case on it, there's no chance it belongs to anyone besides Anna.

I touch the twin thin braids Anna insisted on doing under the pretense of helping keep my hair out of my face and watch the two of them in the mirror above my dresser. My best friend has been trying to get her hands on my hair for months now. I'm so out of it today that I finally gave in.

It's still undecided if that was a good or bad call.

"What are you giggling about?" I ask.

Rory answers without peeling her eyes from the screen. "Poppy is texting the group chat."

"Which one?"

"Titty Committee," Anna says.

Rory adds, "She's wondering if you and Daisy matched for today and if you're nervous to be meeting her parents."

"I've already met her parents."

But not like this.

My phone's lying face up on the dresser, yet the screen remains dark. I muted that group and Poppy personally shortly after she started using it as a way to bug me religiously about Daisy. The spam of messages was quite literally waking me up at night.

Poppy's the type of person who will slam her finger on the *Notify Anyway* option if you're trying to silence her. A full mute was the only way I managed to sleep the past three nights.

She didn't need me to tell her that Daisy had spent the weekend with me at my parents' house. Darren spilled it to her the moment I got back home and sent him an *I'm alive* text.

I'm ignoring him, too, because of it. The loudmouth.

Actually, there's a whole lot of ignoring people going on right now in our inner circle. Me and Poppy, me and Darren, and as of Sunday night, Daisy's been avoiding me.

I've never seen a bedroom door shut as often as hers has been since the moment we got back from my parents' place five days ago.

She hasn't noticed the new wicker basket in the living room that's currently overflowing with her blankets. The written list of songs from her playlist that I wrote out and slipped beneath her door went unnoticed, maybe even crumpled and tossed out.

I haven't been able to shake my discomfort for days. I've been home by dinnertime every night and have taken to refusing clients left and right because I know my absence had hurt her, and I'd rather not do that shit again. The only thing that's done for me is remind me what it feels like to eat dinner at the table alone every night.

Something feels wrong, but fuck, I don't want to think about the possible reasons for her pulling back. Not when the one at the forefront of my mind is that it was our kiss that ruined everything. That she hated it so much she's decided not to go through with this anymore.

We need to talk and air shit out before I go insane. This avoiding one another act we're both pulling is immature, and I'm ready for it to be over.

"She wants to know what you're wearing," Rory says, watching me in the mirror.

"Tell her to come here herself if she's so interested in my outfit."

Anna looks up next, worrying her lip. "Are things okay between you two?"

"Why wouldn't they be?"

"Well, you haven't really been talking to each other as much," Rory puts in.

"She's been gone."

Anna dumps the phone on the bed and perches on her knees, her hands cupping them. "It's okay if you're upset that she's gone, Bryce. I miss her too."

My throat tightens as I grip my phone and tuck it into the back pocket of my jeans. The sleeves of my black shirt reach my wrists, and the matching puffer vest Anna forced me into is constricting. She was very confident in her outfit advice, and I hadn't wanted to argue, given that I stood naked in my bathroom contemplating my life choices for twenty minutes. That's where she found me.

"I always knew she would outgrow this place. It's fine. I'm happy that she's happy," I say, fighting a flinch.

"Daisy's home, right? She's here?" Rory asks, changing the subject.

I shoot her an appreciative glance, even if Daisy isn't my ideal topic right now either.

From the first day we met Rory, I knew she was more like me than the other girls. Not only do we both have complicated familial relationships, but we're harder-walled than other people are.

Anna and Poppy are kind and thoughtful, but sometimes, they forget that not everyone is that way. There are some things I don't want to talk about, and being pushed to do so will only make me retreat further into myself.

It's nice to have both types of people in my life. I don't know what I did to deserve them, though.

"Yeah. She's somewhere," I answer.

Anna's brows climb her forehead. "Somewhere? Aren't we all going together?"

I turn away from them and shove my shirt sleeves up my forearms, needing to not feel so fucking covered. "She's in her room, Anna. I don't keep tabs on her every move."

"But you live together," she argues, tapping her knees. "I would have liked for her to be here with us. We could have gotten to know her a bit better."

My tongue burns from the dig of my teeth into it. I push away from the dresser and start digging through the pile of boots cascading out of my closet. The pair I constantly gravitate toward are missing, and my temper flares.

"If she wanted to be here for some kumbaya girl chat, she would have been, Anna. She's the one hiding away in her bedroom. I haven't locked her away like a fairy-tale princess," I snap, standing straight and tipping my head back before cursing under my breath.

A sharp inhale fills the room before Aurora clears her throat. "Alright, so, obviously there's some trouble there, then. And I'm guessing you don't want to talk about it?"

My jaw pulses from how hard I'm clenching my teeth. There's nothing right to say. It's all a giant mess of hurt and regret and this stupid fucking yearning sensation that's been driving me out of my goddamn mind for three years. I'm one breath from ripping my hair out of my skull from pure frustration.

Suddenly, I'm wishing the only person here was Poppy. The two women watching me right now have no idea that my relationship with Daisy isn't real. I can't talk to them about this. Not the truth of it.

"She's upset with me for something," I reveal cautiously.

Anna blinks, a soft smile appearing. "Have you apologized?"

"How can I apologize if I don't know what I did wrong?"

"You could go to her and ask. This barbeque is at her parents' house, Ice. Not to mention, it's supposed to be your first time meeting them as their daughter's girlfriend. Don't go into it with bad energy," she says.

Rory twists her mouth. "Hashing shit out right before leaving isn't always the right thing either, Anna. It could make things worse."

"Great. So, I'm fucked either way, then."

"You know, maybe *that's* the problem. Have you two been intimate at all?" Anna's question is innocent, but I physically reel from it.

Not out of anger but because I know deep down that that's the problem. Daisy's issue is me and what kissing me made her feel. Which was clearly nothing good. Talk about a sucker punch to the fucking gut.

"Let's go. I don't want to be late," I force out, snatching a random pair of boots from the floor.

My best friends jump off the bed and race after me, attempting to keep up with my furious pace. I keep my mouth shut, knowing if I open it again, I'm going to ruin everything that Daisy and I have done up to this point.

I'll expose the truth.

"Wait up, Bryce! I didn't mean to overstep. You've never shied away from talking about those things before, and I just didn't think it was different this time. I'm sorry."

Guilt slashes deep, leaving me with a gaping hole in my chest. "It's okay, Anna. I didn't mean to snap at you either."

She grabs me by my arm and tugs hard enough that I'm forced to spin to face her. My guilt transforms to annoyance before disappearing altogether.

It's not Anna holding me. The eyes that dig into mine with a startling familiarity belong to Daisy. I should have known from the searing warmth of her touch.

My pulse hammers. She's so close, so fucking pretty it hurts to look at her. To see the perfect image she makes in a pair of leggings and bright yellow blouse that she's hiding beneath a leather jacket.

The leather jacket I haven't been able to find since I offered it to her our first night at Peakside.

I don't realize that I've been fisting my hands until she takes one and pries it open.

"What's going on?"

The concern in her voice almost has me spilling everything to her, but it's not enough to make me forget what's been going on. How we went from sleeping in the same bed with her fingers running a constant path through my hair and having our first kiss in an exhausted haze under the pretence of practice to this utter silence. It's been jarring, to say the least.

"Where have you been?" I demand.

"I've been getting ready."

"Don't, Daisy. That's not what I meant, and you know it."

"Work was busy. I stayed late a few nights this week," she tries again.

"That's not good enough."

I shake free of her and lean against the wall before shoving my boots on. My socks have folded at my ankle, and I grip one, prepared to tug it back up, when I feel Daisy's attention slip. Her stare burns the skin of my ankle. The exact area where I got lost in my mind and inked a soft yellow daisy.

She folds an arm across her stomach, mouth falling open. "Is that a . . . daisy?"

I cover the tattoo with my sock and hide it further in my boot. I'm so close to lashing out at her, my emotions threatening to get the better of me for the second time today.

"Are you ready to go?" I ask through my teeth.

"Bryce."

"Daisy."

We're not alone, nor is she really my girl. If things were different, it wouldn't matter where we were—in the front hall with my friends nearby or in the safety of my bedroom—I'd have her spilling why she's pulled away from me with her legs spread and pussy oversensitive.

Honesty matters to me in a partner, and yeah, I know how much of a hypocrite that makes me. I've been hiding my feelings from her for years.

I thought I had patience in spades, considering the people I keep close to me, but when it comes to her, I'm barely hanging on by the thread that's been fraying day by day.

She sighs heavily and shifts on her feet. "So, we're going to pretend in front of my family, then? Is that the plan?"

Darting my eyes upward, I keep my mouth in a firm line. "You tell me, Sunshine. Pretending feels fitting, doesn't it?"

"Not like this."

Hurt twinkles in her eyes, but I don't allow it to wound me further. Instead, I kick her out from behind the steel wall in my mind and slam it closed in her face.

"I'll keep myself busy. I won't ruin all of your hard work this week and hang around you. We wouldn't have wanted it to be for nothing."

She hangs her head slightly and nips at the inside of her cheek before bending to grab her sneakers and putting them on in silence.

"Do you guys want to drive separately? Maybe we should go ahead of you," Anna offers, appearing at the end of the hall.

"No. I'm not planning on staying long. We'll go together," I mutter.

It's Aurora who slips past Anna and fixes me with an understanding gaze. "Together, then. I'll sit in the back with Bryce."

"What? You always call shotgun," Anna says.

Rory shrugs. "Not today."

Her words are the last ones I stay for. While everyone else puts on their shoes, I step out into the bitter afternoon and trample my emotions until I don't feel consumed by them.

It's always easier this way.

28

Bryce

The Mitchells' annual barbeque has been happening since I was a child. One day every summer, they host the entire town in their backyard and grill from sun-up to sundown. This year, they postponed it until the end of September and got lucky that the ground hasn't turned white yet.

We all arrive as a group, but Rory ditches us first, sneaking off to where Johnny's manning the smoking grill, smiling like a lunatic at Eliza Steele. Anna's next, blushing as Brody swoops in and ushers her away with an arm around her waist. At least the traitor has the thought to offer me a silent *sorry* over her shoulder whilst abandoning me.

"Giana is supposed to be here today," Daisy says, brushing her body up against mine.

I feign relaxation and press my palm to the centre of her back, too aware of the curious glances aimed our way not to give them something. "It's been a while since she's been at one of these."

"That's why the moms waited until now to have the barbecue. Once they heard Gi was coming home for a few days, they decided she had to be here. Mama hasn't stopped gushing about it for two weeks now."

I nod, finding a spot on the back fence to stare at. "They're all looking at us."

"Let them. We're ready."

"I wouldn't put it past my mother to show," I warn her.

Daisy's laugh sounds almost . . . devious. "You mean I'll have another chance to tell her how badly she's failed you? That doesn't sound so bad."

She's too at ease right now. Her effortless teasing and friend-liness are out of place, considering her actions this past week. It doesn't feel fake, and that's confusing me most of all.

As subtly as possible, I drop my hand from her back. Touching her isn't helping me keep myself sorted right now. Fuck a performance.

"I'll go get us something to drink," I mutter, taking a step forward to leave.

"Bryce." My name is nothing more than a puff of air on her lips.

It makes it impossible to move any further. "What?"

"We'll talk after, okay? Let's just get through the next couple of hours. Can you please stop pulling away from me until then?"

The hurt in her eyes smacks me across the face. But she's not the only one hurt, and I'm not the person to let my own feelings go unanswered. Never have been and never will be. It's better she learns that now before I get even more fucking obsessed with her.

"I'm just following your lead, Sunshine. I'll find you later."

And with that, I force myself to leave her there, alone and odds are, being the good girl she is, pretending nothing's wrong. It makes me feel like horse shit to know I've hurt her feelings and stolen her sunshine. Still, communication works both ways.

If she wants it from me, she has to be willing to put in the work too.

The four blue and white coolers set up beside the picnic table and between camping chairs are open, each one overflowing with ice and an assortment of drinks. I snatch a cold can of Fanta and frown when I notice the lack of boxed iced tea.

The two women on the chairs closest to me are trying way too hard to look like they're not staring, but I've been around my fair share of busybodies to know better. Pinning them beneath a cold stare, I raise my brows in a silent question.

The one with the platinum-blonde hair and seaweed-coloured eyes pales and laughs awkwardly while her friend ignores me altogether, growing the colour of a tomato.

With a huff, I bypass them and carry my drink into the house. Cherry Peak is a small town, which means everyone knows everyone. To an extent. Those two women were in my graduating class, but we've only spoken out of obligation in the past. The same can be said for the majority of those who live here.

If I had to speak to and know every single person who lived here the way someone like Eliza Steele enjoys doing, I'd have left a long fucking time ago.

The interior of Rachel and Jennifer Mitchell's house is the opposite of my parents' place. While their yard is a huge corner lot, the house itself isn't that big. It's spacious enough to have housed four kids, but they've made it appear larger with the way every room has been decorated for ease of use instead of appearances. A small breakfast nook cluttered with random papers and mismatched décor pieces, a dark-stained dining table for six with its fair share of dents and scrapes, and a massive fabric sectional in the living room that could easily fit all of them.

The abundance of childhood photos hung on the walls and placed in funky frames all over the kitchen counters, wooden shelves, and tables has always been hard for me to see at these parties purely out of jealousy. This time, however, it's a bit easier.

I'm glad that they're out in the open for me to look at. Daisy deserves to have a family who's so proud of her that they can't spare one inch of the wall or tabletop to be without a photo of her.

Having been inside the house more than a dozen times, I know they always keep iced tea boxes in the fridge for Daisy. When I open the door to find a similar stock to the one I've started keeping at home, I grab one and then head back outside.

The first person I see when I step onto the patio deck is my mother. Her natural scowl ensures the other partygoers give her a wide berth but in turn makes her look like a total cold-hearted bitch. It's a shame she shared that gene with me.

Past my mother's head, I catch a glimpse of deep red hair flying in the wind. When I shift my feet a step to the left, Daisy appears beneath the giant oak tree, rendering me speechless once again.

The laugh that bubbles out of her is wild and free, and the spread of her lips lights up the entire backyard. It hits me like a kick to the ribs that I'm not the one the reason behind either of those things. I want to be. So fucking badly.

My mood takes a nosedive once I look away from her and to the lucky soul who's gotten to be the recipient of her happiness.

Jealousy taints my mind like poison. It's an emotion meant for insecure idiots. But if that's really the case, then I'm both insecure *and* a giant fucking idiot.

Giana Mitchell stands beside Daisy, her head moving up and down as she nods along with what's being said. It's been a while since I've last seen her, but she looks the same. Short with flared hips and thighs and a freckled face that doesn't hide her disinterest, she's the tightest-strung of the Mitchell daughters, and I'd bet that has to do with her job. Spending every day every day with sweaty, arrogant men is my personal definition of hell. Especially when the majority of them know how attractive they are.

But Giana isn't why I'm feeling the way I am. It's the woman beside her that I don't recognize. The one who's watching my girl with a sincere interest that chafes.

Daisy holds simple, polite eye contact with her, and my grip on the box in my hand turns brutal. It crumples a beat later, the liquid inside gushing from the popped bottom. It soaks the tops of my boots and the grass surrounding them, making everything as sticky as my fingers.

I lower my eyes to the ruined box and glare at it with the fire of a thousand suns.

"Fuck," I mutter, stretching out my fingers around the cardboard.

With my attention stuck on the mess I've made, I block out all of the surprised, prying glances I can feel pricking my skin like a hundred tiny needles. I'll scold myself for this later, but right now, I'm too close to exploding. The walls are closing in around me despite the cool fall air I keep gulping into my lungs. It was a bad call to come today when I knew I was all fucked up inside.

"Was that for me?" Daisy asks, having snuck up on me.

I don't flinch in surprise despite not hearing her approach, and that's a great example of how close she's gotten to me emotionally. With a flex of my fingers around the ruined box, I meet her calm stare and say, "It's for the grass now."

"I see that."

"I'll get you another one."

She hums, low and soft. Her tongue wets her lips before she digs her teeth into the lower one. I lean forward on my toes, a magnetic force yanking me closer to her. Even my brain says to back up.

"Thank you, but I'm craving the taste now."

"Wha—"

I gawk at her, the word disappearing into thin air when she uses a soft touch to lift my hand between us. She takes the ruined box from me and then brings my fingers to her lips, holding them there for a long, weighted moment before pushing two into her mouth.

Her tongue flicks out and wraps around the tip of the digit before sliding down the sides and over to the next. Then, with her eyes slashing into mine, she pushes both fingers further into her mouth and sucks.

A dimple appears when she smirks around my fingers and releases them with a pop. "Your mom wants to murder me and bury me in the mountains."

I think I'm the one buried in the mountains. Twenty feet below the surface where air no longer exists.

"I could have used a napkin," I croak, speaking without thinking.

She winks, and there's something so vibrant and alive in the simple act. "I like my way better, but we can always go find you one after."

"After what?"

A small, sly smile transforms her expression as she glances from me to the space behind me and back again. "This."

Her hands cup my cheeks, and then she's bringing her lips to the corner of my mouth, to the same spot she kissed me in my dream.

I slam my eyes shut and immediately allow myself the time to soak in the feeling of her lips on mine once again. It's different than the full press of her mouth that night, where my mind jolted awake after hours of dozing and my very bone marrow sang with bliss. But it's still just as right.

Her thumb strokes the curve of my cheek, and I shudder at the care behind the touch. My heart flutters, the ache behind my ribs disappearing. She lingers when her lips part. The kiss should end now, but neither of us moves.

I open my eyes, and suddenly, it's as if the past week never happened. Somehow, we've closed the gap between us, and every molecule in my body screams at me to take it just one step further. After tonight, it could be the last time I'll ever have the chance to.

Driven by pure instinct, I drop the box to the ground and move. Her hair is so soft between my fingers when I shove both my hands into the thick mane of it and use the hold to guide her head back. She doesn't pull away from me, even as she trembles in my arms and reaches up to touch my wrist, as if she needs the contact for stability.

A tease of the pupil-blown eyes beneath her fluttering lashes steals my next words. With a steadying breath, I bring my mouth to hers in a full, time-halting kiss.

It's a silent declaration from me to her that if given the chance, I'd do this every minute of every day for the rest of time. I wouldn't need anything else. No wealth or success. I'd toss my tattoo guns off the top of a snow-peaked mountain for the chance to kiss her like this even once more, let alone the rest of my life.

There's too much to say and not enough time to say it. We're not there yet, and I don't know if we ever will be. Calling Daisy Mitchell mine is a dream that I never planned on coming true but always hoped would.

She tightens her grip on my wrist and steps forward, the toes of our shoes touching. The firm press of her lips on mine grows more frantic as she takes control and releases a soft sigh.

It's as close to a moan as I've ever heard from her, and it drives me to utter insanity. I have to tear my mouth away before she winds up with her back against that oak tree and my touch between her legs.

"Daisy," I whisper, pressing my fingertips against her scalp.

Her eyes appear dazed and glossy when she lifts her lashes. I don't have to look in the mirror to know mine are just as lost.

I'm forced out of my haze when she blinks back to reality and shakes off my touch. Red blotches appear on her neck before drifting up her cheeks and the tip of her nose. Her smile is the fakest I've ever seen her wear. It's somehow worse than the one I saw in my bedroom after our first kiss.

Confusion punches me in the chest, and I don't keep quiet about it this time. "What just happened?"

"Not here, Bryce," she pleads.

"Yes, here. I'm real fucking done with the disappearing act. You're not going to do it to me again."

She crosses her arms and leans backward in an adorable attempt at an aggressive stance. "If you get to pull away from me every time we kiss, then I get to disappear on you afterward."

"What are you talking about?" I ask, tightening my gaze as my heartbeat stutters.

"I'm so stupid to think that this time would have been any different . . ."

I press a finger to her mouth, and she stops speaking, that spark of anger igniting into an out-of-control wildfire.

"My mom is coming," I whisper, grazing her temple with my knuckle. For a second time, she subtly shakes my touch away, and my pussy tightens in excitement.

Fuck, I love when she gets angry with me and lets her fiery spirit out to play. Even if it should piss me off.

"You're not off the hook. We'll be talking about what you've apparently convinced yourself of. Even if I already know you're so fucking off base," I add before giving her another inch of space.

My mother tears up the grass on her way to where we stand, and knowing that the reason behind her anger is the best kiss I've experienced in my entire goddamn life?

It tastes almost as sweet as my sunshine.

29

Daisy

"Qu'est-ce que tu fais? C'est pas l'endroit pour ça."

Bryce rolls her eyes and faces her mother. Like wiping marker off a whiteboard, she erases the entirety of her teasing demeanour with a single blink.

I wish it were that easy for me to let my feelings go. It's already taking more than enough effort not to draw her back to me and kiss her again. Pretending to be completely unbothered in the face of her mother's approaching wrath isn't possible.

Keeping my arms crossed to form a boundary between me and the woman I desperately want to touch, I steel my spine.

"You didn't tell me you would be here, Mom," Bryce drones.

"Was I not welcome? Is this not your Daisy's childhood home?"

Her Daisy.

"Of course you're welcome here, Claudine." It's Mama who speaks, joining us with Mom in tow.

Claudine pauses and then quickly tucks her hair behind her ears, her posture erect in a prim and proper way.

"Hello, Rachel." Her smile is small but honest, taking me by surprise. "Jennifer."

Mama settles beside me and rubs my back in a show of silent

support. "I'm glad you decided to join us today. Both me and Jen have been wanting to meet with you now that our daughters have found each other."

It's Mom who speaks next, her tone a bit sharper as her eyes fall on me. "Although, we sure would have loved to hear about their relationship from them instead of through the grapevine. It was quite a surprise when *Josette* called to let us know."

Josette's sitting in one of the camping chairs with her head back and eyes closed, completely naive to the silent promise I make to get her back for this.

I jut my bottom lip out just enough for Mom's glare to weaken. "I was planning on doing it today."

"Oh, I had no doubt about that," Mama reassures me.

Leaning into her side, I give her a quick hug that she returns immediately. Bryce is making an obvious effort to not look my way now that Claudine appeared, and I release my mom when I catch her shifting awkwardly.

It's instinct and a drive to soothe that has me reaching for Bryce and taking her hand, interlocking our fingers. She squeezes me so hard that I have to hide my wince, but I don't for one second contemplate releasing my hold.

"I don't know about you, Claudine, but I think my heart nearly exploded just now when I saw them together. It's been a long while since I've seen our Daisy girl look so enamoured by someone," Mama gushes.

Her statement takes me by surprise. Not because of how observant she is, but because I didn't know I had been so obvious. Has Bryce noticed? Is it playing a part in why she's always the first to break our kisses? To set a boundary?

I flush with embarrassment and stumble over my next words. "Don't be so dramatic, Mama."

"She's only being honest. The both of you look very happy together," Mom says, her eyes soft as she stares at me.

Bryce seems to snap out of whatever thoughts she was trapped within and flashes a close-lipped smile. For a reason that

I won't deny stems from my rapidly growing possessive instinct, I'm glad it wasn't a toothy grin. I want those to be for me and nobody else.

Her palm is slick against mine when she lifts the back of my hand to her lips and drifts them across my knuckles. The hint of a spark in her gaze lights me up inside. "I won't speak for Daisy, but I'm happier than I've ever been."

It sounds so real. So believable. My mind runs laps trying to figure out how it's so easy for her to say these things and convince my silly heart it's the truth.

"Me too," I whisper, not caring if anyone but her hears.

Claudine clears her throat and fusses with her hair again. "I do not know yet. It feels so sudden."

My breathing stutters. Bryce brings our hands to her chest, appearing unbothered. I search her face for any tell that she's surprised by her mother's comment or her lack of belief in our relationship, but her every thought and emotion are hidden behind an impenetrable wall.

"Believe what you want. It won't change anything," she says coolly.

Mom stares at her for a long, silent second before the corner of her mouth tugs up, and she nods in approval. The wink she shoots me has me huffing a laugh.

The look she gives Claudine, however, is not as lighthearted. It's safe to say that her Mama Bear instincts have been awoken.

"Ultimately, we will always choose to believe and support our daughter. Even if I couldn't see what I am with my own eyes, I still wouldn't voice my doubt. Daisy has always been very sure of herself, and from the way we know Bryce, I'm confident that she is the same way. If not even a little more headstrong."

Mama nods along with her wife. "We are very happy for the two of you. Hopefully, you'll come by again soon so we can get to know you a bit more, Bryce?"

Bryce doesn't hesitate. "Just say when."

My stomach flutters, and I blink to fight the sting behind my eyes. Maybe I'm close to getting my period, but her certainty hits me too deep. It picks at the scabs that have grown over the rejection and doubt I've been struggling with, making every wound fresh and sensitive.

As subtly as possible, I pull my fingers from Bryce's and paste a smile on my face. "I just remembered that I have to make a phone call this afternoon. I'll be right back."

It's a miracle my voice doesn't shake as I lie. My moms don't stop me as I head for the house, keeping my emotions hidden beneath a mask of nonchalance.

I don't wait to hear if Bryce has stayed, and I tell myself that it doesn't matter if she has. I'm not her real girlfriend, so she's not obligated to check on me.

Once I pass the kitchen, the rest of the house is empty. Everyone's too busy enjoying one of our last few days of semi-warm weather to bother with hiding inside.

Muscle memory guides me to my old bedroom, and I grip the door handle with a sweaty palm. With a swing, I send the door cutting through the air. Something smacks against it, and the force stops it in its tracks.

My eyes widen as Bryce sidesteps the door and enters my room with tension lining her every movement. I take two steps back, putting space between us that I don't want. She narrows her eyes on my legs and closes the door, sealing us alone inside my room.

"They're going to think something's wrong now that you've followed me," I ramble.

"I'm going to be honest with you, Daisy," she begins, slowly dragging those piercing, angry eyes up my body until they dig into my face. "I don't fucking care."

My chest tightens to the point of pain, and I rub at it with the heel of my hand. "What's wrong?"

"You first."

"I'm not the one who looks ready to rip someone's throat out, Bryce."

Her jaw tenses. "I want to rip something apart, Daisy, but it isn't your throat."

"What do you mean?"

"Tell me what's wrong first. And don't leave out the part where you explain the reasoning behind your disappearing act this week," she demands.

My cheeks pulse with their own heartbeat. "You want to have this conversation at my parents' house?"

She shrugs a shoulder. "We could have had it at home days ago, but you chose to avoid me instead."

"You've avoided me before, too, in case you've forgotten."

Her lips curl in a smug smile. "So you admit you were avoiding me, then."

"I'm not in the mood for sarcasm," I snap.

"Oh? What are you in the mood for then? Honesty? Because I sure as fuck am."

Her lean legs eat up the space I created between us, and then she's right in front of me, her hot, quick exhales caressing my nose. My swallow is audible, the only sound in the room besides our heavy breathing.

"You want honesty, yet you don't tell me that you don't want me to kiss you or that you aren't comfortable with it. I asked you for your boundaries weeks ago, Bryce. You told me you had none, yet every time we kiss, I'm the one left feeling guilty afterward! Like I've taken advantage of you or forced you into something you'd rather never do."

I've never seen her look so surprised, so much so that she stumbles back a step as her wide eyes blink rapidly.

Then, she's laughing. It's a low, hoarse sound that scrapes down my skin in a downright delicious, sexy way despite the cool meaning behind it. I'm a breath from begging her to laugh like that again when my head empties, only the drone of white noise remaining.

With a firm yet gentle grip, she grabs my hand, tugs her shirt down, and presses the bull's horn on her chest. Her gaze is demanding, so completely focused on me that for a brief moment, I fear she's actually stripped my skin off and can see all of my interior pieces and where she could fit between them.

"Stop thinking and *feel*, Daisy." The order is soft but leaves no room for argument.

"Feel what?"

Oh.

The fierce pounding sensation against my palm is so obvious I should have noticed it instantly. My eyes fall to where my hand lies between her breasts, and I spread my fingers slightly, enamoured by how warm and smooth her skin is.

"It's racing," I whisper.

She strokes the pulse in my wrist that has to be just as wild. "Every time you look at me, touch me, or speak to me, this is what I feel, Daisy. Sometimes, it beats so fast that I've imagined it giving out because there's no way it should be able to keep up with such a fucking disbelieving pace for hours on end."

"Why are you telling me this?" I ask, trying desperately to piece it together myself but failing. "I'm really trying not to speak out of place here, but this isn't funny. If you're joking, or think I'll be okay with pretending in private, or saying things that we don't mean just to, what? Learn how to behave as the characters we're playing in public? I'm not. I'm really, really not."

Tucking loose pieces of hair behind my ear, she traces the shell of it. I shiver, and she does it a second time, testing my reaction. This time when my body shakes, she cups the back of my head and holds me steady.

"For someone so fucking smart, Daisy, you've done a great job of jumping right over my explanation and creating one of your own."

I try to pull free of her again, but she doesn't let me go this time. One strong tug and we're even closer, her nose bumping mine on purpose.

"The next time you try and pull away from me, I'm going to tie you to that frilly pink bed of yours and keep you there for as long as it takes for you to understand what I'm saying," she warns.

"And then what?" I'm so breathless it's more of a moan than a dare.

"Don't push me."

Anticipation zips up my spine, an electric buzz building in my veins. "If I don't, then who will?"

Her grin is playful but with a dangerous edge. A recipe for disaster that I'm suddenly starving to try.

"Sit on the bed for me, and I'll explain a few things to you, Sunshine," she coaxes, the pet name making my toes curl into the plush carpet.

My limbs are heavy with anticipation as I follow her instructions and perch on the edge of the mattress, spine straight and head high.

Having shed her vest someplace between the back door and my bedroom, she's in only a tight long-sleeve and jeans. Slowly, with a calm sense of control, she slides the sleeves up her forearms, exposing the endless swirls of designs previously hidden.

My attention lingers on the tattoos before drifting up the length of her arms and to the tight stretch of fabric spread across her chest. It's still moving as rapidly as when it was beneath my palm.

"You have an impressive imagination, Daisy," she says, prowling to the bed.

"Is that so?"

A dirty smirk. "Yeah, it is."

"Explain how."

"You want me to explain so many things. Where exactly do you want me to start?"

"From the beginning," I answer instantly.

She pauses, and I only worry for half a second that I've pushed too hard before she continues toward me. I spread my legs without thinking twice about it, and she settles against the stretching fabric of my skirt with a similar lack of hesitation.

"Remind me where the beginning is," she murmurs.

Eyes falling to watch my mouth, she sets her hands on either side of my body and bends down. I lean back at the same time, allowing her to guide me down on the mattress. My heart rate spikes when I realize I'm lying beneath her.

She's gone in a blink, standing over me with this . . . this feral dominance that has my panties damp and sticking to my pussy. My chest is heaving so hard I lose sight of her behind it.

"The beginning, baby. Remind me where that is," she repeats herself.

It's impossible to answer when I feel the first tease of her fingers on my hip. Every hair on my body rises as I tremble in anticipation of her next touch.

It's lower. So, so much lower. A hot palm cups my ankle, and I gasp. It doesn't move any higher.

"Admit you were jealous of me being out in the middle of the night," she says, realizing I'm in no shape to be starting this conversation.

At this point, is it even going to be a conversation? Because right now, I'll be more than happy to let it go as long as she doesn't stop touching me. We can figure everything out afterward.

I dig my elbows into the mattress and push myself up enough to meet her gaze as she kneels in front of me. The soft fabric of my dress is long enough to hide where her hand remains on my ankle.

"What do I get in return?" I ask on a shaky exhale.

Interest sparks in her eyes despite her blank stare. "What makes you think you'll get anything?"

"We can both get something. A truth for a reward."

"Fine."

"Fine?"

She hums low in her throat. "Don't make me change my mind."

I nod once and pinch the collar of my shirt, hating how restricting it feels in this moment.

"Yes, I was jealous. I never saw you, and I wanted to," I admit.

She listens with intense focus, soaking in every word before pushing her hand up my leg. Her arm disappears beneath my skirt, and she sweeps her thumb across the sensitive skin of my inner thigh once she stops inching higher.

"Why would you ever think that you've forced me into anything?" she asks next, halting her movements.

I frown. A blistering puddle of want has flooded my core, and it poisons my thoughts, making me more agitated by her lack of exploration. Even as I spread my legs and stretch my skirt to the point of risking a tear, she doesn't touch me further.

"That's two questions for me and none for you," I state tightly.

"Just ask me what you want. Don't wait for approval first. You already have it."

"Were you jealous when you found out Kiki was in my room?"

It's not what I should have asked first. If she changes her mind and takes away my ability to have a question answered, I'll have wasted an opportunity to learn about more important topics. But in this moment, I need to know this more.

"Her name is Kristen when I'm between your legs, Daisy," she scolds, her eyes digging into mine with blunt possession.

I roll my lip between my teeth, arousal blossoming with her words. "You're not really between my legs."

"Is that where you want me to be?" she purrs before a rush of cool air envelops my opposite ankle. Another inch of my skin is bared as the skirt rises further. "Would you like me to push your skirt up to your hips?"

"Answer me first."

Fire lines her eyes, and I fear I love their heat on my skin too much to ever go back to a time without it.

"Yes, I was fucking jealous."

A thrill runs through my chest and between my legs. "Take your reward, then."

"This is my reward."

I furrow my brows. "What?"

She doesn't answer with words. One minute, my skirt is draping over her arm, and the next, it's scrunched at my hips. I'm bare from the waist down except for my thin, sheer pink panties. From the cool breeze between my legs, I know I've soaked them completely.

"If you want to reward me, Daisy, offer me a taste of this pussy."

My elbows give out, and I fall down to the mattress with a whimper. It's both approval and an outright plea. I dig my toes into the carpet and push my legs even further apart, offering her exactly what she wants.

"Take more than a taste, Bryce. Please," I moan, writhing beneath her gaze.

My breasts are heavy, nipples beaded and tight to the point of pain as they rub against the padding of my bra.

"I'm not done with you. Not by a long fucking shot. But if I don't get my mouth on you right now, I'm going to lose it, baby."

"Please," I whine, struggling to breathe. "I ache, Bryce . . . please take it away."

Spitting a curse, she curls her fingers beneath the sopping wet fabric of my panties and tugs them to the side, exposing me completely. One puff of her breath on me and I'm curling upward off the bed and gasping.

My eyes roll back at the first swipe of her tongue over my slick skin. A second follows before she shuffles closer and spreads me with two fingers. I'm exposed in the most intimate way, and I'm at peace with that. It feels right, like Bryce is the one I'm supposed to be here with.

"Look at you," she whispers while tracing the shape of my entrance with a gentle finger. "So wet you're dripping onto the carpet."

I moan at the dirty words and spread my arms out on the bed. I've always been vocal in bed, but not usually with words.

I'm powerless to the sounds she yanks from deep in my soul when she licks me again, this time going slow enough to explore and learn what I like best. Circling my tightening hole with the tip of her tongue, she hums and then slicks her finger up with my arousal. She eases it inside, and I lurch up on the bed, grabbing her hair in a savage hold.

She groans, eyes flicking upward, immediately finding mine. Holding my gaze, she pumps her finger inside of me and swirls her tongue around my clit once before flicking it gently.

"Fuck!" I shout, tugging her hair so hard I'm surprised she doesn't cry out in pain.

"You like my tongue on your clit, baby? That feels good for you?"

"Yes! Yes, do it again. Please," I beg, a powerful release already prowling beneath the surface.

"Tell me why you think I don't want to kiss you."

My face crumples with disappointment. "Please, Bryce."

She stops everything, and I cry out, bucking up to try and relieve the pressure inside of me.

I blow out a breath. "Because you pull away and hide your emotions from me the moment we're done. The night you were sick, you reminded me it was just practice. It was like I was the only one who wanted something more and wasn't satisfied with only a few minutes."

Two fingers slide inside of me, and then she's dragging the length of her tongue over my clit and stroking it with a rewarding, consistent pressure. Bliss rolls through my body, transporting me to another universe.

"You have no idea how wrong you are."

"So tell me, then." My voice cracks and morphs into a cry when she curls her fingers to stroke deep and high.

The pace of her licks picks up, and then she's flicking my clit quick enough for my vision to flash with white. Everything happens so fast. I arch off the bed, and Bryce plunges her fingers faster, skilled in the way she never loses my G-spot despite my frantic squirming.

The bed could disappear beneath me, and I wouldn't notice. Not when an orgasm the strength of a world-splitting earthquake sends me soaring high above it.

Yet even as my brain melts and resolidifies in a matter of seconds, I don't miss her next words, and I've never been so grateful for anything ever.

"If I wasn't the one to pull away, I'd have kept you trapped in my bed with me for hours, kissing you until your lips were swollen and sore. I wasn't reminding you that it was just practice. I was reminding myself because if for even one minute I let myself believe otherwise, this fake agreement would be done, and you'd be gone before I'd even had you for one real moment."

30

Bryce

I THOUGHT I WAS OBSESSED WITH DAISY WELL ENOUGH BEFORE today. Thought I knew everything I needed to and was content with taking my time to learn the rest. But now, after sharing this moment with her, I realize that I had no fucking idea how obsessed I could become.

The taste of her sweet pussy lingers on my tongue as I busy myself with kissing and stroking her inner thighs, soothing her through the comedown from her orgasm.

I'll never forget this first one. Every cry and whimper and plea for more has been etched in my goddamn soul. I'm anxious to collect more of them, slowly, quickly, anywhere and everywhere.

It's not the time, though. Fuck, it wasn't the time ten minutes ago either, but that didn't stop me from falling to my knees and feasting on her tight, wet pussy the first chance I had.

Every word I spoke while she thrashed against my tongue hangs suspended above us. An invisible clock counts down the moments left before we're forced to revisit them.

My eyelids droop as I nuzzle my cheek against her thigh and palm her hip bone, touching her with a need that I feel all the way in my bones. I'm tangled up inside, so aroused that even just existing in the same space as her without touching myself is a struggle.

The fingers that were threatening to rip my hair clean from my scalp have relaxed and now stroke the sore places and guide me through the fog of need.

"Did you mean all of that?" she whispers.

"Which part?"

"All of it."

There's no going back now. I'm not diminishing the weight of my words. Not after this.

"Yeah, Sunshine. I meant all of it."

The bed shifts beneath her weight, and then she's sitting on the edge of it, staring down at me with such an honest, open expression. It's who she is, my Daisy. Trusting and kind without judgment. There's no doubt in my mind that if she decided to turn me away, she would still be gentle with her words. Even if she was struggling with doing so.

"Have you felt that way for long?" she asks, the apples of her cheeks burning a bright red.

I hesitate to tell her the full truth. It's never stopped making me feel guilty, and right now, if I admitted that I've been interested in her for years instead of the weeks she's expecting to hear, I won't be able to handle it ruining anything. I've come so close to making her mine, and it feels too good to be true to take even just one more risk.

"A couple of weeks," I say instead.

"So, from before we kissed the first time?"

I turn my face inward and press my lips to her thigh a final time while moving her panties back in place. With a hold on both her knees, I push to my feet. Her skirt is soft in my hands as I lower it over her legs.

She watches with a wide grin as I fuss over her, going as far as to smooth down her hair and wipe away the smudge of mascara below her wet lashes.

"I've wanted to kiss you for a while, Daisy. Before you

brought up the idea of practicing. I'm sorry that I made you feel like I didn't want you."

She shakes her head. "Don't apologize. I let myself overthink and, like you said earlier, convinced myself of something completely off base. Clearly, I'm lacking in relationship knowledge after so long without one."

"So am I. My last one was a total sham, so I guess we both have to relearn everything."

"We're a mess," she teases, reaching for my hand and yanking me onto the bed beside her.

"What happens now?" It's a blunt question, but after waiting so long for this, I don't want to spend any more time wondering.

"We keep doing what we're doing. Nobody will know anything we don't want them to. I'd really like to take the time to get to know you more, Bryce," she murmurs, leaning her head against my shoulder and holding on to my arm.

"Is that your way of saying that you feel the same way I do?"

Her smile is wide enough I feel it against my shoulder. "You mean in the keeping you in my bed for hours and kissing you until your lips are swollen and sore way?"

I breathe a laugh and kiss her hair. "Exactly."

"Yes, Frosty, I do," she admits gently.

"No more disappearing, then."

"That goes for you too."

"I haven't bothered with disappearing in a while."

Her nails dig into my arm as she tightens her hold. "I'm sorry."

"Don't be. Just don't do it again unless you want me to shout your name all over town looking for you."

"I was with Kiki. It's the place I go when I need to think."

"Not your parents' place?"

"Sometimes. But not with this. I needed them to see us together like they did in the yard for them to believe it. If I had shown up here with the way I was feeling before, Mama would have read right through the fake status, and I would have had to tell her the truth."

"You could tell her the truth. If it upsets you to lie."

She drapes her legs over my lap, and my eyebrows jump at the surprisingly confident move. "No, it's okay. If I tell one of my moms, they'll tell the other, and then before we know it, my sisters know, and Johnny's plowing your door down to tell the both of us off for deceiving him."

"Your brother doesn't scare me, Daisy."

"That's because nothing scares you."

I choke on a scoff. "Plenty of things scare me."

"Like what? Don't tease me with this! I'm desperate to know what makes the ice queen shiver in fear."

I lean away from her, making sure she's looking at me before scowling. "I don't shiver in fear of anything."

She rolls her eyes dramatically. "Mhm, if you say so. Now, spill!"

"I don't like when my feet touch the bottom material of a pool."

A long, stagnant pause, and then a laugh explodes from her mouth. "Are you being serious?"

"Make fun of me, Daisy, I dare you," I warn, attempting to sound threatening, but the humour in my tone is a massive give-away that it's a façade. "And stop laughing."

"I'm just . . . what material exactly? The bumpy kind in an in-ground pool or the slick plastic from a pop-up?"

I shiver. "You're having too much fun with this."

She holds my stomach, leaning close, body shaking with bright laughter. "I'm sorry! I wasn't expecting something so mundane to be what scares you. If it makes you feel better, I don't like bodies of water."

"That's not the only thing, smartass, but I'm not telling you anything else until you tell me what you're afraid of. Truly *afraid* of."

Sobering slightly, she nods. "Okay, okay. Well, I think out of everything, I'm most terrified of running out of time."

"In what way?"

"Like, imagine if you had this entire list of things you wanted to accomplish before you died, and instead of making the effort to start crossing them off, you kept putting it off further and further until you woke up one day and realized that you'd wasted too much time. You kept telling yourself that you'd send that text to catch up with a friend tomorrow or that you'd accept that date invite next weekend, then before you knew it, you've grown apart from your friend, and you're spending another night in your bed alone.

"My mama used to tell me that everything that's supposed to happen will happen eventually, but Johnny was the twin who believed in fate and all those shiny things we're told as children. I've always known that if you want something, you need to be the one to take the steps to make it happen. Good things happen to good people, yes, but that doesn't mean you don't have to chase them. So, yeah, I guess my biggest fear is getting too comfortable in the life that I have and forgetting that there's more out there waiting for me. I just have to put in the effort to find it and take it for myself."

"Here I am talking about pool floors, and you go and drop that? Christ, Daisy, you're too good for the likes of me," I mutter, her words banging around in my mind.

She laughs that wind chime laugh, and I melt. "Not at all, actually. I might not believe in everything Johnny and my moms do, but I've never not believed that opposites attract. It's science, as far as I'm concerned."

"And you think we're opposites?" I ask.

She scoots from the mattress to my lap, making a home for herself in the arms I wrap around her. With her head nestled against my collarbone, she traces the black lines at the base of my throat.

"Yes, but in the best way. If we were too similar, I don't think we'd be here right now."

I rub her arm, soaking in the way the simple contact soothes the strike of fear that follows her statement. It's there and gone before I can examine it fully.

"You're right. My relationship with Vic was never meant to last, considering we were almost the exact same person."

Daisy straightens slightly, her head lifting so we can look at one another. "I don't remember her much from before I left for Calgary. You weren't together then, right?"

"No. It was a couple months afterward and lasted just shy of a year. By the time Anna moved to town, we'd been broken up for a few months."

"For what it's worth, I'd have broken his dick too."

A smile rips my lips apart. "So, you do know what happened, then. I wasn't sure."

"I think everyone in Cherry Peak knows what happened, Frosty. It's not every day someone breaks a guy's dick in the supermarket parking lot and gets driven away in the back of an RCMP car. Kristen called to tell me about it in the middle of one of my classes."

My smile slowly falls as the heavier part of the story comes tumbling free. "She'd been cheating on me for months. I figured she was, but I was too headstrong to call her out on it, only to be wrong. When I did find out . . . I might have overreacted."

"It's too late to go back and change your actions now. If you could, would you?"

I roll a couple of answers around on my tongue before going with my gut. "No. The prick deserved it."

She beams, eyes twinkling. "Yeah, that's what I figured. My girl's vicious when she wants to be."

"Your girl?" I rasp.

I've never had such an obvious claim laid to me by someone before, let alone a woman whom I've wanted to claim as my own for a long fucking time.

Her confident smile doesn't waver. Not for a single second.

"Yes, Bryce. My girl. In here and out there and everywhere in between. If that's okay with you, of course."

"More than, Sunshine."

31

Daisy

"SEE YA, MS. MITCHELL!"

"Bye!"

"Have a good afternoon, guys. See you tomorrow!" I reply, waving at the cluster of second graders as they speed off down the halls, backpacks flopping against their backs.

A few still linger at their cubbies, but they've stopped paying much attention to those around them, myself included. After a long day, I'm just as ready to get out of here as they are.

Heading back into my classroom, I smile softly. This job is tiring and stressful, but it's also incredibly fulfilling. I remember being in elementary and middle school and hating every single day of it. Until the eleventh grade, I had no idea that I wanted to become a teacher.

It was a sudden desire that sideswiped me and the goals and dreams I thought I had. I swerved off the path I had previously been set on, and on a day like today, I'm really grateful for that hit.

My book bag is already on my desk when I begin filling it with my scattered papers and laptop. For the last three days, I've been buzzing by the end of every school day, antsy to get finished so I can see Bryce.

Ever since our conversation and . . . *actions* in my old bedroom, things have been different in the best way. Neither of us seem interested in going back to how things were before. We've been spending every moment we can together, just taking the time to enjoy the pace we're moving. It's slow but steady.

My hunt for a new place is non-existent. I gave up browsing after the first week of me staying at Bryce's place, and starting to look again now feels wrong. If I find one, what would be my excuse to stay? We might have made some progress in the romance department, but I don't think Bryce is the type of person to move that quickly.

Living together now is different. It wasn't a decision that stemmed from a previous relationship. Risking changing anything now when we're still on such fragile ice and I've begun to get to know this woman on such a fundamental level isn't a priority.

Slowly, I've started picking up on all of these new little habits and quirks she has that I hadn't before. Like how she never leaves a dirty dish in the sink, and if she finds one that I've forgotten about, she's instantly squirting soap into it and washing it thoroughly before drying it and putting it away. Or the way she's started to fill the fridge with all of the foods and beverages that I've mentioned loving at one time or another.

Half of the fridge is full of my favourite brand of boxed iced tea, and she's even started adding the peach-flavoured kind because I said I wanted to try it once after seeing a commercial for it on TV. And even though I've never seen her eat stringed cheese, there's an entire bulk-sized box of them in the bottom drawer. I take two every day to work.

My collection of throw blankets is now always rolled perfectly into a wicker basket in the corner of the living room, save for my favourite yellow one that's found a permanent home draped over the back of the couch.

Bryce is a giver. She's the kind of person who makes up for her blunt words and sometimes cold demeanour with thoughtful actions in a space she deems safe. But even considering her cold for one moment feels wrong after getting to know her these weeks.

She's not cold. It may come off like that to some, but she's just guarded. And with a family like hers, how can anyone blame her for that? I've enjoyed pushing past her boundaries and getting to see the parts of her not many get to.

There's a knock on the door, and I turn from my desk to where Delaney is waiting. She's looking very fall today with a burnt-orange, plaid T-shirt dress and brown boots. I flash her a grin and wave her inside.

"Are you heading out?" I ask, zipping up my bag.

"Just about. We haven't had a chance to chat this week, so I just wanted to stop by before I left and ask if you were up to grabbing lunch together tomorrow? Unless you have plans, of course."

"I'd love to, Della."

She taps a hand to the brown bag draped over her shoulder. "Great. I'll see you tomorrow, then . . ."

Her words trail off, something catching her eye from the hallway. Hope swells in my chest at who could be showing up here now.

The sight of Bryce passing by Delaney in the doorway has my world brightening. She fixes her dark stare on me and doesn't remove it as she crosses the classroom. I'm grinning like a fool despite the warning in her eyes by the time she reaches me and hauls me into her arms, placing her lips on mine.

It's the first kiss I've gotten since Sunday. Yet, it's a completely different breed. This is more for Delaney than it is for either of us. Bryce is making a statement, and I'm completely weak in the knees by it. It's an unnecessary claiming, but she doesn't know that, and I'm not going to tell her. Not if by keeping quiet, she'll keep her warm lips pressed to mine for a few moments longer, making sure I know that I'm as much hers and she is mine, with or without the labels.

Feeling a bit devilish, I let loose a soft ghost of a moan that I know she hears and maybe even feels when she sinks her teeth into my lip and bites down gently. My smile tugs at the hold she has on my lip.

She releases it and taps a finger beneath my chin. "Those noises are only for me."

"I missed you today," I tease, ignoring her comment.

Eyes fluttering open, I notice hers are already watching me, the fluorescent lights above us intensifying their blue.

"I missed you too."

"Say hi to my friend, Frosty."

She scowls. "I want to take you somewhere."

"You can take me anywhere after you say hi."

Delaney clears her throat behind me, and I giggle at the deeply etched scowl lines that appear on Bryce's face.

While we break apart from the intimate hold, she refuses to let me out of her arms completely. As if I wanted the space in the first place.

"Hello, Delaney," Bryce mutters, her hold on me tight enough that concern slips through the shine of bliss.

My friend stares at Bryce and offers her a weak smile. "Bryce."

"Della was just inviting me to lunch tomorrow," I put in.

Bryce's fingers splay wide over my hip, and her thumb strokes the bare skin beneath my shirt. She keeps Delaney pinned beneath a distrusting stare. "What grade are you teaching?"

"Third."

Bryce nods, relaxing a bit. Her attention falls on me, and I soak it up like a cat beneath summer sun rays. "Ready to go?"

"Are you going to tell me where we're going?"

"No."

Pouting, I break free of her hold and reach for my book bag. She beats me there, hooking it over her shoulder and jutting her chin toward the door.

"Don't pout. You'll like where we're going."

"I'm sure I will," I agree with a sigh.

Bryce shakes her head, the ghost of a smile toying at her lips.

The three of us step into the hall. It's empty now, all of my students' cubbies bare and lockers shut. I take Bryce's hand in mine and settle between the two women.

Awkward silence falls when neither Bryce nor Della makes an effort to speak. To one another or to me. It's obvious there's something going on there, but I don't think it's directly between them. Her reaction to Darren the day we met has always left me unsettled, and now, maybe it makes sense after all.

"So, we'll talk in the morning, Della?" I make the effort to speak when we exit the school.

Delaney breaks off from us and starts in the direction of her car. With a brief look over her shoulder, she says, "Yeah. Bye, Daisy. Nice to see you, Bryce."

It's an obvious lie, but I appreciate her at least trying to be cordial.

Bryce doesn't reply, so I pinch the back of her hand. She jumps but catches my drift.

"Yeah, same."

We watch Delaney get into her car and then start toward Bryce's. As if she weren't being thoughtful enough these past few days, she's taken to driving me to and from work every morning. All it took was me complaining about parking once, and she had her mind made up.

I wait until we're both buckling our seat belts and Bryce starts fiddling with the music on her phone before bringing up my suspicions regarding Delaney.

"Were Darren and Delaney ever involved?"

Bryce fumbles her phone, and it falls between her booted feet. "What?"

I watch her lean down to pick up the phone with my brow raised. Once she sets it in the cup holder, she stares across the console at me.

"That's not a simple question, and the answer is even more complicated."

"I don't need to know everything, and I don't expect you to tell me all the details. I'd just like to know if I should avoid mentioning him or you, for that matter. She looked uncomfortable around you, Bryce. Why?"

She stares out the windshield and pushes out a harsh breath. "They were together officially for four years, but it was actually much longer than that, stemming back to when they were just kids. She's uncomfortable around me because I'm guilty by association."

"Four years? Was this before Abbie?"

"Way before her. They were fourteen when Darren told the entire population of Cherry Peak that she was his future wife."

I blink in surprise, sinking into my seat. "Yet he married someone else."

"It's more complicated than that, Sunshine. Before she left for school, they decided to take a pause. The plan they made was for both of them to focus on getting their degrees, and then they would get back together and live a perfect, white-picket-fence life. It was a stupid fucking plan, and we all told him that," she explains, sounding stressed.

I reach across the car and smooth my hand down her thigh. "Okay, I get it. Don't tell me anything else. I just wanted to make sure I didn't wind up with my foot in my mouth."

Dropping her head, she turns it to the side and focuses on me. "Darren would tell you the whole story if you asked."

"It's not my place. Maybe Delaney will tell me once I've proven myself to be a good friend. Until then, I'm good with what you've shared."

"Thank you."

I shrug a shoulder and pat her leg before reaching for her phone and snaking it. She doesn't try to take it back, just watches as I try to open it only to find it locked.

"1031," she says.

"Halloween?" It's the same code as her front door.

She starts the car while I unlock her phone and open the music app. "I like Halloween."

"Mm, because you're a horror buff?"

"Paranormal buff. Not that fake horror shit."

"So, you don't like to watch scary movies? Not even like *Friday the 13th* or *Halloween*?"

She backs the car out of the stall with an ease that I wish I could steal sometime and then pulls out of the parking lot.

"Those are fine. My problem is with the fake paranormal horror movies. I like the real stories, not the ones that are snapped into thin air with spirits in terrible makeup and fake nails scratching walls. It's all very cliché."

"So, you like ghost-chaser documentaries more than you do the paranormal films."

"Yes. They claim to be based off of true stories, but it's all been so glamorized by the time it hits the theatres."

I nod along with her and find a song I recognize amongst the unfamiliar titles. It blasts through the speakers, and Bryce is quick to turn the volume down.

"You'll go deaf early if you listen to music that loud, you know?" I poke at her.

She reaches over to turn it up one notch. "You sound like my grandmother."

I jump at the new bit of information. "Are you close with her? I don't think I've ever heard you talk about your extended family. Is it big?"

She chuckles. "You're curious today."

"I'm always curious. I just don't like to overwhelm you with my questions," I admit a bit sheepishly.

The phone in my hands grows heavier when I notice the playlist title on the left side of the screen. *My Sunshine.*

Unable to help myself, I open it up and find the same list of songs that were scrawled on a piece of notebook paper and slipped beneath my door last week.

My heart swells and aches, beating so fast I have to take five slow breaths to keep it from exploding.

I haven't mentioned the playlist to Bryce because, truth be told, I didn't want to only see it on a slip of paper. It's supposed to be *more* than that, important. I want to listen to them together.

"My extended family lives mostly in Quebec. I've never been that close to them, and I don't overly want to be. They're stick-up-the-ass, judgmental rich people. As for the size, I have three uncles, a great-aunt, and three male cousins," she says.

I snap my attention from the phone to her, hoping I'm not as red as I feel. "I'm sorry they're like that."

"Don't be. I found another family here that's everything they could never be. I'm content with that."

"Sometimes found family can be everything a blood family never could," I agree.

"I wouldn't have it any other way. Speaking of." She sets a hand on my thigh and pulls it flush to the console between us. "The place I'm taking you is owned by someone important to me."

For the first time since we left the school, I look out the window and take in our surroundings. Crispy, orange trees and yellow fields surround either side of the single-lane highway. Cherry Peak waves goodbye in the side mirror.

"And it's not in Cherry Peak?"

She smiles, letting her head rest against the back of the seat. "No. We're going on a little bit of a drive, Sunshine."

32

Bryce

Maybe I should have warned her that we'd be taking a bit of a road trip, but then I'd have missed out on seeing her nearly climbing the window for a glimpse of where we're going.

I'm fucking greedy with her time. I already know that. After a day at work, she should be home relaxing instead of trapped in a car with me. Knowing that doesn't mean a damn thing to me, though. I'm taking as much time with her as I can possibly get.

"I'm seriously so excited right now. Are you sure you can't give me a hint about where we're going?" she asks, smacking her knees in quick procession.

When I make the final turn and spot the shop up ahead, I decide it's safe to tell her.

"My found family expands a bit outside of Cherry Peak. I don't remember what fucked-up decision drove me to this place, but it . . . It's where I found myself. Shade was the one who shoved my first tattoo gun in my hand when I was eighteen and told me to ink him up. I think the stupid asshole enjoyed the sloppy work. Didn't even wince when I gouged too deep and had him bleeding all over himself."

Her head flies in my direction. "Wait, we're going to a tattoo shop? Is this the same place you got your first tattoo?"

"No. Shade would have kicked my ass out on the street with Wade's signature ripped at my feet. This place is the real deal. One of the most popular tattoo studios in the province."

Into The Shade is the only proper tattoo shop for hours. People drive up to eight hours just to get his work on their skin. I'd drive even further. Apart from my very first tattoo, he's the only artist other than myself who's ever put a needle to my skin.

Daisy gawks out the windshield as we pull up outside the shop. The neon sign is off, but he's inside. For a thirty-two-year-old guy, he's got the most boring fucking life. No wife or kids or pets. Just him, this studio, and his otherworldly talent.

"I wouldn't have thought this place would have been here. Where even are we?"

"Oak Point."

"I've never heard of it."

"Nobody has. Not unless you were born here." I turn off the car and palm the keys. "Come on. I want to introduce you to him."

She quickly unclicks her seat belt and, before I can do the same, leans over and grabs my face. I'm not expecting the peck she lays on my lips. It leaves me tingling and craving more when she flops back into her seat and opens the door.

"What was that for?" I call as she steps out.

Her eyes are twinkling with happiness when she says, "For taking me here. I can't wait to meet him and learn more about your life, Frosty."

In a blink, she's on the sidewalk, and the car door is shut. I want to both squeeze her and spank the fuck out of her ass. Maybe even both at the same time. This woman is my wildest dream.

I meet her on the sidewalk and struggle and fail to keep my hands to myself. The roads are empty the way they always are here, and I take advantage of it.

Daisy squeals when I spin and back her into the brick wall of the shop, her eyes wide, blue-edged with black. Her back arches, pushing her chest up and against mine. Satisfaction thrums beneath my skin, and I pinch her chin with my thumb and fore-finger before lifting it.

"If you're going to kiss me, baby, do it properly," I murmur.

For someone so innocent, Daisy has a devious streak that I can't seem to get enough of. It's such a turn-on coaxing it out of her and seeing just how brave she's willing to be to get what she wants.

"It was supposed to be a peck. A thankful gesture," she explains coyly, enjoying every moment of getting under my skin.

"Not good enough. I have a minimum of at least three minutes per kiss."

"Exactly three minutes? How do you expect that to work in public?"

I lean in, and our lips almost touch. "Do you have a problem with kissing me in public, Daisy? Because we'll have to work on that."

"Did you ever consider that maybe I just like making you work for my public kisses?" she coos, inching closer.

"Have I earned one yet?"

Her mouth slanting over mine in a full, hard kiss answers my question. This time, I don't hesitate to tease the seam of her soft lips with my tongue, coaxing them open before delving deep and tasting her without restrictions.

My hand cups the back of her head, guiding it back as I push forward and slip the control from her hands to mine. She might be too aware of how deep her claws go inside of me, but when it comes to these moments, I'm more than ready to sink mine into her.

Daisy keeps her touch light, a tease when I want something harder. Her fingers glide down my neck and throat, then sneak down to trace the neckline of my shirt, a nail dipping beneath the material like she's about to—

"Public indecency is a crime, you know?"

Daisy freezes, eyes opening wide in panic. I massage the back of her head and turn mine in the direction of the voice.

"If this town cared about shit like that, they'd have locked you up years ago, Shade. You've already scared my girl, and she hasn't even seen your ugly mug yet."

My mentor and friend tips his head back and laughs loud enough for it to echo down the street. It's the kind of roared belly laugh that makes you jump the first time you hear it because your brain hasn't quite recognized it as a happy sound.

It's been a couple of months since I've been back here, and he's let his hair grow out since then. It's as black as mine, long enough to curl at his neck and behind his ears, and has been swooped back out of his face with gel-slicked fingers.

There's a new piece on the side of his throat, the skin still raised and raw: a spiderweb tucked behind his ear with a fat, round spider dangling from it.

Hands tucked into his black jeans, he leans a giant shoulder against the brick wall and smirks. "Don't be cruel. I'd bet that Daisy here doesn't think I'm ugly, do you, baby girl?"

I glare at him, ready to tell him to fuck off, when Daisy urges me back a step with a hand on my arm. She gives him an obvious up-and-down examination.

"I've seen worse, *Shane*."

I slide an arm around her shoulder and plant a kiss on the side of her head as my laugh slips out. Shade lifts both of his eyebrows and pushes off the wall, stretching to his full height of six-four.

"Bryce sold you short. I'm impressed. How about you two come inside so I can give the gorgeous girl a tour of my space?"

"Stop with the fucking compliments," I warn.

Daisy reaches up to cover the hand I've got holding her shoulder and flashes him a sympathetic smile. "Playboys don't do anything for me, I'm afraid."

"I'd be more than willing to let you try me out first before coming to that conclusion."

He falls directly into the trap she's laid for him. I've told him about Daisy more than a few times over the course of our friendship, but I've never mentioned her sexuality before. He knows I'm bisexual, but Daisy wasn't his business.

She was right to call him a playboy, but I prefer fuckboy. He's an ass the majority of the time, a guy who believes he's larger than life and has the good looks and talent to prove it. I always enjoy knocking him down a few pegs.

He eyes Daisy with interest, but I know it's just to piss me off. Maybe as payback for not coming to visit more or ignoring his last few phone calls. Poor guy had a tough time with that, I'd bet.

"Do you have a vagina in those tight black jeans, Shade?" she asks bluntly, almost sympathetically.

He only looks surprised by her question for half a second before that startling laugh makes another appearance, and Daisy giggles along with him.

"Got it, little devil." With a wink in my direction, he gestures around the corner of the brick building. "Come in. I've been looking forward to this all day."

"Looking forward to what exactly?" Daisy asks while we follow him to the front of Into The Shade.

"Bryce's surprise, of course."

He opens the door for us and trails in behind me. A soft calmness blankets me at the familiar space.

The smell of burnt coffee, antiseptic, and expensive cologne. Years' worth of memories come flooding back at the sight of the two leather tables in the open space behind the front desk. A frustrating yearning sensation builds behind my ribs at the reminder that I won't ever have anything close to this. Not living where I do now.

No station of my own, let alone an entire studio. I'll never have the life Shade does, and while that didn't upset me back when I first started tattooing, it does now. The older I get, the harder it becomes to pretend it all doesn't matter.

Shade steps around me to stand in front of us, an arm propped on the desk.

"Welcome to Into The Shade, Daisy. And welcome *back*, Bryce."

"This is amazing," Daisy praises.

His grin is pure male satisfaction. "You haven't seen anything yet. Follow me."

We do, and I waste no time taking in every inch of the space, from the neon blue sign with Shade's name hung above the first of the two stations to the wall of backlit mirrors on the opposite wall. The walls are a cool white with grey wood floors and black light fixtures. Three massive art pieces are hung around the studio, all of which are his own creations. They're similar to the ones I have in my bedroom because I learned how to be proud of my work from this arrogant ass.

The piece closest to his tattoo station is a shot of a woman on the same black felt couch that's only a few feet from the wall of mirrors. She's naked besides a black G-string that's been pulled up high on her hips and has her knees on the cushion with her chest pressed to the back of the couch. The photo was taken of her entire back, showcasing the breathtaking fire-breathing dragon piece that spans the length of it and onto the backs of her arms.

He's Shade for a reason. There's nobody out there better than him when it comes to filling in the elaborate pieces that are brought to him. Whether you want colour or straight black, he will create something incomparable.

"This is where the magic happens. It's also where Bryce here learned everything she knows now," he says, guiding Daisy to the first leather table.

If she's noticed the way it's already prepped and ready to go, she doesn't let on. But considering she hasn't been in a tattoo studio before, I'm confident in her not noticing yet.

The headrest has been wrapped, and the same gun I use at

home is sitting on the table beside the black and yellow ink I asked for.

"Was she a good student?" Daisy asks, flicking her eyes between us.

Shade folds his arms across his chest and pretends to think about his answer. "She was eager to learn but had the same scowl on her face every day she was here that she does right now. Am I bugging you, Bryce?"

"You always bug me," I mutter, intensifying my expression.

He moves to stand at the end of the leather table and sets his hands on it. "Yet, here you are, about to give your girlfriend her first tattoo in my studio. Clearly, you don't hate me too much."

I could never hate him, but I'm not going to give him the satisfaction of hearing that. I'm too focused on the shock that travels across Daisy's flushing features to give a shit about him right now, anyway.

"What? I'm getting a tattoo?" she shrieks, running anxious hands over her hair.

"Not unless you're okay with it," I add quickly.

Shade pats the table. "It's the first thing Bryce told me when she called yesterday. *Please* let me bring my girlfriend to your studio, Shade. I would never, ever bring her anywhere else for her tattoo. *Please, I beg you, Oh Mighty One.*"

His attempt at sounding like me is pitiful. It makes Daisy laugh, though, so I let it slide.

She moves toward the table with only a hint of hesitation. Eying the supplies on the table, it's obvious to tell when she starts putting everything together.

"I'd never force you to do this. I wanted to take you here to show you something personal to me, not just for this," I add carefully.

She looks over at me where I stand a few feet away, the only one not surrounding the table. The corners of her lips fall slightly, and I jerk forward a step.

"It'll be you tattooing me?" she asks.

Shade's smirk makes my palm tingle with the urge to slap him. "Unless you want me, little devil."

"I'd prefer Bryce. No offense."

His smirk transforms into a genuine smile, and my heart expands. "Good answer."

Arching a brow, I watch as he gives me a thumbs-up and strides to my side. He has to drop his head to speak into my ear.

"I'll be back in an hour."

"It'll take me half that time," I mutter, my focus on Daisy and only Daisy.

She sucks on her cheek and examines the supplies on the table. Stray auburn waves droop from over her shoulder to tickle her cheeks before she pushes them back and looks at me. Her shy smile threatens to yank my legs from beneath me.

"An hour," Shade repeats himself. "I'll lock the door behind me and grab dinner."

Emotion catches in my throat. "Thank you, Shade."

For everything, I hope he can read in my expression.

His lips touch my temple for half a second. "It's good to see you happy."

Then he's gone, leaving me and Daisy alone in the one place I always kept just for me, a hidden paradise I feared would get snatched from me.

Yet, with the woman smiling at me from across the room, I've never felt more confident or secure sharing anything in my entire life.

33

Daisy

SHADE KISSES THE SIDE OF BRYCE'S HEAD AND THEN LEAVES. I WATCH him lock the door behind him, tug his hood over his head, and disappear down the street without a second look. He doesn't seem like the type of guy to trust just anyone with this place, and that speaks volumes to their relationship. A friendship that I had no idea existed until now.

He's a very handsome guy, with a towering height, thighs the size of tree trunks, and a dark aura about him that I'd find alarming if I hadn't met him in these circumstances. If that's your thing, I'm sure he'd be a real catch. From his confident, flirtatious jokes, I would put money on him hardly ever striking out with women.

Bryce moves around the table with skilled ease, not fumbling with the supplies or how they've been set up on the rolly cart. She taps the gun and then nods, not having adjusted or swapped out even one thing. They've been perfectly prepared just for her.

"Does Poppy know about Shade?" I ask, unable to help but dig into all of my burning questions.

"I'll tell you everything you want to know once I've shown you my idea and gotten you up on this table."

She's already turning to the thin piece of paper on the cart by the time I realize she's talking about the tattoo she wants to give me. I didn't notice the paper before or the design printed onto it in bright blue.

"I drew it the other night and sent it to Shade to get his opinion before I even contemplated taking you here or showing it to you. It's simple, but with the right colours . . ."

"Let me see," I murmur.

She picks it up with extra caution and slowly extends it toward me. I don't touch it, not wanting to risk ripping it. Instead, I stare at the sketch and blink back the tears that cause it to become warped.

"Good or bad tears?" she asks, the paper beginning to shake before she sets it on the cart of supplies.

I shake my head, sniffling once. "It's perfect. I want you to put it on my skin."

She takes my face in her hands and kisses me softly, content with the simplicity of it. I return the kiss with the same ease and cover her hands with mine, enjoying the affection and the warming effect it has on me.

"Do you have a spot you want it?" she asks against my mouth.

"I trust you to choose."

Her next inhale is shaky, and I kiss her once more before leaning back. "I'll need access to your thigh."

"Pants off, then?" My voice is so breathy, the temperature suddenly cranked in the large space.

"Yes. Then hop up on the table, and I'll get the stencil on."

I swallow past the ball of nerves in my throat and reach for the button on my pink, baggy jeans. Bryce watches my every move with what looks like envy in her eyes. All she'd have to do is ask, and I'd let her take them off herself.

Once my jeans are open, I start shimmying them down my legs. "How do you want me to sit?"

"Just on the edge. Face me."

I squat to grab the jeans at my ankles and lay them on the

table before doing as she said. The leather is cold beneath my bare legs, and I suck in a sharp breath.

"Sorry. I should have warned you that it would be cold."

"It's fine." I'm already warming up because of our proximity.

Bryce rolls a stool over to the table and snaps a pair of black medical gloves on. She reaches for the stack of antiseptic wipes laid out on the cart beside her and rips one open. The wipe is colder than the leather was, but as she leans over my lap, her hair tickling my arm, I don't so much as blink at the sensation.

"I'm going to put it here," she explains with a swipe of her gloved finger over the outer part of my upper thigh. "Are you okay with the length of the design on the stencil?"

"You could tattoo an eggplant on my cheek and I wouldn't have anything bad to say about it, Frosty. The length you chose is perfect."

She rolls her eyes and curls the side of her mouth into a half smile. "No eggplants."

"No eggplants," I agree.

"I'm going to shave the area and then apply some gel to help with the transfer."

"Okay."

The razor she grabs comes from a bulk-sized box of cheap ones, which I imagine is because they're only good for one use. She plucks the cap off the blades and starts to swipe it down my skin. It takes only a few seconds, and then another wipe runs down the area, cleaning away the tiny hairs.

I watch with weighted breath as she works, the focus on her face captivating. Even with something as boring as prep work, she's tuned the world out.

When she wheels the stool back and starts riffling through the rest of the supplies, I pinch the hem of my shirt and shift on the table. My reactions to her passion and adoration for tattooing, combined with her closeness and the fact I'm in only my shirt and underwear, are extreme. I'm flushed from the tips of my ears down to my toes and everywhere in between. My nipples are tight and sore, and the space between my legs is wet, so much so that I worry she'll be able to tell if she comes close enough.

This isn't supposed to be a sexual act. It's sweet and thoughtful and is my chance to see Bryce in her element. Yet, I have to press my thighs together while she's busy and fight back a shiver at the pleasure that sparks.

She hasn't given me an opening to touch her in the same way she's touched me yet. I don't know if that's because we agreed to go slow or if I haven't been obvious enough in my interest in exploring every inch of her body. Either way, I'm struggling with it more and more as the days go on. It's not surprising that I'm turned on right now or that I'm contemplating lunging off this table and pushing her onto it instead.

"—now I'll put the stencil on, and you can tell me if you like the placement."

I clear my throat and look down at where she's bent over my lap again. There's gel on my thigh and the stencil hovering above it.

"Are you okay?" she asks, her eyes narrowing.

"Yes. Continue, please."

With slight hesitation, she drops her stare and smooths the stencil over my thigh. When she pulls it off, the design is in place.

"Do you want to go look at it in the mirror?"

I don't have to think about my answer. "No. It's perfect."

She squeezes my knee and nods. "I'm going to start with the outline and then work my way in. It shouldn't take long to get it drawn, but I'm planning to shade it in with some yellow afterward. If we get to that stage and it becomes too uncomfortable or you don't want to continue, we'll stop. I can finish it another time."

"I'll be fine, Bryce. Just focus on the art, and I'll worry about everything else," I soothe.

"You're always my priority. Everything else is just background noise."

My chest flames. "Your passion isn't background noise. This is what you love to do. I'm just feeling really grateful that you want to share this part of yourself with me in the first place."

She holds my gaze for a moment, and I swear I can hear the combined sound of our erratic heartbeats. We're two complete opposites, yet for some reason, we've found each other. I feel like that makes me one of the luckiest people in the world.

"I like sharing things with you," she admits.

Reaching for the tattoo gun, she faces away from me. I didn't miss the red tint of her cheeks but choose not to tease her about it.

Bryce does a handful of things with the tattoo gun before moving on to the ink. She pours the yellow and black into separate tiny caps and then changes her gloves. The gun starts buzzing for half a second before turning off again.

Wheels move along the floor as she comes to the edge of the table. I stop rubbing my thighs together at the last second and puff out a relieved sigh when she turns her attention to my thigh.

"This should be the easiest position, but if it gets too uncomfortable for you, tell me. I'm serious," she says sternly.

"I will."

"It shouldn't hurt necessarily, but it will feel uncomfortable at first. Like a bee sting or a slight pinch in one spot repeatedly. I always find that it becomes less noticeable the longer it goes on."

The gun starts buzzing again, and I try not to hold my breath as I wait for the needle to touch skin. Bryce's fingers are hot through the gloves as they stroke my thigh and then pull the skin taut.

"Try not to jerk," she murmurs.

And I don't. The first press of the needle to my thigh isn't painful. It's surprising, but I keep my cool, breathing slow and steady.

Folding my hands and laying them between my legs, I say, "That's not too bad."

"Good, Sunshine. I shouldn't take too long with this outline."

I wouldn't mind if she did, which is probably pretty weird. The constant reassurance that her non-tattooing hand provides with only a constant pressure on my thigh has me content sitting here. She's even moving her thumb back and forth as the needle turns the blue lines black, as if she needs the contact as much as I do.

I keep my head down so I can watch her. "So, *does* Poppy know about Shade?"

"Yes. But she's never met him."

"Why not? I thought you two were best friends."

She uses a piece of paper towel to wipe away some of the excess ink from the tattoo and then continues with the outline.

"We are. But this isn't a piece of myself that I was ready to share with anyone before. Not even Poppy."

"But you were ready to share it with me?"

Her eyes flick up to mine before falling to my thigh once again. "You're different."

"How so?"

Okay, yes, I'm digging. *Sue me.* This is my chance to poke and prod inside of her mind, and I'm not going to waste it.

"Poppy's been in my life since I was just a kid. She will always be my best friend. But you're more than that. There are some things that Poppy just doesn't need to know to be my best friend, but that you do if you're going to be more than that."

She pauses to wipe my thigh again, and this time, the gun doesn't start back up right away.

"There are pieces of my life that I've always kept just for me. My relationship with the only person I've ever let get to know me outside of my family in Cherry Peak is one of them. Shade might be an asshole at times, but he's important to me. He's hardly older, but it still feels like he took me in like a big brother the day I showed up here. Keeping him and this place to myself was just instinct. But you're not someone I met in childhood and who knows me the way Poppy or even Anna does. You need to get to know me as I am right now, today, and Shade is an important piece of that."

I pinch a chunk of her black hair between my fingers and tuck it behind her ear to distract myself from the swell of emotion in my chest.

"I'm happy that you trusted me enough to bring me here. Every piece of you that I discover only draws me closer, and I like getting closer to you, Bryce."

"You'll know more about me than anyone else does if I'm not careful," she breathes out before starting the gun back up and continuing to outline the tattoo.

"Would that be a bad thing?"

"Only if you learned it all and decided to leave afterward."

It's the most honest and vulnerable thing I've ever heard her say.

"I don't see that happening."

She sneaks a look at me from the corner of her eye and jerks her chin in brief acknowledgement. It's not acceptance or a sign that she believes me, but I'd never expect her to take my word for something so heavy.

"What was it like growing up in such a full house?" she asks, leaning further over my thigh.

"Loud," I blurt out. Her laugh is instant. "But in a comforting way. If it was quiet, you were alone. I think the lack of loneliness is the biggest benefit of a big family. If you're upset and need to speak to someone about an issue, you have your pick of therapist. But it can also be a bad thing. If you need time alone, it's harder to get it when you have a handful of people worried and knocking on your bedroom door to try and help.

"It took me a while to get used to the silence that came after Giana and Josette left home. First, I was excited because Gi had always had the biggest bedroom of all of us, and I beat Johnny in rock, paper, scissors for it. But I quickly realized that she was actually *gone,* and the girl who was always the first to offer advice or a shoulder to cry on wasn't here anymore. Johnny is the best brother in the entire world, but he isn't my sister."

Bryce has listened to every word I've said, nodding along and humming from time to time. Her genuine interest in my life means everything to me.

"You mentioned that your moms were supportive when you came out. Was everyone else?"

I flex my toes in my sneakers and relax the muscles in my leg that I didn't realize I'd been tensing. "They were. What about you? If your parents accepted you, did your stick-up-the-ass, rich relatives?"

"They don't know what my sexuality is."

My mouth gapes wide. "What?"

"They don't deserve to know. Not to mention that they wouldn't give a shit anyway. They'd probably crinkle their noses and tell me I'm wrong, then pretend I never told them in the first place."

"What happens if you get married to a woman one day? Would you not invite them?"

She wipes my thigh and twists to stare up at me, expression completely open. I lean forward, drawn close by the honesty in her gaze and continued strokes of her fingers across my sensitive flesh.

"*When* I marry a woman, there won't be a single person in attendance who doesn't deserve to be there. Sharing blood and DNA doesn't give anyone access to my most important moments. Those are sacred, and I won't have them tarnished by unwelcomed faces who were invited solely out of obligation," she swears. To who, I'm not sure.

My stomach swoops. Something about her declaration touches parts of myself that I never knew existed. It unlocks a mountain of hidden desires.

"I've never met someone more headstrong than you."

"Is that a bad thing?"

"It's an incredible thing," I correct her.

She furrows her brows and wets her lips. "You're making it very hard to go slow."

"When I mentioned slow, I didn't mean tortoise speed," I tease lightly.

"Are you saying you want to go faster?"

I take a deep breath and drop a bucket into my well of confidence. "We're here alone, and I'm in my panties. If you shifted an inch to the left and watched as I spread my legs, you'd see that they're damp. They have been since you kissed me outside."

Her eyes drift shut as she sets the gun on the table. "Christ, Daisy. I don't know what it is about you that has me second-guessing myself all the fucking time."

"Yeah, you need to stop that."

"I'm just trying not to scare you. I can be a lot when it comes to relationships, and I'm stressing myself out toning it down."

I ignore the way my thighs have stuck to the leather and push myself off the table. My legs are wobbly for a moment before I stabilize myself.

"I might come off as sweet and innocent, Bryce, but there's a time and place for everything. I'll always be kind and gentle and understanding to those who deserve it, but I'm not afraid to be demanding and confident when the moment calls for something a bit stronger. You've mentioned my backbone before, so don't think for one minute that I won't use it when it comes to this," I tell her, my voice steady.

She tips her head back to keep eye contact, and when her pupils expand, eating at the electric blue, my pulse skips.

"And what exactly is *this*?"

"*This* is you being too cautious," I start, placing my hands on her shoulders and pushing her until her back touches the edge of the table. "*This* is you thinking your needs come second to mine."

She grips her knees and heaves in a breath.

I bend forward until our faces are at eye level and finger the button of her jeans. Her throat strains with a swallow.

"*This*," I continue, unsnapping the button and tugging down the zipper, "is me returning the favour from last week like I've wanted to since you first got between my legs."

"Daisy." She chokes on my name.

Thinking back to her words about Kristen in my old bedroom, I taunt, "It's baby when I'm between your legs."

Her head drops back completely, and I grin while dropping into a squat and tugging at the band of her jeans. She lifts her hips, and despite being nearly painted on, they come down easily.

The black lace panties that cup her between her legs are thin and tight as they stick to the curve of her pussy. I drop onto my knees and ignore the slight pain that follows before trailing the backs of my fingers up her thighs. The skin rises with goosebumps as I trace the shape of each peach inked there.

"I saw these tattoos in your room," I confess.

Bryce shivers when I reach the stems of the peaches and linger there, not half an inch from the black lace. "How?"

It's like she knows the answer already but needs to hear it from me.

Shifting further between her legs, I drag my knuckle along the centre of her panties. They're slick, just as wet as mine, yet there's one difference. The small hoop at the top of her seam that bumps against my knuckle isn't something I'm used to, and it excites the hell out of me.

"I snooped in your room a couple of days after moving in. And I don't regret it."

Before she can respond, I have her panties shifted to the side and her bare pussy in front of me. Pink and glistening, the sight of her excitement makes my belly tighten with desire.

Her breathing is so laboured I risk a glance upward to make sure she isn't close to passing out. The feral gleam in her eyes as she fixes her gaze on me proves that she's more focused than ever.

"When did you get this?" I rasp, tapping the black clit piercing with my nail. It looks like a nose ring but with a ball in the centre of the hoop.

She hisses, hips lifting to chase the sensation that just sparked. My eyes threaten to cross, and I lean in to give the metal a soft kiss.

"Fuck, baby," she gasps.

Her fingers strangle her bare knees, and I part my lips over that small ball, taking my first taste of her. A moan claws its way up my throat.

"When did you get this?" I repeat my question.

She releases her knees and reaches one hand behind her to grip the table while the other finds my shoulder. "Three years ago."

I hum against her pierced hood. The metal hoop is cold, but against her hot skin, it's not noticeable as I slip my tongue beneath it and lift. When I pinch it between my teeth and tug gently, Bryce whimpers, the sound so high-pitched and desperate it rattles my brain. Driven by the need to hear it again, I repeat my motions before blowing a stream of warm air over the spit-slicked skin.

"Stop toying with me," she demands weakly.

I smile against her and abandon the piercing, continuing to explore. She slides an inch down the stool, giving me more room to work. It's as much for my benefit as it is for hers.

Parting her lips with my tongue, I dip a finger inside her entrance and close my eyes at the tight grip. She moans, clenching around the intrusion as I slowly work my finger out and then back in again.

Her lower abdomen strains with the effort it's taking to keep from bucking herself off the stool, so I pick up my pace. After today, I'll have another chance to take my time with her.

If Shade were to come back while I have Bryce in this position . . . Fucking worth it.

"Will you tell me what you like best?" I ask before swiping my tongue along the length of my finger.

"There's a reason I got the hood piercing."

I drag my tongue up through her puffy skin until I find her clit and its pretty jewelry and suck. With it suctioned between my lips, I flick my tongue at a quick pace, cutting the foreplay.

Her moans turn into cries, and then the fingers curling into my shoulder move. She slaps a palm to my nape and tightens her hold until her nails prick into the skin. Pride flutters in my chest, and I don't say a word as she uses the hold to pull my face flush to her pussy.

Hips jerking, she grinds against my tongue, demanding her pleasure. Driven by similar urges, I'm unable to stop myself from reaching between my legs and pressing my palm against my panties, rubbing my clit.

They're soaked through, so I shove them down one of my hips and dive eager fingers beneath the fabric. I'm slippery and swollen with arousal as I start working my clit with the pads of two fingers.

"You touching your pussy, baby?" Bryce asks between gasps of air.

I refuse to stop working her pussy with my tongue, so I nod my answer. The pace of her grinding picks up, and I slip another finger in beside the first.

"Fuck . . . Fucking shit. You're going to make me come," she mewls.

Good.

I release low, needy sounds and swirl my clit faster and faster, chasing the release that's bubbling in my core. Bryce clenches around my fingers, and her clit pulses in my mouth.

"Fuck yourself, baby. Two fingers like you've got inside of me. I need to taste you."

I moan, nudging my fingers inside and using my palm to keep the pressure on my clit. Two strokes and I'm there.

My hearing blows, but I hear her cry out in bliss seconds before she sucks my fingers deep into her pussy and smacks the table. I suck harder and hum, sending the rumbles zipping up her body.

A moment later, her fingers go lax around my nape, and I remove my mouth. My laugh is sudden, but once it's out, another follows. Bryce tenses briefly before letting out a laugh of her own.

"Are you okay?" I ask through a giggle.

She runs her fingers from my neck to beneath my chin and then guides it up. Careful not to hurt her if she's too sensitive, I pull mine out from inside of her and wipe them off on the dry part of my panties.

"It's going to smell like pussy in here when Shade gets back," she mutters bluntly.

"I'm sure it isn't the first time," I tease.

Moving to wipe cum off my second set of fingers, the ones from inside me, I pause when Bryce shakes her head, eyes on my hand.

"I told you I wanted a taste." She parts her lips, tongue slightly extended.

I sink my teeth into my bottom lip and offer her my fingers. She immediately wraps her mouth around them and sucks them clean. Regardless of just coming, I clench at the approval in her gaze before she releases me.

"Just as good as the first time."

My cheeks heat. "I hope we learned something from this."

"Other than me having a hood piercing and your pussy tasting as sweet as honey?"

"Well, yes. But also that I'm interested in you, Bryce. Not just emotionally. *Physically.* You don't have to hold back on me, and I won't hold back on you."

Her eyes soften, the fingers beneath my chin curling to hold it. "Okay, Sunshine."

She bends down, and I meet her halfway in a kiss that seals our promise. I feel her smile against my mouth and steal one more kiss before backing up.

"Now, what do you say we finish this tattoo?"

34

Bryce

I'VE JUST FINISHED CLEANING UP MY STATION WHEN A KEY JIGGLES IN the door and Shade saunters inside. He keeps his hood up as he closes the door with his foot and carries the pizza boxes and a white bag of food to the front desk.

"Oh honeys, I'm home," he calls like a douche.

Daisy drops from the table to her feet and turns to face him, grinning. "And you brought food."

Still only in her panties, I have to distract myself with putting all of my supplies back so I don't force her into her pants before she has a chance to see the tattoo. The thought of her half-naked in front of anyone but me feels like a sucker punch to the gut, but it's only Shade. Even if he is one flirty fucker, he won't try anything with her. Not like he would have a shot, anyway. She made that more than clear to him.

"Hope you like pizza and wings. That's just about all we've got in this town."

"I love both."

I tug my gloves off and crumple them into a ball before asking him, "Did you remember my order?"

He shakes his head in disbelief. "You've been gone a couple

of months, Bryce. Not years. So yeah, I remembered, and I even got the extra blue cheese ranch that you love."

"Blue cheese ranch?" Daisy asks, nose scrunched.

Shade winces, setting the bags down and beginning to rifle through them. "Uh-oh."

"I hate blue cheese," Daisy says like that is excuse enough.

I make a pained noise and roll back on my stool to toss the gloves. "No fucking way."

She gapes at me. The irritated, red skin around her new tattoo is angry in the fluorescent lights, but fuck me, it's a good tattoo. So completely her.

"Don't tell me that's a deal breaker?" She balks.

"Normally, I'd say it would be. But that art on your leg tells me that you might stand a chance, little devil," Shade says, butting in with a loose grin.

I catch her stare and wink, loving the way she doesn't bother hiding the flush that smears across her cheeks. "Go look at your tattoo."

With a skip in her step, she moves around me toward the wall of mirrors. I fight off the blast of nerves that hits me the moment she props her leg in front of her and fixes wide eyes to the reflection of the wrapped design.

It's some of my best work, despite the simplicity of it. Two long black stems crossing at the middle and topped with yellow daisies. Script isn't my specialty, but the *Daisy* written in cursive along the left stem was an impulse decision. Once I finished the initial outline, it was like my hand had a mind of its own.

"It's beautiful," Daisy murmurs.

My heart smashes against my ribs. "You like it?"

Nodding quickly, she catches my gaze in the mirror. "I love it. It's so freaking perfect."

"Bryce is one of the best I've ever come across. Obviously, she's not as good as me, but it's a fucking shame she isn't in a space of her own like this one," Shade says with a pointed look in my direction.

I wet my dry lips and flip him off. Daisy answers him before I can.

"Would you ever share this place with her?"

The question takes both of us by surprise. Shade cocks his head and stares at me with those dark eyes of his. We've joked about it before, but he knows just as well as I do from all of my complaining about my parents that it wouldn't work.

As fucked up as it may be, the moment I cut that last cord, I'll free myself from them entirely. It sounds like everything I should and often do want, but at the same time, they're still my parents. Shitty ones, but parents nonetheless.

Who am I without them? Would I regret my choice years down the road?

It's why I've put up with my mother's shit for so long. If I stop, I know what will come next. The family I've made over the course of my life will be all I have left.

Daisy, having pulled her pants back on, abandons the mirrors and starts my way. Once again, it's like she can see straight into my head and the thoughts that run rampant within it.

Shade carries all the boxes of food over to the couch and sets them on the floor in front of it. "There's been a station waiting for her here for years. She's just got to claim it."

"You make it sound so easy," I mutter.

Daisy reaches me and kisses the top of my head. "You deserve to do what you love for a living. Your talent should be seen by everyone. Not just those who call you over in the middle of the night."

"That office job you've got is a waste of time, Bryce. You're wasting the best years of your life and what could be a fucking incredible career behind a desk doing your mother's bidding," Shade adds with a flip of the first pizza box lid.

The longing I felt the moment we stepped into this place returns with a vengeance. It takes too much effort to keep my face blank.

"What is this? Gang up on Bryce day?"

"Sure, if that will help you take us seriously," Shade states.

I stand and kick the stool to the side before turning to Daisy. She doesn't budge from where she stands, concern lining every inch of her face.

"You deserve the best of everything, sweetheart. That's all."

I'm at risk of falling in love with this woman. It's already right there, so close I can touch it with my fingertips.

Fuck, what if I'm already there?

"What she said. Now, sit your asses down and eat dinner with me. I'm already beginning to wither away," Shade huffs.

"You'd be the last person to wither away from starvation. What do you weigh, two fifty?" I ask.

He flops onto the floor with his back to the couch and grabs a slice of meaty pizza. With a leg pulled toward his body and an arm slung over his knee, he looks unbelievably large.

"Two thirty," he corrects me before flexing beneath his hoodie. "And it's pure muscle, baby girl. Wanna see?"

"No."

He shifts his stare to Daisy, but I'm already moving in his direction. Once I've joined him on the floor, I smack him upside the head and snatch a buffalo chicken wing, covering it in the special ranch.

Pointing it at him, I drop my voice into a growl. "Don't even think about it."

"Are you threatening me with a chicken wing?"

Daisy's laugh steals my attention. I watch her sit beside me and criss-cross her legs before taking a honey garlic chicken wing and sinking her teeth into it.

She's immediately fit in with Shade, like she hasn't only just met him today. It's a superpower of hers. No matter where we are or who we're with, she can become a member of their circle with a smile and a few honest words. Everyone loves her and doesn't for one second hesitate to accept her.

I wonder what that feels like. To make such a good first

impression on everyone you meet to the point they're accepting you into the fold with no hesitation.

When I was younger, it was easier to make friends. We didn't know better back then than to take every smile and hello as an olive branch. But as an adult, friendships have been far and few between for me. People can be judgy and cruel but also completely opposite of you in views and dreams. It's a miracle to find even one person that you connect with, and that's not even the hard part.

It's keeping them around once you've started letting them see who you are past the surface level.

I found Shade when I was in my late teen years and let arrogance convince me to pop into this place with a pile of angst and anger and demand the best artist in this part of the country ink me up. If he hadn't taken one look at me and recognized my pain as a similar kind to the one he knew, we wouldn't be here right now.

Anna and Aurora were driven to Cherry Peak with suitcases' worth of their own pain. A cheating ex-fiancé and secret celebrity father. It wasn't a coincidence they were both led here and that we stumbled upon each other when we did.

Daisy . . . she's something more. A blessing from the universe that I know I won't get lucky enough to receive twice.

Every friendship I've made in the last few years has stemmed from a shared experience of pain and anger. All except for the one I've found with my sunshine.

Ours is full of light and excitement. A deep yearning and desire. It's the first ray of sun streaming through the clouds of a lifelong rainstorm.

When I zone back in, it's to the sight of Shade reaching across my body to show Daisy photos on his phone. I blink at the bicep in my face and then lean into Daisy to see the photo on the screen.

"How many of Bryce's tattoos have you done?" she asks,

swiping to the left and rolling her lips to hide a smile when the python with its fangs in the peach on my thigh appears.

Shade looks at me, twisting his mouth as he thinks. "What would you say? Eighty percent?"

"Around that," I confirm.

"And that hasn't been weird? I'm assuming you did the bull piece on her chest?" Daisy asks, hesitation mixing with something else in her voice.

"I did. But no, it's not weird. It's work. We take that shit seriously," he answers between bites of pizza. I shove his arm away, and he drapes it over his knee again.

Daisy brings her eyes up to mine and holds them there, searching for whatever she didn't get from Shade. It takes me a moment to realize what it is.

I stroke the inside of her arm and bring my mouth to her ear. "No, Daisy. It's never been like that between us and never will be. You're the only one I've ever shared an intimate experience with while giving or getting a tattoo. *Only* you."

She shudders as my words drift across her skin. I take the shell of her ear between my teeth and apply soft pressure before releasing it.

"Okay," she whispers.

"Have you ever asked to tattoo Bryce?" Shade asks, attention fixed on Daisy.

"You mean, like, *I* would tattoo *her*?"

I take a bite of chicken wing to keep from laughing at her surprise.

Shade swallows a bite of pizza. "Yeah. I let her do it to me the first day she showed up here. It should be a tradition or something. You come here, you get some ink. Every single time."

Licking the hot sauce and ranch from my lips, I quirk a brow. "I already put everything away."

"Okay, so next time you come here, we'll let the little devil give you a piece of her own. Nobody leaves this place without some ink, yeah?"

"It's only fair, I suppose," Daisy agrees easily.

I've never had many traditions in my life. But this one could be my new favourite.

"You know he's saying that you'll have to get a tattoo every time I bring you here, right?" I ask to be sure.

Her eyes brighten. "I can agree to that."

"Don't let him pressure you. You've only just got your first piece," I add, ignoring the pressure swelling between my legs at the picture in my mind of her with a tattoo gun in her hand.

"And I loved it. A lot."

"You heard her. Stop trying to change her mind," Shade scolds me.

I let it go for now, but considering I'm going to do everything I can to make sure I get the chance to bring Daisy back here, it's not the last time we'll be talking about it.

She's not going to be forced into liking something just because I do. Not when a hobby like mine is the permanent kind.

"Fine," I relent.

Shade tears his pizza crust in half. "And while we're on the topic, you're not staying away for months again. I'm not the clingy type, but I nearly spam texted you to come visit me."

"I'll make sure she comes back soon," Daisy promises.

Yeah, I'm falling in love with her.

35

Daisy

JOHNNY'S TEXTS FLOOD MY PHONE A FEW MINUTES AFTER DELANEY and I order our lunch. I read them between sips of iced tea and roll my eyes before replying.

"Do you have any siblings, Della?"

My friend uses her straw to mix the whipped cream piled on top of her milkshake deeper into the glass.

"I have a younger brother."

"How old is he? And is he as needy as my brother, or is that just a twin thing?"

Her lips twitch. "Is that who was making your phone light up? Grayson is twenty-five."

"Wait, how old are you? I can't believe I haven't asked you that before!"

"I turned thirty a couple of months ago."

"Oh, so a few years older than me. It feels like we could be the same age."

"I'll take the compliment," she says, taking a sip of her milkshake.

The milkshakes from the Rustic Ridge diner are really good. I remember getting one every weekend until I turned fifteen and realized how badly that much dairy upset my stomach. That's when I found an uncurable addiction to iced tea.

"To answer your question, yes, it's Johnny that's blowing up my phone. He's feeling a bit unloved because of how busy I've been the past couple of weeks. Honestly, I'm not used to being home so much anymore. It's more difficult to balance life and work and relationships than I remember from before I left for school. I used to come home for the summer, but I was staying at my parents' house, and having a girlfriend wasn't really anything I had to work my life around," I admit, dumping my entire life story on my poor friend.

Delaney doesn't seem to mind, at least. She offers me a soft, understanding smile and pushes her drink away with her knuckles.

"I get it. And I don't think it ever gets easier. At least not while you're surrounded by so many people. I haven't had that issue in quite a while now."

"Why? You've just been keeping to yourself?"

"You could say that. It's been a long time since I've had to share my life with anyone."

I tongue my cheek, debating whether or not to say the words that have formed on my tongue. It could be how much time I've spent around Bryce that's encouraged me to be more honest, or maybe it's just the type of person I'm growing into. Either way, I decide to go with my gut.

"When was the last time? Was it . . . with Darren?"

Hesitation flashes in her gaze as she looks up. I keep my expression open and honest, hoping she can tell that I don't mean any harm with the question. I'm just unbearably curious recently. Especially after speaking with Bryce and learning little bits and pieces.

Della inhales a long, heavy breath before snatching her cup back and taking two long drags of the milkshake. Once she's done, she drags the tip of her finger through a piece of icy snow on the table that's fallen from the side of her frozen cup.

"Bryce has told you about me and him, hasn't she?"

"Only because I asked. She didn't tell me too much. Nothing specific. I wanted to hear it from you, whenever you were comfortable sharing," I rush out, my cheeks so hot they have their own heartbeat.

"It's okay. I know Bryce isn't the type to gossip. She never was." Delaney tucks her hair behind her ears and then spreads the melting ice along the edge of the table. "Darren is my past. I've tried not to let that time of my life dictate my present and future, so no, the last time I shared my life with someone was not Darren."

"Is it too early in our friendship to ask what happened?"

She tries to smile, but it looks more like a wince. "I'm too embarrassed to tell you the entire story. But the short version? I was young and in love with a boy who wasn't meant to be my forever.

"It was naive love, the kind where you thought the world started and ended with them before you had barely even stepped one foot into it. One day, I was sure I was going to marry my childhood sweetheart, and the next, I was coming home after my final year of university to learn the reason he'd cut me off months before was because he got someone else pregnant. We agreed to take a break while I was gone, but I should have known better than to hope we'd be able to pick things back up afterward. Like I said, I was naive."

My stomach sinks, the pain in her voice so evident it's like I can feel it carving a hole into my chest.

"I'm sorry, Della. That's . . ." I shake my head, unsure what to say.

She offers a weak smile. "It's okay. It was a long time ago. I've made peace with it."

But has she? Because the haunted look in her eyes tells a completely different story. And who can blame her? I don't know the whole story, and it's not my place to search for more of it, but come on? From what Bryce told me, in addition to Della, my heart hurts for the young girl who was broken by the knowledge that the boy she loved had moved on with someone else and, worst of all, gotten her pregnant.

From the handful of times I've met Abbie in passing and spoken to her at school, it's obvious she's a sweet, kind girl. But how does seeing her every day at school make Delaney feel when it was a life with Darren that she had pictured for so many years?

I take a long, long drink of iced tea to clear the ball of emotion in my throat.

She laughs weakly, waving a hand through the air. "Please don't pity me. I'm fine, truly. It all happened a long time ago."

"I don't pity you, Della. But I am sad for you. I can't begin to imagine what that was like. How could you stay here? Cherry Peak is so small."

"My life is here. My job and family. I wasn't going to be run out of town because I made a mistake," she says, tone growing sharper with every word.

I nod, letting it drop before I touch too raw of a spot.

"Well, on a bit of a happier note, I wanted to invite you to a pole class with me and Bryce this weekend. Obviously, you don't have to come, considering Poppy will be instructing, and, well, she's obviously Darren's sister. But I thought it could be fun to get out of town and have a bit of a girls' day if you were up to joining us? You don't have to worry about being new to it or anything. So am I!"

"What day?"

"Sunday? We can pick you up on our way out of town?"

A contemplative pause. "They don't mind if I come along?"

"Nope! When Bryce brought it up to Poppy, she seemed really excited."

After I convinced Bryce that it was a good idea in the first place. It's not that she didn't want Della to come, but she didn't see the appeal of losing time that was supposed to be just for us. Not to mention her worry about my tattoo. It's been healing up well over the past couple of days, but she's such a mother hen.

She was putty in my hands once I straddled her lap on the couch and kept her there for another hour, lips locked—

"Alright. If you're sure I won't be third wheeling or anything," Delaney says.

My grin is instant as I clap loudly. A few of the people around the diner turn to look at me, and I ignore them. If they wanted to dine in complete silence, Rustic Ridge wasn't the place to choose.

The diner belongs to Kiki's family, and they never meant for it to be a quiet place but one for families and happy chit-chat.

Speaking of Kiki, she comes rushing to our table with a plate in each hand. We move our drinks and napkin-wrapped cutlery out of the way for our food.

"A grilled cheese with a garden salad," Kiki announces, sliding the first plate in front of me. The second is set in front of Della. "And a veggie burger with onion rings."

"Thank you," Della says.

I look up at my best friend. "Sit for a minute?"

"If you insist." Kristen slides into the booth beside me and lets out an exhausted sigh. "How much of your lunch break do you have left?"

I check the time on my phone, a new text from Johnny flashing. "Twenty minutes."

It only took three minutes to get here and another fifteen to get our food. Quick service is a bonus when it comes to living in a small town.

As long as we're anywhere other than Peakside on a Saturday night. Then it's like every person in town and two hours outside of it has come in for a drink.

Delaney squirts extra ketchup onto her burger before taking a bite of it. I opt out of ketchup and eat my grilled cheese dry.

"Classes are going good?" Kiki asks, the question not directed specifically at either one of us.

Della finishes her bite first. "It's hard to not enjoy your days when the kids are so cute. Even if they can be total assholes sometimes."

"I don't think we're supposed to call kids assholes, Della," I tease between bites.

Kiki reaches for my iced tea and drinks from the side of the glass before saying, "Why not? I've known some real asshole kids. Two of them are my nephews."

Della laughs, unrolling the napkin around her cutlery and using it to dab at the ketchup that's streaked over her mouth.

"We can think it, at least."

"Fair enough," Kiki agrees.

An older woman around Eliza Steele's age lifts her hand and waves at us, and Kristen pats the table. I give her a quick side hug before she slips from the booth.

"I'll text you later, Didi. And I'll see you around, Delaney."

Delaney nods, and I watch Kiki leave before tearing my teeth into my grilled cheese.

"She's a nice girl," Della notes.

I hum past the food in my mouth, and she snorts a laugh.

"Is she coming this weekend too?"

With a forceful swallow, I shake my head. "No. She works here pretty much every day."

"I haven't seen Poppy in a long time."

"Not even at Peakside?"

"I don't go there," she says quietly.

I shrug and focus on appearing nonchalant, even as a weight boulders my chest. "It's crowded and loud, anyway. And they upcharge for drinks."

"Thank you, Daisy. You don't have to try and downplay the place for my benefit, though," she says, seeing straight through me.

"I'm sorry."

"How about you tell me a bit about Bryce and Poppy? I've missed a lot, I'm sure."

"Okay, well, first, Poppy's dating someone, and it's pretty serious."

"I heard about that. Cherry Peak grapevine and all that. He's not from here, right?"

"Not in the slightest. He's from Toronto. A city boy through and through."

Our conversation goes on until both of our plates are scraped clean and we're paying the bills. We avoid any and everything to do with Darren, and by the time we're heading back to the school, I think she's feeling a bit more confident in her decision to join us this weekend.

I just can't wait to finish the day.

Seeing Bryce once the final bell rings is the only thing on my priority list, and I think I love that.

I'm falling in love with her more every day. And I don't think I've ever felt such excitement for the future than I have with her by my side. A future that she's now a focal point of.

I just hope that once I finish making the fall, she'll be there waiting to catch me.

36

DARREN TRIES TO CALL ME FOR THE THIRD TIME SINCE WE GOT INTO Calgary. Shielding my screen from Delaney, I decline again and then shove my phone into the inside pocket of my shorts.

It's obvious as fuck that he's not happy I'm spending the day with his ex-girlfriend, but quite frankly, I don't care. There was no way I was going to tell my girl that her friend couldn't come when she batted those sky-blue eyes at me and crawled into my lap to beg. And once she kissed me?

Game over.

"This place is gorgeous, Poppy," Daisy exclaims mid-spin.

The second Beautifully Bold location is somehow better than the first. It's brighter, with more space and a water heater that doesn't require a monthly checkup. And Poppy's here. She's the best part of the place.

I'm hanging back by a window, letting Daisy fill the silence that followed an awkward chorus of hellos once we arrived.

Poppy and I haven't spoken much recently. She's the one person who I've always shared almost everything about myself with and who knows the truth about my relationship with Daisy, yet I've held back from her out of pure selfishness.

I'm angry with the hours between us and have been taking it

out on our friendship. What I'm doing is unfair to the both of us, and I won't deny that. Still, that doesn't make it hurt any less or her absence any easier to swallow.

My best friend tightens her ponytail of thick, hazelnut-coloured hair and smiles at Daisy. "Thank you. It's my love child."

"When did you dye your hair?" I ask sharply, catching the two women off guard.

Daisy tugs her brows together as Poppy turns to me with a frown and says, "Two weeks ago. I sent a picture to the group chat."

"I haven't checked it."

"Yeah, I know."

Delaney, who hadn't moved from her place by the door, shifts enough to glance between the two of us with wide eyes. She's not a stranger to either of us, but we've made her feel that way over the years.

For fuck's sake, she was always around when we were growing up. Poppy used to refer to her as a sister, always asking Darren when her big sis was going to be coming over. We were quick to release her like a fish we didn't want to keep on the line once everything went down.

Now she's here, and having her stare between Poppy and me like she has no idea who we are . . . it hits harder than I was anticipating.

Daisy moves to my side and gazes up at me with warmth and understanding that I doubt I deserve after the mess I've made.

I focus on her and let her presence smooth a calming balm over some of my most anxious parts. She doesn't have to do much more than just stand beside me, offering her silent support, to have me ready to confess the feelings swelling in my chest.

"Can we just talk, Bryce?" Poppy asks. I keep my eyes

hooked on Daisy's. "Please? The class doesn't start for a half hour."

"I'll take Della to get something to drink," Daisy announces. "Coffee?"

Poppy smiles appreciatively. "There's a nice smoothie shop about a block away."

"Got it," Daisy chimes.

Cupping my cheek, she pushes forward and skims a kiss across my mouth. I chase her lips, but she pulls back before I make contact, already expecting my move.

She drops her voice to a whisper. "Sort this out, Bryce. Don't miss your chance."

I hook a finger beneath her chin the moment she makes to move and turn her face toward me. This time when our lips meet, I don't let her slip away so quickly. I spread them with my tongue and steal a proper taste before tapping her chin and releasing her.

"Don't be long," I mumble.

She smiles at me, revealing a flash of white teeth, and I reluctantly let her walk away this time. It's not until she links her arm through Delaney's and they disappear out the door that I pull my attention to where Poppy stands watching, her mouth gaping.

"I missed a chapter," she notes carefully.

"What?"

Her brows shoot up to her hairline. "That wasn't fake. Not for you, and sure as hell not for her. When did that happen?"

"It was never fake for me."

"I know that. Does she?"

Guilt squeezes my stomach. "No."

"How are you handling that?"

"Have you been taking counselling lessons in your spare time?" I snap, my protective instincts flaring wide.

"No. If I had been, I'd know better than to ask you these questions head-on. I'm your best friend, Ice."

"Are you?"

She flinches. "Am I what?"

"Nothing," I mutter, shifting my body so I face the windows along the side of the studio instead of her.

Feet pad along the floor, and then hands find mine, clasping them in a tight hold. I don't pull from the touch. If anything, I want to pull her into my arms and squeeze her instead.

"Look at me, Ice," Poppy demands, pulling at my hands.

I force myself to. The deep-rooted sadness I've buried over the past few months is yanked back to the surface at the helplessness in her expression.

"I fucking miss you, Poppy."

Her face crumples, tears filling her eyes. "I miss you so much."

When she wraps me in a hug, I'm powerless to the sting behind my eyes. Her vanilla-scented perfume smells like home and comfort, and I hug her close, squeezing too hard.

"I'm proud of you, Pops. For your success and the love you've found. But I don't know where I fit into your life anymore," I whisper.

Her hold on me tightens to the point of pain. "You fit where I need you to and where you want to be. There will always be a spot reserved for you right at the centre of me. I'm sorry I've made you feel like you weren't a focal point in my life. I've been trying to find a balance, but I'm doing a shitty job of it."

"I'm used to the lives we all had years ago before everything started to change. First, it was Anna on tour with Brody for months on end, then you moved to Calgary, and it was like everyone was outgrowing Cherry Peak but me."

"Bryce," she says on an exhale. Loosening her hold, she stares at me, eyes glistening. "Not everyone needs to outgrow their home. I might be gone, but nowhere I go will ever be Cherry Peak."

I wipe away the lone tear that's escaped. "I'm just having a hard time adjusting."

"So am I. And if there was a way that I could move back home with Garrison and make it work with his job, I would. You know that, right? I never would have left."

"I know, Pops."

She'd have been content with only one studio as long as she had everyone she loved and needed in her life around her. But she also deserves this success more than anyone else.

"There hasn't been a single day that's passed since I left where I haven't hated being away from you. I'm sorry, and I'll do better with splitting my time."

I'm a fucking mess of emotions. That's the only explanation I have for the words that explode from my mouth.

"I love her."

Poppy blinks a few times, her lips parting on invisible words.

"Daisy," I add, shoving a hand through my hair. "I love her."

"Oh, wow. Okay. You love her."

"I do," I confirm.

"When did that happen? When did all of this happen? Because from what I saw, she might be in love with you too."

I laugh on instinct, shaking my head. "She's not in love with me. But things started changing a few weeks ago. Just small things, like her taking care of me when I was sick and we were trapped at my parents' house, and me always keeping the house stocked with her favourite shit. I was interested in her before, but it's so . . . it's so fucking different now."

Poppy's lips pull into a soft, understanding smile. "Different how?"

"Watching her from afar, I knew she was caring and kind and beautiful. But there's so much more to her than that. She's brave and confident and loves to get a rise out of me. I've never had anyone push me as much as she does. It's like she's dug into my brain and found my instruction manual," I ramble.

"You do love her."

My laugh is brighter than usual. "I do."

"So, it's safe to say it's not fake anymore?"

"We've agreed to go slow."

"Is that a yes?"

"I haven't told her that I was interested in her before."

"Will she even care about that?"

I bite the inside of my cheek and dart my eyes around the studio. "I don't know."

"For what it's worth, I don't think she will. Look where you are now. Who cares about you being interested in her before? But you need to own up to it, even if just to clear your conscience. Don't start a relationship with a lie, even one like that."

I don't disagree with her. I've always known that I would have to tell Daisy about my preexisting infatuation eventually. Even if it was only a crush, I went into this knowing I was interested in her.

"When did you become so knowledgeable with relationships?"

"Ever since I learned what real love feels like. The kind that shifts the world beneath your feet not once but every single day."

"Yeah, I think I'm starting to get that."

"There's nothing I want more for you than to get to experience a love like that, Ice. *Nothing.* You deserve someone who's going to make you wake up with a smile on your face, even when you slept like shit the night before," she says, tears leaking down her cheeks at a quick pace.

My stomach swoops as Daisy's name repeats itself in my mind. "Don't cry, Pops. I've already been gushier than I wanted to today."

She shoves my shoulder. "You can never be too gushy."

"Are we good now? You and me?" I ask cautiously.

Poppy pulls me in for another hug. "If you're good, I'm good."

"I'm sorry for pulling back. You're my best friend."

"No more apologies. I love you."

I nod against her shoulder. No more apologies sounds just right to me.

"I love you too."

IF I HAVE to watch Daisy bend over in front of me one more time, I'm going to burst into a giant ball of flame and accidentally burn this place to the ground. My grip on the pole is punishing as she follows Poppy's instructions and sways her round ass in my face. It's one of the only moves I approved of with her healing tattoo, and now I'm regretting us coming here at all. I should have insisted we wait another week or two.

Poppy is ignoring my death glare, smirking to herself while moving from student to student and giving them tips on how to improve their form. I haven't been listening for shit. God help me, I've barely broken a sweat because I've been stuck in a standing position, watching my girl all class.

The pole beside Daisy was empty when she and Delaney got back from grabbing us smoothies, and I knew I should have chosen that one. Instead, I parked myself directly behind her, thinking that would be the best possible fucking spot.

It was my possessive streak that forced my hand. I didn't want anyone else to be able to stare at her ass, and now I'm paying the price.

"Lower, Daisy. Let your shoulders go loose as you hold the pole in a lower spot. Yes! Now, sway your hips and let the music guide your movements," Poppy encourages her.

The wink my best friend shoots me over her shoulder has me baring my teeth like a feral dog.

Daisy is oblivious to my struggles. Her hair falls around her face like a curtain as she drops her head and puts her entire focus into Poppy's instructions.

I let loose a pained noise and attempt to put effort into the beginner move. It doesn't fucking work, and instead, I bend forward only to become eye level with her ass. If I thought the leggings she wore hiking were bad, they were basically a Mrs. Lemieux–approved work skirt compared to the tiny fucking shorts she has on right now.

My eyes nearly cross when I take in how high they've ridden up. At least an inch of both her ass cheeks are exposed, the rounded, plump skin directly in front of me. So close I could take a bite out of them with my teeth. I'm seriously considering banging my head on the metal pole just to shake all of the dirty thoughts free of it.

Like how little effort it would take to sneak up behind her and yank the shorts up even higher, wedging them between her cheeks and tight pussy. Would she soak right through them? Could I taste her if I licked her through the fabric?

My breathing shallows, and I loosen my hips as I hike my ass in the air and sway. Daisy's shorts are hot pink. I'd bet her cunt would soak right through them with two strokes across it. The pink wouldn't be able to hide the wet spot. Not the way my black ones are hiding mine.

"You're drooling," Poppy drawls, passing by me to help Delaney.

I nearly kick my foot out at her.

"I'm not used to this sort of thing," Delaney huffs.

"That's fine. You're doing really well. Here, let's try this next."

It's impossible to look at what they're doing. One second, Daisy's swaying, and the next, she's snapped upright. The air in my lungs burns when she curls her entire torso backward and stares directly at me. Her head hangs upside down, and her tits heave with her panted breaths as she uses her tight hold on the pole to swing herself side to side.

Knees bent and legs parted around the pole, she swishes her hair in the air and blows me a kiss.

I grit my teeth, nipples threatening to stab through my sports bra. Daisy's eyes brighten with mischief, and her biceps contract with the subtle shift of her arms. She adjusts her hands on the pole and uses her arms to squeeze her tits together.

They bulge against the material of her bra, and I glance at the ceiling before focusing back on the crease of her chest.

I tighten my stare and lift an eyebrow. "Keep it up, Sunshine."

"Am I in trouble, Bryce? What's with the tone?" she asks, one pouty lip quivering.

"The moment I get you in private, I'm going to have you beneath me."

A shit-eating grin. "Promises, promises."

She has no idea what I have planned, and that's only going to make it more fun for me. If she thinks she can tease me like this somewhere I can't have her, I'll just have to spend hours reminding her that she's mine somewhere I can.

We've taken things slow, but I think it's obvious that we both need more now. I'm going to have the time of my life exploring all of the different ways I can make her come and scream my name. Once I'm done with her, there won't be a doubt in either of our minds that we're the exact type of love Poppy was explaining to me.

If I don't have it with Daisy, then I never want to with anyone else.

37

Bryce

"I can't believe that you don't like cowboy boots. Either of you!" Poppy guffaws, flicking a finger between Delaney and Daisy as we pass endless aisles of dresses. "You're fake Cherry Peakers."

The dress shop is overstocked and busy, but I haven't had it in me to complain about either of those things. It was Poppy's idea for all of us to come to the mall before we left town. She pulled the *I have nobody here to go shopping with* card, and I still felt too guilty from our conversation earlier and the lack of communication between us to turn her down.

It doesn't matter what we do as long as we can spend more time together. Even if I have to suffer through hours of shopping for a wedding that isn't even happening until this summer.

"Anna didn't wear them when she first got to town," I point out in a weak attempt to help take the heat off them.

Poppy shushes me while shoving hangers along a metal rack and flipping through the dresses. "That doesn't count. She was from big-city Vancouver. These two were born and raised here!"

"Does your boyfriend wear them?" Daisy asks innocently.

"He does."

I release a rough laugh. "Liar."

Poppy shoots fire-lined eyes in my direction. "Have you forgotten that he worked on Steele Ranch? He's worn them a time or two."

"That doesn't count, and we both know it. And he only worked there for a couple months. Don't get carried away," I say.

"Speaking of boyfriend," Daisy cuts in and slides between me and Poppy with a loopy grin. "Is it going to be boyfriend for much longer, or are we finally going to see you with a ring the size of the moon?"

Poppy's sigh is dramatic as fuck but so very her. She lifts her hand in front of her and stares at the bare ring finger.

"You're asking the wrong person. I'd have married him two years ago."

"Do you think he's dragging his feet?" Delaney asks.

She's the one of us who doesn't know all that much about Poppy and Garrison's relationship. I'm guessing what she does know, she's heard from gossipers in town.

"Garrison isn't really the type to beat around the bush. I think it's more to do with his career and all of the changes in our life recently than dragging his feet," Poppy explains, letting her hand fall.

"He could not want to overshadow Brody and Anna's wedding either," Daisy offers.

It will be the biggest wedding Cherry Peak has ever seen. They recently chose Steele Ranch as the venue, and yeah, it's an important location for the two of them, but I think it's also the only place with enough space.

Delaney feels the sequined straps of one of the dresses before pushing the entire thing away with a grimace. "I thought the wedding wasn't until summertime?"

"It's not. But planning has already started. I've told Garrison that I don't want a long engagement either. So he knows that when he proposes, the wedding has to be at maximum three months afterward. I'm not giving him time to change his mind or swooping in to tie the knot before Anna and Brody do."

"He wouldn't change his mind regardless of how long you waited," I say.

"Realistically, I know that. But insecurities are a bitch."

Daisy gifts her a soft, honest smile. "He couldn't do better than you. Something tells me that he's more than aware of that."

"You're the sweetest, Daisy. If Bryce doesn't keep you, I'll have to revoke our best friend status," Poppy threatens teasingly.

It's Daisy's eyes I latch onto. "I don't plan on letting her go."

She blushes all the way to her ears and ducks into another aisle. We all follow, and the scratch of hangers grinding against the metal rods makes the hair on my arms rise.

I tuck my arms into my sides and step back into a puffy dress when a group of teenage girls rush by me with high-pitched squeals and arms full of fabric.

Daisy notices my discomfort a beat before Poppy does, and then the both of them are taking my arms and leading us out of the aisle.

"What do you say we find somewhere else to look?" Daisy asks.

Delaney answers. "I saw a few other shops on our way here."

Daisy takes my hand and links our fingers. I give them a thankful squeeze, and then, side by side, the four of us leave the store as a unified front. My chest fills with appreciation.

"Actually, I saw another shop I wanted to check out. It's only a little bit further," Poppy says.

I think I'm the only one that picks up the slight wiggle in her voice.

"What kind of shop?" I ask, narrowing my eyes.

She grins and points to a place on my right. "That one. I've been needing something new."

"A sex shop?" Delaney barks before laughing.

Daisy walks a little quicker, pulling me with her. "Oh, fun! I've never actually gone into a sex shop before."

"What?" I ask, surprised.

She shrugs. "I just order toys online."

"It's easier that way," Delaney agrees.

The shop is dark on the outside, and when we step through the door, it's just as dark inside. Majority of the light comes from the toy displays, making them the focal point of the store. It's smart.

We're approached by a tiny Black woman who asks if we need anything, but Poppy's too excited to show Daisy around to accept any help. With a grin and a reminder that she's there if we need anything, the sales associate leaves us to wander around on our own.

Another few people enter the store, and they take the associate up on her offer for help.

"Who needs a dildo this big?"

Delaney pokes the shaft of a hot pink suctioned dildo standing tall on a shelf and stares wide-eyed when it bounces around. The balls at the base are massive, and Poppy laughs like a hyena when they shake alongside the shaft.

"Garrison's bigger."

Daisy chokes. "Your poor vagina."

"It's not just my—"

I cut her off and shove her down the line of toys. "We're close, but I don't need to know about all the places Garrison puts his cock."

Poppy shoots me a wink and then focuses on Delaney. "So, you don't have a lot of dildos, then?"

"Not like that one."

"Do you need one, or do you have a real dick in your life?" Poppy asks, blunt as hell.

"Are you single, Della? I think that's what Poppy was trying to ask," Daisy says.

I snort a laugh while Poppy rolls her eyes.

Delaney taps the edge of the dildo display. "I'm single."

Poppy hums, the corners of her mouth twitching in a way that reeks of potential meddling. It's not a good sign for Delaney.

She tries to keep her expression nonchalant but fails. "Were you invited to Anna's wedding?"

"No. I don't really know her at all."

A sneaky hum is Poppy's reply.

"What?" Delaney asks her suspiciously.

I mutter, "Just ignore her."

Delaney nods. "Are you all in the bridal party?"

"I'm the maid of honour, and Bryce is a bridesmaid. Daisy's going to be Bryce's gorgeous date, right? And not a fake one anymore."

I tense at the use of the word "fake." Daisy freezes in front of the butt plug displays.

Delaney looks at each of us, confusion sparking in her eyes. "A fake one?"

"Bryce and Daisy were only fake dating at the beginning to get Bryce's mom to stop setting her up on dates. That's done now, though. They're the real deal, and I'm so damn happy for them," Poppy explains, her voice not loud but carrying across the store regardless.

How did I not notice how quiet it is in here until now?

"How about we don't talk about this in public, Poppy?" I ask, my heartbeat a bit too fast.

She blanches. "Shit. I'm sorry."

The group of people pretend not to look in our direction as I usher us all away from them, but there's no doubt in my mind that they heard every word Poppy spoke. I couldn't care less about Delaney knowing the truth. I'm not on edge about it or worrying that she'll tell anyone. It's those I don't know that make me anxious. If Poppy had noticed them lingering so close, she wouldn't have said anything.

I remind myself we're not in Cherry Peak and try to settle my nerves.

Daisy doesn't seem as worried as I am about anyone over-hearing. She just looks at Delaney and smiles.

"I'm sorry I didn't tell you. We'd only told a couple of people."

"We didn't know each other. You shouldn't have felt like you needed to tell me something like that," Delaney replies, staring between me and my girl. "I could never tell that it wasn't real."

Poppy's attention falls on me, and I know what she's thinking. *It wasn't fake for both of you.*

"It didn't stay that way for very long," Daisy muses.

She moves to my side, and I curl an arm around her hip, tugging her close. With her bright blue eyes caressing my face, I'm too weak to deny my need to kiss her and do exactly that.

It's quicker than I'd like, but better than nothing.

My desire for her is the only thing I have no fucking control over. I want her near me all the time, and even when she is, I'm not sated unless her lips are on mine and I can feel her skin beneath my fingers.

It's been torture keeping my thoughts of straying to the memory of her in the pole studio, but I can't risk losing my head in the middle of the mall.

I'm addicted to her and proud as fuck of it.

A sniffle snags my attention. It's Poppy who's crying while trying to hide her face behind her shirt sleeve. I frown at the sound of her sobs, and Delaney turns to me, alarmed.

Daisy gives me a light push in Poppy's direction. I swallow and wrap my best friend in my arms for the second time today.

"I thought we said no more tears earlier," I murmur.

The arm she's using to hide her face presses painfully against my chest, but I don't have the heart to tell her to move it.

"We did. But that was before I got to watch the two of you together like this. I've missed so much being away! You're the cutest couple I've ever seen, and I'm not there to see you fall in love. You're so—you're so happy," she blubbers.

A hand sweeps up my spine, and I know it's Daisy's from the

way my body melts at the touch. Poppy shakes in my arms, and I bite my cheek hard enough for it to bleed so I don't cry alongside her.

"You're not missing anything. When you're home next weekend, we'll still be there. Just like this."

"Promise?"

Daisy hugs me from behind, her lips finding the back of my ear. It's confirmation enough.

"I promise, Pops," I declare.

38

Daisy

AN EVIL, MANIACAL LAUGH HAS BEEN TRAPPED IN MY CHEST FROM the moment the pole class started to now as we watch Delaney wave around her sex shop bag from her front door. It's dark out, the time on Bryce's dash reading a few minutes past 9:00 p.m.

Delaney goes inside, and then Bryce is pulling out of her driveway and down the street. The engine revs as she pushes us past the speed limit.

"Is your foot feeling a little heavy tonight?" I ask innocently.

"Mmhmm."

"You were also going quite fast on the highway."

"I was."

"Is there any particular reason for that?"

I'm asking for trouble. Every time I open my mouth, something devious falls out. I think it's the horniness festering in my brain that's driving me to push and push until she finally snaps and ravages me.

My not-so-subtle actions in the studio were affecting her so openly that I almost took pity on her and invited her into the shower with me afterward. My frosty couldn't have been cold then or now if her life depended on it. She'd burn me the moment I touched her.

I've never felt so desired by someone before.

"I'm just ready to be home," she says tightly.

I smirk, fisting my knee. "Any particular reason why?"

Her eyes flare with blue fire when she pins me beneath them. "When we get home, go straight to my room."

"Manners, Bryce," I murmur.

"Not a fucking chance. My manners are non-existent at this point, and that's your fault."

"My fault?" I ask with a mocking gasp.

"Keep digging the hole, baby. I'm going to have the time of my life making sure you lie in it."

I laugh brightly, feeling the shine of bliss in every inch of my body. "Will you join me, at least?"

She flattens a palm to my thigh and holds it in a tight, reassuring grip. "I'd join you anywhere."

"That's a confident statement."

"I'm a confident person."

"You're supposed to be my fake girlfriend."

Her nails dig into the material of my jeans, and her jaw tightens before relaxing. "I'm not your fake anything. Use that term again and I'm more than happy to keep you in my bed until you forget it."

The car comes to a jerking stop, and I realize a beat later that we've made it home. Bryce is moving instantly, and I get the feeling that I've maybe underestimated her promises. My excitement only grows, ramping up to an extreme that has sweat beading along my spine.

Without a word, she has the car off and is already slamming her door shut. In the dark, her figure looks like a shadow as she rounds the hood and heads right for me. I fumble with my seat belt and toss it across my body before my door opens, and she's *right* there.

"I'll have you here on the street, Daisy. Hiding in the car won't save you," she warns, voice thick with desire.

"I'm not hiding."

I hold her blistering gaze and slide out of the car, making sure my chin is tipped high. She may be a predator, but I'm no easy prey.

Her warmth is almost jarring in comparison to the evening chill, but I lean into it on instinct.

"My room," she reminds me.

My skin feels like it's melting to my bones as a flush of arousal ripples through me. I blink slowly and reach out to touch her, only to have her shake her head and lean back.

"I told you about the hole you dug, Sunshine. If you want to touch me, you have to earn it. Starting with going inside to my bedroom," she says before I have a chance to grow offended.

"You're not being serious."

But she doesn't look like she's kidding.

"Inside, Daisy."

I don't stay to argue about it any longer. She may have been unable to hide her reaction to me in the studio, but that doesn't mean I wasn't just as affected by her. I've been walking around all day with soiled panties and even had to use water to rub the slick from my pink shorts in the studio bathroom before changing back into my jeans.

I keep my pace controlled as I head up the sidewalk, refusing to glance back to see if she's nipping at my heels. Her presence isn't banging against my back, but I shove that thought out of my mind.

I'll do what she tells me to because I want everything she's planning. I'm safe with her, my trust rock solid without a crack in sight. I know that tonight will be perfect. It would be even if all we did was curl up in bed and watch a ghost-hunting documentary like we've done every night for the last week. For Bryce, I've worked past my fear of ghosts just so I can watch her movies without freaking out.

I enter the door code and then slip inside. Bryce isn't behind me, so instead of searching for her, I shut the door and toe off my sneakers.

The house is dark, so I flick on the hall light. It's bright enough to illuminate the living room and the yellow blanket thrown along the back of the couch. A few schoolbooks and glitter pens are strewn over the glass coffee table, but the space is clean and tidy otherwise.

With my pulse jumping, I reach for the hem of my shirt and pull it up and over my head. It falls silently to the floor as I move further inside.

Ignoring the kitchen, I turn down the hall and unbutton my jeans. With my shirt behind me, my jeans add to the trail as they fall to a heap at my feet. I step out of them and drop my bra in front of the bathroom.

By the time I'm tucking my thumbs into my panties, I'm looking into Bryce's bedroom. They come down easily, and I'm too hot with desire to care about the wet fabric as I hang them on the door handle.

I've been in Bryce's room several times over the last couple of weeks, but we've been very tame within its walls. That's about to change. For good, I hope.

I'm completely naked as I wander over to her bed and run a hand over the velvet blanket. She always lies on the left side of the bed, and now, with her outside somewhere, giving me time to do whatever I need to before joining me, I settle in front of her nightstand.

I haven't told her that I walked in on her masturbating yet, but the memory of it hasn't left my mind since. It's there at night, when I'm alone in my own bed after an evening of holding each other and an ache grows between my legs. She's the one I think about when I thrust my fingers inside of myself and pinch my clit. It's her tongue I picture lapping at me. Her moans in my ears.

I take the silver nightstand handle between my fingers and pull. Inch by inch, the drawer opens, and my eyes grow larger and larger.

I've never seen so many toys in one place outside of a sex

shop. The collection is extensive. There are tiny vibes, a wand vibrator, grinding pad, glass and silicone dildos, and a handful of different-sized butt plugs. If I reached into the drawer and shuffled things around, I'm sure I could find more hidden beneath all the others.

"Oh, my God," I whisper.

"Pick one."

I jump at the sound of her voice. My thigh digs into the corner of the drawer when I spin toward the doorway, pain exploding in the muscle.

The pink panties hanging from her finger have my cheeks throbbing with a blush. She rubs the crotch with her thumb, right over where I know I've soaked them.

"Pick one," she repeats herself.

"Anything?"

"What do you prefer?"

She's leaving it up to me, I realize. Regardless of her own desires, she's giving me the chance to be in control, at least when it comes to this part of the night.

I dip a hand into the drawer and follow my gut, knowing what I do and don't like.

"Anything with a vibration. I need clit stimulation to come," I start, grabbing the round-headed vibrator. "And I don't shy from ass play."

There's a rough exhale from the doorway, but I keep focused on the drawer of toys, tapping the glass butt plug with the rose-shaped base.

"They're all clean. But if you'd prefer, I can wash them again first. I haven't had sex in over three years, and my tests were clear the last time I was at the doctor's," she divulges.

"I trust you. And mine were clear as well." With a swallow, I ask, "Which toys do you like best?"

"Everything in that drawer. Vaginal and anal penetration and clit play."

I shiver in anticipation, tightening my hold on the simple

vibrator. Without looking at her, I know she's closing in on me. The air shifts and pulls taut, like it's trying to force us together.

Her breasts brush my arm, and then she's reaching for the vibrator, taking it from me.

"On the bed. Legs spread nice and wide," she murmurs.

I look at her and moan, the sound of it low and needy. Without so much as touching me, she makes me pulse between my legs, arousal slicking the inside of my thighs.

It's the obsession in her eyes and the way they rake across my face inch by inch in a silent claiming. There's something powerful about having someone stare at you like they need nothing but your mind, body, and soul to survive. It makes me feel invincible, like a goddess.

With bated breaths, I climb onto the bed and spread out on my back. She follows every shift of my body with her dark, possessive stare, and I feel the weight of it like nails gliding over my bare skin.

Pressing my palms into the velvet blanket, I slowly part my legs. The air is hot on my arms but cold between them. If I looked down, I know I'd find myself dripping onto the blanket.

"Christ, you're gushing."

I give a jerky nod and track her as she moves to the end of the bed, directly in front of my naked pussy. My thighs fall completely open as she inspects me.

The vibrator in her hands is silent, but she traces the buttons along the side of it, toying with me.

"Are you going to use that on me?"

"I am."

"Take your clothes off first."

She lifts a brow. "Why?"

"The only time I've seen you completely naked is when you were sick. I want to see you again, for real this time."

"You should have thought about that before you teased me in the studio and the entire drive home."

The vibrator rumbles to life, and I press myself into the

mattress on instinct, clenching around air. Bryce joins me on the bed in her jeans and cropped shirt, but I don't have a chance to be angry about her lack of nakedness before—

"Oh! Bryce!"

The thick, round head of the vibrator makes contact with my core, and Bryce must have skipped the first few levels of intensity. The vibrations are fierce and sharp, yanking the air from my lungs.

She crawls between my legs and stares into my eyes as the wand moves in slow, controlled circles over my clit. I whine at the relentless contact, and then a moment later, I'm jerking my hips up into it, grinding against the head.

The intensity goes up a notch, and I squeeze my eyes shut, moaning and moaning and moaning until I'm starting to drown out the buzz.

Bryce leans over my body, her fingers tracing shapes up my stomach and waist. "Tell me before you come, baby."

I can only nod in answer. The bed sinks deeper as she moves further up my body, exploring with firm touches. My nipple grows hot before it's sucked into her mouth, a soft, flat tongue lapping at it.

She swaps breasts and sucks at the opposite nipple before kissing and nipping at the skin around it. It's like she's enjoying driving me out of my mind. No, I'm sure she is.

With a twist of her wrist, she adjusts the vibrator, lifting it just enough for my pussy to spasm, pleasure building and building—

"I'm going to come," I whimper.

Just like that, the vibrator disappears, taking my orgasm with it. I make a growl-like sound and snap my eyes open only to glare at her.

She crawls the rest of the way up my body and kisses me, swallowing all of the angry words I wanted to say. My eyes fall shut again, and I thread my fingers in the hair at the back of her head before she can push me away again. She can deny me orgasms, but I'm not going to allow her to deny me the ability to touch her.

I lick at the seam of her lips, and she parts them for me as if she's as desperate for more as I am. A stroke of her tongue against mine, and I'm grasping her waist to pull her against me, needing the reassurance that this is really happening. That I'm in Bryce's bed, beneath her body, and with her lips on mine.

"Let me see you, Bryce. All of you," I beg.

She drags her mouth across my cheek and down beneath my jaw, sucking the skin. I sigh in pleasure and bare my neck. Her fingers slip between our bodies and find my nipples, brushing and tugging at them.

"If I take my clothes off, I'm not letting you leave this room tonight. You'll be coming all over my sheets and sleeping beside me on top of them."

"Yes. Do that."

Her chuckle is pure sin. "Okay, baby."

I nearly reach out to pull her back to me when she pushes backward and steps off the bed. It's a miracle I can even keep myself pinned down on the bed and not tear across it to be the one to take her clothes off.

She removes her jeans first, the material tight enough around her thighs that she has to wiggle them down to her ankles. The black thong cupping her pussy is next. It disappears into her jeans.

In only a cropped black tee with Nirvana written across it in vintage writing, she stands so confidently before me that it's like a blast to the face. Bryce is the most gorgeous woman I have ever laid eyes on, and right now, like this, I know exactly how lucky I am to be the one in her bed. To have her want me in it.

A myriad of colours and designs are scattered over her legs, groin, and midriff. Some of them I've discovered, have touched and kissed. But there are so, so many more to explore.

"I haven't seen your very first tattoo yet," I whisper.

She doesn't answer with words. In a blink, she's begun

sliding her shirt up her body and over her chest. Discarded, it joins the rest of her clothes on the floor.

I suck in a hot breath of air. It may not be the first time I've seen her shirtless, but it feels like it. I didn't give her the proper attention that first day, and I'm ready to spend the next several begging for forgiveness for my mistake.

"You're gorgeous," I declare softly.

A deep pink colour spreads across her high, round breasts. It's so similar to the rosy shade of her nipples as they tighten, becoming hard peaks accentuated by black jewellery.

I cut off my next inhale when I notice the small tattoo I hadn't in her old bathroom or the photo in her bedroom. The middle finger shaded in purple, pink, and blue inked into the soft skin beneath her left nipple.

"Thank you, Sunshine," she all but purrs, climbing back onto the bed to straddle my thigh.

My lips spread in a happy, lazy smile when her body weight returns. I run my hands up her sides and then down around her back. She's so smooth and warm and curved in all the right places. I'm lost to how right she feels beneath my hands and how addictive it is to touch her like this.

"Let me please you," I whisper before licking a stripe up the side of her throat. "Let me earn my forgiveness."

She moans, dragging her breasts against mine and then upward until a cool, pink-tipped nipple brushes my lips.

"Open," she commands.

I part my lips and take her nipple into my mouth. Circling it with my tongue, I listen for every slight sound that escapes her, letting them guide me. When I graze the sensitive peak with my teeth and tug at the piercing, she rocks forward, and wet, hot skin glides along my thigh.

"Bite it. Gently," she breathes out.

I follow her instructions, and she grips the blanket beside my head before grinding down on my leg. An exhaled whimper escapes her gaped mouth, and she continues to ride me, slicking my thigh in her arousal.

Acting out of impulse, I take her breasts into my hands and squeeze gently. I pinch her second nipple before rolling it between my fingertips, careful of the metal hoop.

The ball at the centre of her clit piercing is prominent with every roll of her hips, and I imagine it's pressing right against her most sensitive spot.

My lips tingle when I pull them from her nipple and shift to lick the other one. "What does it feel like to grind your pussy against me with the piercing?"

Her eyes flash, but her words are weak, breathy. "Extra stimulation."

"I want to feel it against my tongue again."

"Not yet."

She shifts, feeding her nipple into my mouth to distract me. The first glide of her fingers through my slit forces her breast from my mouth.

"Please," I plead brokenly.

I'm sensitive and aching deep after my stolen orgasm. I need relief so badly I'm willing to do anything for it.

Sinking two fingers into my opening, Bryce shifts her position on my thigh until she can watch them glide deep. A puddle of arousal coats my thigh beneath her as she keeps us pressed together but doesn't glide forward again. Instead, her attention has fallen on me.

I preen beneath her wide-pupiled stare. The pleasure blooming in my core is instant and intense after being teased. I only need a few more strokes to come. Release is so, so close—

"Bryce! Oh . . . Oh, I'm going to come. I'm going to . . . Please let me come," I plead brokenly.

She hooks her fingers inside my walls and brings a second hand to play with my clit. An orgasm stronger than I've ever felt knocks the wind out of me. It grows in intensity the faster she rubs her thumb against my clit, and I forget to breathe.

"Eyes open, Daisy. Watch me when I make you come."

I arch my neck and suck in a strangled inhale, forcing my eyes open. It gets stuck in my throat as my body begins to shake, the pleasure lasting hours upon hours, like it'll never end.

"Don't pass out on me. You're not done."

My pussy cries at the loss of her fingers. My head feels empty, nothing inside but the desire for more. For both of us.

Bryce must be thinking the same thing as me. I do nothing but lie beneath her, my muscles still jelly, while she swivels and brings her thighs to either side of my head. She's glistening between her puffy pink lips, and I dart my tongue out to get a taste before she's settled in place.

An animalistic sound escapes me. My hands find her ass, and I squeeze it in two tight fists. She drops her hips and leans off the side of the bed. Her pussy rubs against my mouth, and I waste no time before swiping my tongue over the length of her again.

She groans, thighs tightening against my cheeks. "Not yet."

"Then when?"

A low, almost undetectable buzzing sounds, but I can't see where it's coming from with her on top of me. Her arousal coats my lips, and I decide that I don't care what it is or what she's planning on doing with it.

"Now, Sunshine," she says before breaching me with something round and slick.

The vibrations are weak compared to earlier, but combined with the thick width of the dildo, the pleasure is sharper, more intense.

"Look at you, stretching so wide for my toys. Do you want it deeper?" she asks, her praise setting me on fire.

I nod, and my words get swept away as I plunge my tongue into her opening and then flick it against her pierced hood. The dildo bottoms out, leaving me so full it's almost uncomfortable, before she pulls it free and soothes the ache with the pressure of her thumb to my clit.

"Louder, Daisy. You've had such a busy mouth all day, but now you don't have words to say?"

I take the hoop piercing between my teeth and pull just enough for her to feel it.

"Oh, *fuck*," she curses, starting to jerk her hips into unstable movements. "I can't get enough of you or this gorgeous cunt. Could spend the rest of my life right here."

I don't understand how I can already be so close to coming a second time only a few minutes after the first, but it's there. It's building and building, and if she keeps up the double stimulation, I'm going to explode.

I lift her off my mouth just long enough to say, "I watched you come riding a toy in your bed weeks ago. It's been on my mind since, and after tasting you for the first time at the shop, I knew I wouldn't ever get enough of this pretty pussy, even if I had an entire lifetime to spend between your legs."

Bryce comes with a cry that I'd bet her neighbours can hear without even one of my fingers inside of her. She pulses against my tongue, and I slide my tongue through her opening, craving a taste of her cum.

The dildo continues to thrust into me, but when Bryce collapses forward and drops her face between my thighs, I know it won't matter. The moment the tip of her tongue circles my sensitive clit, I come again.

The second orgasm doesn't last as long as the first, but it's more intense. My temperature rises, then falls, and my pulse beats in my ears as I suck in quick breaths to try and bring myself back into my body.

Bryce tugs the dildo free, discarding it somewhere on the bed before sealing her mouth over my slit and licking me clean. I moan, both at how sensitive I am and how comforting the act is, and then loosen my punishing grip on her ass. The half moons I left indented in her skin make me frown.

A moment later, she rolls off me and onto her back on the

mattress. Her toes are painted a dark blue that appears almost black, and they wiggle as she sighs.

"Are you okay?" she asks, her voice barely above a whisper.

"I can't feel my legs, but yes. I'm better than okay. That was everything I thought it would be."

She hums, rolling onto her side. "You've imagined this?"

"Of course I have."

"Was that before or after you spied on me?"

She's too good at hiding her emotions, and while usually I can see right through whichever act she's decided to put on, I stumble this time.

"I didn't mean to spy. Really. It was late, and I didn't even know you were awake. Then, I saw you in bed, and I just—I stayed. I'm sorry."

The bed shifts and creaks as she pushes up and around until she's lying with her head beside mine. I turn onto my side, and she follows.

Her hand moves up between us and cups my cheek. I lean into her touch, rolling into her body as my eyes drift shut.

"I'm teasing you. I don't care if you watched me, on accident or otherwise."

"Really?" I ask, suddenly too tired to keep my eyes open.

She strokes a knuckle along my jaw and drapes an arm over my waist. "Really. Now, rest."

"You'll rest too?"

"I'll rest too, baby."

It's all I need to hear before letting stealing a few minutes of sleep.

39

Bryce

THE SMELL OF BACON WAKES ME BEFORE MY ALARM DOES. I STRETCH my arm out at my side and feel cold sheets instead of the warm body I remember falling asleep beside.

After Daisy woke from her nap with my tongue tracing the shape of her breast, it was late by the time we managed to tire ourselves out again. But I wasn't so far gone that I imagined sprawling across Daisy's chest and falling asleep.

She was here, and now she's gone. Even if she's only in the kitchen, I wanted her here when I opened my eyes. Maybe to give me some sort of validation after what we did last night and the steps we took, or who fucking knows. I just wanted her to be the first thing I saw.

The whole "sex is a good way to relax" saying is bullshit. Sex with Daisy makes me clingy and desperate, not relaxed.

I groan and throw my arm over my eyes. Maybe if I go back to sleep, I can have a redo.

"I heard you groaning, so you can't pretend to be asleep just so you don't have to go to work this morning."

Baring my eyes, I push up on my elbow and glare at her. It's hard to keep it up once I spot the plate of food in her hands and the bright grin on her sleepy features.

"Stop glaring at me, Frosty. I left to make breakfast."

"I wanted you in bed when I woke up," I grunt.

She teases me with a pout and hovers the plate of food over my lap. "You could have told me that last night."

"Neither of us were doing much talking then."

Snatching a piece of crisp bacon, I rip off a chunk and begin chewing. There's more than enough food on this plate to feed three people, let alone the two of us.

"That's fair. I'll keep in mind that you're needy in the morning."

I swallow the bacon and curve a hand over her nape before bringing her in for a kiss. Her lashes flutter shut as she kisses me back and pushes my messy hair over my shoulder, running her fingers through it.

She entertains me for a couple of minutes and then pulls back with a bump of our noses.

"Eat, Bryce. We both have work today."

"I'd rather stay here."

"Me too. But it's too short notice to find a sub, and I want to keep my sick days for the next time you find yourself kneeling over a toilet."

I chuckle, propping myself up against the headboard and folding my leg to make room for her to sit on the bed. "How do you know it won't be you puking next time?"

Her chin tips toward the ceiling when she sits and places the food on the mattress beside my stretched leg. She holds my knee and takes a peanut butter–smeared pancake between her fingers.

"I never get sick. It's a Mitchell family blessing."

"Must be a sham because Johnny's gotten sick plenty of times."

"You mean he's *pretended* to be sick plenty of times," she corrects me.

I lean forward and steal a bite of the pancake held to her lips.

"Do you like peanut butter on pancakes?" she asks, taking in my expression as I chew.

Swallowing, I take another pancake from the stack. "I've never had it until now. Who doesn't like peanut butter?"

"You'd be surprised. But I love it. It's been a while since I've had it on pancakes, though. Johnny hates peanut butter and used to hide the jars our moms would buy for me."

"Johnny's a shit disturber."

She giggles, and I decide right here, right now, that I never want to start a day again without hearing that sound.

"I had a good time yesterday," she murmurs.

"Poppy's going to meddle into Delaney's life, you know?"

"Would that be such a bad thing?"

"It will be if she's doing what I think she is and getting herself involved in Delaney's relationship with Darren."

"I'm assuming he won't be any happier about that than Della?"

"I told him she was coming with us yesterday, and he called me six times while we were gone. I haven't answered him yet, but I'll need to soon."

She rolls her lip between her teeth before letting it go. "He's mad at you for letting her come? You should tell him that it was my idea."

"I won't be doing that, so he needs to get over it. I'm glad she came. It was nice."

I mean it too. Delaney is good company. And Darren is a grown man with a child old enough to learn from the examples he sets. He can sort himself out before he self-destructs. They've been separated for nearly a decade.

Daisy nods, accepting my explanation without a doubt, showing her trust in me. I take her hand and guide her up onto my lap. She hovers over my thighs and sucks a smear of peanut butter off her thumb.

I zone into the movement, desire coiling low in my belly. Depending on what time it is, I could convince her to get back in bed for a few minutes . . .

She releases her thumb with a loud pop, and her lips curl high when she notices my stare. "Don't even think about it, Ms. Punctuality. Eat and then get dressed."

"I'm not thinking about anything."

"Liar," she whispers, leaning forward to kiss the tip of my nose.

"I want every morning to be like this," I admit, pushing past the voice in my head that tells me not to be so obvious with my love.

"The being served breakfast part or the being with me part?"

"You know the answer to that already. Although the breakfast is nice too."

She sweeps her knuckles across the hair tickling my forehead, a serene warmth lighting her eyes.

Eating breakfast in bed in the early morning with someone you love is such a mundane thing, but it means more to me than most others do. It's a step in the right direction. A look into the future I hope to have with Daisy.

The words *I love you* bubble up my throat, and I'm one heartbeat away from telling her how I feel. It's a risk, but if I keep it inside any longer, I'm going to burst, and she'll learn about my feelings from the doctor after I'm left with a heart-sized hole in my chest.

I steel my spine and open my mouth—

Someone starts pounding on my front door, making it rattle on the hinges loud enough for me to hear it all the way in my bedroom.

"Who is that?" Daisy gasps, hopping off me.

She rushes to my dresser and starts riffling through the first and then second drawers. I don't have a chance to tease her about looking through my panties before she's whipping a shirt and shorts at me. They're tiny fucking things that Poppy forced me to buy over a year ago, but I put them on without complaint.

"No clue," I reply tightly. "But stay here while I go look."

"As if. Who are you, Captain America? If you're getting hit with a baseball bat, I want to be hit too," she says, and suddenly, I wish she hadn't gotten dressed already this morning.

I scroll my eyes up and down her body and would have smiled at how weird she looks with all-black clothes on if I wasn't so annoyed with whoever it is threatening to plow through my door.

"Fine, Daisy."

She doesn't wait for me before leaving the room, so I fumble out of bed and jog to catch her in the hall.

I knew I should have spanked her last night.

The knocking gives for a second, but the silence doesn't last for long. Johnny's voice blows right through the door, and I freeze, feeling Daisy's attention shift to me.

"Open up, Bryce!"

"Were you expecting him this morning?" I ask, quietly enough her brother won't be able to hear.

She shakes her head. "No."

"Great," I mutter.

I slide past her and unlock the deadbolt before opening up the door. Johnny Mitchell doesn't wait for an invitation inside. He just storms right past me.

"Sure, come inside," I tell him, no hint of a joke to be found in my voice.

He's clearly pissed off about something, but when he doesn't take his boots off before disappearing into the living room the way he always does, something sours in my gut.

"What's wrong, J?" Daisy asks, quick to chase after him.

I trail behind and linger beneath the archway. Johnny faces his sister with raging eyes the same shade as hers. "Why haven't you checked your phone this morning?"

"I was busy."

He spins to face me, and his anger swells. "And you?"

"Not like it's your business, Jonathan, but I was with Daisy. Now, knock it down a few pegs when you're speaking to her."

"Oh, you're takin' this whole thing really far. You can cut it out now that I know the truth," he snaps.

That sour feeling grows in intensity, turning to queasiness. Daisy isn't able to hide her emotions from me, and as she starts piecing together what he's saying, her face pales beneath flaming red cheeks.

"Watch it," I warn again. "What are you talking about?"

He plants his hands on his jeaned hips and stares me down. "This whole sham! You've been lyin' to us. *All of us.*"

"It's not a lie—" Daisy starts.

Johnny keeps me trapped beneath a stare flickering with betrayal. "You used my sister for your own benefit. I trusted you with her, and you stabbed me in the back. We were all so happy for you, and then first thing this mornin', I had Eliza Steele pull me aside and explain the rumours flyin' around town about you and my damn twin sister."

"What rumours?" I snip, letting his other words slip away for now, not giving them space in my mind. They'll hit really fucking hard in a few minutes.

"You and Daisy! Your fake relationship that was only created to trick your parents into leaving you alone so that you didn't have to actually stand up for yourself."

"Johnny," Daisy says, a threatening edge to her tone that I haven't heard before. "You don't know the whole story."

He snaps his head in her direction and scrunches his brows. "I don't want to talk to you right now, Daisy. Me and Bryce have some shit to work through."

"Okay, macho man. That's not going to work. You need to take a breath and really think about whether you want to continue acting like a bull in a china shop."

"I like you, Johnny, but I'm not going to stand here and let you attack me in my own house," I say coolly.

He laughs humourlessly. "You lied to my family and my friends. I'm sorry for not being cool-headed."

"They're my friends too," I snap back.

"Then why didn't you tell us the truth? Actually, it doesn't matter. I don't even trust you enough anymore to stand here and listen to whatever it is you have to say in your defense."

"You're being dramatic, Johnny. Just calm down and listen to what we have to say," Daisy says.

He shakes his head hard. "What do you even have to say? That you felt it was okay to just lie to everyone you know and care about in order to help someone who should have known that it's okay to ask for help straight up? Do you have any idea how badly this is going to hurt the moms when they find out the truth? If they haven't already."

Daisy winces, her face crumpling. "They weren't supposed to learn about the fake part. Not now, considering it's not like that anymore."

"That's not for you to decide. Word broke in Peakside last night when one of the ranch hands started runnin' his drunk-ass mouth to anyone who would listen. The others mentioned it to Eliza this mornin', but I'd put money on it being all over town by now."

Alarm spears through me as I start to panic. *My mom.*

She has fingers in every social circle in Cherry Peak. I wouldn't doubt if she was one of the first few people to find out.

"How did that guy even learn about this?" Daisy asks.

Her twin blows out a harsh breath. "His sister was up in Calgary yesterday. Apparently, she was in a goddamn sex shop and recognized Poppy when she overheard everything."

I shove trembling fingers through my hair and keep breathing steadily. The odds of that happening are one in a million.

I've never given a shit what the people in this town think or say about me, but I do care what they say about Daisy. She doesn't deserve to be spoken about and judged by people who don't know a damn thing about her because of something she was doing for me.

And Poppy . . . She'll never get over knowing that her innocent words were stolen by someone and used to create a burst of harmful gossip.

I force myself to speak. "Which ranch hand was it?"

"Doesn't matter. It's too late to get ahead of it. The truth is out now, and it won't pass until somethin' else comes along. You know how it works here," Johnny answers roughly.

It's not what I want to hear but knew was coming.

"I have to go," I mutter.

Johnny scoffs. "What? We're a long way from done talking about this."

Daisy ignores him and comes to stand in front of me. She takes my face in her hands and forces me to stare at her. My lungs feel like they've shrunk as I can't seem to get enough air into my system.

"Go see your mom. I'll talk to Johnny," she whispers.

Her touch doesn't soothe me the way it always has before. Instead, it makes me feel worse. Like I'm undeserving of it.

I don't have it in me to smile, even just to soothe her temporarily. Instead, I use my words. "Don't let him make you feel small. You're the furthest thing from it."

Johnny is one of the kindest people out there, but everyone is capable of having a villain moment when they think they're protecting someone they love.

I'm one drive away from experiencing exactly that.

Daisy presses her lips to mine in a fierce kiss that I know is meant to reassure me, but I keep it short for the very first time. It feels wrong to pull away, but the alternative is to take her back to my bedroom and lock her inside for the next few months until all of this blows over.

Despite our mutual agreement to fake date, I was the one who benefited from it. It was my parents I needed help pushing out of my business so I didn't lose them completely and my best friend, who unknowingly exposed our secret. We lied to not only my best friends but to her family too.

The blowback for this needs to catch me before it so much as considers touching her. And there's only one place to go to try and make that happen.

My parents' house.

40

Daisy

BRYCE HATES SHORT KISSES.

I've lost count of the number of times she's pouted about them, so having her be the one to pull away quickly makes me more unsettled than everyone knowing our secret.

"What's wrong with you, Johnny?" I ask, a bubbling pit of anger growing inside of me.

He huffs. "What's wrong with me? What the hell is goin' on, D? This isn't you. You're not a liar."

"I'm not a liar. And I don't appreciate you making me out to be one because you're upset."

"You lied to all of us. What else do you want me to make you out to be?"

"I didn't lie to anyone because I thought it would be fun, Johnny. You know that because you know *me* and the type of person I am. We never set out to hurt anyone, especially you and the moms."

"What you set out to do doesn't really matter now."

I collapse on the couch and reach for the yellow blanket, bringing it to my lap. Twisting the corner of it, I stare up at my brother, the other half of myself, and hate the way he looks back. Like I've disappointed him.

"I was the one who suggested the idea to Bryce. She was struggling with her mother, and since I was staying here when she definitely didn't want a roommate, I offered to play the part of her fake girlfriend as a way of paying her back. The first time we went to Peakside together, we barely knew each other. We didn't know how to touch one another or how to make a stranger believe us, let alone those closest to us."

With stiff limbs, Johnny sits beside me. I keep speaking.

"Bryce isn't who I thought she was months ago. I should have known there was more to her than what I'd previously seen, considering how many of you love her so much, but witnessing it firsthand and having her show me her heart, it was hard not to fall for her.

"The more we got to know each other, the easier it was to see how amazing she is behind the masks she wears. Things happened quickly, and before I knew it, our touches weren't fake, and neither was the yearning I felt toward her. At the barbecue, I realized that I wanted her to be mine. I didn't want to only kiss in public or when we felt the need to put on an act. Things stopped being fake after that day, and I think we both were just hoping we could forget that's how it ever started. It doesn't matter if we were only pretending before because now, it's serious. The only person who will be punished for what we chose to do at the beginning of our relationship is Bryce. I'm grateful for the push it gave us because I don't think we would have been here otherwise, but her mother will never let this go. Even if we only lied to her for a few weeks."

"Daisy," my brother says on a sigh. He shifts, opening his posture and stretching an arm along the back of the couch behind me. "Maybe you just got confused in the role you were playing."

I fist the blanket, glaring at him and his stupid, pitiful frown. "Are you sure you just didn't think Aurora was so beautiful the first time you saw her that the next time you did, you got confused by your feelings and are actually just attracted to her physically?"

He recoils, jaw pulsing. "Touché."

"I know myself well enough not to mistake what love feels like. Alluding otherwise when you've only been around us a couple of times hurts me."

Scrubbing his hand down his face, he mutters, "I'm sorry. I just feel blindsided. You're not just my sister, Daisy, you're my goddamn twin. If there was anyone who you should have trusted to tell about this, it's me."

"I don't say this to be mean, but I didn't trust without a doubt that you wouldn't let it slip to someone. You would have had to keep it a secret from Rory, and I didn't want to put you in that position."

"I'm not a town gossiper, Daisy."

"The only person I told was Kiki. That's it."

"And Bryce? Who did she tell?"

I smooth the blanket over my thighs. "Poppy."

"Did she tell Garrison?" he asks, hurt panging in his voice.

With how close he is with the grumpy billionaire, I can understand where that hurt comes from.

"Not as far as I know. She didn't tell anyone. Even him."

He doesn't appear relieved. "So, Poppy could be trusted not to tell her boyfriend, but I couldn't be trusted not to tell my girlfriend?"

"Please just stop. You're allowed to be upset, but I didn't do anything to hurt you on purpose. And honestly, this isn't even about you. It's about me and Bryce. And she's out there taking care of this all on her own because she wanted me here to fix the relationship I have with you. She's the most incredible person I've ever met, and this is only another example of why."

Johnny glances away from me and to the mess of my books, pens, and the empty iced tea box on the coffee table that I forgot to throw out. Then, he finds the basket of blankets and the pillows between us on the couch. He touches a fringed edge of the one closest to him with a callused finger and releases a rough exhale.

"You're really with her now? No more pretendin'?" he asks.

"Yes. Bryce is my girlfriend."

"You need to tell the moms, then."

The weight on my chest grows heavier. "I've got work this morning, but I'll head over after. Do you think they've already heard?"

He spreads his legs further apart and bends over them, elbows digging into his thighs. The manspreading would annoy me usually, but now's not the time.

Propping his cheek in his hand, he looks at me. "Yeah. They've always known everything hours before everyone else."

"Are you going to have words with the guy who spread this?"

His grin is wicked. "Yeah, Daisy. I'll be havin' words with him. Carved out an entire time slot in my schedule for it."

"I'm honoured. I know how busy you are."

It's only partially a joke. My brother is one of Wade Steele's most trusted ranch hands. I've heard over the years about how much more responsibility he keeps handing Johnny, as if testing him or preparing him for an even bigger role on the ranch.

If there's anyone who deserves it, it's my brother. He's been working on Steele Ranch since he was sixteen and hasn't ever loved a place or a job more.

"You're my sister, and I love you to bits," he declares before dropping his arm to my shoulders and pulling me in for a hug.

"I love you too, J," I whisper.

He keeps me tucked into his chest until my warning alarm goes off, letting me know I have to leave for work in fifteen minutes.

"Work," I tell him when he sits back and arches a brow.

"Got it. I'll go, but let me know if there's anythin' I can do to help get this sorted, okay? And please, for the love of God, talk to me more."

"Communication goes both ways," I push but eventually nod. "I'll call you later."

We stand, and I walk him to the door. He lingers, and I know he's got something else he wants to say.

"Out with it, J."

His lips tip in a tiny smile. "I'll talk to Bryce. Apologize for blowin' up on her."

"I'd appreciate that. And in return, I won't tell the moms that you walked through our house like a madman with your work boots on."

He blanches, dropping wide eyes to the dark brown cowboy boots flaked with dried mud. "Shit."

I laugh and open the door for him, feeling some of the weight lift from where it's been crushing me.

"We'll talk later."

He kisses the top of my head and slips by me out onto the porch. "Have a good day."

"See you."

It takes me until my brother hops into his truck and drives off to realize that I called this place our house. Bryce's and mine.

I smile to myself. Yeah, I think that sounds just right.

Bryce

I SCROLL through the text messages that have filled my phone since last night and swipe them away without replying.

Anna: Are we okay? Can we talk today?

Darren: Call me so I know you're okay.

> Pops: I'm so sorry Ice. This is all my fault. Call me please.

> Johnny: What the fuck are you doing with my sister?

> Johnny: I trusted you with her.

There are a shit ton more, especially from Johnny, but I don't read through them all before removing them from sight.

The collection of voicemails has only come from one set of numbers. My mother's, and then when she realized I wasn't answering her calls, my father's.

Parked on the rounded driveway outside of their house, I listen to the first voicemail and prepare myself for the attack.

"Hello, Bryce. I've had something very alarming come to my attention. Something you must explain to me now."

Beep.

The second is along the same lines as the first. I play the third.

"Enough of this. Answer your phone. Your father and I are so embarrassed. *T'as poussé trop loin!*"

I don't bother with the rest of the voicemails. The only thing I'll accomplish is hurting my own feelings. There's no point in hearing how terrible of a daughter I am before I even make it inside the house. She'll only repeat it in my face.

As prepared as I possibly can be, I head inside. There's nobody to welcome me in. My mother must know I'm here, but she's going to make this as hard for me as possible, starting with forcing me to search for her.

"Mom?" I call out from in front of the staircase.

"Upstairs," she snips from the second floor.

I take the steps slower than usual, stalling this meeting without outright leaving. As much as I'd like to walk right back out the front door and never come back, it's time I grow up and take care of this. If there's one thing being with Daisy has taught me, it's that I deserve more than what my mother has offered me. And if holding my tongue and dragging people into my messes just to avoid ruining whatever remains of our relationship is what I have to look forward to with her, it isn't worth it.

I wish it hadn't taken me so long to make this decision, but when my first reaction to Johnny's news was fear as to what my mother will do not only to me but to Daisy . . . that's a sign as clear as any.

The door to my parents' bedroom is ajar, so I walk inside without knocking. Mom is sitting at her vanity, swiping a powder puff over her cheekbones. When she notices me, she catches my eyes in the mirror and sets her puff down.

"You did not return my calls," she snaps, her accent as thick as it was in her voicemails.

"I figured it would be easier to speak with you here."

Taking a full look at me, she scrunches her face in distaste. "What are you wearing?"

"Pajamas. And I'm not here to discuss my choice of clothing."

"You should not wear those things outside of the house."

I take a calming breath. "Is Dad home?"

"*Non.* He's at work. Where you should be."

"I hate that fucking job, Mom."

She gasps, her blue eyes flaring wide in alarm. "Don't be so crass."

"I'm twenty-eight years old. This is the kind of language I use," I argue.

"Not in this house."

"Do you really want to argue about my language right now? I'm telling you that I hate the job you forced me into taking."

She swipes her hand through the air. "Sometimes we must work jobs we do not enjoy. Until you get married, that will be your job."

I can't stop my laugh from dropping between us. "And then what? I get knocked up and raise a rich man's babies? That's not fucking happening. Not in this life or any other."

"Oh *my*. Who are you today?"

"I'm me, Mom. This is who I am outside of this prison. I'm crass and blunt and cold. I am everything that you taught me how to be."

She presses a hand to her throat and shakes her head, staring at me with such disdain. Like she's staring at a stranger that she can't believe had the audacity to speak in her presence.

"This is Daisy Mitchell's influence," she declares.

I wet my lips, scoffing a dark laugh. "The only thing Daisy has done is offer me more love than I have ever seen from anyone in my entire life. So, yeah, I guess this is her influence. Because of her, I know that I deserve better, and I'm not afraid to shed all of the relationships in my life that have done nothing but drag me down."

"I am your mother, Bryce. You cannot simply wish away our relationship because I don't support the decisions you're making."

"Yes, I can. And I'm finally ready to do it. You haven't been here for me for years."

"The past is not why you're here. We need to speak about you lying to me about your being in a relationship. I have cancelled dates on your behalf and upset several men who were excited to meet with you because you wanted to play pretend. But that is over, and now, we can go back to what we were doing before," she says, straightening her spine with a smile.

"No. I'm done with those fucking dates. The only reason I put up with them was so I could avoid this exact conversation. I don't. Want. To. Date. A. Man. Ever. Not now, and not in five years from now. Daisy Mitchell is my girlfriend."

She laughs, but it's a weak, disbelieving sound. "You say that now, but you could always change your mind. And stop it with the lies. I know the truth."

"The *truth* is that I was too afraid of you to tell you how I felt and instead pulled Daisy into my mess. But that's over now. I love Daisy Mitchell, and she *is* my girlfriend," I declare, my chin up and shoulders straight.

Mom balks and stands from her chair before striding toward me. I hold the doorframe.

"Do you have any idea how it makes your father look to have the town gossiping about his daughter lying about dating a woman only to be caught? It makes you look desperate and makes us look ridiculous to have believed you."

"Is the problem here that I was lying about dating a woman or that I didn't choose to pretend with a man?"

My question shocks us both. I've never dug into my mother's opinion on my sexuality, but she's never been outwardly upset by it. It was more that she had a preference, and I couldn't blame her for that any more than she could blame me for not having one in the first place. But now, with all of this drama and the lies and hurt, I don't know what to think. Maybe I just need to hear her say that she doesn't care who I love, as long as I'm happy.

Her expression falls, eyes gleaming with unshed tears. I don't know whether to believe they're real or expect the worst of her.

"Your sexuality does *not* define you, Bryce. I have never thought differently."

"You may have never thought differently, but your actions tell another story."

"I just want the best for you."

"I don't believe you!" I shout, my voice bouncing off the walls.

She falls back onto her chair, as if I've shoved her down. "I will not deny that I am old-fashioned. There was a life I imagined for you when you were just a little girl, and I suppose . . . I suppose I have let that poison my mind over the years. You are my Bryce, *ma fille*, regardless of who you love."

My throat tightens to the point I feel like I'm breathing through a straw. A swell of emotion rocks into the anger I've grappled, threatening to sweep it away.

"You have disregarded what I want for years now. It wasn't a secret that I had no desire to go on the dates you continued to set up for me," I say, refusing to back down.

"You created such an elaborate scheme to get me to stop. Is that the truth? I have broken that much of the trust between us?"

I swallow. "Yes."

"I am the cause of this," she mumbles to herself, a harsh slap of reality hitting her.

Her sob startles me. I can't move from my spot in the doorway, and I don't think she expects me to. As her shoulders curve and she cries, I blink back my own tears, refusing to let them fall.

"I won't be going back to the town office. This is my formal resignation," I start. Maybe I'm a terrible daughter, but a few tears will not fix this. And even if they could, I'm not ready to forgive and forget. "I've been tattooing the people in town for over a year now, and that's what I want to do with my life. I'm going to open my own shop one day, and my girlfriend will be there with me when I do it."

Maybe.

Daisy is my main concern right now, and knowing that there are people in this town talking about her has me livid. I want to protect her from all of this, but at the same time, what if I'm the one she needs to be protected from?

This is all my fault. She should have a say in what we do going forward. If there is any *we* in the future. How could I blame her for wanting to distance herself so she isn't bunched in with me anymore?

Who is going to believe us now? Will the judgment continue once we're seen out together and acting the way we have been for weeks now? The last thing I want is for Daisy to be the subject of a bad joke.

There will be doubt in everybody's eyes from now on. Her parents included.

"Bryce . . ."

"Can you tell Dad that I want to talk to him?" I interrupt.

"Yes, I can."

"Thank you."

I turn to leave, needing to get the fuck out of this place before I say something stupid. For the first time in over a decade, I might have gotten through to her. I feel like an idiot for not asking her those questions earlier and continuing to pussyfoot around, wasting so many years away being unhappy.

But there's nothing I can do now. I can't go back.

Mom clears her throat, and I pause. "I do not know how things got so out of control."

Me either.

With nothing else to say, I walk out of the room and the house that I've dreaded for so long. And this time, I don't have a clue when I'll be back.

41

Daisy

It's a miracle that I managed to get through the day in one piece.

I looked at the clock more times than I think is normal for any one person, and I had the kids doing more free reading and chatting than I would ever allow on a normal day. By the time the final bell rang, I was packed up as quickly as they were.

It was my first day in weeks without either a lunchtime visit from Bryce or one of her small meals packed into my lunch box. I miss her so much already.

Sitting in my car outside of the school, I send her another text.

> Me: I'm about to leave work. Are you home?

It joins the other unanswered messages, and I wait anxiously for a reply. There's an annoying, restless feeling prowling beneath my skin that only grows stronger with every minute I sit and stare down at the screen.

Clicking on her contact name, I smile at the photo that pops up. It's from our mountain hike with the runoff sparkling behind our heads. Bryce is mid-eye roll, but I'm grinning so wide I remember the way my cheeks ached afterward. Until now, I never noticed the slight crook of her mouth, like she couldn't help but smile just a little bit but didn't want me to know she was really enjoying having her picture taken.

I call her, but she doesn't answer. With worry nipping at my stomach, I send off another text.

> Me: Should I be worried that you haven't messaged me? Are you okay?

I let the phone fall into my lap and lean my forehead against the steering wheel. There was this feeling in my gut all day that told me something was wrong, but I pushed past it, too excited to just see her again. I should have paid more attention to it.

Bryce's mother is a soft spot for her, and I swear, if she made things worse, I'm going to—

My phone starts vibrating, and Bryce's name, along with our photo, appears before I answer the call.

"Hello?"

"Hey." Just hearing her voice makes me smile.

"You didn't answer any of my messages. I was worried."

"I didn't know what to say. I've been doing a lot of thinking today."

My smile drops. "Thinking about what? How did it go with your mom?"

"She started crying when I brought up her not being supportive of my sexuality. But honestly, I don't think that matters. She can cry and tell me anything she thinks I want to hear, and I don't actually think it would make much of a difference right now."

"I'm sorry, Frosty."

"I quit the office job and told her I was done with the dates."

"I'm proud of you."

A pause on the line over the droned buzzing noise of a tattoo gun. "I want you to do something for me, Daisy."

No Sunshine. For some reason, that has me sitting up a bit straighter.

"What is it?"

"I'm going to crash somewhere else tonight, and I want you to take the space to think about whether you're sure about us moving forward."

"I don't need a night alone to decide that. I already know the answer, and it's yes," I rush out, fear swallowing the last few words.

"Please. Just, please think about it. I'll be home tomorrow, and we can sit down and talk. But tonight, just see if you change your mind. Things will be different for us now, and I need you to be sure that you're okay with that."

This is the part of Bryce that's been hidden beneath layers and layers of ice. The woman who, like every other person who cares about someone with such an incredible fierceness, still needs reassurance but always feels uncomfortable asking for it. Like she thinks it will make her appear needy or insecure.

It's the opposite. It makes her brave and confident enough in herself to know what she needs from someone she cares about.

"Okay, I'll take the night. But I want to see you tomorrow morning before I leave for work."

"If you're sure."

"I am. And Bryce?"

"Yeah?"

"Add another Daisy beside the one you already have on your ankle. Or even better, just make it a whole bouquet."

I hang up before she replies, a ridiculous grin on my face. There was no way I was forgetting about seeing that tiny little yellow tattoo. Though, I have wondered if she had it the day I helped her into the bathtub. If she did, I'd been too busy staring at the rest of her to search her ankles for secret tattoos.

Not to mention that if she did have it by then, it would mean that she was interested in me weeks before my parents' barbecue.

I roll my lips together and finally leave the parking lot. But I don't head home. Instead, I take the main street out of town, knowing exactly what I need to do in order to convince Bryce that I'm here to stay.

INTO THE SHADE is slow for a Monday night. Or I think it is.

There's only one person in the building in addition to Shade when I walk inside, the door jingling above my head. A woman about my age is propped up on the same leather table I was on only days ago.

Shade is hunched over her side with an open jar of healing lotion in his hand that he's spreading over her hip. The wrap goes on next, and then he's snapping his gloves off and looking my way.

"Little devil," he says in greeting, his dark eyes warming slightly as he takes me in.

"Hey, Shade."

"Gimme one sec, yeah?"

I flash a soft smile and turn to face the wall of photos behind the reception desk. They weren't really a focal point for me the first time I was here, so I take the time Shade's using with his client to search for any familiar tattoos in the photo frames.

It doesn't take me very long to spot one. I've seen it often, considering the placement of it on her left forearm.

There's a forest background set behind a cherry tree that's been shaded in black with grey leaves. A cobra with a flared collar is twisted around and hanging from a lone branch, and a leopard pokes its head around the thick trunk with one paw extended. The jaw of the beast is wide, almost like it's midgrowl. Storm clouds tie the design in with the rest of her sleeve.

Sneakers squeaking on the floor have me blinking and

looking at the woman settling at the desk beside me. Her eyes, a unique shade of blueish green, meet mine as she smiles.

"That's Bryce, right?" she asks.

I look back at the picture, curious as to how she knows that. "It is."

"Don't tell her, but I think that's one of the best pieces I've ever done," Shade boasts, joining us.

He moves behind the desk and grabs a portable debit machine before tapping on the pad at the bottom. A beat later, he hands it to the woman.

"It's amazing, Shade," I agree. "Did you do all of these?"

"I did." His eyes fall to the edge of the desk. "How's yours healing up?"

"I haven't noticed it much, honestly. Bryce said it was healing well, though."

The woman quickly pays for her tattoo and then hands the machine back to him. I tap my thigh where my first tattoo hides beneath the skirt of my dress.

"I'd bet she's been checking it over every day just to have an excuse to take your pants off," Shade teases.

I giggle, and the woman who's still lingering raises both of her eyebrows at me.

"Wait, are you *with* Bryce?" she asks me.

My giggle slowly fades. "I am."

"Oh! Can you please, please, *please* tell her to say yes to my request? I've been trying to get her to give me this tattoo I've been dreaming of for weeks now, but she turned me down. Sent me here to Shade instead," she rambles, pushing her hands together in a praying position.

Shade gawks at her. "Are you saying I was your second choice? I bumped you ahead of the queue because Bryce asked me to."

"She said she wasn't taking any female clients for the time being," she explains with an intense pout.

My cheeks burn while butterflies fill my stomach. I've never asked her not to take female clients, and I never would. In my mind, it doesn't matter who she tattoos, but the gesture is so incredibly thoughtful that I know my decision to come here was the right one.

Bryce is the right decision. Always.

"I can talk to her, but I can't promise anything," I offer.

She beams. "Thank you! I'll message her later this week. Thank you for this piece, Shade."

"No problem," he mutters.

I swallow a laugh at his reaction to this. What an overgrown puppy in need of praise.

"I'll see you later, then," she adds, making her way to the door.

Without offering my name, I wave and watch her leave. Shade is quick to lock the door behind her and gesture for me to head through the studio.

"So, Bryce isn't taking any female clients?" he asks, smirking.

He's dressed similarly to the first time I met him, but instead of a black hoodie, he's in a simple black long-sleeve. It's easier to tell how muscular he is without the extra bulk of the sweatshirt, but despite his size, he doesn't intimidate me at all, even when I'm alone.

"I didn't know she'd done that," I answer. We sit on the couch, and I pull my legs up and under me. "I'm sorry to show up without asking first. I should have expected you to have a client."

"You're Bryce's girl, little devil. That makes you family. You're welcome here anytime."

I press a hand over my heart in response to the sentiment and lean my cheek against the couch. "I actually wanted to talk to you about something."

"I figured you didn't show up here alone just to visit," he teases.

"Ha-ha. It's kind of serious."

He sobers up, nodding for me to continue.

I'm not ashamed of how my relationship with Bryce started, and Shade doesn't show a single sign of judgment as I explain it to him. By the time I'm finished, I'm almost positive Bryce has told him far more than I had expected her to.

"I knew it had gotten bad with her mom, but not that bad," he grits out.

"I think she hid a lot of it from everyone."

"Sounds like her."

"You live in a small town, so you know what it's like when the gossip mill starts running. I think she's got it in her head that I'm going to get spooked by what everyone's saying or will think and take off on her."

Even saying it out loud sounds wrong. Worse than repeating it in my mind.

"Again, that sounds like Bryce." Shade pushes his hair back, sighing. "Listen, when she told me about the two of you, I didn't question it for a fucking second. Even if I hadn't caught you two making out outside the studio or seen the way you watched each other and couldn't stand not touching for a single goddamn minute, I wouldn't have doubted it."

"Why not? You didn't know me."

"Didn't I? I'd heard all about you for the last three years."

"What do you mean?" I splutter, staring at him like he's just grown a second head.

He touches his teeth together and pulls his lips back in an oops expression. "You didn't know?"

"No, I didn't know. Now, explain. Please."

"Bryce . . . Well, she's been into you for a while, little devil. Not in the stalking you while you're walking home kind of way, but she's had an interest in you for like three years now. It's why I didn't second-guess you being together. I was used to hearing about all the cute things Daisy Mitchell had done or who you had gifted your smile to at those little barbecues your family throws. Bryce was enamoured by you."

I bring my fingers to my throat, prodding at it to see if I can feel the bulge of emotion that's currently restricting my ability to swallow properly.

"I never picked up on that. Bryce never acted like she was interested in me. She was always so rude. Even when Johnny asked if she'd let me move in for a little while, she looked like she wanted to tell me to get lost."

"It was probably hard for her to imagine you being around all the time when she wanted to smash kissers. Didn't you think it was odd that she agreed to let you stay with her at all? I mean, Bryce isn't really the sharing-spaces-with-strangers type."

"I thought it was a favour for my brother," I murmur.

"Bryce doesn't care much for favours."

She hid it so well. For three years, she thought I was that attractive? *Enamoured*, Shade said. She was enamoured by me.

Sure, I only saw her occasionally, mostly only at the summer barbecues and birthday parties. But still, I didn't anticipate this.

The clearest memory I have of her from before the last couple of months is from the birthday party Johnny's friends threw us at Steele Ranch last Halloween.

Kiki had chosen my costume the week before, and while it was a total cliché, the whole angel thing was cute, and I looked good in white feathers. We got to the party shortly before my brother and Rory did, and I had just snagged a drink when I spotted Bryce in the next room.

I remember being surprised seeing her in the tight red devil costume. My brother had mentioned only a few days prior that he expected her to come dressed as a Ghostbuster like she always did. That night was the first time Bryce had made such intense eye contact with me. For a moment, I thought she was even going to come up and speak with me—maybe about what a coincidence our costumes were—but when Kiki came rushing up my side, Bryce turned and left.

I didn't see her again for months.

"Halloween last year," I blurt out, searching Shade's face for any hint of recognition.

It's there a second later. "Your brother mentioned your costume. I think she was planning on making a move that night, but I never heard how it went, so I didn't ask."

My heart pangs before rattling against my ribs. "I had no idea."

"How could you? She didn't scream it at the top of her lungs."

"If I had noticed earlier, we could have—"

"Nah. Don't play the would have, could have game. It all worked out in the end, even if it did happen a bit later."

"Why didn't she tell me this once we got together?"

"That would be a question to ask her."

Fair enough. I tuck my hair behind my ears and lean forward. "Do you have any other clients tonight?"

"Are you propositioning me, little devil? Because if so, I'm afraid I'll have to turn you down."

I laugh gently. "Not in that sense."

Intrigue brightens his brown eyes. "I'm listening."

"I know you said that the next time I came back here, I was going to tattoo Bryce, but what if you tattoo me instead?"

42

Bryce

Abbie's sitting at the kitchen table devouring a bowl of Lucky Charms when I pull myself out of the spare room. My stomach growls at the sight of that sugary cereal, so I take the seat beside her and grab the box before dumping some into my hand.

I tip my head back and shovel it all into my mouth, then notice Abbie's set her spoon in her milk-drenched cereal and is staring at me like I've just committed a crime.

"What?" I ask, cereal dust falling from my mouth.

"Why are you here, Auntie Bryce?"

"I had a sleepover. It's something adults do."

She cocks her head, sending one of her pigtails flopping into her face. "You had a sleepover with my dad?"

I accidentally swallow some of the unchewed cereal pieces and cough, my eyes bulging. Shaking my head, I press a hand to my sternum.

"What Auntie Bryce means to say, Abbie, is that no, she didn't have a sleepover with me. She just needed somewhere to stay last night and couldn't go home," Darren says, interrupting from where he's just joined us.

He leans against the side of the fridge with a mug of coffee in his hand that I contemplate stealing and a CPFD shirt on with matching black sweats. His hair has gotten too long, but if I tell him to cut it, he'll grow it even longer just to spite me. I'll have to get Abbie to bring it up to him sometime.

The little girl beside me stares up at him with such blunt adoration. She's always thought he was a superhero, and fuck, he sure acts like it with her. Abbie is his entire life. Oftentimes, I've wondered how he even has any room left for anyone else.

Swallowing the broken bits of cereal down my now scraped throat, I nod at Abbie.

"I slept in the spare room."

"Oh. Why?"

"I forgot my house key," I lie.

Darren coughs to cover a laugh. "You finish up your cereal, bug. I'm going to talk to Auntie Bryce in the living room for a couple of minutes."

"Can I come to the living room too?" she asks, already starting to lift her bowl from the table.

Darren leaves his spot and goes over to her. She focuses her doe eyes on him, but he only tightens her curly pigtail, not giving in. "Not this time. I'm going to tell her about all the new additions to your Christmas list, and we can't risk you hearing, or we won't be able to get you the things you want."

She gapes, nodding enthusiastically. "Okay, Dad."

I head to the couch and flop down on the thick cushions, shutting my eyes. It's an expensive couch, but it fits the space, considering his fancy tastes. The entire house was designed by him and then constructed by one of the top companies in the province.

He originally bought the lot with the original house five years ago for a few pennies and then tore it down and built this place from the ground up. Sasha, his ex-wife, hated what he decided to do with the new house, but then again, I don't remember her liking anything about Darren besides the things he did to try and make her happy.

"You know I don't have a problem with you coming here whenever you need to, Rye. But if you're going to use my house as a hiding spot, you can at least tell me what's going on," he says.

I open my eyes when he lifts my feet from the last cushion and sits in their place. He drapes them over his thighs and pats my ankle.

"Don't pretend like you have no idea why I'm here. You called and texted a million times yesterday."

"And you didn't respond once before I found you hiding out on my porch."

"I'm not a raccoon."

His deep laugh fills the room. "You're not. But you are upset, so talk to me."

I rub my temples, my shitty sleep last night catching up to me. "I'm sorry for lying to you about Daisy. It was never supposed to come out like that. Fu—Frick, it wasn't supposed to come out at all."

With a glance at the little girl humming under her breath at the table, I rule out her hearing my slip-up.

"You don't have to apologize to me. I was more worried about you," Darren says.

"I'm fine, D. You know that I don't care what's being said about me. My concern is Daisy."

He nods. "And that's why you're here. Let me guess, you told her that you felt too guilty to go home last night, even though this isn't your fault."

"It *is* my fault. That's the problem."

"Alright, let's say it is your fault, then. What are you going to do about it?"

"I gave her the chance to walk away."

Darren blows out a long breath, pushing further into the couch. "Of course you did."

"What does that mean?"

"When you said that to her, what did she say?" he asks, ignoring my question.

"She said she didn't want to. But how can she make a decision that important so quickly? It's not just that people are talking but that from now on, we'll always be second-guessed. *Are they really together? Is this another joke?*"

"So what? You know the truth, and so will those closest to you. Bryce, I'm going to hold your hand when I tell you this." He does exactly that, humour glinting in his eyes. "You're far more obvious than you think you are when it comes to Daisy. I've known for a long time that there was something there for you. Even if it was only from afar, you were interested. The only reason I kept it to myself was because I knew you weren't ready to talk about it. Every time I tried, you were quick to clam up.

"I'm sure I can speak for all of us when I say that even if you had told us from the beginning that the relationship was a show for your mother, we wouldn't have believed you. Johnny's the only one who didn't see it, but Daisy's his twin. He'll always see things differently."

I don't know whether to laugh or cry or both. It could go any way at this point.

"Screw you, Darren," I mutter.

He squeezes my hand and chuckles. "Screw me? Screw you, Bryce."

"I still left the decision up to her, even if you do have a point. It felt right to give her control, considering I did get her into this mess, even if it wasn't intentional."

"You need to give your girl more credit."

"I know."

"Does she know about that?" he asks.

I follow his stare to where it's been glued to my forearm. The clear wrap over my most elaborate piece feels suffocating, but this is one time I'm not going to risk fucking up the healing process.

"I only did it last night" is my answer.

"Is there a love language that specifies getting tattoos for your significant other? If there isn't, there should be."

"Isn't that just acts of service?"

He gives his head a shake and releases my hand to scratch his jaw. "No. Too broad. You're not going out and buying her a puppy. You're altering your body."

"Okay then. Let's hear an idea."

"What about love codes?"

My jaw goes slack. "Did you actually just come up with that on the spot?"

"I did," he says through a smug smirk.

"Love codes," I repeat, testing the feeling of it on my tongue. "I think Daisy would love that."

"What about you?"

"I'd say yes, but you're already a cocky ass without getting any extra praise from me."

I might as well have just told him he was an artistic genius. The proud expression on his face is nice to see, though. He's got light back in his eyes.

I'm beginning to think it's back in mine too. While I might have dimmed it with my own actions, even just talking about Daisy is enough to fill me up with warmth. I don't regret forcing her to take the time to think things through.

I'm not interested in her for only a few more weeks or months. I want her for the rest of them. And I need to know that she's sure about taking that step with me sooner rather than later.

"You say the nicest things . . ." He cuts himself off and shoves off the couch, staring past me at the front window. An incredulous grin flips his entire expression into one that immediately has me on alert. "There's no way."

"There's no way what?" I ask, shooting to my feet.

Darren sets his hands on my shoulders and brings me to the centre of the living room, directly in front of the window.

The laugh that comes out of me is so rare that it makes

Darren's hands tense on my shoulders. I feel the vibrations of the laugh all the way down to my toes and deep into my very bones.

My stomach cramps as it continues, but I don't want it to end. Not when I shake out of Darren's hold and whip open the front door, and not when I stand on the front porch and stare at where Daisy's standing on the sidewalk.

I'm in rumpled, borrowed pajamas with my hair a greasy mess, but Daisy looks at me now the same way she always does. Like she couldn't care less what I wear or how much makeup I've put on as long as I'm here, close to her.

"What are you doing?" I ask, gripping the porch railing.

The thin costume-store angel wings on her back ruffle in the wind, and the feathers around the hem of her short white skirt and sleeves of the matching long-sleeve look just as fluffy as they did the first time I saw them on her birthday last year.

"I haven't really gotten started yet. You weren't supposed to see me until after you heard me," she replies, tugging at the ends of her wavy hair.

I curl my lips into a cheesy grin. "Would you like me to go back inside, then?"

"No, but maybe cover your ears?"

"What?"

She doesn't answer me. Instead, she picks up the megaphone I hadn't noticed at her feet and brings it to her mouth.

"Good morning, Cherry Peak! This is Daisy Mitchell speaking, and I wanted to make a special announcement."

I stare at her, dumbstruck, my fingers growing weak around the metal railing. A second later, they slip from it entirely.

One of Darren's neighbours watches us from his porch across the street with a newspaper in his hand, his rocking chair remaining completely still. The front curtains of the house two doors down from him part as a woman gawks at us and waves to someone behind her. A second person joins her, and I look away, uninterested in anyone but Daisy.

"I love Bryce Lemieux! I love her so much, and I don't care

what anyone thinks about that because I'm going to love her forever!"

Her eyes don't waver as they remain fixed on mine, gleaming with more affection than I've ever seen. I don't know how I manage to walk down the steps and through the grass to meet her, but somehow, I get close enough to take the megaphone for myself.

Bringing it up to my mouth, I palm her bare waist and say, "I love Daisy Mitchell, and I will for a long, long fucking time."

Her smile destroys me just to build me back up again, this time with all of my crooked, mismatched pieces in their proper slots.

"Do you mean that?" she asks softly.

I drop the megaphone and reach for her face instead. The weight of her cheeks in my palms is just right. Fucking perfect. She holds my wrists, locking them in place.

I tap our noses together. "Love codes, Daisy."

"Love codes?"

Her hold on my left wrist tightens when I try to pull my hand back, but once she looks just a bit higher, she gasps and releases me.

"What—when? Oh, Bryce," she rambles, tugging my arm closer while leaning in to look. "Is that for me?"

"Love codes was Darren's idea, but it's . . . it's us. I've always been able to express myself with art better than I ever could with words. And these tattoos, Sunshine, the one on your thigh and my ankle and now my arm, they're my love language. I could ink your name into every inch of my skin and still try to make room to keep going," I confess, staring down at the new addition to my sleeve.

The cherry tree isn't the focal part anymore. Both the snake and panther aren't watching over it so much as they are the field of daisies now surrounding the trunk. The only colour amidst the grey and black is yellow.

"I found myself in the basement last night with my tattoo

gun in my hand. It's not the first time I let my feelings for you control me while in that type of headspace. But this time was different. The piece I altered is complete now. It's whole."

Her eyes glitter with tears as she guides my arm to her mouth and kisses the raised skin. My nerves sizzle beneath her lips.

"Close your eyes," she whispers, hot breath fanning over the field of daisies.

I shut them instantly and keep them that way while she shifts in front of me.

"Okay, open them."

The moment I do, my heart rips through its restraints and tries to soar through my chest.

I've never had someone give themselves a tattoo for me. Daisy allowed me to give her one, but—but this is something completely different.

"Shade told me about the party last year. I meant to throw this costume into a donation bin a few days after, but for some reason, I couldn't. I kept it at the back of my closet on the off chance I ever decided to wear it again. So, I know you're not in tight red leather, but I think this counts as a redo," she says.

Her nail traces the outline of the tattoo on the inside of her wrist that I can't seem to look away from.

"I wanted to commemorate that night because even if nothing came of our matching costumes, I think I felt something when our eyes met. A spark, there then gone. And while I wish we could go back and have that proper moment, I think what we got instead was more than worth the wait."

"Baby," I croak.

The ice cube is small but detailed in the same way all of Shade's designs are. Every crack and frozen detail is well placed, but it could be a fucking blank square for all I care. It's the water dripping off the edges and the letters they've been designed to spell that has me lost for words.

Bryce.

The end of the *e* has been curled into a devil's tail, and above the left corner of the *B*, two angel wings are spread wide.

"It's small, but—"

My mouth smashes against hers in a hard, rushed kiss, but there's plenty of time for slow and gentle later. Right now, I've really just fucking missed my girl and could very well die without tasting her.

Daisy responds to my desperation with one of equal force. She's the one to slip her tongue past my lips and moan low and long at the overwhelming sensations that follow. I swallow each one of those sounds.

"I love you. I love you," I repeat against her warm lips.

She smiles and strokes my jaw. "I love you, Frosty."

"Say it again."

"I love you."

Daisy Mitchell loves me, and I think that might be my greatest accomplishment to date.

43

Daisy

Bryce takes us home.

Home.

Ours.

Grateful to have walked to Darren's instead of driven, I follow her inside and pause just beyond the front door. The wings I refused to take off in the car are itchy as they hang off my shoulders. Still, I keep them on.

When she notices my absence behind her, Bryce turns and raises two eyebrows at me. "What's wrong?"

"Nothing's wrong."

Her blue eyes fill with suspicion. "Why are you standing in the doorway, then?"

"Well, you haven't actually officially welcomed me into the house as your girlfriend yet."

Suspicion shifts into a bright humour. "Oh, my bad. How do I fix this great mistake?"

I roll my lip between my teeth and push my hair over my shoulders, chest starting to rise a little faster.

"Well, kissing me here would be a good place to start."

She's on me in a single heartbeat. The soft yet controlled

press of her lips makes my head empty of anything but her name on repeat.

"Is there anything else I can do?" she murmurs between slow kisses.

"Well, you missed your shot to carry me through the door, but—Bryce!"

With a beaming grin, she sweeps me into her arms and carries me through the living room archway. I cling to her, my fake wings smacking into her, and let our laughs intertwine. They make a beautiful sound, one that I want to hear a million more times.

"Please forgive me, your majesty. Let me rectify my mistake," she teases lowly, nipping at the tip of my nose.

I sigh dramatically, pressing the back of my hand to my forehead. "Well, if you insist."

Bryce slowly lowers me to the couch, and I watch with a loopy smile as she climbs onto my lap, pinning me beneath her weight. Her hands find purchase on the couch, bracketing my head as she leans in, our faces mere inches apart.

"I love you, Sunshine," she declares, her eyes flicking between mine.

The blue in them is so bright, so alive, that I swear I can make out every tiny ridge of the black surrounding them.

My eyelids droop when she skims her lips across mine. "I love you, Frosty."

"I'm going to make love to you now, so I hope you've thought ahead and called for a sub."

My stomach flutters, a zip of excitement shooting up my spine. "I might have."

"Might have? That's not good enough."

"Play me my playlist, Bryce," I whisper.

Recognition flickers across her features. "Right now?"

"Right now."

She slowly climbs from my lap and pulls her phone free of

her pocket. With a few swipes across the screen, music begins to play from the speaker.

"I wrote out every song on a piece of paper for you," she says.

"I know."

"You never said anything."

I gaze up at her and smooth my hands down my thighs. "I wanted to see you and hear the songs. Not have them slipped under the door like a dirty secret."

Taking my movements as the invitation I meant them as, she comes back to me, reclaiming her place on my lap. Her phone falls to the cushion beside us.

"Hear them and see me, then, baby."

With a finger to the underside of my jaw, she tilts it to the side, baring my neck. I stretch it a bit further just to be a smartass, loving my ability to get under her skin. She presses an open-mouthed kiss to my throat and chuckles.

My voice is breathy when I ask, "Is it true you've been turning down female clients?"

She rakes her teeth against my pulse. "Yes."

"You don't have to do that for me. I don't care who you tattoo as long as you get to do it."

"I don't want to touch another woman, Daisy. Period. Just *my* woman. And before you ask, I haven't wanted a man in three years. They may as well not exist."

"If I say that I love you again, will it start getting annoying?" I ask, shivering with desire when Bryce sucks at my throat.

My skirt is high and tight, and the feathers keep tickling me, only making my sensitivity to touch that much more intense. I'd be happy if we were both naked already, but that would mean Bryce getting off me, and that's just not acceptable right now.

I like being her plaything, and right now, she's enjoying toying with me in any way she can.

"That's impossible," she states.

Guiding my head the opposite way, she starts giving the

other side of my neck the same love as the other. My toes curl when she swirls her tongue around the love bite I already feel the sting of.

With her distracted, I carefully move a hand between us and start hitching my skirt up my thighs. I'm pulsing between them, and I'd prefer to wear this skirt and costume again without having it to have it dry-cleaned first.

Bryce is too zoned into my movements. She swats my hand away and bites the underside of my jaw as punishment.

"Are you uncomfortable in your skirt, baby?"

"I don't want to ruin it."

I can feel her smile against my skin. "How would you do that?"

"Why don't you reach beneath it and find out?" I taunt.

She hums, sending the vibrations racing down my body. Too slowly, she palms my knee and then slides her hand up my leg. Her fingers brush the daisy tattoo on my thigh before swivelling inward.

"Are you wet, Daisy?"

"Yes," I answer without delay.

She brings her mouth to my ear and whispers, "Me too."

I quiver beneath her fingers. "Oh, God."

"God is a woman after all."

My brain short-circuits as she speaks the words while also bringing her thumb to press over my swollen clit. I jerk up off the couch, but she's there to settle me back down by making a slow circle over my wet panties.

With a strangled noise, I snap a hand out and cup her breast, needing something to hold on to. Her nipple is hard against my palm. It scrapes against it with every one of her inhales, and her lashes flutter against my cheek.

"There are too many layers between us," I croak, the songs coming from her phone beginning to grow deeper and throatier as the minutes pass.

"Your costume stays on."

I wiggle my hips. "At least take off the skirt so I can spread my legs."

"You're perfect like this. Just like you were the first time I saw you in these ridiculous white feathers and fake wings. It shouldn't have surprised me that you could make something so cliché look like it was pulled from a runway show. You didn't even have to do anything, and I was ready to carry you off somewhere we could be alone."

"Why didn't you?" I ask on a shuddered exhale.

"You weren't mine to carry off, Daisy. I knew that before I'd even considered changing my costume."

"But you still did. We were all expecting something else, and you wore what you knew would match me."

"I wanted you to notice me," she reveals, her face remaining hidden in my neck.

"There was never a time when I didn't."

The soft noise that escapes her strokes something inside of me. Something raw and sensitive.

"Maybe it wasn't in the same way that you noticed me, but you were never invisible. I always saw the black-haired woman with the startlingly blue, don't-piss-me-off eyes and the take-no-shit attitude. You couldn't blend into a crowd if you tried."

"I wish I'd said something earlier," she whispers.

Six words and I know her remaining walls have dropped completely. There's an honesty to her tone that strikes that raw, sensitive spot all over again.

"I love you, Bryce. This was the perfect time for us. I *feel* it."

She pulls back, her teary gaze lifting to meet mine. I kiss away the two that fall first and wipe the next few. She doesn't look away from me.

Her thumb makes a single pass over my slit, and then she's pushing my skirt up to rest at my waist before taking my panties off. As soon as I'm bare, her fingers are back, this time running up and down my slick lips.

She parts them, and I gasp, nuzzling my cheek against her temple. "You're perfect."

"I need—I need you, Bryce."

"What do you need from me?"

"Anything. Everything."

She watches me, eyes lined with bold desire, as she sinks a single finger inside my opening. I inhale sharply and dig my teeth into my lip.

She presses the pad of a finger to that same lip and pries it from where I've trapped it. "Be loud for me. Paint the walls with your moans and make this house officially your home."

I let my eyes roll back and rock my hips with every pump of her finger. "It's already my home."

"Then do it for me. I want to hear you cry my name."

With a nod, I lean up as far as I can and kiss her while she brings a second set of fingers to toy with my clit. The dual sensation is intoxicating, but it's her presence that's going to send me over the edge.

I feel her everywhere. Between my legs, in my blood, and tucking herself in the walls of my heart.

She swirls an expert touch around my pulsing clit, and a second finger slides inside of me. I rip my lips from hers as my head falls backward, and a whimper escapes.

"Louder," she coaxes, curling her fingers and stroking them deep inside my pussy.

Reaching for her, I grip her wrist and use the hold as an anchor. She strums my clit at a quick pace that only seems to grow faster as the seconds pass. I forget to breathe and then gulp down air, repeating the same motions until my head feels too light.

"Bryce! Bryce, Bryce, Bryce." I repeat her name like a chant, a plea.

It hits me suddenly. One second, I'm lurching my hips in search of more, and the next, I'm going boneless as release rips into me. I think Bryce moans at the sight of my pleasure because that can't only be me . . .

"You're so beautiful. Let it go, baby. I love you so much," she murmurs, continuing to work her fingers.

"I can't . . . I can't take any more," I whisper a beat later, pulling at her wrist.

She removes her fingers instantly and is quick to bring them to her mouth, licking them clean. I'm so wrung out that it takes more strength than it should to cup her breast again and pinch her hard nipple between my fingers. But I want to bring her the pleasure she brought me.

"Come to bed with me, Sunshine," she says, gently removing my hand and using it to stabilize her when she swings off my lap.

"You need to be the one coming."

Her smile is soft. "Not right now. I didn't sleep well last night, and I just want to lie with you."

"Okay," I say, voice barely audible. "That sounds perfect."

She helps me up, and we head to her bed. Our bed now.

I stall only a handful of steps from the couch. "Can I bring the yellow blanket with us?"

"Already trying to redecorate?" she teases.

"What do you think I've been doing the last few weeks?"

"Bringing sunshine to my life. I think I've stolen some of it along the way."

I squeeze her hand as tight as I can and snag the blanket, pressing it to my chest.

"Keep it. I think it's always belonged to you, anyway."

EPILOGUE

THREE MONTHS LATER

Bryce

"ARE YOU NERVOUS?" DAISY ASKS, TWISTING IN MY ARMS, HER pretty blue eyes locking with mine.

I pepper kisses along her hairline. "No."

"Good. Everyone is so proud of you."

"Including you?" I fish for her approval.

She reads right through me. "Oh, honey, I'm the proudest of all. Don't slot me in with everyone else."

"So sassy today," I coo, tapping the underside of her chin before guiding it back and swooping in for a kiss.

Her eyes twinkle when she pulls away. "You're rubbing off on me."

"Better me than anyone else."

"So possessive today," she pokes, echoing my tone.

"Fucking right I am."

Her giggle is music to my ears as I look around the studio and take in the familiar faces filling it.

Into The Shade has always been a safe space for me. But now, it's more than that. Starting today, it's my new home away from home. I'll be working here until I can save enough to open a shop of my own in Cherry Peak. The station beside Shade's is mine, and the small sign above it glowing in yellow will one day be ten times bigger in size and hung outside of my tattoo shop.

Love Codes.

A reminder that I'm no longer afraid to chase my dreams.

Every one of our friends is here today to celebrate. Brody and Anna, Johnny and Rory, and Poppy and Garrison. Darren and Delaney are here too—not together, of course, which is something Poppy spent a solid hour complaining about this morning. She's taken it upon herself to try and play matchmaker, and I haven't had it in me to tell her it's a lost cause.

Originally, I didn't want to make a big deal out of this day, but Daisy had everyone hyped before I got the chance to tell them it wasn't necessary. Poppy's even been staying at the guest house on Steele Ranch with Garrison all week under the pretense of helping finish all of the preparations.

There's been a lot of these moments over the last three months. Poppy's been here more recently in the past few months than in the year prior, and I've spent enough time in Calgary not to need my maps app to get to her house and Beautifully Bold anymore.

"You'll have a sore hand by the time we go home tonight," Daisy murmurs, staring past our friends and to those who've come for the flash tattoo sale Shade suggested we hold.

Flash tattoos aren't my favourite, nor are they Shade's, but fucking hell, the guy has done so much to help me with this new job that I couldn't turn down another one of his attempts to bring more traffic into the shop.

I bring my mouth to Daisy's cheek and linger there. "If my hand's out of commission, I guess you'll just have to ride my face, then."

Heat presses to my mouth as her cheeks blaze. She rolls her eyes at me.

"You're ridiculous."

"No, Sunshine. I'm happy."

Her features soften immediately. "I love you."

"Awe, I love you too, little devil," Shade purrs, appearing out of nowhere to plant a fat, wet kiss on her forehead.

I shove him off and away from my girlfriend. "Go kiss someone else, asshole."

His grin could blind someone. "Who are you calling an asshole, asshole?"

"Ooh, I love this game. Can I be an asshole too?" Poppy asks, kissing the back of my head.

Garrison slides up to her side and pulls her against him. "What's with all the goddamn kissing?"

"Shade started it," Daisy says.

The man himself stares at her like he's never seen her before. "Oh, how quickly you throw me under the bus, little devil."

"I still don't get why you call her that. Daisy is an angel," Poppy sings, winking at Daisy.

Garrison's always been overprotective of Poppy, so I ignore him when he glares at Shade so fiercely it's like he's trying to make him poof into a cloud of dust.

It isn't the first time my friends are meeting Shade. With some encouragement from Daisy, I introduced them a couple of months ago. Once I got it into my thick skull that they weren't going to steal him from me, it was easier to let it happen.

Poppy was upset at first that I'd kept him a secret, but she got over it quickly. Everyone else was just excited to have another person join the group.

"See, Shade? I'm an angel," Daisy taunts, batting her lashes.

I know better than that. She might look like an angel, but she's got a devilish streak that would shock everyone. I'm a lucky bitch to get to see that side of her so often.

The bell above the door dings, and I look toward it on habit. My skin turns cold as if I'm out in the frigid January air when my mother steps inside and shakes the snow from her heavy coat. Her eyes are wary as she examines the space, but even as I wait for judgment to fill them, they stay cautious.

"What are you looking—oh," Daisy mumbles, stroking a reassuring hand down my arm. "Did you invite her?"

"No."

"Do you want to speak with her?" Poppy asks, noticing my divided attention.

"I should."

We haven't spoken since the day I quit and told her that I would be pursuing tattooing. She's called a few times over the last few months, but it's been Dad who I've spoken with instead. It's always been easier to talk to him, and with my disaster of a relationship with Mom, he's all I have left. I guess I latched onto him and the opposite approach to parenting he's always taken.

He isn't perfect, but I've never felt judged or pressured with him. His quiet understanding is what I'd been needing for a long time, even if I doubt he has or ever will stand up to Mom.

"I'll come with you," Daisy offers, already interlocking our fingers.

"We'll be back, then," I tell no one in particular.

Poppy catches my words and touches my shoulder before Daisy guides me away from the group and toward where my mom is hovering awkwardly by the reception desk.

The wall of Shade's favourite pieces falls prey to her stare, and I'm suddenly on edge, unsure if she'll recognize which are on my body.

"Mrs. Lemieux," Daisy says, taking the lead without hesitation. "How are you?"

My heart swells with the strength of my love for her, somehow still growing as the days pass.

My mother turns to face us. The emotion that ripples across her face startles me.

"I'm good, Daisy."

I swallow and offer a stiff smile. "I wasn't expecting you here, Mom."

"Oh . . . Yes, I know." She fidgets with the rings on her fingers, and I feel guilty when the fluorescent lights highlight the bags beneath her eyes. "I just wanted to come see this place. See you."

I don't know what to say, so I say nothing.

Daisy rubs the back of my hand with her thumb. "Well, what do you think?"

"It is very busy. And the artwork on the walls is special."

"Do you recognize any of the pieces? Shade, the owner of Into The Shade, did all of them. But soon, Bryce's work will be up there too. If I have anything to do with it, at least."

Mom turns back to the wall and the frames, staring intently at each one. She points to one with a perfectly manicured fingernail.

"That one is my Bryce."

Surprised, I focus on the piece she's pointed out. It's one I usually forget I have. A neck of a guitar that's been smashed on one end. It's small, hardly three inches long, and fits into the collection of random art on my right bicep.

"And that one," she adds, spine straight with pride.

It's the snowflake Shade put behind my ear four years ago.

"How did you know that?" I ask.

She smiles sadly. "That is your ear."

My chest feels too tight. I grip Daisy's hand and stare at my mother, seeing too much of her heart exposed for the first time in years.

Daisy moves forward and starts gesturing to the rest of the frames that my body is featured in, explaining what the designs are and the meanings of some of the harder-to-understand ones. The woman who raised me, the same one who didn't show a single ounce of care about my passion for art, listens intently to my girlfriend, as if she genuinely wants to learn everything.

I don't know what to make of that. It feels sudden, but in reality, it's been three months. Could she actually have spent that time trying to better herself?

"That one is my favourite," she declares.

I look to the end of the pointed finger, and a slight smile curls my lips.

"It's mine too," I tell her.

My forearm is already exposed as I offer it to her and wait for her eyes to fall on the tattoo. It healed perfectly and is, without a doubt, my most popular piece. I've caught myself staring at it more times than I can count.

"*Un champ de marguerites*," she whispers before glancing up at my girlfriend. "A field of daisies."

The translation she offers shocks me more than the warmth in her tone.

A sheen moves over her eyes as she keeps them on Daisy. "Thank you."

"For what?"

Instead of answering the question, Mom focuses on me. "Will you come over for supper next week? Both of you."

"Will Dad be there too?" I ask, rubbing my palm over my sternum. We've talked, but I don't think our relationship will ever be anything special, as sad as that was to admit to myself.

"Yes, yes, he can be. He *will* be. And there will be no fish."

Daisy giggles near silently beside me, and I pull our hands up to replace the one I was using to rub my chest.

"Okay. We can come," I say.

Mom sucks in a relieved breath and clasps her hands. "I will call you with details?"

"Sure."

"For now, could you show me more of this place? I would like to meet this Shade."

I don't know if I can take any more surprises. My head swims with the effects of her genuine efforts. Yet, my heart is fuller than ever.

Daisy leans into my side and watches me and my mother with pride and relief. Like she's been hoping for something like this to happen just as much as I was.

It's too early to let bygones be bygones, but the effort is there, at least for today. That seems to be good enough for me right now.

With my girlfriend beside me, I take another look around the studio and ignore the burn behind my eyes. There's so much light in my life, and somehow, it grows brighter every fucking day.

I have Daisy to thank for helping me see it.

"Yeah, Mom. I think it's time you properly met my family."

Thank you for reading Stealing Sunshine! If you enjoyed it, please leave a review on Amazon and Goodreads.

The fifth and final book in the Cherry Peak series is coming in July with Darren and Delaney and their second chance, angsty romance.

While you're waiting for more of these characters, jump into my backlist! Want to learn a bit more about Garrison before he met Poppy? Or meet Anna before she came to Cherry Peak? Jump into my Greatest Love series.

To be kept up to date on all my releases, check out my website!
www.hannahcowanauthor.com

Acknowledgements

This story is and will always be one of the most important to me. Bryce and Daisy's love story was yanked from my soul and smeared all over these pages. I can't put into words how fully these two captured me during the 8 weeks that I spent writing them. I'll never forget them or the emotions they made me feel.

Bryce deserved Daisy and the family Daisy offered her. As a bisexual woman myself, I felt every ounce of Bryce's struggles and hope that I was able to do her justice.

Here we go with thank the yous. As always, my biggest thank you goes to the women in my life who helped inspire the women in this series. Hayley, Nicole, and Becci, you are my girl gang. Thank you for loving me both when I'm a raging bitch and an overemotional turtle hiding in my shell.

To Sierra, I love you endlessly. Thank you for reading my words as I blurt them onto paper and loving them and me. I'm so grateful to have you in my life.

To Lauren-Brooke, thank you for keeping the wheels turning. We already know I'm a hot mess on a good day. I love you.

To my team of creative masterminds, Sandra, Julie, Mary, Andra, Silver, Jordan, and Cassie. Thank you for turning this book into a masterpiece, inside and out.

To everyone who has helped share my books to the world and helped bring so many new readers to Me and my stories, thank you. You truly don't know how much I love and appreciate you for everything you do.

Chante, Chelsey, Bree, LB, and Shelby, thank you for sensitivity reading this story. I adore you so much.

Sierra, Glav, Courtney, Christina, Jenine, you deserve a shoutout above the rest for always going above and beyond. I wish I could squeeze each and every one of you.

About The Author

Hannah is a twenty-something-year-old indie author from Canada. Obsessed with swoon-worthy romance, she decided to take a leap and try her hand at creating stories that will have you fanning your face and giggling in the most embarrassing way possible. Hopefully, that's exactly what her stories have done!

Hannah loves to hear from her readers, and can be reached on any of her social media accounts.

Facebook Group : Hannah's Hotties
Website : www.hannahcowanauthor.com